Disclaimer

The events, characters, businesses and organisations described in this story are fictitious. Any resemblance to actual persons, living or dead, is unintentional and entirely coincidental. Any representation of organisations portrayed in this story is purely fictional. This story is not meant to cast aspersion upon any current or past branch of the United States Government or any government contractors. The locations and facilities described in this story did exist, however, and were operated for over three decades to support the United States nuclear weapons stockpile as a deterrent during the cold war. While entirely fictional, the events in this story illustrate the possibility that the risk to the public of operating these facilities may have been greater than was realised at the time.

Assault on L

Acknowledgments

I would like to thank my wife, Stella, for her tireless editing and proofreading of the manuscript for this book.

Jacket design courtesy of David Smith at 49th Floor Graphic Design, United Kingdom (david@49thfloor.co.uk)

Several photos courtesy of the United States Department of Energy

Assault on L

Glossary of Terms

- <u>Actuator System ("Forest")</u> – The collective system of telescoping tubes that latch onto the top fittings of individual control rods and safety rods, used to withdraw these rods from the reactor, into the vertical space above, in any desired pattern or grouping.

- <u>Alpha Emitter</u> – Radioisotopes that emit particles consisting of two protons and two neutrons from the nucleus during radioactive decay (called alpha decay). A layer of paper or plastic provides sufficient shielding to prevent significant alpha particle exposure.

- <u>Annunciator</u> – A bell, light or other device that provides information about the status of a piece of equipment or system. A green light typically indicates the status is normal. A red light typically indicates an alarm condition or malfunction that needs attention. Alarm conditions are normally 'announced' by the sound of a buzzer, bell or siren.

- <u>Berm</u> – Horseshoe shaped mound of earth designed to provide cover for security personnel who are attempting to repel an attacking adversary.

- <u>Control Rod</u> – A column of small diameter lithium-aluminum slugs encased in a seamless aluminum sleeve to form a long cylindrical rod; used for controlling neutron flux in a nuclear reactor by vertically withdrawing portions of these rods from interstitial positions between fuel assemblies in the reactor core.

- <u>Criticality</u> – A condition within fissile material (e.g., uranium, plutonium) where each fission event releases a sufficient number of neutrons to sustain an uncontrolled nuclear chain reaction, producing heat and large amounts of radiation, often accompanied by a visible blue flash of light.

- <u>Critical Mass</u> – The minimum amount of fissile materials needed to sustain a nuclear chain reaction.

- <u>Critically Safe</u> – Physical arrangement of fissile material (e.g., uranium, plutonium) that prevents a nuclear criticality from occurring, usually by ensuring a safe distance between items of fissile material that are each less than a critical mass, and/or placing neutron absorbing material (e.g., borated paraffin) between the items.

- Deuterium – An isotope of hydrogen in which the nucleus consists of one proton and one neutron, rather than one proton only. Deuterium has double the mass of ordinary hydrogen.

- Filter Compartment – One of five very large aluminum boxes containing 1) 'demisters' made of Teflon coated wire to remove entrained moisture, 2) high efficiency particulate air (HEPA) filters to trap smoke and fine particles, and 3) activated charcoal filters to adsorb fission product radioiodine. Air is exhausted from the reactor building through a three-foot diameter duct at the bottom of the filter compartment, flows through the demister, HEPA, and charcoal filters, then flows back to the exhaust fans through an identical duct at the top of the compartment.

- Fission – The splitting of a large atomic nucleus (e.g., uranium) into smaller nuclei, producing heat and a new generation of neutrons that can cause additional atoms to fission.

- Gadolinium Nitrate – A chemical solution injected into the primary reactor coolant that interrupts the nuclear fission process by absorbing neutrons and stopping the nuclear chain reaction.

- Glock 19 – A mid-size pistol, shooting the 9x19mm pistol cartridge (9mm Parabellum), a standard military round.

- Graphic Panel – Instrument panel displaying cartoon or silhouette representations of equipment that make up a system to accomplish a desired purpose; for example, all the supply fans and dampers that make up a building ventilation system. Vital information about each piece of equipment (pressure, temperature, etc.) is typically displayed on each silhouette.

- Half Life – Interval of time required for one-half of the atomic nuclei in a radioactive isotope to decay.

- Heat Exchanger – Large cylindrical tank containing thousands of tubes used to transfer heat from the primary reactor coolant (heavy water) to the secondary coolant (ordinary water). The heavy water flows through the tubes, while the ordinary water flows in one end of the tank, around the outside of the tubes, and out the other end of the tank.

- <u>Heavy Water</u> – A form of water (deuterium oxide) made of the hydrogen isotope deuterium and oxygen, rather than ordinary hydrogen and oxygen.

- <u>M16</u> - A family of military rifles adapted from the ArmaLite AR-15 rifle for the United States military, 5.56mm automatic usually with a 20-round magazine.

- <u>MILES Equipment</u> - Multiple Integrated Laser Engagement System, employed by the U. S. Military using lasers and blank cartridges to register 'kills' during simulated combat exercises.

- <u>Mothballed</u> – Term used to describe a complex mechanical or industrial system that is no longer used or operated for a period of years but is maintained in a state that would allow it to be upgraded and restarted, given several years of refurbishment.

- <u>Neutron Flux</u> – The number of neutrons crossing through some arbitrary cross-sectional unit area in all directions per unit of time. Neutron flux gives a measure of the 'power' or heat being generated in the reactor core, and is a major parameter used to control the reactor and measure the production rate of various nuclear materials within it.

- <u>Neutron Poison</u> – A substance (other than fissionable material) that has a large capacity for absorbing neutrons, used to prevent or retard nuclear fission.

- <u>PIDAS</u> – Personnel Intrusion and Detection Analysis System, consisting of infrared and microwave motion detection equipment enclosed in a double fenced area surrounding the facility to be protected, along with video assessment cameras and computer systems to correlate sensor and alarm data.

- <u>Plenum</u> – A large flat pancake shaped tank with 600 holes in the bottom, used to distribute heavy water to 600 individual fuel assemblies in the reactor core located below the plenum. Heavy water is supplied to the plenum through six identical inlet nozzles equally spaced around its perimeter.

- Rad - a non-SI unit of absorbed radiation dose, used prior to 1990.

- <u>Radioactive Decay</u> – The process by which an unstable atomic nucleus loses energy by radiation, usually in the form or alpha, beta or gamma emissions. Some isotopes may emit neutrons as well.

- <u>Radioisotope</u> – Any of the species of a chemical element that have different masses and unstable nuclei that emit radiation.

- <u>Safety Rod</u> – Rods composed of neutron absorbing material that are withdrawn from interstitial positions in the reactor core before control rods are withdrawn during reactor start up. These safety rods are held out of the core by gravity and fall into the core for rapid reactor shut down in the event of electrical power failure, or other conditions, including operator initiation of a SCRAM.

- <u>SCRAM</u> – Emergency system that shuts down a nuclear reactor by dropping the safety rods into the reactor by gravity. A SCRAM action drives the control rods into the reactor as well.

- <u>Supplementary Safety System (SSS)</u> – Emergency system that shuts down a nuclear reactor by injecting a neutron absorbing chemical (gadolinium nitrate) solution into the heavy water coolant to stop the fission chain reaction.

- <u>SWAT Team</u> - A SWAT (special weapons and tactics) team is a tactical unit that uses specialized equipment (e.g., body armour) and weapons to combat an armed adversary.

Assault on L

Prologue

Captain Brownlie dropped his third cigarette butt and pressed it gingerly into the ground with his left boot. They were far enough inside the wood's edge that it wasn't likely anyone at the facility could have seen it. And even if they had they were expecting him sometime before midnight anyway. There had to be an element of convenience to these things. His boss didn't really want to keep the Department of Energy (DOE) people waiting all night for the result. 'Why did they have to do this on my poker night', he wondered?

The obvious conflict of interest that had concerned Brownlie for the past year weighed on his mind more than ever. His instructions were clear: 'Your team should do its best to win, but it will be best for our business if you don't'. 'Understood Sir' was the correct reply! What annoyed him even more right now was the noise of the cicadids. The bug people at the University of Georgia Ecology Lab had predicted 1986 would be a bad year for cicadids. It was the 14th of March and already they were everywhere. Damn things made so much racket at night you couldn't hear yourself think.

About eight meters away Brownlie's second in command was also annoyed, first by the mosquitoes and second by the dense underbrush they had to negotiate to get to their designated launch position. 'Jonesy' was the newest member of the team, having been hired straight out of the U.S. Marine Corps only a few months earlier. And by the way he hated being called 'Jonesy'. What annoyed him about the woods in South Carolina was that you couldn't just walk through them like you could in southern Illinois where he grew up. These woods were more like a jungle. In addition to your weapons you needed a machete to hack your way through the tangled vines and undergrowth. At least tonight they had been 'deposited' on a nearby road while it was still daylight, leaving less than a thousand meters on foot to reach launch point.

Brownlie whisper-yelled to Jonesy, "Five minutes". "Roger" came the reply, as Jonesy turned to pass the word down to the other three members of the strike team, each about eight meters from the next. Brownlie had some discretion about the exact launch time, but not much else. 20:50 hours saw a sliver of a moon finally disappear below the horizon. It was nearly 'Showtime!' Suddenly the flash of a red laser caught Brownlie's eye. With both the strike team and the Protective Force firing blanks, MILES (Multiple Integrated Laser Engagement System) 'laser hits' was the only way to keep score. A laser hit meant you were dead for the purposes of this exercise.

"Hey Jonesy. Tell your guy to knock it off. No MILES until we reach the perimeter." Just then a live round impacted the trunk of a large pine tree about a foot behind Brownlie's head with a loud whack. It was close enough that splinters hit him in the back of the neck. He froze for an instant, then realized that turning toward Jonesy's position during the last second must have saved him from taking that bullet in the left eye. But from where?

Jorge couldn't believe he'd missed at such close range. This certainly wasn't the weapon he was used to. He was sure he wouldn't have missed otherwise. Would he get a second chance? Jorge held up five fingers to let his team know there were five members in the site security contractor's Force on Force strike group. Even though those five were firing blanks, they had to be swiftly eliminated before they could contact anyone and sound an alarm. There would indeed be an assault on L Reactor tonight, but the script had been altered. The DOE wouldn't need to tally up the laser hits. They could count the bodies instead.

Assault on L

Chapter 1

Thursday is 'Barbeque Day' for those who are fortunate enough to work in the Main Administration area of the Savannah River Site. Employees are only supposed to take thirty minutes for lunch, and it takes that long just to drive to the famous Barbeque House in New Ellenton, South Carolina and back again. Nevertheless, the queue for the best pulled pork in the state is always full of Savannah River employees, starting well before 12 noon on Thursdays. And it stays that way until just before 1 pm.

Dining arrangements are quite informal. The tablecloths are printed and delivered before dawn every morning. Today's edition is dated March 13, 1986. No fine china, just paper plates and cups – only the metal utensils go into the square grey bucket to be washed. Find a seat at one of the two dozen long wooden bench tables and share a plastic squeeze bottle of barbeque sauce with whomever happens to be sitting nearby. Of course, carpooling there is more fun, and you can talk 'shop' with your co-workers while you're eating, even though you are cautioned not to.

"So, tell me why you have to work tomorrow night?"
"I can't say exactly. We're not supposed to talk about it."
"You're seeing another woman, aren't you? I knew this would happen..."
"No, no. Really!"
"You said you were working the day shift for the next month. Now you tell me you have to work on a Friday night. I'm not buying it, OK!"
"If I tell you, you mustn't say a word to anybody, agreed?"
"Yes, agreed." She leaned forward, arms folded tightly and still frowning. He spoke softly.
"L Area flunked its last Force on Force exercise two months ago. We're doing a rerun tomorrow night. Now that's all I can say." He motioned for her to lean back.

A man who had just turned 30 was sitting two places down. He adjusted his Clemson University baseball cap while picking over a last bit of coleslaw. The tiny directional microphone above the 'C' in 'Clemson' looked like just another ventilation hole. Shaggy blond hair hid the wire to a tiny receiver in his left ear. He waited three minutes after they had left before dumping his paper plate, cup and utensils into the waste bin near the door. He didn't see the dirty look the cashier gave him.

She had to make the next customer wait while she went and fished the silverware out of the waste bin. "Some people!", she grunted as she returned to ring up a double portion of pork with coleslaw, and large iced tea. Once in the parking lot the young man waited again for a few minutes before slowly pulling out onto South Carolina Highway 19 that runs through the center of New Ellenton

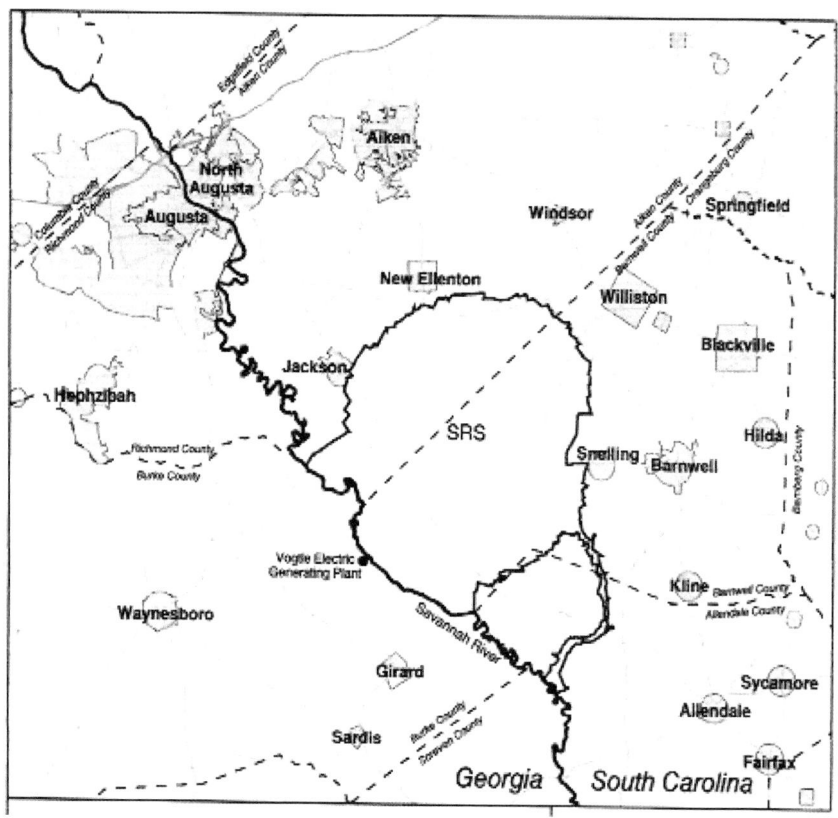

Silas (his American name) had lived alone in one of the few apartments available in Aiken, South Carolina for almost three years. He kept to himself and paid cash for everything, including his rent. None of his neighbors could claim to know anything about him beyond his name and the fact that he drove an old Ford F-150 pickup, faded brown with one rusted out fender. Every day Silas scanned the real estate page (actually less than half a page) of the Aiken Standard for rural property for sale. He needed a farm, even though he had never spent a single day farming in his 48 years, not in America and certainly not in the country he came from, where farming was practically impossible. It was a cloudy September morning in 1984 when Silas suddenly spotted what he was looking for.

Assault on L

'Ole McDonald had a farm', as the nursery rhyme goes but, in this case, Mr. and Mrs. McDonald had both died within a month of each other and left no heirs. Their 145-acre farm was being offered at the October State Auction, in the hope that enough could be raised from the sale to cover the property taxes that hadn't been paid for years. Of course, Silas had to see the property for himself. It had to be remote, away from prying eyes, and irritatingly troublesome to access. Check.

In fact, the dirt road contained so many washboard ruts Silas was relieved his F-150 held together long enough to reach the house and barn. The house was large but needed a new front porch. There were several loose boards – some were missing entirely. Silas had to step carefully, or he might put his foot completely through to the ground about a foot below. The plumbing only worked in the kitchen as far as he could tell.

Outside, the fence was only half in place and the gate was off its hinges. The barn had no doors at all, and he could see blue sky through several holes in the roof. There were several exits in the rear that the builder clearly had not intended. The grounds had not seen a plough or lawnmower in at least a year. He couldn't find either in the barn. The north side of the property was heavily wooded. The south side was open field. Silas judged the entire estate to be barely habitable. In fact, it was absolutely perfect! Anyone attempting to drive a decent car down the first half mile of that road would quickly abandon any curiosity about what might be found at its end. Silas wasn't really surprised to find himself one of only three bidders for the property. He paid twenty-seven thousand dollars in cash.

Silas wasn't all that anxious to leave his apartment in Aiken. It had been hard to get. There just weren't many in the area. At a very early age he discovered the advantages of living alone, with no brothers or sisters he knew of. As a boy his clothes were the only thing he had of value. Five different men kept appearing and disappearing throughout his youth. None ever stayed more than a few months. He wasn't really sure which of them was his father. He thought about asking his mother, but doubted she knew either. In his culture women were often considered property, to be shared occasionally in return for payment, some of which went to her. That all stopped when his mother reached the age of 40. It was a custom that hadn't changed in thousands of years. When Silas reached the age of 14 his mother had to trade him for two mules and a 50 kg. sack of flour. He managed to escape when the ship made port in Istanbul. Silas's skin was much lighter than his mother's, which gave him an advantage. A quick mind and strong back gave him a future.

Assault on L

South Carolina was nothing at all like the land Silas left 34 years ago. He judged the small town of Aiken to be a very pleasant place to live, with beautiful tree lined boulevards and quiet lanes. Some of the locals told him Aiken was the first town in South Carolina to be laid out with double lanes going east and west separated by wide grass-covered medians. Founded in the 1830's, the local government voted in 1877 to plant over 500 hardwood trees along the avenues of South Boundary.

Silas was never sure why it was called South Boundary, but it did display some of the most beautiful old oak trees he had ever seen. The huge trees on both sides formed a canopy completely enclosing the road for as far as you could see. It was like driving through a lush tunnel of green. There was also a 'small town' feel to the place. There were lots of small shops in the town center where you could have a leisurely stroll most any afternoon. Unfortunately, he didn't want to be seen doing such things.

It took another four months to collect some meagre furnishings and various other necessities to make the farm more hospitable. Being a minimalist, Silas had no intention of providing the team with any luxuries. Like him, they must be willing to make a few sacrifices for the mission. Eight single beds, bought in pairs from different local suppliers in different months, all survived that horrible road in the back of the old F-150. Whatever Silas thought of western or American culture he had to admit Ford made good trucks. By February everything was in place except for fixing the toilet – there were no plumbers willing to 'come out that far'. One more small sacrifice they would all have to make.

Silas used the phone at the local hardware store in Aiken to let his handler know all was ready. His handler then placed an ad in all the major newspapers, nationally and internationally. Silas only knew one other name besides his own. Jorge was to be in charge once he arrived. No word as to when that might be. Regardless, his instructions were to be followed without question. The number of mercenaries in the world was far more than the public realized. There were those who performed covert activities for national governments, while others worked for wealthy private interests. Most were amateurs, but an elite few at the top of this guild considered themselves consummate professionals. The 'best of the best' either knew, or knew of, the others. Some pretended to serve some noble cause, but it really was all about the money. For the right fee they would take on the most daring of missions. The fee in this case would be $25 million each!

It was late March before Silas spotted a bearded man with wavy brown hair wearing faded jeans and sweatshirt walking up the road toward the house. He looked to be in his middle thirties, but extremely fit. In the months Silas had been there no living soul had ever come to visit. Why should they? Absolutely nothing was happening there. Even Silas had grown disinterested in the place.

"May I help you", Silas offered? It was the only greeting he could think of. "Maybe", answered the bearded man. "My name is Jorge. I'm looking for a bed for the night". "Well, you can't have mine, but I've got seven others you can pick from", Silas half smiled. His visitor didn't.

Jorge took a quick look around the house and nodded, then walked out toward the barn. "Yes, this will do nicely." He gave Silas that 'alpha male' sort of look that says, 'As long as you do what I tell you we'll get along just fine'. Silas had seen that look before, from his commanding officer in the Turkish Army several decades ago. It's the sort of thing a man never forgets. Back inside, Jorge dumped his backpack unceremoniously onto one of the two beds in the second room on the left. His dark brown eyes scanned the small living room for signs of a phone.

"Got to make some phone calls. Don't suppose you have a phone here?" "Sorry, no", Silas replied. "OK, probably shouldn't use it anyway. I'll hitch a ride into Aiken. Must be a payphone there somewhere." "You can take the truck if you want", said Silas. "Nope, rather walk." With that he was out the door, quickly disappearing down the two-mile dirt road back to the highway. Silas wasn't really sure he wanted other people there. He was anxious about what was coming next.

Indeed, there were plenty of payphones in Aiken. Finding one that actually worked was another matter, however. Jorge decided he needed three, a different one for each newspaper ad he needed to place, as a precaution. Each ad contained a coded reference to an obscure location in rural in South Carolina. It was almost four hours before he arrived back at the farm. "Any luck", asked Silas? "Won't know until the New York Times comes day after tomorrow. Don't suppose you have it delivered here by any chance?" "Sorry, I let my subscription lapse last month", Silas replied, with a smile and a shrug of the shoulders. "Right...", Jorge replied, again dismissing Silas' attempt at humor.

"Guess I'll have to walk back to town for a paper then." Silas considered offering Jorge the use of the truck again, but then thought better of it. "I could drive you", he offered instead. "Absolutely not! We must never be

Assault on L

seen together. And certainly not in that rust bucket!" Jorge slammed his coffee cup down, rose from the small dining table, and left the room. Another day came and went. Hardly a word passed between them. It was 6:15 the next morning before Silas saw him again. Neither said a word as Jorge made his way out the front door, stepping around the broken planks in the front porch, and down the dirt road.

Two hours later Jorge returned clutching the March 17, 1985 edition of the New York Times in his right hand. He didn't look pleased. Silas' pulse quickened. He stood just inside the doorway as Jorge brushed by him at full stride to take a seat at the table. Neither said anything for almost five minutes. Silas knew better than to ask. He would have to be patient. "Five out of six", Jorge finally announced. "Five of six – that's not too bad is it?" Silas didn't know whether to answer or not. "If we can't get the girl, then we'll have to do without her." Jorge spread the newspaper out on the table. He circled five items in the classified section. Each was an offer to sell two tickets to an international sporting event; two in Frankfurt, Germany; one in Barcelona, Spain; one in San Francisco and one in Washington, D.C. "I don't get it", said Silas.

"Look again", replied Jorge. "Look at the dates. The dates on the tickets don't match the scheduled dates of the events." "So, they are fakes", said Silas. "Somebody is trying to sell fake tickets." "No, not just any 'somebodies'", Jorge replied. "Five very special 'somebodies', each replying to my newspaper ad. A date on the ticket of the 10th means they're unavailable. Count them out. A date on the ticket of the 12th means they're in."

"Each of these five ads in the classified section of the Times shows a pair of tickets dated the 12th. They're in! They're on the team. The two in Germany and the one in Spain will be here within a week. The ones from San Francisco and Washington will be here the day after tomorrow. Unfortunately, the girl didn't respond. Maybe she never saw the ad. That could be a problem – we'll have to work around it somehow."

If you wanted to remain anonymous there were a few things to remember. Always pay with cash. Never write anything down. Anything written down can be used to find you and, in most cases, incriminate you. Never use the postal system. Mail can be read by somebody before it gets to you. Newspapers were a way to communicate without traceability. Nobody could listen in or trace it back to you. You just needed to know which newspapers to look at, when to look, and what to look for.

Assault on L

Silas kept staring at the copy of the Times on the table. He couldn't believe it was that simple, five messages hidden in plain sight in one of the most widely read newspapers in the world. "What's this", he remarked, pointing to an ad for tickets to the Annual Chicago Craft Fair the week of May 21st? "Someone's transposed the digits on these tickets as well." Jorge's face slowly morphed into a broad smile Silas hadn't believed possible. He was grinning from ear to ear. "That's her", Jorge shouted, jumping to his feet. "That's her! She's in! That makes six!!"

As darkness fell over the McDonald farm, Jorge realized the only lights that worked were in the kitchen and the living room. "Nice place you've got here", he said out loud to nobody. Silas came through the front door about a minute later. "What's wrong with the toilet anyway, Jorge asked? "Plugged water pipe under the house, I think. It's not busted 'cause it looks dry under there and we've still got water pressure in the kitchen. You can carry water from the kitchen sink to make it flush." Jorge grimaced at such an inconvenience. "So obviously the electric pump at the well still has power. Why no power in most of the house then?" "Don't know", Silas replied.

"Maybe one of your guys can fix the electrics when they get here. And maybe the plugged water pipe too." The frown on Jorge's face turned to a smile. "These guys have survived machine gun fire, mortar attacks, roadside bombs, and just about everything else live combat can throw at them. And you think one of them might be willing to share that two-foot crawl space under this house with 'South Carolina snake and bug city' long enough to belly-crawl ten meters to reach a plugged water pipe?" He shook his head while starring at the weathered wooden floor. "Not a chance in Hell!"

An hour passed without another word being said. Jorge's mind was clearly in another place and another time. When he was a boy, he used to sit next to his maternal grandmother on a small stone pad in the garden. She would tell him the names of all the flowers, and he would try his best to remember them all. The pond had fish in it, too. Some were as long as his arm. "Why can't we catch one of the fish", he would ask? His grandmother would reply, "Because the fish have as much right to live out their lives in the way they choose as you and I do. Just because we can catch them doesn't mean we have the right to do so. You must think about your actions and decide if they are just and proper."

"But what if I'm hungry and want to eat the fish", Jorge asked? "Then you must decide if the fish's life is more important than your life." "My life is more important, of course", he replied. "According to who?" "According to me." "Suppose it was a choice between your life and the life of another person?" "I would choose my life over theirs", he replied. "Let's hope it's your choice rather than theirs, when that time comes!"

Suddenly Jorge's thoughts jumped a quarter of a century into the future. He was wondering about the mission. Should he be planning out how the operation would do down, or trying to think of a way out of the whole thing? "What's our chance of pulling this off", Silas finally asked? The question seemed to catch Jorge by surprise. He sat up straight. "No problem. We've got the right people for the job. I have every confidence in them. We just need the right opportunity. We have to be patient. It will happen. Trust me." Jorge was an experienced liar. He estimated the odds of completing their mission at one chance in five. Either way every one of them could end up dead. For some it might take only minutes, for others maybe days...., a week at best.

Silas spotted him first, walking slowly down the rutted dirt road toward the house just after 7:00 hours. Now there were three! Henry looked to be about five years younger than Silas, clean shaven with short red hair that showed early signs of receding. Both could boast the same number of years in active combat. Silas had always expected to be the most senior member on the team. That wasn't necessarily a good thing. It was young man's game after all. "Henry!", Jorge shouted, as he pushed past Silas and into the open doorway. "I suppose you expect us to have breakfast waiting for your arrival?" "As any great hotel should", Henry replied.

Both turned and looked at Silas. "And you must be the cook", said Henry offering a firm handshake. "Looks that way, doesn't it", Silas replied grudgingly. Cooking wasn't what he had planned for this morning, but then one had to be flexible. That afternoon Jorge and Silas gave Henry a round of applause for rigging a hosepipe from the kitchen to the bathroom at the end of the hall. No more carrying water from the kitchen to flush the toilet or fill the old cast iron bathtub. 'Things were looking up', thought Silas.

It was nearly 15:00 hours the next day when the fourth one showed up. He was young, too young by Silas' measure. 'Late 20's at best', he thought. Samuel had the kind of shaggy blonde hair that always looks like it hadn't been combed since he was born. The girls probably liked it, but Silas didn't care for it. Just looked 'unprofessional'. As soon as he was inside the house Samuel pulled a weathered baseball cap out of his hip pocket and pulled it down onto his forehead. Silas couldn't resist asking. "Why do you wear a cap indoors?" "'Cause I don't wear it outdoors. Sun fades the colors", Samuel replied with a half-smile.

It was plain to see that the colors had already faded into a few subtle shades of grey. Silas considered pursuing the matter further, but then thought better of it. Only thing worse than a smart-ass was a young smart-ass! Jorge introduced Henry and Samuel by name only and asked that everyone keep the small talk to a minimum until the rest of the team had arrived. More formal introductions would have to wait until then. With all four bedrooms at the farm taken, the next to arrive would have to share, whether she wanted to or not.

She looked even younger than Samuel, barely old enough to drink. 'Definitely too young to die', thought Jorge. But even lambs have to be sacrificed on occasion. In the meantime, he had to admit she was 'something special' to look at. Janine wore her jet-black hair in bangs just above the eyebrow. With a Chinese mother and American father, anyone could see she had inherited the best genes from both. Her blue-green eyes were impossible to ignore if she was interested, and impossible to access if she was not.

Samuel was the first to attempt a somewhat less than polite conversation with Janine, in spite of Jorge's admonition about small talk. It didn't go well. She suggested ripping off a part of his anatomy and feeding it to him. "I wouldn't mess with that one if I were you", Jorge offered. "Several of her martial arts teachings have been banned from international competition." Samuel always fancied himself a 'lady's man'. He was convinced as early as his high school days that he was 'God's gift to women'. Many women had tried to convince him otherwise.

Samuel's other claim to fame was his expertise with electronics. With an electrical engineer for a father and a professor of mathematics for a mother, he was destined to make his mark in the world. But it was the Western world he wanted to tame, not the Russian world he was born into. His criminal career began when he defeated the electronic alarm systems at a major bank in Moscow and stole over a million rubbles in gold coin at the request of the Russian Mafia. His career ended when he decided to keep the gold rather than give it to the mob. Samuel had spent most of it over the past five years perfecting his English into a perfect southern drawl and establishing an identity in North Carolina, while evading more than a dozen Russian mobsters determined to retrieve their money, or peel the skin off his body as compensation.

Assault on L

As the afternoon wore on it was obvious to everyone that a difficult decision had to be made. Jorge passed the dilemma to Janine, suggesting she choose whose bedroom she would prefer to share. "My grandmother taught me to honor my elders. Who here is the oldest", she asked? Silas slowly raised his hand. "It will be your treat, then", she announced, with a slight bow in his direction. Silas instinctively returned the gesture. He had never been called 'elderly' before but decided he would forgive her that slight.

As he nodded his acceptance, his middle-aged heart skipped a few beats. He had never taken a wife or even a girlfriend, partly because of the memories of how his mother and other women were treated when he was growing up. He had never seen a live woman 'in the flesh'. It would be his treat indeed, as Janine proved she wasn't shy about dressing and undressing in front of a man she barely knew. She had a sense for these things, however, and seemed to know he would grant her as much or as little privacy as she wanted. It was out of respect for him that she maintained a certain degree of modesty. Silas decided being the senior member of the team was a good thing after all. And now there were five.

Another week passed before the others made their appearance. Luis considered himself lucky to get a flight from Barcelona to Washington's Dulles International on such short notice. Those flights were usually fully booked several weeks in advance. There were plenty of flights from Dulles into Hartsfield Jackson International in Atlanta, Georgia, but only a few from Atlanta into Augusta. Then there was the cab ride from Augusta to Aiken, which Luis judged to be much more expensive than it should have been, especially since he asked the driver to drop him off at the side of the highway next to a dirt road before even reaching the Aiken city limits. It was good thing the cab drivers in Barcelona didn't know how much their counterparts in America were charging!

By the time Luis walked the two miles to the farmhouse he had twice considered that he might die of exhaustion before the mission even began. His favorite pastime, rock climbing, was surely easier than traversing these dusty dirt roads in South Carolina. Jorge's cheerful greeting and a glass of lukewarm tea improved Luis' outlook somewhat, although he wasn't entirely convinced he'd made a wise choice in coming all this way. He was only 31. Maybe he should live a bit more before risking his life on such a mission. But then Jorge could be very persuasive. And now there were six.

Assault on L

The last two members of Jorge's team, Otis and Ansel, sat nine rows apart on the flight from Frankfurt to Hartsfield Jackson International in Atlanta, but not for operational security reasons. Both were in their mid-thirties and were known to Jorge, but although they happened to live within a mile of each other in Frankfurt they had never met. Otis and Ansel first spoke to one another quite by accident in the Augusta Airport baggage claim area. Augusta enjoys a larger airport than most cities its size due to the huge influx of visitors for one week a year. Nevertheless, its baggage claim area is quite small. It's impossible for anyone there to not overhear the conversations of others, especially if they have a foreign accent. In Augusta anyone not from either Georgia or South Carolina readily qualifies as having a 'foreign accent'.

Two German's in Augusta, both wanting to go to the same small town in rural South Carolina. What a coincidence? It wasn't until they both asked to be dropped at the same place on a lonely highway next to a dirt road that things clicked. Unlike the others, they had the luxury of keeping each other company, in German of course, while they walked the two miles to the McDonald farm. Now there were eight.

With the team complete the time for more formal introductions had arrived. And none too soon. The players were getting more restless by the hour. Jorge took center stage. "Now that we're all here I will ask each of you to reveal as much or as little personal information you wish to share so that we can all get to know one another. Each of you has a speciality vital to this mission. It is critical that each of us know each other's roles in this operation. It is too early to reveal exactly what that mission is. At this time it is enough for you to know that it involves one of the operational facilities at the Savannah River Site less than twenty-five miles from here.

Several things were obvious. Except for Janine, all of them had extensive military experience and were excellent marksmen with a range of weapons. All of them were known quantities to Jorge, either by direct observation or unimpeachable reputation. Some might have their own reasons for wanting to be part of this team. None of that mattered to Jorge, as long as it didn't interfere with accomplishing the mission. As their leader he had to establish trust between the members of the group.

Silas knew more than the rest but pretended otherwise. His pockmarked face and unkempt greying eyebrows added five years to his true age. "Name's Silas. Last name is not important. My initial role is one of support. Procuring and furnishing these 'luxurious accommodations' was first on my list. I trust you are all enjoying the fine cuisine and stunning architecture." He extended his hand and gracefully panned around the cracked walls of the small living room. "Twenty years in the Turkish Armed Forces, five in Special Operations. I have only one rule – pay cash for everything! One other thing. I'm not a farmer, but I have managed to grow some carrots and cabbage in a small plot out by the barn. Please don't walk on them. Thank you."

Samuel considered Silas 'obsolete' in all respects, but he had to admit the old man had done his tour. "Samuel here. Spent the last five years helping some government nerds in Arlington, Virginia design new ways to keep the bad guys, like us, out of their precious facilities. Why they gave me a security clearance I'll never understand. Not too sharp these guys!" He paused to push his baseball cap back a bit from his forehead. "Grew up in North Carolina, 'bout a hundred miles from here. Some of you've probably never been to North Carolina. That's OK. You might still be forgiven when you reach the Pearly Gates, if St. Peter's in a good mood." He started to sit down, then stood back up. "Oh, and I'm facing the big 3-0 next month. No birthday cake, please." Samuel saw no point in revealing his Russian heritage. In his experience most people in the west had an innate distrust for anyone or anything Russian.

Henry rose to his feet slowly, one hand on his hip, then paused to take a wad of chewing gum out of his mouth. He threw it toward the garbage bin near the kitchen door but missed. "All this sitting around is putting my back out", he exclaimed! "I'm Henry. Jorge hasn't said, but I guess I'll be second in command, just in case he gets taken out early in the mission. Gave up a perfectly good pharmaceutical job in San Francisco to attend this party. Jorge hasn't told me why he needs somebody with a Chemical Engineering Degree from MIT. Suppose that will become clear later on. Idaho's my State. Lots of wide-open spaces where a boy growing up can do pretty much anything he wants. Can't say I've ever found anyplace better." All that was a lie of course. Henry had never been within a hundred miles of Idaho. Lying was a favorite pastime of Henry's, like breathing. He gave a mock salute and sat back down slowly.

"Luis", he announced, with a strong Spanish accent. "Can't recommend your hotel here to the international crowd." He was looking at Silas with faint smile. "Still, it beats ten hours a day of cutting up fish in Barcelona. Looks like I've got Samuel beat by a year. Reminds me of my little brother, except for the baseball cap." Samuel didn't show even a hint of a smile. "My thing is rock climbing. I've done El Capitan twice! But I've never seen anything as bad as the dirt road to this place, Silas." "Thank you", Silas replied with a tip of the hat. "And I know a bit about explosives, too", Luis added.

"I'm Janine", she announced in a soft voice while still seated. "I teach martial arts in Chicago, or at least I used to. Hopefully I can get my job back when this is over. I suppose I must be the youngest of the group. I was only seventeen when I got involved in saving our planet from being destroyed by humankind. The more I've seen in recent years the more committed I am to the cause. Like in any war, there will be casualties. If that includes some us, so be it. Our planet's future depends on the sacrifices we are willing to make." Samuel couldn't help thinking that wasn't the woman he talked to several nights ago. She would happily pluck his eyeballs out and use them for olives in her martini! Silas leaned over to Jorge. "She's good isn't she." "Extremely good", Jorge replied, turning back toward the group. "You're up Ansel."

Ansel was still thinking about Janine's blue-green eyes. "Yah, uhh.. "I come from Austria. I work in air freight warehouse at Flughafen Frankfurt am Main International Airport. The things that come through air freight, you would not believe. These things I can get for you. Weapons, explosives, night vision equipment, whatever the mission requires. Some things quickly, other things take more time. You let me know, yah?" "We'll discuss that later", Jorge interrupted.

Otis was last as usual. It seemed to be his lot in life. "Hello, I am Otis. I work as assistant chef at a five-star hotel in Frankfurt. Hope you have enjoyed the meals I have prepared for you the last few days." All heads nodded their approval. "Anyone unhappy with the food, you are welcome to cook, instead." "No, no", replied Henry. "Food's great!" "Anyway", Ansel continued, "I come from Noordwijk in the Netherlands and have a master's degree in physics from Heidelberg University." "Why would someone with a degree in physics want be a chef in a German hotel", Janine asked? "Physics is boring", replied Otis. "Cooking is much more exciting!" Janine lowered her head slightly and smiled. She was interested. Samuel noticed. He wasn't happy. Maybe Otis would have an accident or something....

For Otis there was one thing more exciting than cooking up great food. That was cooking up radioactive cocktails for very particular Russian customers in high places. On one occasion it was Polonium 210. Another time it was a mixture of Strontium 90 and Uranium 234. He had provided Actinium and Thorium isotopes in answer to other requests. The Russians seemed to enjoy poisoning those who dared to publicly disagree with the government's position on political matters, especially when they managed to acquire asylum in the west. Officially such deaths were recorded as 'cause of death unknown', but the message to other dissidents was clearly understood. Someday someone would do a thorough autopsy on one of these people and discover the truth. Otis knew that would lead back to him eventually. But he hadn't actually killed anyone, and he was being well paid.

That left Jorge. "All of you know me or have heard about me", he began. "That I am on Interpol's 'most wanted' list in several middle eastern countries should not concern you. Those charges and my past freelance activities have nothing to do with our mission here. What's important is that I am the team lead for this mission. This mission will only succeed if you follow my instructions without question. Is that understood?" All heads nodded in agreement.

For operations security here are the rules:

1. Silas, Samuel or I will normally be the only ones leaving the farm until the mission is launched. If you need something one of us will get it for you. Anyone leaving the farm for any reason must have my express permission, even if it's a medical emergency.

2. Specific information about the target will be revealed when the mission launches. Speculate privately all you like, but do not share those speculations with anyone else. It will only cause confusion during training and strike simulations.

3. There will be no fires (i.e., smoke) or any other activities that might attract attention to the fact that the farm is occupied. The condition of the dirt road leading to the farm has been an effective deterrent to the curious. Let's keep it that way.

4. Once weapons arrive no rounds, live or blanks, will to be fired without sound attenuation. Our nearest neighbour is approximately two miles to the east. We don't want them hearing gunfire and calling the police.

One more thing. Some simulations will assume early loss of certain team members, including myself. Don't take it personally! Any questions?

Samuel couldn't resist asking the most obvious question. "Any idea when the mission might launch?" "That will be determined by events", Jorge replied, a bit annoyed at being pressed for more information. "The less you know right now, the safer it will be for all of us." He didn't mean it as a personal put down, although Samuel took it as such. The truth was nobody could say if they might have to wait two months or two years for the right opportunity to present itself. But they had to be ready within twenty-four hours when it did. It was a strike team leader's greatest challenge.

Jorge projected a cold hard exterior. It helped him maintain discipline and discipline was critical to accomplishing this mission. The eight of them represented the minimum number required to pull it off. He couldn't afford to lose any of them, but fully expected to lose maybe half during the initial assault. As far as taking a human life, he had done so many times without a second thought. He had to assume based on what he knew of the others that they were the same. The slightest hesitation in this business could be fatal. His real concern was tension between team members before the mission ever started. The longer they had to wait the more that tension would build. That was his second challenge. They needed time to train and develop as a team; after that, time was working against him. Keeping them from killing each other might not be easy.

Jorge had witnessed first-hand in Iran and Iraq how morale can make the difference between success or failure on the battlefield. The leader was often the key. A charismatic leader could inspire his troops. But if he was lost early, a successful charge frequently became a rout. He made certain no one thought of him as charismatic. Personal rivalries were the problem with this group. Each member of the team was a 'highly tuned thoroughbred'. He knew enough about horses to know they liked to run. And when they ran, they liked to win. Strict discipline and possibly a bit of primal fear were the only tools he had to keep the competition under control. He had to use them to maximum effect and hope it would be enough. They had to fear him more than anything else.

Unfortunately for Jorge fear was no stranger. From his first year in school he learned to fear the gangs of older boys who would steal anything you had of value. Jorge never had anything of value, but they singled him out anyway just for being different. "Why are your eyes round", they would ask with a sadistic grin? He didn't know of course, and his grandmother dismissed such questions as unimportant. As he grew older, Jorge experienced all the stigmas associated with 'being different'. He explained the bruises as just being clumsy, although he suspected his grandmother wasn't fooled. Indeed, she wasn't. She taught Jorge how to turn fear into a weapon rather than a weakness.

Assault on L

Growing up in a society that didn't accept him taught Jorge to be inherently suspicious of others. His grandmother was the only one he trusted, and on occasion he even worried about her. Once he was old enough to leave her care he vanished into the world without a trace. There were other countries more accepting, who's military forces were only too happy to teach him the skills he needed to defend himself. After being discharged from the armed services in one country he would simply relocate to another and start over, never using the same identity twice. He found military life to be safe, anonymous, and much to his liking. Jorge frequently supplemented his military pay by taking on ever more ambitious 'jobs' for clients who wished to have their political enemies 'disappear'. Fear no longer kept him awake at night. Fear of him kept others awake instead.

Assault on L

Chapter 2

Captain Brownlie had never been in the Protective Force Main Administration Building, let alone the Head Office. What could he possibly have done to warrant a reprimand at this high a level? Why couldn't they just fire him without all this fuss. He was told to wait in the main lobby until called. It was only fifteen minutes, but it seemed like a lifetime. The door opened. "You may go in", the secretary announced.

Inside were his immediate supervisor, and his boss, and his boss. Surely, they didn't need three senior levels of management just to fire one Captain! "Please have a seat, Captain Brownlie." His immediate supervisor gestured toward the only chair on the left, while the other men all took the chairs on the right. "Captain Brownlie, I'll come right to the point. It seems we have an opportunity for you." Brownlie knew what that meant in military speak. There was a most undesirable job nobody wanted. 'Congratulations Brownlie, you're it!' "But you must keep this information in strictest confidence. Do we have your word on that?"

"Yes, sir", he replied, without the faintest notion what he was agreeing to. "As of March 1, 1985, effective at 8:00 hours the Department of Energy Threat Guidance has been revised to require periodic real-time testing of Protective Force operations at DOE facilities, to include Force on Force simulations by an elite strike team constituted from Protective Force personnel. This letter dated March 3rd instructs us to begin such actions immediately. After consultation with other members of Staff we have selected you, Captain Brownlie, to lead this elite strike team."

"I'm not sure I understand, sir. Do you mean live fire demonstrations", Brownlie replied? "Not demonstrations, Captain Brownlie. Actual simulated combat, using blank ammunition of course. Your team will attack the target facility and the Protective Force personnel will respond and repel the attack in real time. Fatalities will be simulated by using Multiple Integrated Laser Engagement System (MILES) equipment attached to your weapons. MILES equipment has been used by certain elements of the U. S. Military for some time and with satisfactory results. I would suggest you become familiar with this equipment as soon as possible."

Once outside, Captain Brownlie began to wonder how an organization could be ordered to attack itself without bias. Even though his identity and the identity of his team would remain a closely guarded secret, even from his own organization, the conflict of interest was obvious. His first thought was 'OK, make it look realistic but let the guys inside the facility win'. Surely there would be swift and certain criticism for any other outcome! Over the coming days members of his strike team were selected and began to report for instructions. He could only keep them in the dark for so long. When he finally briefed them on the task they had been assigned, it was no surprise their reaction was the same as his.

"So, we're supposed to storm the place, kill all our mates in the building, and then what", asked O'Hara, a ten-year veteran of the British Royal Marines. "Then we call up the boss and tell him the bad news", replied Brownlie. "Bad news for us, you mean", quipped O'Hara. The pained look on Captain Brownlie's face was all the answer they needed. "Look, we're being paid to do a job. So, let's do it in as professional a way as possible." That was the end of the briefing.

The Savannah River Site comprises over 300 square miles of federally owned land on the South Carolina side of the Savannah River. Finding remote locations on site for Captain Brownlie's team and other members of the site Protective Force to practice with MILES equipment was not difficult. Within six months all appropriate personnel were sufficiently trained so that Force on Force exercises could begin in earnest.

The first of these involved a simulated attack on a nuclear materials storage facility in the 200-F Separations area of the site. For the strike force team, winning meant getting into the facility, achieving 'hands on' access to simulated nuclear material, and escaping back out of the facility with their prize. For the Protective Force personnel charged with defending the facility, winning meant capturing or killing all of the attacking forces before they could escape with the nuclear material, or better still, killing or capturing all the attackers before they reached the nuclear material.

The first Force on Force exercise was primarily a learning experience for Captain Brownlie and his team, as well as for the Protective Force personnel in the facility. A few minutes after the attack was launched all of the attacking forces had been killed without ever getting inside the facility, giving senior management for the site security contractor a great deal to brag about for the next month.

There were those within the DOE, however, who felt the Protective Force personnel in the facility had been given an unrealistic advantage. Captain Brownlie wholeheartedly agreed. There was an element of pride amongst his team members, who were a bit embarrassed at being defeated so easily. Perhaps the timing of the attack and other information given to the defending forces should be less specific. Two months later the exercise was repeated. This time the attacking forces made it into the facility by using explosives to blow open a side door to the building. Of course, no explosives were actually used – the door was simply left unlocked for purposes of the exercise.

On this occasion two of the attackers made it to the location of the simulated nuclear material but were killed before they could gain entry into the storage room. Another rousing success for the site security contractor, but another mark against Captain Brownlie's strike team. There were hints that perhaps his team might not be trying hard enough. Most of Captain Brownlie's team began to view their efforts as just a series of 'no win scenarios'.

O'Hara was again the most vocal of the group. "How can we be expected to win when everyone knows exactly when we're coming?" "We aren't expected to win", cried Thompson. "It's so artificial. It doesn't prove anything about what might happen in the event of a real 'unannounced' attack on one of these facilities." "Maybe it isn't supposed to", added Sarco. "It's DOE's game – they can make the rules any way they like." Captain Brownlie was thinking he might soon have a mutiny on his hands if this continued. He needed to convince his management, and the DOE, that these exercises were a waste of time and money unless a greater degree of realism was allowed. The need to keep operations personnel in these facilities 'out of the way' during these Force on Force exercises meant that a relatively large number of people were free to witness these events. What would happen if one of these witnesses judged the whole thing to be a farce and confided in the newspapers?

It took several months but Captain Brownlie's persistence finally paid some dividends. The rules of engagement changed significantly. It was agreed that the target facility would be given a six-hour window during which the simulated attack would take place. In addition, the strike team could use diversions and other ploys to distract the Protective Force personnel in the facility during that six-hour window. Methods to defeat or confuse the Perimeter Intrusion and Detection Analysis System (PIDAS) equipment could also be employed so that information about the exact time and location where the attackers penetrated the secure area might be slightly delayed and/or inaccurate. Captain Brownlie explained these changes to his team two weeks before their next exercise. Moral improved almost immediately as they began considering diversionary tactics and other methods they might use.

The next Force on Force exercise was completely unlike any that had been conducted at the Savannah River Site before. Not only had the rules of engagement changed but the target had changed as well. This time the target was one of the three operating nuclear production reactors on site. The protection strategy for reactor facilities was different than for facilities that store nuclear materials. The protection strategy for nuclear materials is one of 'containment', i.e., preventing the attackers from escaping with the nuclear material. The protection strategy for a nuclear reactor is one of 'denial'. No member of the attacking force can be allowed to reach certain sensitive locations in the reactor building, where they could take actions that would result in a reactor meltdown and release of radioactive contamination across the entire eastern seaboard of the United States. Much more stringent demands are placed on the Protective Force personnel under a 'denial' protection strategy. For both Captain Brownlie, and the entire Protective Force organization, the stakes in the game had been raised substantially!

For most people, the week between Christmas and New Year's means enjoying the holidays with friends and family. Many businesses are closed or running with minimum staff. Some operations at the Savannah River Site slow down but most continue as though Christmas week was just like any other. Nuclear reactors require a minimum staff of personnel 24 hours a day, 7 days a week, but the number of people in a reactor area during Christmas week is usually below normal. Management's decision to conduct the next Force on Force exercise during that week made sense. Fewer people, particularly outside the reactor building meant fewer chances of someone getting in the way. "We will be launching a simulated attack on the L Reactor Area approximately 72 hours from now", Captain Brownlie announced the day after Christmas. I know the timing sucks but that is the direction we have been given. My apologies to your families for the inconvenience."

"Although we have been given a six-hour window, moonrise on the 29th will be approximately one hour after sunset. The pines along the eastern boundary may block direct moonlight for fifteen or twenty minutes, but that may not be much help. So, we effectively have one hour instead six. You can scratch the element of surprise off your list gentlemen. On the other hand, they will not know our direction of approach. We may be able to confuse them on that point at least. One of us will create a diversion at the east corner of the PIDAS, while the other five approach from the west just after sunset. Our objective is for at least one of us to reach a location in the center of the main building at the minus 20-foot level where critical piping, known as the 'crosstie header', is located. Placing a simulated explosive charge at this location will end the exercise. I will be able to give you more information on the 29th. Are there any questions?" "I take it the 'bad guys' plan to blow the piping with no expectation of escape", Thompson inquired? "That is correct", Brownlie replied. "Wow", replied O'Hara! "Yes, WOW", said Brownlie!

At precisely 10:00 hours on the 29th, 8 hours before the launch window, Captain Brownlie assembled his team again. "Gentlemen, this will be your final briefing before tonight's exercise. We can expect to be transported to a location in the woods on the west side of L Area at approximately 14:00 hours. Thompson will move through the woods to a position on the east side and begin random diversionary activities at approximately 16:00 hours using his MILES equipment and aluminium balloons that inflate on impact inside the PIDAS. By the time we launch our attack from the west, facility personnel monitoring the PIDAS should be at their wits end trying to respond to all the spurious alarms and camera tracking error messages. Sometime after 18:00 hours the rest of the team will emerge from the wood line and scale the outer fence of the PIDAS.

In the unlikely event that monitoring personnel can distinguish our activities from those created by Thompson, we will have fifteen seconds to cross the detection zone and scale the inner fence before the Protective Force can respond to our location." Any questions so far?" "I thought we couldn't start our attack before 18:00 hours," remarked O'Hara. "The rules of engagement say we can't launch our attack before then. But they don't say we can't harass the poor bastards inside the facility before that time", Brownlie replied. A round of applause erupted. It was just the emotional boost Brownlie needed.

"Once inside the inner fence", Brownlie continued, "our destination is a personnel doorway on the west side of the building slightly below grade. This doorway will give us access to an area of the building where the diesel generators are located, known as the '108 building'. This doorway and its twin on the east side of the main building have been identified as 'soft entry points' that lead directly into the minus 20 foot elevation of the building." Brownlie displayed several drawings on the overhead screen showing the east and west 108 buildings and corridors on minus 20 level leading directly to the 'crosstie header'. "Distance from the fence to the 108 building doors", asked Sarco? "About 100 meters", Brownlie responded.

Assault on L

"We may encounter defensive personnel and grenade screens inside the 108 building. Or perhaps not. Either way, we must reach the inner doorway about 25 meters from where we came in. There is a large diesel engine and several other smaller diesel engines along the wall to provide cover. The smaller diesel engines will be running so don't touch them. Once through that inner door we will have to fight our way past defensive personnel behind grenade shields along several corridors. Distance to the crosstie header location is currently unknown but it shouldn't be more than 80 meters as judged from these drawings."

At precisely 16:00 hours Thompson began diversionary activities on the east side of the PIDAS, initially from beyond the wood line and later on from the cover of a shallow ravine that ran parallel to the outer PIDAS fence at a distance of about 40 meters. Lasers used as part of the MILES equipment could temporarily blind cameras used in the PIDAS for visual assessment. Repeated laser flashes would cause repeated error messages, annoying monitoring personnel until they turned them off. Once turned back on, these cameras needed at least 20 seconds to reboot. Prior to sunset Thompson couldn't risk moving out from behind the wood line. Once it was dusk, however, he could use another tactic, one that he was actually quite proud of.

Aluminized balloons were commonplace, often filled with helium for children's birthday parties, etc. On his own initiative, and without authorization, Thompson had designed a system that would cause a balloon to inflate upon impact, using small helium cartridges with impact sensitive valves. "Can we use these things", Thompson had asked? "What things", replied Captain Brownlie, after witnessing a brief demonstration?

As dusk set in Thompson began lobbing his rolled up uninflated 'balloon balls' into the detection zone between the two PIDAS fences. As they hit the ground each one inflated into an aluminized sphere, that quickly began moving around in the wind, setting off all the motion detectors. Alarms from the east side of the PIDAS began to flood into the monitoring consoles. Personnel had to be sent out to physically assess the alarms. Upon arrival it was plain to see these balloons were causing the problem, but removing them meant someone had to go inside the detection zone, pick them up, and dispose of them. Sending someone inside the detection zone required that all the motion detection equipment in that zone had to be temporarily switched off, and then the system had to be rebooted when everything was switched back on again. This was not a good thing to be doing when a Force on Force exercise was imminent.

By tossing one 'balloon ball' into the PIDAS about every fifteen minutes, Thompson was able tie up a large number of Protective Force personnel, while simultaneously degrading confidence in their detection capabilities. By 18:30 hours Protective Force personnel were totally confused about which alarms were real and which were false.

The line of trees to the east did provide a few additional minutes of darkness before moonlight lit up the area. Captain Brownlie's team exited the woods at 18:40 and reached the outer PIDAS fence in about 90 seconds. Using car floor mats to cover the stands of razor wire topping the eight-foot cyclone fence, all five were over and into the detection zone in 10 seconds. This set off several motion detection alarms on the west side of the PIDAS. It took the Protective Force about ten seconds to isolate those alarms from the ones created by Thompson on the east side, and another ten seconds to switch their monitors to the cameras in that sector of the detection zone for a visual assessment. By then Captain Brownlie and his men had cleared the second PIDAS fence and were on the move toward the west side 108 building.

A Protective Force response team arrived in time to catch the strike team on a dead run about twenty meters from the 108 building entrance. One laser beam painted Sarco in the chest, setting off his MILES receptor. He immediately stopped and sat down in place. He was to remain there pending the preliminary critique to be held at the end of the exercise. Others missed their targets. Three members of the strike team reached the exterior door of the 108 building. Brownlie and Jonesy held off the Protective Force response team with weapons fire, while Brennen simulated blowing the door with explosives. For the purposes of the exercise the door was left unlocked.

A MILES laser painted Brennen just as they moved through the doorway. Once inside the 108 building Brownlie, Jonesy and O'Hara met no armed resistance. They moved quickly to the inner door leading into the minus 20 level of the main reactor building. Finding this door already propped open, they ran down the open corridor to the first corner. A quick assessment of what lay around that corner revealed two grenade screens positioned on opposite sides of another long corridor.

MILES fire from behind the grenade screens indicated there was only one defender at the moment. Others would be arriving within seconds, so it was critical that Captain Brownlie get past these positions with minimal delay. O'Hara tossed three flash-bang grenades toward the left grenade shield, before taking a laser hit to the chest. On detonation of the flash bangs, Brownlie and Jonesy stormed the grenade shields and took out the lone defender. The last corner before the corridor leading to the crosstie header was more heavily defended. Several attempts to overcome this position with flash bang grenades failed.

In desperation, Captain Brownlie managed to leap across to another area of cover on the opposite side of the corridor. He and Jonesy took out all but one of the defenders with crossfire. Jonesy finally eliminated the last defender, but not before Brownlie took a hit to the chest. To his surprise Jonesy encountered no further resistance, reaching the crosstie header location only 20 meters away. Dropping his weapon, he placed a simulated explosive charge on the 18-inch pipe just over his head, only seconds before taking three laser hits. "Sorry", he announced. "I think you're too late!"

DOE protocol requires that several 'independent observers', in remote locations, witness each Force on Force exercise as it unfolds in real time. Their evaluation is factored into the overall performance assessment during the final critique and is intended to provide assurance that both adversary and Protective Force actions are realistic and not contrived toward a predetermined result. No one could have suspected that events transpiring in L Area on the night of December 29, 1985 were also being observed by someone without authorization to even be present on Savannah River Site property.

Captain Brownlie's team was quite proud of their performance. Brownlie had mixed emotions. It probably meant that more restrictions would be placed on them in the future, particularly when it came to diversionary tactics. Afterall the objective of these exercises was to prove to the DOE customer that the Protective Force organization could defend any of the Site's facilities against attack by a real adversary. During the formal critique of the L Area exercise Captain Brownlie's senior management was repeatedly embarrassed. On this occasion they had failed to do what they were being paid to do.

One could argue that Thompson's knowledge of the intrusion detection system and the ways it could be degraded gave the adversary team an artificial advantage. An actual adversary would not likely have such knowledge. Brownlie argued on the other hand that a real adversary team could strike at a time of its choosing, and probably wouldn't pick 18:30

hours on a moonlit night. Surely no one could pretend this exercise included an element of surprise. This being the first Force on Force exercise on a reactor building there were a number of lessons to be learned.

First was the realization that outside entrances to the 108 buildings clearly represented 'soft targets' to a real adversary. Physical hardening of these entrances was needed. Delaying the strike team at this location for even another 30 seconds might result in the entire adversary team being killed without ever getting into the building. Second, once the strike team was inside the 108 building there were no fighting positions for the Protective Force in that part of the facility. With only one path from there into the main building, the inner doorway of the 108 building was an obvious choke point.

In fact, Captain Brownlie's team had encountered no resistance at all until they were well inside the main building and within 90 yards of their target. Third, the exercise highlighted numerous deficiencies in the Perimeter Intrusion and Detection Analysis System (PIDAS) monitoring protocol, which made response to false alarms and diversions irritatingly ineffective. Some means of isolating spurious alarms in one zone from valid alarms in other zones was needed. Camera technology that was less susceptible to laser interference should be investigated as well.

At the conclusion of the critique the site's senior manager for the Protective Force organization graciously accepted that there was work to be done, apologized for failing to meet the DOE's expectations, and pledged the support of his entire organization in quickly correcting the deficiencies noted.

Captain Brownlie fully expected his supervisor would want to discuss his team's performance in greater detail. The summons was immediate. "What the hell were you guys doing", his boss yelled! "You're not supposed to win these things! They're raising hell all the way up on the fourth floor of the Forrestal Building in Washington right now!! We could lose the contract at this site, and maybe even other sites, over this." This was what Brownlie had always feared.

Pride and commitment were the core of any military organization. The guys on his team didn't understand about business models, about profit and loss statements, or company stock prices. None of them had ever read the contract language the company's Chief Operating Officer had signed off on. All these guys cared about was doing the job they were assigned to do to the best of their ability. They were justifiably proud of their win in L Area. How could he explain to them now that they had done the wrong thing? There's an old saying that 'sometimes you have to just stand and take'. He could do that as well as any man. When his boss finally finished his rant, Captain Brownlie simply replied "Yes sir", and walked out the door.

Two weeks later Captain Brownlie was again called to this boss's office. He had heard nothing about his future or the future of his team. If they were being fired, why should they have to wait two weeks to be told? His boss had few words for him. "Captain Brownlie, the DOE has agreed after much negotiation to give us another chance, a 'do over' in L Area. You have less than two months to prepare. And this time, for God's sakes, get it right!" "Yes sir", Brownlie replied.

Outside he contemplated whether he should just barge back into his boss's office and resign on the spot. It would be easy to do. He could probably find another job within a few weeks. He had no wife or kids to consider. Maybe some time off would do him some good. No stress. Travel for a month or two. Until the money ran out of course. But where would that leave his team? A new team leader would be assigned, with little knowledge of past events in L Area and very little time to learn. It wasn't fair to the team for him to take the easy way out. They wouldn't blame him, but they wouldn't respect him either. So, what would he tell them this time….?

"Gentlemen, due to some issues with the conduct of the Force on Force exercise on December 29th, we've been asked to repeat the exercise in approximately eight weeks. "They're pissed 'cause we won, huh", quipped O'Hara? Brownlie paused, then decided to ignore the comment. "There will be a few changes, notably in the use of diversionary tactics. Thompson, I'm afraid your 'balloon balls' are out. However, there may be other things we can do to improve our chances." Thompson's face dropped. But then he smiled. It was too good to be true. He knew that all along. "The good news is that it'll be warmer in March and there will be no moon after 21:00 hours. Maybe we can surprise them this time."

Throughout the next eight weeks Captain Brownlie had determined he would say nothing to his team about what might happen if they succeeded in reaching their target again in the March exercise. If they won, then it's likely they would all be fired the next day. So be it. There were other jobs. And people with their qualifications were in demand all over the world, especially for those unwilling to sell their integrity.

Assault on L

In other areas of the Protective Force organization programmers were working feverishly to rewrite the PIDAS monitoring software to allow segmentation and prioritization of alarm signals. The list of potential vulnerabilities had grown. Some were relatively easy to fix. Others would require a complete rewrite. That was not possible in the time available. At least two weeks would be required to test and validate the new software. Another week would be needed to upload it to the operating system in L Area. Then there was retraining required. Monitoring personnel would have to be retrained to recognize and activate the new software features. Procedures would have to be rewritten to reflect the changes as well. Above all the newly integrated system had to be tested and declared operational. The last thing they needed was for the system to crash on the night of the exercise, leaving them blind to the adversary's location and activities.

Other Protective Force personnel were fabricating and installing grenade shields in each of the 108 buildings in L Area. These would delay the adversary team's entry into the minus 20 level of the main building, giving more time for the response team to take up their positions in the corridors. That assumed, of course, that the adversary team would be attempting to reach the same target as before, i.e., the crosstie header on the minus 20 level. Little thought was given to the possibility that an adversary might choose a different target somewhere else in the building. In fact, there were several.

Captain Brownlie's poker group met around 19:30 hours every Friday night. It was his turn to host on this occasion, and he was running low on supplies. One of the other men offered to make a 'beer run' before the serious business got started. Serious business was when the ante got up to 50 cents a hand. Brownlie was having a good night for a change. Surely, he was due after losing nearly $64 over the last two Fridays. Those 'second best hands' were his weakness – three kings losing to a straight, full house losing to four jacks. He played the odds, but somehow he seemed to be one card short most of the time. Maybe he should find a cheaper hobby, but then the camaraderie was definitely worth the price.

"Don't you guys out there at Savannah River ever get tired of carrying your guns around with you everywhere you go?" Vick was a legal clerk working in an office every day in Augusta. Working outdoors appealed to him, as long as it wasn't cold or raining, and he didn't have to carry a lot of heavy stuff around with him. "You get used to it", Brownlie replied. "Have you ever had to shoot any bad guys", Charlie asked? "Nope."

Assault on L

"You think you could if you had to?" "Of course, that's our job." "So, this bad guy comes running out of the woods and you shoot him, right?" "It doesn't work quite that way actually", Brownlie replied with a forced smile. He was holding three queens. "I'll see your $1.00 raise and raise you $1.50." It was nice to spend one night a week with people who really didn't have a clue about what you did for a living, even though they could be a bit obnoxious at times.

"Do you practice shooting people out there", asked Vick? "We have to qualify with various weapons on the target range." "No, I mean do you ever pretend that the bad guys are trying to take over one of your buildings and blow it up, or something? 'Cause I heard someone say you did that sort of thing out there." Charlie could get on your nerves sometimes. "Sorry Charlie, that's not a subject I can talk about. Now are you going to call my raise or not?" "I call", said Charlie. "Full boat, tens over sixes." "Damn", replied Brownlie.

Brownlie lived alone in a two-bedroom apartment in Augusta. Losing his wife to cancer after only six months of marriage was the hardest thing he had ever had to survive. Twice he had seriously considered using his Glock 9mm pistol on himself. Five years later he still couldn't hold back the tears when he thought about her. Brownlie had resigned himself to a solitary lifestyle, devoting most of this time to his eight-year career with the Protective Force at SRS. He used every opportunity to practice on the target range, maintaining expert marksman qualifications on every weapon his employer provided. When he wasn't at the target range he was in the gym. At forty-one years of age meeting the physical fitness requirements for his job was getting tougher. He knew there would come a time when he couldn't make the grade any longer. What would he do then?

Jonesy was new to the organization, having retired from the U. S. Marine Corp after ten years in the middle east. At thirty-four he wasn't the youngest man on the team - the years were beginning to catch up with him. Coming from a rural upbringing in southern Illinois, Jonesy had somehow avoided settling down. He never found the right woman to marry and had no children, at least none that he knew of. Considering himself a younger version of Brownlie, Jonesy spent a lot of time on his fitness. He could run the 100-yard dash quicker than anyone he had ever met, maybe quicker that anyone at the Site. "I want your job!" he told Captain Brownlie the first week on the force. "You can have it, just as soon as you're able to take it away from me" Brownlie had replied.

Assault on L

O'Hara could be a pain in the ass! One look this six-foot four-inch goliath with his short red hair and bushy moustache and you knew he was going to be difficult. A true professional, O'Hara had volunteered for the British Royal Marines as soon as he was of age, retiring five years ago to join the organization at Savannah River. Only a few years younger than Brownlie he looked considerably older – 'well-seasoned' as he like to put it, possibly the result of being a confirmed bachelor. Irishmen have a reputation for being quick tempered. O'Hara was certainly no exception. Someone once asked Captain Brownlie, "If you were stranded at sea in a lifeboat and you could have only one member of your team with you, which one would it be?" He answered immediately. "O'Hara. Whatever trouble you're in, he can get you out of it!"

Thompson was visibly the youngest on the team, having just turned thirty. He was also the shortest, at only five foot ten inches. What he lacked in height he more than made up for with enthusiasm. Thompson was always the first to volunteer and the first to 'bend' the rules of engagement when there was an opportunity to do so. He loved to 'think outside the box'. Only Thompson and Sarco had families to worry about. Thompson spent time with his six-year-old daughter every other weekend, and sometimes on Tuesday evenings while his ex-wife was at her bridge club.

Sarco was the one Brownlie worried most about. In his early thirties, Sarco had a full plate of responsibilities at home, with a young wife and three children to take care of. Short black hair, dark brown eyes and overgrown sideburns gave Sarco the look of a street wise punk selling drugs on the east side of Chicago. Nothing could have been further from the truth. Sarco was a soft touch for anyone who needed someone to talk to. He was the team's 'therapist'. He was also the team's instructor in the martial arts, having won several Tai Kwon Do titles while in his twenties. Brownlie's only concern was whether Sarco would put his life on the line if he had to. He had so much to lose.

The only thing Sarco and Brennen had in common was their age. Brennen was the quietest most reserved member of Brownlie's team. Brownlie had to admit he never quite knew what Brennen was thinking. He never mentioned any family or even a girlfriend. With his sandy blonde hair, blue eyes and youthful appearance he could certainly have had his pick of women. Everything Brownlie knew about Brennen was listed on the questionnaire he submitted for his security clearance. The team had to have an explosives expert and Brennen was it. Beyond that the man was a mystery. Brennen followed orders, did what he was told and did it well. Brownlie had to leave it at that!

Assault on L

The day of the repeat Force on Force exercise finally arrived. Captain Brownlie still hadn't made up his mind what to say in his final briefing before they boarded the truck that would take them out to their launch position just inside the wood line on the west side of L Area.

Assault on L

Chapter 3

Summers are long in South Carolina. Silas made a trip into town once a week to buy groceries and other supplies needed at the farm. He made a point of never going to the same grocery store twice in the same month. Someone might notice the old rusty brown F-150 and wonder why one man needed to buy a month's worth of groceries every week. He padded the bed of the pickup with an old mattress the McDonalds had left in the barn. That way the groceries wouldn't be shaken to pieces on the return trip down that horrific excuse for a dirt road. Jorge's team had been training for almost four months now without being given the slightest hint what they were training for. All they knew was that the target was a facility at the Savannah River Site not far from there. It was now August, typically the hottest and driest month of the South Carolina summer. And 1985 was turning out to be one of the hottest years on record.

Jorge was pleased with the team's progress but realized there wasn't much more they could do without knowing more about the target facility. He called the team together, all except Samuel. He sent Samuel to get his backpack. "I think it's time to share some information about the facility we are interested in." Samuel arrived and began taking packets of paper out of his backpack, laying them on the table. There were five packets, each labelled with a letter of the alphabet. As Jorge began to open up each packet, the group could see they were drawings of both rectangular and complex shaped buildings. There were elevation and floor plan drawings for each level within each building showing entrances and hallways.

For the complex buildings there were elevation drawings as well as floorplans for building levels at 40 feet below ground, 20 feet below ground, at ground level, 66 feet above ground, etc. For the rectangular buildings the floorplans were simpler, but again showed multiple levels at various elevations.

Assault on L

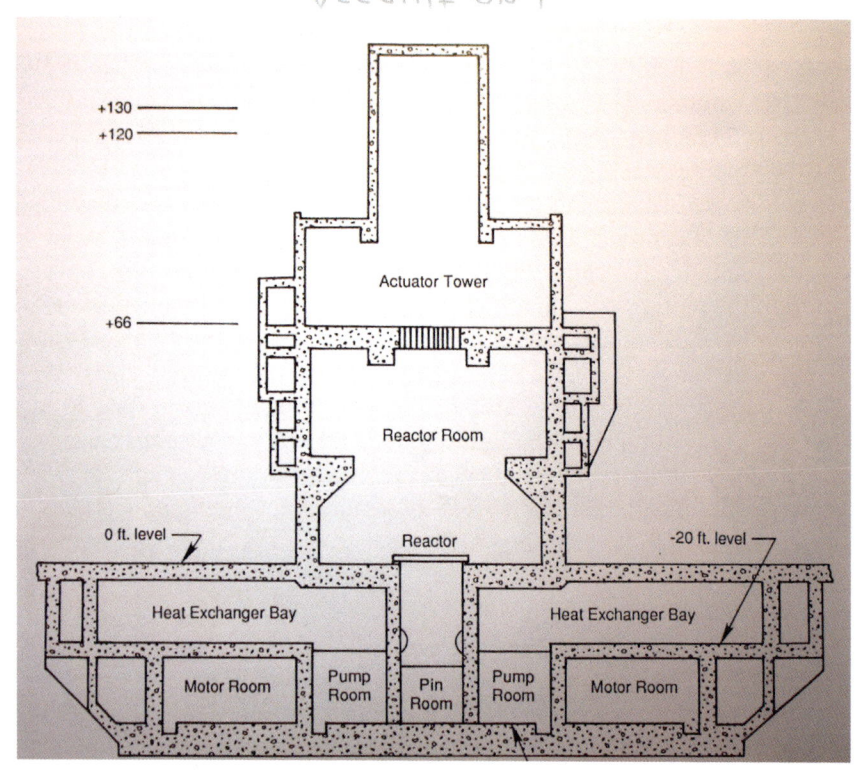

[Diagram: Cross-section of reactor building showing Actuator Tower, Reactor Room, Reactor, Heat Exchanger Bays, Motor Rooms, Pump Rooms, and Pin Room. Elevation markings: +130, +120, +66, 0 ft. level, -20 ft. level.]

Samuel also found several research papers that described activated charcoal and high efficiency particulate air (HEPA) filters used at the Savannah River Site reactors. These filters were expected to prevent release of 99.9% of the radioiodine and radioactive particles should there be a reactor accident. "We'll have to take those out as well", Jorge remarked, with no further explanation.

After everyone had given the drawings a cursory look, Jorge began to describe what they were looking at in detail. "Our friend Samuel here was a day late arriving at the farm last March. That's because he spent six hours in the Library of Congress in Washington printing off copies of the original construction drawings used during the early 1950's to build some of the facilities at the Savannah River Site. Some of these drawings even show equipment they planned to install in these buildings after they were constructed." Samuel commented, "Of course, these drawings may not be totally accurate compared to what is there today, but you will note the walls are eight feet thick reinforced concrete. Some are even thicker. Since it is quite difficult to move concrete walls that are eight feet thick, I think we can assume that the layout of these buildings today is essentially the same as shown on these drawings.".

Assault on L

Jorge continued. "Our 'client' would like to be able to announce to the world that they have the capability to detonate a nuclear weapon in a major city in America, as a negotiating tactic. Our mission is to deliver enough plutonium to them to make one or several such weapons. The original plan was to enter one of these rectangular buildings and remove plutonium buttons estimated to be worth at least 300 million dollars on the world market." He pointed to a location in one of the rectangular buildings. "However, the intelligence we've been able to gather over the past two years indicates such a mission would have almost no chance to succeed. Our analysis of their defences showed some vulnerabilities and identified several ways to successfully enter the building and reach the material. However, the Protective Force response time and the numbers of their forces would make escape virtually impossible."

He pushed two packets of drawings off onto the floor, while shuffling one of the remaining sets of drawings to the top of the pile. "Our new plan is to seize this facility instead." He pointed to the center of the main reactor building in L Area. "This is our target!" With that he stepped back to let everyone get a better look. Otis pointed to a seventeen-foot diameter round hole in the ground level floor and a similar hole in the floor below. "This must be where they put the reactor vessel itself", he noted. "Control systems must come in from above. There is no space anywhere else."

"Do they store plutonium there as well", asked Luis? "No, not in a form we can use", Otis replied. "Sorry, I don't get it", said Henry. "What's in that building that we should risk our lives breaking into it?" "Enough radioactive fission products to contaminate the entire eastern seaboard of the United States, making it uninhabitable for humans for about thirty years", Otis answered. "Cool", Janine remarked! "Think how wildlife in the Appalachians would thrive with no humans around for thirty years!" Jorge couldn't help rolling his eyes. He hadn't realised he had a 'tree hugger' on the team. He let out an audible sigh. "Taking over an operating reactor gives us leverage. We won't have to steal anything. They're going to give it to us. They'll let us walk right out with it. Otherwise we blow up their precious reactor making Washington, Charlotte, Richmond, Greensboro, Durham, and every other city on the east coast a dead zone for decades." The group was silent for a few minutes. This was a substantially different mission from any they had been speculating about.

"So, after they deliver the material to us, how do we get out", Henry asked? "I'm afraid one of us will have to stay behind to maintain the threat of a reactor meltdown until the others have left." Jorge paused to let that soak in. "That will be me, in case anyone was thinking of volunteering." None of them were. "And we just walk out with the prize?" Henry remained sceptical. "Actually, there will be a helicopter to pick you up in L Area and take you to a location of safety." "With the plutonium", Ansel asked? "No, the plutonium will be delivered to a third party, who will have already paid us by depositing $220 million in our Swiss bank account. We get our money before they get their plutonium." "Cool", quipped Janine.

Silas had remained silent throughout the discussion. "Suppose the DOE decides to call our bluff? Suppose they refuse to give up the plutonium? Then what?" "Then we teach them a painful lesson they won't forget for at least the next thirty years", said Jorge. There were frowns all around at that remark. "Look", he said. "The American government is a big believer in 'risk analysis'. This is clearly a trade-off of one risk against another. If they refuse our demands 10% of their population and 20% percent of their economy will have to relocate, maybe even west of the Mississippi River. No one even knows if that is possible, much less how to do it."

"On the other hand, if they give us what we want it's just possible they will catch up with those who have their plutonium and maybe recover it. And even if they don't, it's far from certain that whoever has the plutonium can make a weapon that works", Jorge continued. Otis added, "At best such a weapon could kill half a million people in a single city, say New York or Chicago. That's got to be better than losing most of the east coast. There would probably be ten thousand deaths just trying to evacuate Washington and all those other major cities."

It was several days before anyone had very much to say. Everyone on the team was trying to process the new information they had been given. Jorge had to wonder about their individual commitments to the mission. He hadn't expected them to really care that much about how the mission was to be accomplished, only that they would be paid their share. Afterall the outcome was the same as what they had originally agreed to. Several members of the team were privately wondering about Jorge's plan to stay behind and guarantee their escape. Would he change his mind at the last minute? Once they were gone Jorge would eventually reveal their identities under interrogation. Unless he ate his Glock 19 9mm. Jorge had one more bit of information he hadn't revealed. The offences he had committed years earlier in the middle east were punishable by hanging. Interpol had come very close to finding him a year ago. In another year they would surely succeed. He didn't like living on borrowed time. He just needed to get this one last job done.

Luis found the south wall of the old barn on the McDonald farm quite boring after scaling El Capitan two years in a row. He considered that to be his crowning achievement, even though it was nearly six years ago. Abella de la Conco, only a few hours from Barcelona, and El Chorro were his favorite local challenges. He had done both at least a dozen times. The gable on top of the old barn was only 43 feet from the ground. According to Samuel's drawings he would need to scale a solid concrete wall 55 feet high to reach the roof of the reactor building in L Area. Once on the roof he would have ample time to place his explosive charges, one on the intake duct to each of the five filter compartments described in the research papers Samuel had found.

In the photographs they looked like oversized railroad boxcars. The charges didn't need to be very big since the filter compartments appeared to be made of simple sheet aluminum. Destroying the compartment intake ducts would do two things. It would interrupt proper airflow in the reactor building. And it would allow fission products, including Iodine 131, Cesium 137 and Strontium 90, to disperse into the atmosphere at an elevation of 55 feet above the ground, rather than at the discharge elevation of the 200-foot stack. The filter compartments would be downstream of the discharge point and therefore totally useless.

Janine maintained her physical prowess with a rigorous workout regimen that consumed almost three hours of every day. She had discovered a clearing not far to the north of the barn, but out of sight of the others who might serve as a distraction. Unlike most of them Janine needed several hours each day of isolation. Her mental health depended upon it. A brief visit from Otis was the only thing she would tolerate. Others, including Samuel, appeared at the clearing from time to time just to watch, but Janine had a way of looking at them that was intensely uncomfortable, especially in Samuel's case. She was aware of the rivalry between him and Otis. She didn't encourage it, but she didn't dismiss it either. It was a source of entertainment in an otherwise sterile environment.

Janine's view of the universe, and her place in it, were completely different from the others. It was pointless to try to make them understand. It would only waste her time and theirs. Janine was a firm believer in the multiverse. Whatever she did in this universe would be balanced against her actions in other parallel universes. If she killed in this universe, somewhere in another universe she saved a life. Wherever she failed in this life, she succeeded in an alternate life. Balance across all universes – that was all that mattered.

There was one thing everyone at the farm agreed upon. The meals Otis prepared were second to none. His only problem was getting some of the ingredients. Silas simply wasn't able to find some things he needed. Otis would voice his annoyance at not having any saffron from time to time. No one else seemed to notice. He hadn't assumed any of them had what he considered to be an 'educated pallet'. However, he was determined not to let his standards slip, no matter the clientele.

Ansel had arranged to have a large number of straw bales delivered to a local freight depot in Aiken, just four each week to avoid suspicion. Deliveries of straw and hay were commonplace because of all the stables in the area. For over a hundred years the 'rich and famous' had been stabling thoroughbred horses in Aiken, where polo was played every Saturday afternoon. In fact, there were several polo grounds in the area. The annual Steeplechase in Aiken brought in large crowds around mid-March every year. Many of the locals in Aiken often commented that the all-brick air-conditioned stables were superior to the homes they lived in.

Each week, in addition to groceries and other supplies, Silas would pick up four bales of straw at the depot, load them into the rusty brown F-150 and ferry them out to the farm. Once they were moved into the barn Ansel would cut the metal bands, allowing the straw to spread out across the dirt floor. Each straw bale contained two or three weapons wrapped in plastic, including M16's, Glock 19 9mm pistols, grenades, and night vision equipment. The last straw bales to arrive contained a wide variety of plastic explosives, caps, and radio-controlled detonators. "Halleluiah", yelled Luis. "It's Christmas in October!"

Silas had not been idle during the time spent in Aiken. There were plenty of fast food places in Aiken, New Ellenton, Jackson and other local communities where one could read the newspaper, have coffee and overhear people's conversations. He was never comfortable in public places, but there was no other way to collect the intelligence he needed. In the thirty-four months prior to buying the McDonald farm, Silas had managed to learn a lot about the Savannah River Site. Much of it was trivial, but some of it was priceless. The site was going through some fundamental changes, mostly driven by ever more onerous environmental requirements. In particular, discharging hot water from the reactors back into the Savannah River was coming under intense scrutiny.

Assault on L

Even the slightest increase in river temperature could no longer be tolerated. Requirements for silt and trace chemical content in the reactor discharge were tightened to the point that the water had to be returned to the Savannah River cleaner than when it was withdrawn a few miles upstream. These problems drove the Department of Energy to construct a cooing pond for L Reactor by damming the effluent canal leading to Steel Creek. Over 99% of the water used to cool the reactor could then be recirculated rather than returned to the river.

Since moving to the Aiken area, Silas had driven along the public highway that passes through the Savannah River Site nearly thirty times. The Savannah River Site consists of 310 square miles of federally owned property in south western South Carolina, bordering the Savannah River for about 17 miles. On the opposite side of the river are several communities in the state of Georgia. Augusta is the largest of these, with a population well over 100,000, and lies about twenty miles to the north west of the Site. The United States Department of Energy operates five nuclear production reactors, a fuel assembly fabrication facility, two chemical separations areas, waste processing, storage and disposal facilities, and a number of other support facilities on the property. Access to the property and the facilities on it is strictly controlled. For reasons of security there are no publicly available maps of facilities on the site.

Most of the property outside the boundaries of the Site is farmland that is privately owned. There are a number of small communities surrounding the Site as well. The largest city to the south east is Charleston, South Carolina, a large metropolitan center and major port on the South Carolina coast. Both Augusta, Georgia and Charleston, South Carolina are historically important 'Cities of the South', and contain a great many historical monuments and other memorabilia from the United States Civil War era of the 1860's.

Assault on L

Since 1938 South Carolina Highway 125 has served as a direct route between Allendale, South Carolina and Augusta, Georgia. When the Savannah River Site was first built no public traffic was allowed on Site property. Closure of Highway 125 resulted in significant inconvenience to the local population. The highway was finally reopened for public access in 1970. However, traffic on the 17.3 mile stretch through the Site was closely monitored. Private vehicles were prohibited from stopping except for emergencies.

Mile-markers going north to south helped travellers count the miles before they are out of the restricted area. Though the highway is maintained by SCDOT, it is patrolled by federal security; the speed limit throughout is 55 miles per hour. Security barricades were located at both ends of SC 125. When arriving at the entrance checkpoint, drivers received a pass and might also have their vehicle searched. Drivers were required to

Assault on L

return the pass at the exit barricade. Upon exit, security personnel compared each vehicle's time of exit against time of entry. A difference of significantly more or less than the expected twenty minutes was treated as suspicious. Drivers might be questioned and delayed for a period of time.

Public traffic through the site was typically light. In fact, Silas rarely saw another vehicle during the time it took to drive his F-150 from the north security barricade to the identical security barricade at the southern border of the site. There were numerous side roads where one could turn off the public highway, but each lead rather quickly to a security barricade. Without a security badge you would be directed back onto Highway 125.

Of course, Silas was interested in what facilities or operations he could see from the highway. To his disappointment there were virtually none. Observation of any of the operating facilities was impossible, obviously by design. South Carolina 125 was essentially a corridor through a heavily wooded pine forest, with one notable exception. Ongoing construction for an earthen dam for L Lake, as it was called, was clearly visible as he drove past. According to information provided in the government's environmental impact statement for the new lake it was to be about three miles long when completed. That would place the L Reactor Area about 5.5 kilometres distant. While the dense forest prevented any of the buildings in L Area from being seen, one could safely assume that following the edge of the new lake for about ninety minutes would lead you to it.

Silas chose his moments to pass bits of critical information on to Jorge, usually in the evenings when things were quiet. Jorge suffered from a short attention span. Too much information at one time just seemed to irritate him. There were a few things about L Area that Silas had picked up in places like Burger King and McDonald's fast food joints. But he had to admit no one had a really clear picture of what was there, beyond the thirty-year-old drawings and other information Samuel had provided. In particular, they had no idea how many Protective Force personnel were assigned to L Area or how they were deployed. They also knew nothing about distances from the wood line to the buildings or what barriers or detection zones might be in place.

"The mission can't possibly succeed without a lot more information", Silas cautioned. "Yes", Jorge shouted. "Yes, I know that!" The others in the room looked up with a start. Jorge lowered his voice. "One of us is going to have to get close enough to the target to assess those things and a lot more. I've been thinking about ways to do that."

Jorge began to realize this was not something he could figure out all on his own. He needed the entire team's input. Silas began, "I can get you as far as a drop off point along the public highway that runs through the Site. You can enter the woods just before we get to the L Lake dam, then make your way along the edge of the lake until you see the buildings in L Area. You'll know the reactor building when you see it. Probably best to drop you off around mid-morning, then pick you up again about the same time next day. We may have to abort the drop off or the pick up if there is any other traffic in sight. Stopping is not allowed so there can't be any witnesses. Also, they count heads when you enter the site and again when you leave. You'll have to hide when we enter for the drop off and again after I pick you up the next day."

"There's nowhere to hide in that old rust bucket of a truck you've got", said Jorge. "No, I'll rent a small U-Haul truck for a couple of days. We'll stack some hay bales in it so you can hide behind them." "Don't they search the truck", asked Henry? "Not very thoroughly." "They probably don't have 'heart monitors' or anything sophisticated like that", Samuel added. "Besides, they've seen me nearly every month for the past three years. I doubt they'll give me much trouble", said Silas.

"What happens if you and Silas get caught", Henry asked? "Then you all go back to your day jobs and pretend none of this ever happened. You never met anyone called Jorge or Silas. You spent the summer in sunny South Carolina, on the beach maybe. You'll think of something", Jorge replied with a shrug of the shoulders. "But if you can get twelve hours of intel on what goes on in that place, we'll know what we're up against", said Ansel. "Exactly", Luis added. Jorge looked around the room. All heads were nodding in agreement.

It had to be done. But when? Silence fell over the room. "Why not the week after Christmas" offered Janine. "A lot of people will be off during the holidays. Less chance you'll be seen when Silas drops you off. Less chance you'll run into someone in the woods. Less chance you'll be seen in L Area." "That makes sense", Jorge nodded. "Meanwhile I'll continue to listen around town. Maybe I'll hear or see something", said Silas. "You mean like a bright star in the east", Janine added, with a smile? "Yeah, just maybe."

Assault on L

'We may be able to get one man in and back out again. But how do we get all eight of us to the target without being detected when the time comes', Silas wondered to himself? He had noticed one other thing in his monthly trips through the site on South Carolina 125. Security guards didn't bother to look all that closely at employee badges when they arrived for work each day. One employee in the car would hold his badge up to the windshield. If the face and the picture on the badge matched, that was good enough. They were promptly motioned through.

No bright star appeared in the east before Christmas, but two days later Silas returned from the Walmart in Aiken with some curious news. He overheard a delivery driver complaining to his friend in the parking lot that his scheduled delivery of supplies to L Area on the evening shift of the 29th had been cancelled. "They're telling everyone to stay away from L Area that day. 'No nonessential personnel in the area', they said. So now I've got a loaded truck that I've got to unload and reload with something else. What a pain in the ass these people!"

"What does that mean 'no nonessential personnel in the area'," Samuel asked? "Either they expect to have a problem that day or something is planned that they don't want anyone to see", Otis answered. "Sounds like maybe something we DO want to see", Jorge suggested. "Silas, you think you can get me in there that morning?" "If I can get a U-Haul on short notice", he replied. The demand for truck rentals in the Aiken area wasn't that high during Christmas week. Even so Silas had to settle for a 25-footer.

Assault on L

Chapter 4

Silas' heart rate began to climb as he approached Jackson on South Carolina 125. Once through Jackson it was only about a mile to the north security barricade. He was sweating in late December! Hopefully the security guard at the barricade wouldn't notice.

"Morning", he said, as Silas rolled down the window on the driver's side of the truck. "Morning", Silas replied with a smile. "What happened to your old brown Ford", the guard asked? "Oh, had to leave it at the U-Haul place. There's a farmer down south wants more hay than that thing will carry." "OK, let's see in the back." He was already walking toward the rear of the truck. Silas climbed down out of the cab and opened up the rear doors. Twenty-two bales of hay were neatly stacked inside. There was clearly room for another forty bales. The guard peered in. "Looks like U-Haul saw you comin'. You could have done with a truck half this size. Did the same thing to me when I moved my mom's stuff last year. Make you pay for a truck bigger than you need!" "Yeah, well what can you do? Seems everyone's out to rip you off these days," said Silas. The guard looked at the hay bales again. Silas' heart skipped a beat. "OK" said the guard, motioning him to drive on through. Silas closed the rear doors but left one door unlatched. He looked at his watch. He now had twenty-one minutes to make it to the other barricade, driving at exactly 50 miles per hour.

As Silas was getting the truck up to speed, he noticed a security patrol car pull out onto the highway behind him. His heart skipped another beat. Were they going to follow him? That would screw up everything! The security patrol car continued to follow about 100 yards behind. Silas banged on the rear wall of the cab. "We're being followed", he yelled, hoping Jorge could hear him. There was no response. About five miles from the north barricade the security patrol car slowed down and turned off the public highway onto a side road. Silas watched closely in the big oversized rear-view mirror. There was no sign of the patrol car, and no other traffic in front of him. He banged on the rear wall again. "I think we're clear. I'll bang three times if it's clear for you to jump out." "Got it", Jorge replied.

As he approached the L Lake dam Silas checked again to make sure there were no cars ahead or behind them. He slowed to less than five miles per hour while banging the rear wall three times as hard as he could. In the rear-view mirror he saw Jorge dive onto the shoulder of the road, then disappear into the tree line at 10:14 hours. He hit the gas and the truck lurched forward. Silas estimated he would need to drive sixty-two miles per hour for the next eight minutes in order to reach the south security barricade at the proper time. Hopefully there wouldn't be another patrol car to catch him exceeding the 55 miles per hour speed limit.

Jorge stayed low in the undergrowth among the stand of young pines about twenty meters from the highway. If he had been observed, they would be coming in minutes. There was no response. In fact, he couldn't see another human being anywhere. The entire open area around the dam was apparently deserted. What had been an area of virgin forest had been scraped clean. The earth had been dug up, turned upside down and reburied so many times nothing would be able to grow there for many years. Along the top of the earthen embankment there was a concrete ridge, much longer on the left side of the point of intersection than on the right. There were no boats on the water that he could see. He quickly made his way toward the northern edge of the lake where foliage was just beginning to reclaim the land that had been disturbed.

Staying just inside the line of pine trees he was able to make good time. The normally dense undergrowth had not yet grown back in that area. It was easy walking. He wondered about the blackish water reaching across to the opposite shore. It looked completely devoid of life. Being so recently completed the lake would have no fish in it, of course. He wondered if there ever would be any. Maybe it was so contaminated by the reactor operation, or the temperature of the water was so high, that life more complex that mosquito larvae wasn't possible. Several intrusions of the lake into the forest forced Jorge to take a crooked path toward his objective. It might be only 5.5 kilometers as the crow flies, but his journey would be a bit longer. Even so, the buildings in L Area should be visible by noon at his current rate of progress.

Silas arrived at the southern security barricade on South Carolina 125 about half a minute early according to his calculations. The security guard walked slowly over to the driver's side of the truck and motioned for him to roll down the window. He had a serious look on his face. "You've got a problem", he announced. "Please step out of the cab." Silas couldn't figure out where he'd slipped up. "You left one of your doors unlatched", said the guard. "They spotted it as you were driving away from the other barricade." "Damn", Silas remarked, as he walked to the rear of the truck. The door was slightly ajar. "Thanks for letting me know."

Assault on L

"Let's have a look", said the guard as he pulled the unlatched door back and climbed up into the truck. Of course, he couldn't know that the hay bales were stacked differently from when they were inspected at the other barricade. Jorge had stacked them all along the side walls rather than being two or three high as before. "OK, you can go through", said the guard. "And make sure your doors are latched this time." "Absolutely, and thanks again", Silas replied. 'I'm getting too old for this crap', he muttered to himself as he drove away. And this was just the beginning. After a night in a cheap motel room in Allendale he would have to do it all over again. The pick-up promised to be even more difficult!

Jorge approached the edge of SRS Road B, as indicated on the road sign on the far shoulder, separating L Reactor Area from the northern edge of the lake. His watch read 11:55 hours. He could clearly see the rectangular tower on top of the reactor building, about 700 meters away, without having to get too close to the road. It was mostly small scrub hardwoods here, so he had to approach the road cautiously, then dash across and into a more densely wooded area on the other side. Now he was only about a few hundred meters from the cleared area around the reactor building. Moving as swiftly as he could through the undergrowth and thick pine forest to the west of the reactor building Jorge found a location just inside the wood line where he could observe personnel coming in and out of the secure area enclosed by a double fence. The space between the fences was obviously a 'no man zone', equipped with electronic devices to detect any attempts to gain unauthorised access to the facilities inside. The fences didn't appear to offer much delay, however. They didn't appear to be electrified. Jorge estimated they could be crossed in less than 15 seconds.

Using his Nikon 16 x 50 binoculars he could see three earthen berms in the courtyard surrounding the reactor building. He assumed these were intended as fighting positions for security personnel defending against an attacking force. Over the next two hours he counted four armed security personnel going into and moving around the main entry portal and another three patrolling areas between the reactor building and the double fence. No doubt there were more armed security personnel inside the main building. Weapons appeared to be conventional side arms and M16's. There did not appear to be any active patrolling of cleared areas outside the double fence or the wooded area where he was. Jorge figured he could stay at his present vantage point for as long as he wished, or even move to a better one without fear of discovery. Suddenly he heard noises coming from the woods behind him. Had he made a huge mistake?

Assault on L

Maybe they did patrol the wooded areas around the reactor building. If so, and if they had dogs, he was only minutes from being caught. It was too late to run. All he could do was squat down and wait to be arrested.

He could hear them approaching rather noisily. They couldn't be more than thirty meters away. From the sound of their voices he guessed there were five of them, and no dogs. Why such a large group for a simple patrol procedure? He could see one of them now. Then the second. They were wearing camouflage fatigues, not the dark uniforms of the security personnel inside the facility. And dark colored vests, but the material was too thin to provide protection against an M16. A rush of adrenaline rushed through his veins as he realized the truth. All of his efforts to date had been in vain. These men were about to attack this facility before his own team had the chance. He could only guess at their motives or mission objective. But it didn't matter. If he was lucky enough to make it back to the farm, he would have one hell of tale to tell. Then he would have to dismiss his entire team back to where they came from. Somebody had quite simply beaten them to it!

Jorge could see all five of them now. They seemed to be content to remain inside the wood line about twenty-five meters from his location. He didn't dare move and he wasn't armed. If they discovered his presence, he was surely dead. All he could do was remain as silent as possible until they launched their attack. That would not likely occur until dark, another four hours at least. It became the longest four hours he could ever remember. As dusk finally set in, he could hear them stirring. He could also hear some activity on the east side of the building during the last hour, but his view of that area was blocked. Protective Force personnel were running around the building periodically, but he couldn't hear any gunfire. About a dozen employees had entered the secure area through the entry portal building between 15:50 and 16:10 hours and about the same number exited the area between 16:30 and 16:50 hours. Otherwise nothing seemed to be happening. It was like he had arrived at the movie theatre four hours before the movie was supposed to start. He had often thought about what today might bring, but boredom was not on the list.

Suddenly the five of them began to run out of the woods toward the nearest section of double fence. Jorge looked at his watch. It was 18:40 hours. All five were over the double fence and on the run toward the reactor building when Protective Force personnel opened fire with M16s. All five adversaries continued to run while returning fire. About halfway to the building one of them suddenly stopped and sat down on the ground.

Assault on L

The others seemed unconcerned and continued to run until they reached a side door to the building. Protective Force personnel completely ignored the man sitting on the ground and pursued the other four attackers. Was the man on the ground suddenly invisible? Jorge studied the man with his binoculars. He didn't appear to be injured and he didn't get up and walk away. He just sat there. Then he saw another attacker sit down near the side door of the building while the other three went inside. Again the downed man just sat there, apparently uninjured but refusing to move.

At this point all the Protective Force personnel he could see seemed to lose interest entirely. All of them shouldered their weapons and began to walk casually back toward the entry portal building. It was as if nothing had happened. Except for the two men sitting on the ground. Then he burst out laughing. "It was all pretend", Jorge said out loud to nobody! "It was all a game. They must all have been firing blanks. Two were killed and three made it into the building." The whole thing seemed hilarious. He had just witnessed a simulated attack on his target, providing far more information than he could ever have hoped for. How could he be so lucky. "Wait until they hear this", he said, again to nobody!

Picking up Jorge from the woods near the L Lake dam required precise timing. Being late would leave him vulnerable to being discovered so close to the public highway. Being early was much worse. Silas could only stop for a moment, and then only if there were no other vehicles in sight. If Jorge wasn't there yet, Silas would have to proceed without him. It would likely be hours or even the next day before he could return to try again. The U-Haul arrived at the southern security barricade promptly at 09:50 hours. Silas was relieved to find the security personnel on duty were different from the ones the day before. He hoped they would pass him through without significant delay. By now he knew the drill. As requested, he opened both doors at the rear of the truck for inspection. With all the hay bales stacked along the sidewalls the truck obviously contained nothing else. "OK, go on through", grunted the security guard. It was easy to tell this man didn't enjoy his job very much! No matter, Silas was on his way, on schedule to pick up his passenger at 10:10 hours.

In fact, he arrived one minute early. He pulled off the road onto the right shoulder. Jorge was nowhere in sight. Just then a security patrol car appeared around the curve about half a mile from his location. "Damn", Silas shouted, giving the steering wheel a smack with his fist. He only had seconds to react. He pulled the hood release and climbed out of the cab. Lifting the hood, he did the only thing he could think of. He quickly retrieved a small pocketknife from his right pocket and stabbed a hole on the underside of the radiator hose. A small stream of water spewed out onto the hot engine block, filling the space under the hood with steam. He had barely replaced the pocketknife when the patrol car drove slowly past him, then off on the shoulder in front. "You're not supposed to stop on this road", yelled the lone security guard as he walked back toward the front of the truck. "I know", Silas replied. "But it's running hot. I'll burn up the engine if I keep going, and it's not my truck." The security guard looked down into the cloud of steam, then raised his head. "I see your problem. You're losing water through that hose. Must be a hole in it. I've got some duct tape and a water can in the car. Be right back." Silas couldn't believe his luck. This guy was going to help him! But where the hell was Jorge?

They had to wait a few minutes for the water pressure to drop enough that the security guard could wrap duct tape twice around the hose covering the hole Silas had made. It took almost a full can of water before the water topped up at the radiator cap. "That should get you to Jackson at least", said the security guard. "U-Haul will probably charge you for fixing that hose." "No problem", Silas replied. "Thanks very much for helping me out." "We all carry stuff in our patrol cars in case someone gets in trouble. I do need to look at what you're hauling." Silas started for the rear of the truck as the security guard dropped the hood shut on the truck. He arrived in time to open the doors before the guard could see that one of them was already unlatched. Two rows of hay bales were stacked three high against the front wall of the truck bed. The security guard frowned. "Ugh, I'm allergic to hay – makes me sneeze. You can close it up. I'll call the north barricade and tell them why you're late." Silas watched him walk back to his patrol car and drive away. 'Seems a shame to kill someone like that who's just doing their job', he thought.

Once back on the highway, Silas banged on the rear wall of the cab. "You there Jorge?" "Yep", came the reply. "You are a clever man, Silas." "I wish", Silas replied. There was still one more inspection before they were out of danger. "You need a truck this big just to haul some hay bales", asked the security guard at the north barricade? "Smallest one I could get", Silas replied. It was the truth after all. "Some guy in Beech Island wants some special hay for his horses" he added. "Claims he can only get it from Allendale." "What's special about it. Just looks like ordinary hay to me", said the guard. "Beats the hell out of me. I'm just the delivery boy", Silas replied. The security guard climbed up, walked to the front for the truck bed, and pulled a long piece of hay out of one bale.

Assault on L

He sniffed it, looked at it, and sniffed it again. "Ain't nothing special about this hay. Get on out of here", said the guard, as he climbed down out of the U-Haul. Silas closed both doors and latched them securely. He climbed back in the cab, started the engine and slowly drove on through. A few minutes later, as they were passing through Jackson, Silas heard a banging behind his head. "Yeah", he queried? "What's all this crap about 'special hay'?" "It was all I could think of", Silas replied. "Don't do that again, OK." "OK"

Silas returned the U-Haul without mentioning the duct tape on the radiator hose. They would surely discover it, but he had given a false address and phone number. Even though they had a copy of his South Carolina driver's license it was unlikely they would be able to track him down. And since he paid cash, there was no credit card number to trace either. He could see Jorge was champing at the bit to tell the team what he had learned, although he remained suspiciously silent during the bumpy ride back to the farm in the old F-150. There was a round of applause when they came through the front door. "You didn't get caught and you didn't get killed, so what's your excuse", asked Henry? "Learn anything important", Samuel added? Jorge knew how to keep his audience in suspense. "Oh, I picked up a few bits here and there", he began with a wry smile.

Half an hour later none of them could believe their good fortune. "But", Jorge interrupted, "the bad news is that I don't think we have the resources to complete the mission." He began to explain how things would be different in their case. "For one, the doors probably won't be unlocked like they were during their little game last night. They only did that to avoid actually destroying the doors into the building. It was all part of the 'pretend'. We will have to use real explosives. And there will be a real delay while we move away and back again after detonation. Second, I couldn't see what went on in the building. The Protective Force response inside may have wiped out the adversary team as soon as they got in. They will be firing real ammunition, not blanks like last night. I think we would need a team twice this size to pull it off. And that's not going to happen. Besides, I haven't figured out how to get even the eight of us onto the site property, much less a group of sixteen!"

They had all worked hard and weren't ready to give up just yet. There were lots of ideas thrown around in the coming weeks but none of them seemed to gain much traction. Silas suggested they give it another six weeks before disbanding. Maybe they would think of a different plan to accomplish the mission, or maybe it was just too tough after all.

Assault on L

The team was struggling with mixed emotions. They were excited to know what they were up against. Now they could practice under realistic conditions until they were confident they would succeed. On the other hand, they might be practicing for nothing if Jorge was convinced they would fail without a team twice as big. Henry and Silas took down what was left of the fencing on the property and used it to create two fences in parallel, each two and a half meters tall. They topped each fence with old rusty barbed wire they found in the barn to simulate the razor wire Jorge had seen on the PIDAS fences in L Area. Old carpet remnants Silas found at a furniture store in Aiken were perfect for getting them over the barbed wire. After drilling for a month, the entire team was consistently able to clear both fences in 14 seconds. All except for Janine. She took no interest at all in the fence drills. She had something different in mind. Maybe Luis could give her a little instruction.

It was now the second Thursday in March. Some were already packing up to leave. Samuel had gone to the Bar-B-Que House in New Ellenton. He was supposed to bring back enough for everyone. Ansel and Henry were waiting for theirs before walking out to the highway and hitching a ride to the Augusta Airport. Samuel drove the old F-150 up the rutted dirt road much too fast with a big smile on his face. "How's the Bar-B-Que", asked Ansel? "Better than you could possibly imagine", Samuel beamed!! All were amazed at what he had learned. "Wait a minute", said Henry. "Where's OUR Bar-B-Que?" Samuel looked stunned. "Oh, uh… I forgot and left it in a bag on the table. Sorry!"

It was finally time to try Silas' scheme for getting all eight of them onto the site property and as near the target as possible without either being arrested or killed. Personally, he gave it one chance in ten.

The loading dock in the rear of the Aiken Walmart store was mostly hidden from public view. Activity there varied from frantic, when full delivery trucks arrived, to nearly deserted, when one of Walmart's delivery trucks was being loaded. Once a delivery truck was loaded, everyone other than the driver vanished back inside the building.

As usual, timing was everything. It was 18:14 hours. The delivery driver was just about to climb back into the cab of his truck. "Excuse me", said Janine. "I've gotten myself lost walking back to my apartment. I know it's somewhere around here. Can you point me in the right direction, please?" The driver took one look at her and decided he might even take the time to escort her there himself. Even stay for coffee. As he raised his arm to point in a westerly direction, Janine shoved an eight-inch kitchen knife between his third and fourth ribs. He looked at her in disbelief! She used the palm of her left hand to slam the butt of the handle, driving it in the full eight inches. The driver's mouth fell open as he collapsed onto the concrete.

Henry came out from behind one of the dumpsters to give her a hand in lifting the body into the back of the truck. "We'll have to wash all that blood off the truck bed", Henry commented. "Yeah, you can do that", Janine replied with a smile.

They couldn't just dump the contents of the truck and the driver's body at the farm. Silas had found a place in the country, about halfway between Aiken and Augusta, where kaolin clay was being mined. There were lots of narrow dirt roads leading nowhere. It was already getting too dark to see properly; Silas wasn't exactly sure which one he had driven the Walmart truck down. "Don't take everything out of the truck", said Henry. "Leave some stuff we can hide behind." Anyone walking down that dirt road in the next few days was going to find a huge cash of canned goods, light bulbs, and other household items. They might find a body as well, but that would be well after Jorge's mission had either succeeded or they were all lying in the Augusta morgue. "How about all these boxes of Kotex sanitary napkins", Henry asked? There were at least fifty boxes, all quite large but not very heavy. "Yeah, we'll keep those. Put them all back on the truck and button it up", Jorge replied.

The Walmart truck only needed to make one more bumpy trip to the farm. The old barn was easily big enough to hide it for the rest of the night. Silas figured the police wouldn't begin searching for either the truck or the driver before noon the next day. By midnight it was loaded with all the gear the team would need. At 6:45 hours the next morning it was on a small country road headed toward an intersection with South Carolina 125 somewhere north of Jackson. "Damn", said Henry! He could hardly believe what he was looking at. The traffic on SC 125 was nonstop. Getting the truck across the northbound lane and onto the median was easy. Only a few cars were heading toward Augusta at that hour. But pulling out into either of the southbound lanes looked to be impossible.

It was like watching a parade moving at 70 miles per hour that never ended. They just kept coming and coming! It was nearly 20 minutes before he saw a break. He pulled the truck out into the near lane as fast as it would go, fully aware that if there was an accident South Carolina Highway Patrol would quickly discover a truckload of automatic weapons

Assault on L

and explosives, along with six people dressed in military camouflage. Several cars blew their horns in disgust as the entire inside lane had to slow down. Occupants in three cars gave Henry the finger as they sped by.

Luis was thinking how much this reminded him of traffic in Barcelona at certain times of the day. He thought about commenting on their situation, but then decided it might only antagonize Henry, who seemed pretty stressed out at the moment. Everyone slowed down to around 45 miles per hour as they passed through Jackson. Obviously, those who lived on the west side of SC 125 were doomed to stay there between 6:30 and 7:30 each morning. And the same if you lived on the east side. Traffic got even slower as they approached the turnoff for employees who worked in the Main Administration Area of the site. Then the pace of the traffic going straight picked up again for a short distance.

Both Henry and Luis found their lips were dry as they pulled up to the security barricade. Henry put the badge Ansel had made for him up to the windshield as Silas had instructed. It was an excellent copy of the deceased Walmart driver's badge but with Henry's photograph. The security guard looked down the side of the truck and motioned for Henry to roll down the window. 'Had Silas been wrong thinking they would be waved on through if they arrived during the rush of shift change?'

"Don't remember seeing you guys before", said the security guard. "You're early. Didn't think you liked getting caught up in all the rush this time of morning." "Special delivery", Henry replied, thinking they were all going to be in a security van on the way to jail in a few minutes. "They've run out and needed this stuff in a hurry." "Where's Charlie anyway. This is usually his route, isn't it", asked the guard. "Yeah, Charlie's got the flu. We came over from the Columbia Walmart to help out." Henry licked his lips again.

The guard looked down the side of the truck for a second time. He could see a never-ending line of cars, with drivers getting more and more irritated at the delay. "OK, go ahead", he motioned. Henry put the truck in gear and pulled slowly on through, picking up speed as he moved further down SC 125. "Wow", said Luis! "I thought he was going to ask to touch your badge and ask for mine as well." As good as Ansel was, they both knew neither badge would stand up to close inspection. "We're not in the clear yet. There's another barricade at Road B. That one's going to be even tougher", said Henry.

Assault on L

SRS Road B intersected the public highway about a mile before reaching the L Lake dam. Henry slowed to make the turn off SC 125, then proceeded another 100 meters to the small security barricade. He looked at his watch. It read 08:05 hours. There were only two security guards. One came out to meet them. "Would you both get out of the truck please", said the guard? He gave their badges a cursory look, then motioned them to follow him to the rear of the truck. "Open up", said the guard, acting as though he had performed this routine about 10,000 times. Henry opened up both doors to reveal four columns of boxes covered in the word Kotex and their company logo. Each column went nearly to the ceiling. If the guard was surprised, he didn't show it. "What the hell do they use these things for anyway", he asked? Luis answered, "Not sure. They don't tell us that stuff".

Just then the other security guard arrived to take a look. "My brother works in 400-D Area. They use tons of these 'things' to clean up spills of heavy water. Then they send them to the burial ground as low-level radioactive waste. Except they call them 'atomic swipes'." "Really", said the other guard? "Yep, must be millions of them in the ground out there." The first guard looked back at Henry. "What else you got?" "That's it", Henry replied. "Whole truck's full of them." The second guard climbed up and pulled down one of the boxes on top. There was another box just like it right behind. It was obvious neither of the two guards wanted much to do with the items in question. And they certainly didn't want to unload box after box of these 'things' onto the roadway. "OK, close it up", said the first guard. Both men headed back to the guard house. As soon as the barrier was raised Henry dropped the truck into gear and proceeded through it.

Three miles down Road B they came to a location Jorge had found during his previous trek to L Area. It was large ravine in amongst a lot of small scrub hardwoods about 50 meters from the edge of the road. They ditched the Walmart truck there, where it couldn't be seen from the road. It was unlikely anyone would notice a few small trees broken over. Site security wouldn't discover the truck for at least twenty-four hours. All they needed was twelve. It took less than 20 minutes to gather up their gear and move across Road B, then about 700 yards through the dense pine forest to the west of L Reactor building. Now it was just a matter of waiting. As they neared the edge of the woods the spectacle of the huge building came into full view

Assault on L

The structure before them was massive, built to withstand just about anything other than a direct hit by a nuclear weapon. It was 170 meters long, 100 meters wide and over 45 meters high in several places. Luis immediately spotted the aluminium boxcars on the roof at one end of the building, and the huge concrete stack rising over 60 meters between them. "That tall square tower with the fins on it must be for the control rods", observed Otis. "The reactor will be right below." What Otis also noticed was the absence of a containment dome. In fact, the building was much too large to be enclosed in such a structure.

From the drawings that Samuel had found it was obvious this building was designed and constructed long before nuclear power plants. That made Luis's job a lot easier. But why the fins on the tower in the center? They weren't shown on the original 1950's drawings. Since they were made of concrete, they certainly weren't for heat dissipation. "Maybe they got worried that an earthquake might shift or topple that tower and then the control rods wouldn't work", said Henry. "They don't have earthquakes in South Carolina, do they", Luis asked? "Maybe", Otis replied.

L Area emerged like a sterile concrete island in a thriving sea of green forest. All agreed the building looked like a fortress, surrounded by double fence instead of a moat. The double fenced area ran completely around the reactor building and other smaller structures. Samuel had seen several designs like this one while working in Arlington, Virginia. "It's just a detection zone, not really a barrier", he began to explain. "Neither fence is electrified. The two fences are only there to keep animals and people from walking in front of the motion detection equipment. Most systems like this have multiple types of detection devices, including microwave and infrared."

"The white gravel between the fences is there to give a flat level surface so someone can't find a low spot to crawl under the beams. It also prevents someone from digging their way under." "What about where it crosses over a building", Janine asked? "The system is continuous all the way around. They're very careful not to leave any gaps. Experts come in every so often and performance test the system to see if they can find a way in." "So it goes across the roof of that entry building as well?" "Yes", Samuel answered. "The roof has to be very flat."

"It might look like a fortress", said Jorge, "But it has many doors. And they will be open tonight only, just for us." It was that rare opportunity they had been waiting for. "They're expecting an imitation tonight. We'll give them the real thing. They are expecting us to go in that door, pointing to the 108-building entrance. We'll be going in that one instead."

Jorge's watch showed 10:12 hours. He didn't expect the Protective Force strike team to arrive until 14:00 hours at the earliest. With their target in sight adrenaline was already flowing. Regardless, they had to remain quiet and out of sight. Jorge assumed the Protective Force strike team would take up the same position in the woods on the west side as before. There were five in the group on December 29th. He had to guess the number would remain the same this time. They would have to be eliminated, of course, before the exercise was scheduled to begin. But not too early. Otherwise their management might become suspicious at not being able to contact them. Once again timing was everything.

Assault on L

Chapter 5

Following World War II, several countries including the United States began development of two types of nuclear reactors. One would use the heat generated by uranium fission to generate electricity, discarding the exotic isotopes these reactors created as highly radioactive waste. The other was designed to produce isotopes needed for nuclear weapons and, to a lesser degree, for other purposes. In this type of reactor, the heat generated by fission was discarded as waste energy. There were even a few designs (e.g., N Reactor at the Hanford Site) that attempted to achieve both in one reactor. Such designs were not very efficient at either task.

In 1946 the United States Congress created the Atomic Energy Commission (AEC) to oversee construction of reactors to produce electricity. Water is heated by nuclear fission to very high temperatures and pressures, then released as superheated steam through a series of turbines which turn electric generators. These reactors were initially seen as economical, environmentally clean, and safe by utility companies who built them. Expansion of the commercial nuclear power industry was based on the idea that electricity from nuclear power plants would eventually become so inexpensive that it would no longer be worth the effort to meter it. The idea of nuclear generated electricity expanded quickly during the 1960's.

The United States Atomic Energy Commission was also given responsibility, at least initially, to oversee development of nuclear reactors to produce isotopes of plutonium and other fissile materials needed for nuclear weapons. In fact, this effort preceded the development of the nuclear power industry by a decade. The production of fissile materials for use in nuclear weapons was of the utmost urgency since at least one other country in the world (The Soviet Union) was creating its own nuclear weapons arsenal in competition with the United States. Development of reactors for plutonium production required a completely different design approach. Water/graphite moderated reactors initially used for plutonium production at the Hanford Site in Washington State were superseded in the early 1950's by more efficient and versatile heavy water moderated and cooled reactors at the Savannah River Site in South Carolina.

In 1971 there were twenty-two commercial nuclear power facilities operating in the United States, producing 2.4% of the U.S. electrical needs. The Energy Reorganization Act of 1974 divided the functions of the AEC between two new agencies. The Energy Research and Development Administration (ERDA) was created to oversee nuclear research and development. The Nuclear Regulatory Commission (NRC) was given responsibility to regulate the commercial nuclear power industry. In effect, the NRC became the agency responsible for all things associated with reactors owned by commercial utilities generating electricity, leaving ERDA as the agency responsible for all things associated with government owned reactors that produced plutonium and other materials for nuclear weapons.

In the 1970's growth of the nuclear power industry slowed significantly as demand decreased, leaving a number of commercial nuclear services companies looking for work. The public had also become concerned about the safety of commercial power reactors, their environmental releases, and disposal of radioactive waste, especially highly radioactive spent nuclear fuel. During that same period of time, the U.S. nuclear weapons stockpile was demanding increased production of isotopes for their weapons. The public's interest, however, remained focused primarily on issues surrounding reactors in the nuclear power industry. Information about the operation of the government's reactors producing weapons materials was classified and not available to the public. In 1977 President Carter signed the Department of Energy Organization Act, transferring all ERDA functions to the new Department of Energy.

A loss of coolant accident in 1979 at the Three Mile Island nuclear power station near Harrisburg, Pennsylvania sparked renewed public interest in the safety of both commercial and government reactors. Questions about government reactors were dismissed, however, based on the substantial differences between commercial power reactors and those used by the government. A typical power reactor operates at a primary coolant pressure of 150 atmospheres and temperature of 325 degrees C. At this pressure the coolant does not boil but transfers its heat energy to a secondary coolant that becomes the steam to drive the turbines and electrical generators. A great deal of energy is stored in the primary coolant itself and would be released catastrophically if the coolant boundary (piping, etc.) was breached. By contrast, reactors operated by the Department of Energy at the Savannah River Site never exceed 1.3 atmospheres pressure and 129 degrees C. The primary coolant stores very little energy compared to a commercial power reactor, and thus can sustain a primary coolant breach with only minor effects, as long as sufficient coolant continues to reach all the fuel assemblies in the reactor core.

Assault on L

The NRC and the DOE each developed their own approaches and analyses to ensure the safety of their own reactor types. When challenged, DOE's position with regard to the possibility of NRC type oversight of the DOE's reactors was that measures provided by the government to ensure reactor safety were 'different but equivalent' to those employed by the NRC. Both organizations based their methods on lessons learned from several previous accidents, including:

- October 1957, Fire at Windscale Unit 1 in the United Kingdom
  A release of energy in the graphite core of Unit 1 lead to higher temperatures than expected. The core temperature eventually reached more than 750 degrees Fahrenheit. When air was vented to cool the core, the reactor caught fire. Carbon dioxide was initially used to put out the fire, but this failed. Using water, workers finally extinguished the fire after it had burned for three days. During that time radioactivity escaped through the chimney, contaminating much of the surrounding area, even reaching parts of mainland Europe. More than 200 cancer deaths were attributed to this accident.

- July 1959, Sodium Reactor Experiment in Los Angeles, California
  A partial meltdown occurred at the Sodium Reactor Experiment when the flow of coolant was blocked causing the reactor core to overheat. Thirteen of forty-three fuel elements overheated when tetralin, an oil-like fluid, leaked into the primary liquid sodium loop and blocked coolant flow to these elements. The overheating caused failure of the reactor core. Fission products were released from the damaged fuel into the primary sodium loop, and then leaked from there into a region inside the building housing the reactor. Other fission products mixed with the helium cover gas, which leaked into the building as well. The air containing these fission products was processed through filters in the ventilation system and discharged to the atmosphere.

- January 1961, SL-1 Reactor at Idaho Falls, Idaho
  Manual withdrawal of a single control rod caused a catastrophic power surge and steam explosion, killing all personnel who were present. Workers were reattaching drive mechanisms for the control rods. They manually lifted the central control rod approximately 20 inches instead of the 4 inches that was required. This action caused the reactor to go critical, with a power surge 6,000 times more than normal in less than a second. Nuclear fuel

vaporized, creating a steam bubble. The steam bubble expanded so rapidly that it pushed the water above it against the reactor vessel, causing it to rise off its support structure. All the water and some of the fuel was released from the reactor vessel in the process. All three workers on duty received lethal doses of radiation.

o October 1966, Enrico Fermi Unit 1 at Frenchtown Charter Township, Michigan
   Partial meltdown of two fuel assemblies at Fermi Unit 1 resulted from a coolant flow blockage in two fuel channels. Fermi Unit 1 was the first and only commercially operating liquid metal fast breeder reactor. A component in the reactor vibrated loose and was carried by coolant up to the fuel assembly's inlet nozzle, blocking coolant flow. The blockage was not noticed until core temperature alarms alerted the operators. Several fuel assemblies reached 700 degrees Fahrenheit and melted. After repairs Fermi 1 returned to partial operation until 1972. It was decommissioned in 1975.

o March 1979, Three Mile Island in Middletown, Pennsylvania
   A partial meltdown at Three Mile Island Unit 2 resulted from failures in the non-nuclear secondary coolant system. A manually operated pressure relief valve in the primary coolant system then stuck open, allowing much of the primary coolant to escape. Human error compounded the problem, resulting in substantial core melting. However, the containment structure around the reactor prevented most of the radioactive contamination from being released to the atmosphere.

By the mid 1980's DOE's insistence on 'different but equivalent' measures to ensure the safety of the government's reactors was being challenged more and more. Events at other at DOE sites weakened their argument further. There was a call for increased scrutiny of the government's reactors. By January 1985 it was inevitable that the DOE would have to accept some NRC type oversight of the Savannah River Reactors. As of late 1985 there were nearly 100 nuclear power reactors operating in the U.S., compared to only three DOE reactors still operating at the Savanna River Site.

The NRC made a convincing argument that the measures employed by the many needed to be imposed on the few, whether they fit or not! This included alternatives to existing reactor safety analyses, changes to operational protocols, enhanced control of equipment and design changes, and enhanced demonstrations of defence against threats posed by armed terrorist groups. 'Independent experts' from the commercial power industry were brought in by the DOE to inspect and review the operation of reactors at Savannah River Site, with the aim of identifying improvements that could be made. Since many of these people were looking for work, it was not surprising when they found that indeed the government's reactors needed a great deal of work, which they were imminently qualified to perform, of course.

The DOE suddenly found themselves in a dilemma of their own making. They didn't have the money to correct all the deficiencies that had been identified, but they also didn't want to be blamed for doing nothing to resolve these newly highlighted issues. One issue in particular proved to be very expensive to correct. That involved a management practice known in the commercial nuclear industry as 'configuration management'. In a commercial power reactor, a component or piece of equipment could not be replaced or redesigned without first changing all the engineering drawings and records associated with that piece of equipment. The process often took months, but then very few such changes were required since these reactors operated for years between refuelling outages. In the DOE's reactors the need for such changes was much more frequent. Often changes were made and approved on an urgent basis. Drawings in the field were marked up in red to show the changes. Formal changes to the master drawings had to wait for months or longer.

'Independent experts' insisted this was unacceptable. Any component change in a reactor building would have to wait until all the drawings and documents were formally revised and approved. The backlog of drawings and documents that need to be changed had already become enormous! DOE management at the Savannah River Site didn't have the money to support a huge program to work off the backlog. When they asked for more funding, they were told to take it out of some other part of the Site's operations. That simply wasn't possible. The Site DOE Manager was faced with a problem for which no solution existed. It seemed certain he would be blamed for failing to respond to issues arising from the independent investigation he had sponsored.

'Independent experts' from the commercial reactor industry also took issue with the operations protocols in the reactor control rooms. Some came from the Nuclear Navy Service and were accustomed to strict communications protocol, requiring every verbal instruction to be repeated back to the officer in charge. This practice was completely foreign to operations personnel at Savannah River Site. Another difference was reliance on highly efficient filter systems in the event of a reactor accident. These filter systems did not meet the NRC's definition of 'containment' in the same way as a steel and concrete dome constructed over a power reactor. However, in this case no one could suggest an alternative that was any better than what already existed.

Several 'experts' even recommended that pipes in the reactor buildings be painted various colors for identification, like the carbon steel pipes in commercial reactor buildings. That idea was abandoned when they were shown how intergranular stress corrosion cracking (IGSCC) had already caused the permanent shut down of C Reactor at Savannah River. IGSCC is caused by chlorides, found in most paint, attacking stainless steel vessels and pipes. Such cracking was found to spread rapidly when attempts were made to weld patches over the cracks. Painting stainless steel piping would surely result in irreparable damage.

The unusual burden placed on reactor operations and technical personnel at the Savannah River Site over the period 1984 through early 1986 was unprecedented and resulted in a great deal of additional work and stress for those who worked in these facilities. The increased level of 'independent inspections' and vague questions from those who claimed to be 'experts' but who misunderstood the design and operation of the heavy water reactors became a serious morale issue. Both reactor operations and technical personnel resented the inferences that they were incompetent or professionally deficient. Most feared there would be fundamental changes in the way they did their jobs, simply for appearance sake or to shift blame. All of this made their jobs more difficult and less rewarding.

The impact on reactor operations staff included distractions from their duties, interruptions to explain why tasks were being performed in a certain manner, and documenting discussions or answers to questions being asked during their rounds. Each morning each reactor area spent more time reporting all the 'findings' of some 'independent expert' during their operating shift than on the status of the reactor. The reactor operations manager was shadowed almost constantly by an 'inspector'.

The reactor technical staff fared no better. Their methods and procedures were questioned repeatedly. Reactor safety questions were asked and answered, then asked again in almost the same form. New novel analyses were requested, without basis. The reactor technical manager had to explain every decision and the rationale for it. All questions had to be answered in writing. Both the reactor operations and reactor technical managers were expected to attend meetings after normal business hours and even on most weekends. They were clearly outnumbered by those attempting to find fault with their work. Managers at all levels put in a great deal of unpaid overtime just to keep up with the extra workload. During the summer of 1985 many managers and staff never saw their families or lawns in the daytime. The site security organization wasn't spared either. They were treated with a bit more courtesy, however, maybe because they carried side arms.

A significant portion of the engineering support staff at the site had to be devoted to creating program plans and schedules to track all the 'findings' being created daily. By February 1986 there were over 21,500 findings to be dealt with. Every finding, no matter how trivial, had to be addressed, tracked, corrected or otherwise dispositioned, and finally closed out. It was the ultimate example of bureaucratic overkill. Staff in both reactor operations and technical often felt they were being harassed for no valid reason. The DOE's 'independent experts' were often arrogant and disrespectful.

Assault on L

Chapter 6

There's an old saying, 'Operating a nuclear reactor is like flying an airplane. Both involve endless hours of sheer boredom, interrupted by moments of sheer terror!' MacMahon had been a pilot before qualifying as a Senior Reactor Operator in the Reactor Operations Department at the Savannah River Site. It took him only four years to get promoted to Shift Supervisor. In January 1985 MacMahon was promoted to Shift Senior Supervisor and took over B Shift just prior to L Reactor restart. He had to change his carpool arrangements, but the additional money was worth a temporary inconvenience.

L Reactor was the only production reactor in the DOE Complex to have been shut down and mothballed, then refurbished and restarted. It seemed to attract a greater number of visitors than other similar facilities. MacMahon often found himself acting as tour guide for groups of three or four who were curious to see what the government had spent so much money on. In fact, he was happy to show them in most cases. He didn't like those who insisted on debating the facts he was giving them. There seemed to be more of that type of visitor lately.

"Beginning on the left side of the control room, you can see a graphic panel depicting our building ventilation system, with its three exhaust fans and five filter compartments located on the plus 55 roof. We keep two of the three fans running constantly. To the right of that is the hydraulic graphic panel showing the six pumps and twelve heat exchangers that remove heat from the heavy water that circulates through the reactor itself. We used to take water from the Savannah River to cool the heat exchangers, but now we recirculate that water from our new L Lake. AC and DC motors that drive the heavy water pumps are depicted on the next panel to the right. We have several sources of 13.8 KV power for the AC pumps. In the unlikely event that all those fail, you can see there are six DC pumps driven by their own dedicated diesel engines located at the minus 20 level, three on either side of the building. We don't have to start these diesel engines – they are running all the time, just in case."

Moving across an empty space separating the instrument panels, MacMahon continued. "This panel contains the annunciators for systems that monitor important equipment in the building. Our operators respond to these alarms according to written procedures that have been approved by our operations management and by our engineering staff. Next to the annunciator panel you can see four chart recorders, known as High Level Flux Monitors. These recorders continuously monitor the neutron flux in the reactor and produce charts that can be analysed in the event of any deviation from what is expected. Our operators watch these four recorders and take immediate action should they see an anomaly, to include dropping the safety rods into the reactor to shut down the nuclear chain reaction if needed. That's called a SCRAM." "Why is it called that", a United States Senator once asked? "It's an acronym. When the first atomic pile was built in a squash court at Stagg Field in Chicago in 1942 there were three control rods. One of them hung from a rope over the pile. If the reactor started to go wrong, a man with an axe was standing by to cut the rope and drop the safety control rod into the pile, shutting down the nuclear chain reaction. SCRAM stands for Safety Control Rod Axe Man." The Senator nodded.

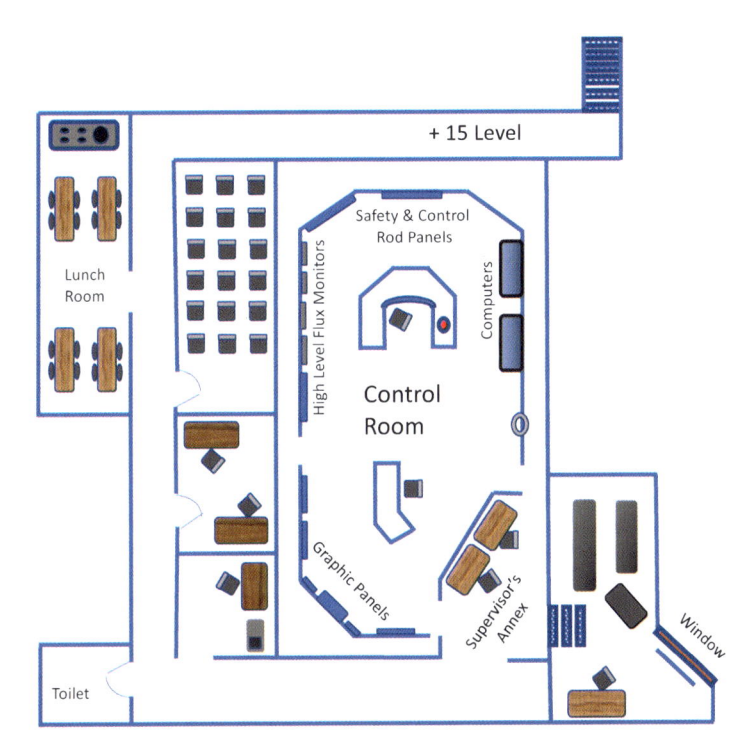

MacMahon moved to the right again, "Behind me you can see two large round panels, each containing a hexagonal pattern. The right panel contains dials and knobs that allow us to bias, or 'trim' individual groups of control rods as necessary to maintain a uniform neutron flux across the pattern of fuel assemblies in the reactor. The left panel shows the status of our safety rod system. As you can see, they are all in their fully raised positions, as they must be whenever the reactor is operating. These rods are held by electromagnetic clutches and drop into the reactor by gravity upon loss of electrical power, or when any of a number of instruments indicate a problem requiring the reactor to be shut down."

"On the right-hand side of the control room you can see two banks of computers. One of these acts like the automatic pilot on commercial aircraft. It maintains the reactor at a constant predetermined power level. The other computer monitors the effluent temperature for each of the 600 fuel assemblies in the reactor, and automatically shuts down the reactor if any of these temperatures exceed predefined limits. Last but certainly not least, you will notice a square shaped hole in this instrument panel and a large metal ring just inside the hole. Pulling this ring will shut down the reactor by injecting a neutron poison, gadolinium nitrate, into the heavy water coolant. The mechanism for this shutdown system is completely mechanical and requires no electricity or other external power source. Once this system is activated the reactor cannot be restarted until all the gadolinium nitrate poison has been removed from the heavy water using a series of deionizers that must be mechanically connected into the system. This process typically takes four to five days."

"The center of the control room contains two consoles. The horseshoe shaped console in front of the control rod trim and safety rod panels allows operating personnel to control reactor power by moving control rods, in gangs or individually. This operator can also initiate emergency shutdown, using control rods, safety rods or the gadolinium nitrate system. The other rectangular console is the Automated Incident Action system, AIA. This system monitors various locations in the building and can automatically open valves to supply emergency cooling water (light water) to the reactor if the normal heavy water circulating pumps are disabled by flooding due to a rupture of normal cooling water piping inside the building. Ladies and gentlemen, are there any questions?" There always was at least one question, but MacMahon could say that he had never been asked the same question twice, with one notable exception.

Assault on L

B Shift in L Reactor was generally considered the best of the four rotating shifts. They had a reputation for getting things done promptly, professionally, and without complaint. MacMahon's leadership had a lot to do with that. He did have one 'bur under his saddle' though. He had his doubts about management's decision to conduct security exercises while his reactor was operating at full power. The Shift Supervisor on B Shift understood MacMahon's concerns. "It's like this", MacMahon offered. "Everyone needs training. The flight crew on a commercial airliner needs training so they know what to do if there is an emergency during a flight. But the airlines don't conduct that training in a plane full of passengers at 35,000 feet. They do it on the ground where their people can make mistakes without any serious consequences. We should only be doing these security exercises when the reactor is shut down for refuelling. That would give them two or three opportunities a year. Isn't that enough?"

"I suppose the Protective Force might become lax if they knew a simulated attack could only come when we're shut down", Murphy replied. MacMahon responded, "But they're told when these exercises are going to happen anyway, just like we are – plus or minus a few hours. I'm just not comfortable with a bunch of trigger happy ex-military people running around my building while we're operating, even if they are firing blanks. We're told to stay out of their way, which means our building people have sit in the lunchroom for four hours rather than being out in the building taking their readings. The security people are told to stay away from the control room and not touch any 'sensitive equipment' in the building. Do they know 'sensitive equipment' when they see it? I doubt it!" "Have you talked to the Area Superintendent about all this", Murphy asked? "Yes, twice. Apparently, no one wants a shutdown just to let these guys play their war games. And they don't want to wait until our next refuelling", said MacMahon. "I just pray it all goes well."

MacMahon chose not to share his other concerns with the personnel on B Shift. One was the number of self-proclaimed experts who wanted to inspect his building, and then argue that he was 'doing it all wrong'. His management never treated him that way. Neither had any other visitors up until recently. It was annoying and he had complained to the Area Superintendent about this as well. MacMahon noted the only good thing about these security exercises was that all the 'independent experts' were suddenly nowhere to be found, leaving operations personnel free to do their jobs without interrogation or interference. It seemed ironic that now it was the security exercise that was preventing them from getting anything done.

Assault on L

MacMahon's other concern was that his building was being cluttered with grenade shields that partially blocked hallways at various levels, as well as other 'modifications' to doors and passageways. These were designed to 'fortify' the building against attack. All of this made it more difficult to keep the building clean and corridors free of litter that has a tendency to accumulate in a large operating facility. It just made more work for his staff, whose job it was to operate a nuclear reactor, not clean up after the 'local troops' every week. While none of the building operators had complained, he could tell it was having a negative effect on morale.

"I think they've started already", remarked the Building Foreman on B Shift. Tyler had the same misgivings about these 'war games' as MacMahon. Everyone in the control room had just finished getting turnover from the day shift going off. Tyler had come up to read the day shift log entries. "Only one problem in minus 40 that might give us some trouble tonight", he said. "One of the sensors for the AIA in the pump room sump on the near side is acting up. Procedure says we can bypass it for this evening. Day shift tomorrow can get an E&I mechanic to replace it." "Yeah, OK", MacMahon replied.

Normal shift compliment during reactor operations included one Shift Senior Supervisor, one Shift Supervisor, one Building Forman, two Senior Reactor Operators and two Reactor Operators in the control room, and four Reactor Operators that roamed areas inside and outside the building. One Maintenance Mechanic and one E&I (Electrical & Instrument) Mechanic were typically assigned to each shift as well. Tonight's shift compliment was short two Reactor Operators in the building, a Maintenance Mechanic and an E&I Mechanic because of the security exercise. There was no point in having everyone sitting around in the lunchroom most of their shift. The requirement for a minimum of nine members of the operations staff was met.

"It won't be dark for at least two hours", Murphy noted. "Well, something's going on already. Security guys are watching the PIDAS fence on the east side of the area", said Tyler. "I don't like it when those guys get nervous", MacMahon remarked. "Better call all our guys upstairs just in case they start early. We won't be able to get much done tonight! C Shift won't be happy when they show up at midnight and we haven't taken all our readings." It was normal for the oncoming shift to have to clean up one or two messes the shift before them left behind. But the next shift would have to do the same for them, so everybody came out even in the end. In general, there was more camaraderie than competition between the four shifts in a reactor area. Competition between reactor areas could still be fierce, however! If you pressed him MacMahon would admit that L Area was the best, and B Shift was the best in L Area.

Each reactor area was operated by four eight-hour rotating shifts, designated A, B, C and D. MacMahon was the oldest of the four Shift Senior Supervisors in L Area, being just four months shy of 40. Unfortunately, his black hair and dark complexion only served to highlight the premature greying around the temples. His true love was flying. He owned two small planes at one point, and even worked as a commercial pilot for a small airline for several years. He lost his pilot's license when he was diagnosed with a mild form of epilepsy, even though it was completely controlled with medication. The other members of B Shift weren't even aware of his medical issues, as far as he knew. MacMahon's wife and twin teenage daughters knew about the epilepsy, of course. It was just something they learned to accept. Murphy was MacMahon's right arm. He knew the Shift Supervisors job like the back of his hand, having served in role since January 1982.

Although he had been in reactor operations two years longer than MacMahon, Murphy held no resentment for the man who got the promotion Murphy had expected. He was nearly five years younger than MacMahon, after all. Murphy's wife was understanding about such things, or so she said at the time. "Your time will come", she had said. Patience was one of Murphy's virtues, but definitely not something he learned in the Marine Corp. The Marine Corp. didn't teach him how to show compassion or empathy either. His father taught him that, and how those traits can project strength rather than weakness in a leader. Everyone on B Shift in L Area knew they could discuss any subject with Murphy without being judged or ridiculed.

What the Marine Corp. did teach Murphy was the value of loyalty. Not the sort of loyalty that's demanded, but the kind that's born out of respect and earned anew every day. Everyone on B Shift was proud of the job they did. Murphy had that effect on people. He saw the best in them and that made them do their best in return. For Murphy there was a coldness about the reactor building, however. All that concrete between you and the natural world. Day or night, sunny or raining, warm or freezing outside. There was no way to know. It was like being in a dragon's cave - if you could turn out the lights it would have been total darkness. And you sensed the dragon was alive. It had a great fire in its belly even though it didn't move. L Reactor was a clean safe place to work, but

Assault on L

Murphy would readily confess it wasn't the sort of place where a naturalist like him would spend time if they didn't have to.

It didn't help that Murphy had been hearing rumours about a number of major changes that might be coming, changes in how B Shift would operate. He suspected that others on B Shift had heard them too. There hadn't been anything official, but there was talk of converting to methods used by Nuclear Navy Officers to give orders on nuclear submarines. He had seen it in movies, where everything the commanding officer said had to be repeated back to him for confirmation. Maybe that was necessary on a nuclear-powered submarine, but it seemed completely useless in the L Reactor control room. Nobody in the Marine Corp ever made him repeat back an order. He didn't see why he should have to do so now. He had also heard that getting a maintenance mechanic to replace a piece of equipment in the building might require a much longer chain of approvals than it did now. That could seriously affect operations, even to the point of having to shut down the reactor unnecessarily because a component couldn't be replaced in a timely manner. That didn't make any sense at all. Perhaps none of these rumours were true.

Murphy and Tyler were exact opposites, something MacMahon took full advantage of. At 32, Tyler was the youngest member of supervision in L Area. But Tyler had worked in reactor operations since 1976 and was on the L Area restart team since its inception in 1981. He knew every nook and cranny in the building. When a new operator or mechanic arrived in the area the first thing the others would do is warn them about Tyler. There were places in the building where you could make a bed of coveralls and take a quick nap when things were slow. Tyler knew every place there was. He would find you before you could even doze off! His light brown hair and soft eyes would lead you to think he might be a soft touch. Two operators who had lost their jobs in the last few years could tell you that he wasn't. He was a stickler for following procedures. And so was MacMahon.

Blythe was the only problem employee MacMahon had. He had to admit it wasn't her fault. Most of the reactor operations staff were men. It seemed a more natural career for men than for women. But every once in a while, some bright young woman would challenge that notion. Blythe was very bright indeed. With a degree in chemistry from University of South Carolina, one might wonder why she wanted to be a nuclear reactor operator. "Because I find applied physics fascinating", she would reply. It took her less than a year to qualify as a Senior Reactor Operator, scoring significantly higher in the reactor simulator and other certification examinations than any other candidate. She was quick to spot a problem and consistently accurate with her solution. She was also 28, single, tall, blonde with blue eyes, i.e., stunningly attractive to the opposite sex. And in L Area she was surrounded by the opposite sex. That was MacMahon's problem. How to keep them away from her so she could do her job. Never slow to spot an asset, MacMahon usually arranged to have Blythe sitting at the nuclear console whenever he had VIP government visitors. They never failed to notice.

Like all L Area personnel, B Shift had been briefed shortly after the first Force on Force security exercise that took place two months earlier on December 29th. Fortunately for MacMahon and crew the critique of that exercise didn't reveal any mistakes or deficiencies on the part of the operations personnel. Nevertheless, they had been cautioned against doing anything that might interfere with Protective Force activities this time around. If the adversary team won again it had better not be because of anything operations people did! In a building with eight-foot-thick concrete walls there are no windows that let you see out. If MacMahon wanted to know what was happening with the security exercise outside he had to send Tyler down to ground level to look out the main personnel door of the building. But that violated his instructions about keeping everyone up on plus 15 level and out of the way of the exercise.

It was a potentially hazardous guessing game. But MacMahon still had to have some idea of what was going on. After all it was HIS building! He decided to send Tyler down once every hour and hope he didn't get caught in the middle of things. At 5:10 pm Tyler reported nothing was happening. At 6:05 pm his report was the same.

Murphy hated these times MacMahon referred to as 'endless hours of sheer boredom'. He found himself lost in thought, standing in front of the three-foot thick lead-glass and oil-filled window that looked into the huge room containing the reactor vessel. To the casual observer the window could pass for a still photograph of the reactor tank top and 'forest', as they called it, of control rod and safety rod latch mechanisms resting on top of the giant cylindrical tank. When MacMahon gave tours of the control room his 'grand finale' was to take his visitors down a few steps into the dimly lit room adjacent to the supervisor's area, so they could look out and see the reactor itself. The one question he was asked repeatedly was, "Is it 'on'?" "Yes, of course it's 'on'", he would reply. Nothing moved in that room except for the imperceptible changes in positions of control rods from time to time. It was like watching paint dry. Not very exciting, he had to admit. But he kept it in the tour because visitors always wanted to 'see the reactor'.

Murphy believed there WAS something exciting about looking out that window. He marvelled at the eloquence of design on display. Even more impressive was what was below that ten-foot-thick concrete floor, and below the floor below that. A sixth of America's entire production of stainless steel for a year and over a thousand cubic yards of concrete were there, just for starters. Pushing huge quantities of heavy water around in six symmetrical loops to collect the heat generated by nuclear fission, and then removing that heat with twelve giant heat exchangers wasn't that difficult. All you needed was half a dozen pumps and motors to drive them. What could be simpler, except for the fact that you couldn't just switch it off. Decay heat from fission products would melt everything he was looking at if the water suddenly stopped moving. Even worse if it disappeared entirely!

Tyler came down the steps quietly to join him. Murphy turned with a start. "Is it still there", asked Tyler with a smile? "Yes", Murphy replied. "Hasn't moved an inch." During the first year of his marriage Tyler's young wife used to ask him what he did while he was at work all day. He tried to tell her, but it all went right over her head. She knew all about teaching children ages 6 through 12. But 'pumps and valves and heat exchangers' meant nothing to her. By the second year she stopped asking. Tyler was equally perplexed at his wife's ability to entertain her pupils while teaching them. He had witnessed the process several times when she allowed him to sit in during one of her classes during his day off. She clearly had a talent he didn't possess. For him a room full of 8-year olds was infinitely more complicated than a nuclear reactor ever could be. The fact that they couldn't have children of their own was a bitter pill for them both. They were thinking about adopting, perhaps within a year or so.

Both men leaned on the railing in front of the amber tinted window. "Shame they couldn't have made the reactor tank out of glass so we could see what's going on inside", said Murphy. "Yeah, that would be cool", Tyler replied. The room they were standing in was rarely visited while the reactor was operating, except for the occasional tour. When the reactor was being refuelled however this was where all the action took place. A separate group of reactor operators performed the refuelling activities. There was a lot to see through that lead-glass window then.

During refuelling the 'forest' had to be retracted into the ceiling nearly nearly 70 feet overhead, exposing the top of the reactor tank. Precision cranes were then brought into the room, one for removing spent fuel assemblies and the other for inserting fresh ones. The whole process usually took several days, working round the clock. It was only when the reactor was shut down that a great many other jobs could be performed in areas around the reactor tank and elsewhere in the building. Tyler had to admit he had never seen the refuelling process. He was always too busy. "Seen enough", Murphy asked? "Yep", replied Tyler. Murphy reached up and flipped the light switch to off. The lead-glass window went from amber to black.

It was almost 8:00 pm. Time for Tyler to make another trip down the stairs to the main building entrance to check on the security exercise. From the control room doorway, the plus 15 level personnel corridor formed a perimeter around the outside of the control room, finally arriving at the stairway that lead down to the building main entrance. Along that corridor were a small conference room, a well-equipped kitchen and lunchroom, and several offices used by additional supervisory staff who were typically only present from 7 am until 4:30 or 5 pm Monday through Friday.

MacMahon actually preferred it when B Shift was on from 8 pm til midnight, or midnight til 8 am. The 8 am to 4 pm, or 'day shift' meant that his boss and his boss's boss were there, either generally getting in the way or thinking up extra things from him and his crew to do. Tyler came down the metal grating stairway from plus 15 level with caution. He spoke to the security guard sitting behind one of the grenade screens in the hallway. "Anything happening?" "Nope, not yet", replied the guard. "Mind if I stick my head out the door for a moment?" "Go ahead." Tyler cracked open the door and looked out. He could hear the cicadids singing but saw nothing moving. Back upstairs, MacMahon looked up as Tyler walked in shaking his head. "Nothing yet", he said.

Blythe was on the nuclear console. The main problem with that job was staying alert. Watching the High Level Flux Monitors was like watching a tulip open its petals to the sun. There were changes but it took hours to notice them. When the reactor was not on computer control small manual adjustments of the control rods were necessary to balance the neutron flux across the reactor and compensate for very gradual depletion of fissile material in the fuel. At least it made the job interesting. But with the reactor on computer control there was quite literally nothing to do. The computer made all the control rod adjustments in imperceptible increments.

Only a very disciplined mind could maintain focus on recorder traces that didn't seem to change from beginning to end of the eight-hour shift.

That's why there were two Senior Reactor Operators who rotated on and off the nuclear console. When the computers were first installed some thought the Senior Reactor Operators were redundant. But computers aren't infallible. If an errant control rod suddenly decided to start driving out on its own and the computer didn't stop it there had to be someone there to shut down the reactor.

Leland had just finished his two hours on the nuclear console and was busy taking readings on the various instrument readouts in the control room. He was just happy to be on his feet and have something to do. Being more than a few years older than Blythe he had sort of settled into a groove, as he would describe it. He knew the Senior Reactor Operator's duties so well that he didn't have to think that much anymore. He could instantly spot an instrument reading that was even slightly different than normal. And, most importantly, he was stickler for procedure compliance.

There were two tenets in this business. One was personal safety. Personal injuries just didn't happen in this company. There was a constant emphasis on wearing personal protective equipment, including safety glasses, hard hats, steel toed shoes, etc. The other was following written procedures. Every process or operation was conducted according to approved written procedures. If the job couldn't be performed the way the procedure described, then the procedure had to be changed and approved before the job could continue. Supervision all the way up to the Reactor Operations Manager made it clear a violation of either of these two tenets was a fireable offense.

Tyler picked up the shift roster kept at the desk on entry to the supervisors' annex to the control room. He and MacMahon were on it, along with Blythe, Leland and Crosby assigned the control room. Also listed were the three Reactor Operators assigned to the building and grounds, Jared, Martin and Ferbis. Except tonight everyone was staying out of below grade areas of the building because of the security exercise. Murphy was listed as the Shift Supervisor for B Shift. The Maintenance Mechanic normally assigned to B Shift had the night off. MacMahon had been told at the last minute that he would have his usual E&I Mechanic tonight but forgot to list him on the roster. His name was Grogan.

Assault on L

Chapter 7

Before Brownlie could fully comprehend he was in danger his head snapped backward from the impact of a second hollow-point round. His legs buckled, dropping him to a kneeling position, before he fell face down in the pine straw. Jonesy reached Brownlie in seconds. The back of Brownlie's head looked like the inside of a ripe watermelon that had been dropped on concrete. As Jonesy bent over his commanding officer, a round hit him in the left temple, toppling him onto his right side.

Jorge looked at his watch, then held up three fingers to let his team know there were now three members in the site security contractor's Force on Force strike group. Even though those three were firing blanks, they had to be swiftly eliminated before they could contact anyone and sound an alarm.

At 20:40 hours Janine began moving across the open field on her own. She had spotted a possible way to get inside the L Area PIDAS undetected. The area outside the primary entry portal for authorized personnel wasn't being patrolled. Reaching the entry portal building in just over a minute she silently scaled the outside wall. Once on the roof she slid on her back through a low point that ran just underneath the infrared beam. She then dropped down along the opposite wall of the building. The roof had recently been repaired at that point and the new roofline had not yet been performance tested. That test was scheduled for next week.

The main personnel access door on the west side of the reactor building was only about 80 meters away. She reached it on a dead run in 22 seconds. Fearing it might be locked, she gently tried the handle. It was not only unlocked but slightly ajar. She paused to catch her breath and gain her composure, then calmly opened the door and casually walked in, wearing a slightly soiled pair of grey coveralls like those typically used by maintenance personnel in most factories and warehouses.

"You're not supposed to be out in the building, mam", barked a nervous member of the Protective Force. "There's an exercise going on. You need to leave this area immediately". He was standing behind one of two grenade shields in the main personnel entry corridor. "Oh sorry", she replied. "I'm pulling a double shift tonight and just had to have a smoke.

Assault on L

We aren't allowed to smoke inside the building you know". She noticed several cigarette butts on the floor next to the grenade shield. Her sheepish smile was meant to distract him from noticing she didn't have a badge and that her shoes were specially designed for rock climbing. She had learned a few things from Luis, and even borrowed a spare bit of his equipment.

Blue-green eyes and an innocent smile worked as intended. He motioned her past his position to the open metal staircase leading up to the plus 15 level of the building, then turned back around to face the entrance corridor and access door. As soon as he turned, Janine swivelled on her left foot and reached him in two steps. A side kick to the left kidney brought him to his knees. She quickly reached her left hand around to grasp his chin while the right hand rested on the crown of his head. With one quick snap his neck was broken. As he fell onto his side, she was already checking his carotid artery for signs of a pulse. She counted three rapid heartbeats, then there were none. Because of all the equipment he was wearing she had some difficulty dragging the body about 10 meters to a space under the stairwell. Boxes of coveralls, lab coats and other supplies stored under the stairwell temporarily hid the body until she could find somewhere to dispose of it.

With the main entrance now clear, Janine needed to find somewhere out of sight to wait. She ducked into an open doorway on the right side of the entrance corridor. It was a dimly lit area where the floor appeared to be glowing. She found the entire room to be an enormous swimming pool covered with metal grating. "This must be where the spent fuel assemblies are stored", she said to no one. How beautiful it was! Rows and rows of long cylindrical shapes glowing in the most beautiful shade of blue she'd ever seen! It was mesmerising!

Jorge had been watching Janine's progress. As soon as she entered the main building, he signalled the rest of the team to move toward the PIDAS on a dead run. It took them about a minute to cover 220 meters to the outer fence and another 20 seconds for all seven to get completely over the PIDAS. Two armed Protective Force personnel responded to the PIDAS alarms, taking up defensive positions behind two earthen berms in the yard. Two others came around the corner of the main building, while another came from the entry portal building. Jorge took out the man coming from the entry portal building. Henry and Silas dropped the two responders coming around the main building.

Assault on L

Responders behind the berms hadn't noticed their comrades had fallen and were not moving. Another man came running out of the entry portal building yelling at the other two, but they couldn't hear him for the gunfire. "They're shooting live rounds. Live rounds! LIVE ROUNDS!!" Finally, he got their attention, as all six adversaries had begun running again across the yard to the main building access door. They were all inside in another five seconds.

"What in the hell is going on", yelled the man behind one of the berms. All gunfire had ceased. He stood up slowly and walked over to one of the men lying on the ground. There was a lot of blood coming from a large bullet hole in the man's upper thigh. He took off his jacket and tied the two arms around the wound to stop the bleeding. The man had a stunned look in his eyes. How could he have been shot. They were using blanks. Other Protective Force personnel began to arrive at the scene, only to find two of their comrades were dead. "Somebody's going to hang for this mistake", shouted Captain Lowe. "Call an ambulance. Hurray."

"One's still alive over there", yelled the man holding pressure on his partner's leg. "This one's not", shouted another. The man behind the other berm had caught a bullet that burst his neck. There was no place to even try to get a pulse. No one had noticed that one of the adversaries had separated from the group. In the confusion Luis had circled around to reach the outside wall of the building just below the plus 55 level roof. While the Protective Force was dealing with the wounded, Luis launched a grappling hook onto the roof. It found a firm hold under one of the rails that hold the filter compartments in place. He was up the rope and onto the roof in less than three minutes, pulling the rope up after him. Since he couldn't be seen from the ground, he had all the time he needed to place his plastic explosives on the intake ducts of the five filter compartments.

Once they had assembled in the main access corridor, Jorge made assignments. "Silas, you and Janine stay here in the entrance corridor. Use their own fighting positions and grenade shields against them. Latch the door and inject glue into the lock. Don't let them get through to us." Janine got Silas' attention, pointing toward the door into the spent fuel storage room. "You hide behind the grenade screen. I'll be in here. Perhaps I can distract them – make them think I'm an employee, or a hostage trying to escape."

Jorge continued, "Samuel and Ansel, get inside the room with the reactor. Place your charges on three of the water inlet pipes and set for remote detonation. It looks like there's only one doorway to access that room.

Assault on L

One of you should be able to hold them out while the other places the charges. Once we take over the control room they will have to pull back. Then we can get you out." Otis added, "If you place all three charges on the same side it might shift the top of the reactor enough that the safety and control rods won't drop in." Samuel looked puzzled. "They won't be able to shut down the reactor", Otis added. "Henry, you and Otis are with me", said Jorge. The three of them started up the stairs to plus 15 level.

Tyler realized it was about time to go down for another look. Suddenly there was some commotion down the hallway. MacMahon turned around with a start. "Hey, you guys aren't supposed to be in this part of the building. What's going on?" A bullet hole in his forehead answered the question. He slumped to the floor, as those in the control room stared through the Plexiglas partition in disbelief. Murphy was sitting at the supervisor's desk. He managed to bump the silent duress button with his knee, before being ordered into the control room with the others. Jorge rifled through the papers on the desk until he found the shift roster.

"We'll have to make sure everybody on this list is either in here with us or in one of the rooms we passed in the hallway." He motioned for Henry to go make it so. The phone rang. He motioned for Murphy to come back to the desk and answer it. Murphy picked up the receiver as though it was a priceless crystal vase. "105 L Control Room." He listened for a few moments. "What do they want", Jorge asked in a soft voice? Murphy covered the mouthpiece with his hand. "It's the Site Emergency Operations Center. They're asking for the duress alarm abort code."

Jorge cocked his Glock 19 and placed it against Murphy's forehead. "Then tell them", he whispered. "I can't", Murphy replied, staring him right in the eyes. "You just killed the only man that knew today's number." Being an ex-Marine, Murphy knew how to be cool under fire. Jorge didn't approve of his attitude. His impulse was to just pull the trigger. But then he reconsidered. This man might have other information they would need later. He smiled, then lowered his pistol and stepped back. "Let's go join the others, shall we?"

Murphy gently replaced the receiver back on the phone and walked back to the center of the control room where the two Reactor Operators where standing. The Senior Reactor Operator was seated at the reactor control console but facing away from the controls. "Everyone stay exactly where you are", Jorge shouted. "All except for you." He pointed his Glock 19 at the woman sitting at the horseshoe shaped console at the far end of the control room. "You, stand up!" The Senior Reactor Operator stood slowly, still not fully aware of what was happening. She had heard the shot but not seen her Shift Senior Supervisor fall to the floor behind the desk and partition.

"Everyone keep your hands where I can see them", Jorge shouted. The woman slowly raised her hands in front of her. "Now move slowly away from the console. DO IT NOW!", he yelled. As she moved toward the four High Level Flux Monitors along the wall on the left, Otis quickly slid into the chair at the console. "Everything's on computer control. We're cool!", he announced, looking across to Jorge with his thumb raised. He laid his Glock 19 gently on the console next to the SCRAM button.

Otis had seen several control rooms at nuclear power stations, both in America and in Europe. He had never seen one like this, however. There were no steam turbines depicted on the control panels, no generators, no pressuriser tank, no high-pressure injection pumps, no high pressure relief valves. He couldn't see any pressure gauges. "What pressure are you running at", he asked, looking at the Senior Reactor Operator whose seat he had just taken? "Five psi", Blythe replied. "No, no. In the reactor. What pressure? 2000 psi, 2200 psi, what?" Blythe repeated her answer. "Five pounds per square inch." Otis shook his head. He was confused.

"We don't have a pressure vessel. This reactor operates at ambient temperature and pressure, nearly", Murphy volunteered. "So if we blow a hole in your reactor there won't be any high pressure steam", Otis persisted? "No steam at all", replied Murphy, until the fuel overheats and melts. "Ah, now we are getting somewhere", Otis replied with a smile. Then he looked back at Blythe. He found her quite attractive. Under different circumstances he would have asked her out for dinner. Or maybe he could have her show him some remote part of the building where they would have a bit more privacy. Jorge wouldn't allow that though, would he?

Right now he just needed her help. "You will teach me how to operate your reactor, yes", he added? "No", she replied. "Then we will kill one of these men every minute until you do", Jorge remarked in a stern voice. He walked up to one of the Reactor Operators and placed his Glock 19 against his temple. He cocked it and looked at his watch. "You have 60 seconds.... 40 seconds.... 20 seconds.... 10 seconds.... 5 seconds..." "OK", she yelled. "This lever raises or lowers power. That red button is the SCRAM button, to drop the safety rods into the reactor. And that switch is the Supplementary Safety System or SSS. That will shut down the reactor if everything else fails." "Thank you", replied Otis with a smile and a mock salute.

"What's down there", Jorge asked? "We don't use that room", Tyler replied. "That's not what I asked." Jorge eyes narrowed. He was getting irritated. "Controls for charge and discharge machines. For refuelling the reactor", said Tyler. "Show me!" Jorge waved his Glock 19 toward the open doorway into the dimly lit room. Tyler preceded him down three shallow steps. "Where's the light switch?" "Over there." Tyler pointed to the far wall. Jorge flipped the switch. All he could see was a row of panels and a console with knobs and dials. "What's that", Jorge asked, pointing toward the large black glass panel behind the railing?

"Just a window", Tyler replied. Jorge knew he couldn't see outdoors, with all the concrete walls in the building. "To see what", Jorge persisted. "Top of the reactor", Tyler replied. "I can't see anything", said Jorge. "Flip the other switch", said Tyler. Jorge flipped the second switch.

Samuel and Ansel had reached the personnel entrance to the reactor room in only three minutes. The door was like those used on a ship, with toggles to seal the door airtight. Opening it took another 10 seconds. They could feel air rush through the open doorway and into the room when they pulled back the heavy steel door. "Must be for ventilation control", Luis remarked. The heavy door slammed shut as soon as they were inside, plunging them into complete darkness. The room was pitch black except for a few tiny red lights on some instruments some distance away. Even with the door shut they could hear air flowing through the room. Ansel couldn't see his hand in front of him. Their voices echoed as if in a cavern. He put on his night vision goggles. Now he could make out several very large shapes in the center of the room. 'It must be huge', he thought. Three curved shapes just above the floor were very distinct. He quickly realized these must be the cooling water inlet nozzles for the reactor. Their elevated temperature made them stand out in infrared. Suddenly the lights came on, temporarily blinding Ansel. "What the hell", he yelled, ripping off the night vision goggles. Both men attempted to adjust their eyes to the sudden brightness.

"Wow", Jorge exclaimed! "That's it isn't it?" "Just the top of it", Tyler replied. Jorge retreated back up into the supervisor's area of the control room. "Hey Otis! You gotta see this." Jorge stood watch on the those in the control room while Otis went down to the reactor room window. He had to admit it was impressive. And not like any reactor he had ever seen before. Suddenly Samuel and Ansel appeared from behind the 'forest' of control rod and safety rod latches. Samuel waved to Otis in the window. Otis smiled and waved back. Then he realized Samuel's actions weren't just a greeting. He was pointing upward and drawing his left hand across his throat. He wanted the lights in the reactor room turned off.

"Turn the lights off in there", Otis yelled to Tyler, who had moved to the other side of the room. "The switch is over there", Tyler replied. "I guess they feel safer in the dark", Otis added. "The security guys will be shooting at them soon, with live rounds this time." Tyler shook his head. "No they won't. Security is under strict orders to never ever fire a weapon in that room. Too many important things could get damaged." Otis nodded. He took his point!

With the lights off both Samuel and Ansel were relying on their night vision googles again. Samuel kept careful watch on the only door into the reactor room, while Ansel placed the charges. He was nearly done when they both noticed the sound of air rushing through the room was diminishing. Within a minute the room was eerily quiet. "Luis has blown the intake ducts on the filter compartments", observed Samuel. "The fans aren't drawing air through the building anymore." "No problem", said Ansel. "I think we've got enough in here to last us a few weeks at least!"

The sound of a Mack truck air horn suddenly filled the control room. It was deafening! "What the hell is that", Otis shouted? Jorge came running into the room with his hands over his ears. "Shut that damn thing off", he yelled. "Can't", yelled Murphy. Otis looked at the High Level Flux Monitors, then gave Jorge an thumbs up, signalling the reactor was still at full power. Jorge cocked his Glock 19 and pointed it directly at Murphy's head. "I said turn it off!" Murphy pulled the chair out of the way and crawled under the AIA console. He grabbed the air horn with both hands and yanked with all the strength he had. The air horn tore loose from the metal panel, wires and all. Things went quiet. "What in the hell was that thing", Jorge asked? "That was the containment alarm. It means we've lost negative air pressure in the building." Jorge knew what that meant. "Good", he replied.

Otis returned to the nuclear console in the control room, while Jorge yelled down the hallway. "Everything OK down there, Henry?" "We're just fine here", came the reply. Henry had carefully checked the shift roster against the badges worn by the people in the conference room. Everyone was accounted for. Because of the security exercise they were all in the lunchroom anyway. Henry moved them into the conference where they could all sit down with empty chairs between each person and the next. With Henry standing in the only doorway pointing his M16 at them there was nothing they could do but wait.

Jorge was surprised there had been no attempts by Protective Force personnel to retake the building, or at least some portion of it. Of course, he couldn't communicate with Silas and Janine who were defending the main personnel access corridor. Were they still there? Were they dead already? Were areas of the building below him swarming with Protective Force personnel? Did it really matter? Henry would be the first to know if they tried to storm the plus 15 level.

According to Otis, Samuel and Ansel had succeeded in reaching the reactor room. Jorge could now blow three of the six inlet nozzles on the reactor tank top. That would likely shift the 'forest' of control and safety rods, as well as interrupt heavy water flow in the reactor. He might not succeed in melting all the fuel assemblies in the reactor, but he figured on taking out at least half of them. That threat should be sufficient to get the Department of Energy's attention. For maximum leverage he had to keep the reactor operating at full power. That was Otis's job. So far it had been a piece of cake!

With the main access door glued shut, two Protective Force personnel found entry through the rear door of the spent fuel storage area, known as 'Disassembly'. They moved ahead cautiously before seeing Janine limping toward them. "They're holding everyone in the control room", she wheezed, panting for breath. "I managed to escape. Can you get me out please?" "Yes, of course. Just follow on to the back door over there." When he turned back around his partner was on the floor grasping his throat. He never saw the kick coming. It snapped his head back, leaving him disoriented. He reached for his side arm but found nothing there. He saw his partner get a bullet to the head. He never saw the next one. Silas helped lift one of the floor gratings over the spent fuel storage basin so they could push the two of them in. Their bodies were silhouetted against a beautiful blue glow as they floated face down in the crystal-clear water. The scene appealed to Janine's ethereal senses. She wondered what this moment looked like in one of her parallel universes.

It was pretty clear to Silas he didn't really need to stay at his present location. In the past 20 minutes he and Janine had heard several attempts by the Protective Force to open the main personnel access door from outside. After much banging they had given up. There were too many other ways to get into the building. It wasn't worth their time to get this particular door open. Silas signalled to Janine that he was going upstairs to help watch the hostages in the control room. She gave him a thumbs up and crouched down between two tall cabinets along one wall in the spent fuel storage area where she had a good view of that blue glow. Then she had another thought. Checking inside one of the cabinets she found a stack of freshly laundered grey coveralls. She found a pair that fitted and discarded the ones she had been wearing. The breast pocket displayed the E&I insignia. 'Must be properly dressed for the part', she thought.

Silas' appearance at the door of the conference room was a welcome sight. Henry needed a toilet break already and several of the hostages needed one as well. "One at a time", he announced. Of course, he had to escort each one while Silas stood guard on the others. Silas never liked crowds. Three strangers confined in one room was a crowd. It made him nervous. It was different on the farm where he could go for a walk every day to get away from the rest of them. Here he felt trapped, almost as much as the three souls he was left to watch over.

Once relieved, Henry entered the supervisor's area of the control room. "Ah, you're just in time", said Jorge. "Get this guy off the floor and clean up that blood. I'm tired of looking at it." He motioned to the two male hostages in the control room to help. With Henry waving his M16 at them, they picked up MacMahon's body and carried it around the hallway and down the stairs to main entrance corridor. "In there", Henry demanded, as he pointed to the spent fuel storage area. Seeing the open area where the floor grating had been removed, they dumped MacMahon's body into the water. Henry was surprised to see two other bodies floating nearby. 'Janine', he thought. 'How efficient she was!' She must be around, but Henry didn't see her as she remained out of sight. She was thinking Otis could probably explain what caused that blue glow. But she didn't want an explanation. She just wanted a car that exact color!

When Henry returned to the plus 15 level, he motioned the two reactor operators into the conference room with the others. Silas now had all the operations personnel in the room, except for Blythe and the two supervisors, Murphy and Tyler. It was an even bigger crowd than before. Jorge had decided to keep Blythe in the control room in case Otis needed help at the nuclear console. Besides she was nice to look at, even if neither of them had the time to bother at the moment. Otis had allowed Blythe to take her seat at the console again, with him standing immediately behind her so she could not reach the SCRAM button or the Supplementary Safety System switch.

"Just keep everything nice and steady", Otis told her. He rather liked standing so close to her, actually. Blythe found his presence menacing and repressive. Her older brother was the same, although he never held a gun to her head if she refused to do what he asked. Well, he did threaten her with a rusty machete one time, but he probably wasn't serious. It was the male superiority thing that bothered her. The only good ideas were male ideas, according to most of the men she had encountered. Her fiancé was a notable exception of course. She never made an issue of it at work. Better to stay silent about such things in a male dominated environment, although she had to admit that Murphy had been receptive to several of her suggestions, and publicly given her credit as well. Maybe someday there would be a female Shift Senior Supervisor in L Area. It might even be her.

Blythe's father took her brother's side on every issue as they were growing up, helping to reinforce her brother's behavior. Her problem was that she was much smarter than her brother, and never missed an opportunity to demonstrate that fact. She knew the names of all the animals in the Riverbanks Zoo in Columbia. She could also identify all the constellations in the night sky. Surely that should be worth something. Unfortunately, her father and brother didn't think so. As a teenager she lay in bed at night thinking of ways to prove them wrong. At age 28, with a bachelor's degree in chemistry and fully qualified as a Senior Reactor Operator, she still thought about it every night before she fell asleep.

Murphy and Tyler were in the control room for a reason as well. Nearly 45 minutes had passed. Government officials at the site must know where he was by now. Jorge was surprised the control room phone hadn't rung. Why hadn't they called to ask for his demands? When they did, it would be Murphy answering the phone. Tyler was there as backup. That way he could shoot one of them and still have the other to continue the negotiation.

"When are you going to contact them about our demands", asked Otis? "I won't have to call them. They'll be calling us", Jorge replied. He was getting tired of waiting. He looked at his watch. 22:05 hours. Just then the phone rang at the supervisor's desk. Jorge motioned with his Glock 19 for Murphy to answer it. He slowly picked up the receiver. "This is the Emergency Operations Center (EOC). May I please speak to whoever is in charge?" "They want to speak to you", said Murphy, holding the receiver out in front of him. Jorge shook his head, pointing his pistol more deliberately at Murphy's head. "I'm sorry you will have to speak to me", Murphy replied to the caller. "And you are?" "Shift Supervisor Murphy", he answered. There was slight pause. "Since you did not provide a valid code for your duress alarm earlier this evening, we assume that you are no longer in control of the facility. Is that correct?"

"Correct", Murphy replied. "Is anyone else listening to this phone call?" "No." "Can you speak freely?" "No." There was another brief pause on the line. "I understand", replied the caller. "Have those who have taken control of the facility stated their purpose?" "No." There was another pause. "Have they stated their conditions for release of the facility?" "No", Murphy replied. Jorge reached in his breast pocket and pulled out a neatly typed sheet of paper, laid it on the supervisor's desk, and pushed it across to Murphy. "Wait..., yes", said Murphy. Jorge motioned for him to read out loud what was on the paper. "I have just been asked to read this to you", Murphy added.

> The name of our organization is unimportant. What is important is that you do exactly as you are told. You will assemble no less than 30 Kg of Plutonium 239 in pure metallic form, in a critically safe package no more than 1.8 meters in length, suitable for air transport. A helicopter will land at a location in the 200 F Separations Area to receive the package at exactly 14:00 hours tomorrow. They will be allowed to leave with the package without hinderance of any kind. Once we receive word that the plutonium has been confirmed by onboard assay, and that the helicopter has reached international waters a portion of our party will exit your facility and leave the site by prearranged transport. Twelve hours following their safe departure the remaining members of our party will surrender to federal authorities. Until that time all Protective Force personnel will be withdrawn from all areas of the reactor building.

> Any failure to perform or any interference with these operations as we have instructed will result in much of the eastern seaboard of the United States of America becoming uninhabitable due to radioactive contamination. Any attempt to escort, track or observe transport of either the plutonium or members of our party after they leave the Savannah River Site property will be considered an immediate breech of our instructions. We have placed explosives on pipes delivering water to your reactor. Detonation of these charges by any of several means will rob the reactor of essential cooling and result in displacement of safety and control rods so that the reactor cannot be shutdown. The reactor will remain at full power until our demands are met. We may execute any of the operations personnel being held in the facility at any time if we believe our instructions are not being followed.

Assault on L

"Message understood", came the reply. "We will call you back at this number in exactly ten minutes." The line went dead. "They've hung up. They said they would call back in ten minutes", said Murphy. Jorge thought for a moment. "You stay right here and wait for that call, understood?" Murphy nodded. It would take time for the people running the Site to digest his demands. Jorge didn't expect an immediate answer. What he expected was a negotiation. They would try to determine his motives, what organization, domestic or foreign, he was representing, and so on. None of that really mattered to them. They were just trying to buy time. They needed to confirm that he really did have the ability to destroy the reactor. They would also have to determine how far the radioactive contamination might spread under the meteorology for today, tomorrow, maybe the next several days. All of these questions would require their engineers to make a large number of calculations in a very short period of time. When they discovered that their filter system wouldn't save them there would be more calculations. He was prepared to be patient to a point. But they only had until 14:00 hours tomorrow.

The phone at the supervisor's desk rang again. Jorge shook his head and held up his hand for Murphy to wait. After the third ring he pointed at the phone. Murphy picked it up slowly. "105 L Control Room", he answered. "Who am I speaking to please", the caller asked? "This is Shift Supervisor Murphy." There was a slight pause. "We are working to determine if your demands can be met. Are you the only one listening to this call?" "Yes" "How many adversaries are there in the building? For three, say Barnwell. For four, say New Ellenton. For five, say Aiken. For six, say Augusta. If there are more than six, say Columbia. Do you understand?" "Aiken, but I was born in Columbia", Murphy replied. "OK, there are definitely five adversaries, but there may be more than five, correct?" "That's correct." "How many explosive charges have they placed?" "Barnwell", he replied. Jorge motioned for him to hang up. "What the hell are they asking you?" He was pointing his Glock 19 at Murphy's head again.

Murphy looked him straight in the eye. "They're trying to figure out if I'm one of you. They were asking where I live, where I was born, and where my parents lived. Those are things they can go check to see if they're talking to someone who works here or someone trying to blow the place up. It's what negotiators do. They have to know who they are talking to." Jorge lowered his pistol. He had no idea if Murphy was telling the truth or not. Perhaps it didn't matter. He didn't want to talk to them, and now he'd decided he didn't want Murphy talking to them either.

Either they were going to meet his demands, or they weren't. It was a binary choice, like flipping a coin. 'Heads I win, tails you lose', he thought. He reached down, grabbed the cord on the phone, and ripped it out of the wall socket. "Let them sweat for a while", he said, motioning for Murphy to return to the control room. Henry had placed chairs two meters apart in the center of the control room where Tyler and Murphy could sit. Blythe was sitting at the nuclear console. Everything was going according to plan. Except now Henry was hungry.

Henry stepped into the conference room where Silas was keeping watch over the hostages. "Can any of you guys cook", he asked? There was no response. Finally, one hand went up slowly. "I generally cook for most of the shift", said Crosby. "OK, you come with me." Henry motioned Crosby out the door and across the hall to the lunchroom. "What do you normally cook", Henry asked? "Tonight was going to be spaghetti and meatballs", Crosby replied. "All of us should have eaten hours ago." "So, dinner's a bit late tonight", said Henry. "Let's see how good a cook you are."

Half an hour later Henry walked into the control room with three plates of spaghetti. Jorge quickly took one. Murphy and Tyler took the other two. "Food isn't allowed in the control room", Blythe announced. "So fire me for breaking the rules, then", quipped Jorge with a grin. Henry escorted Blythe to the toilet, while Otis took the seat at the nuclear console. They returned a few minutes later with full plates of spaghetti. Jorge looked at Blythe. "Guess you're fired too, huh." Blythe didn't respond. When she was finished Otis gave her back her seat. Silas and Henry moved everyone in the conference room into the lunchroom. Leland and Martin had to wash up after everyone had finished.

Samuel and Ansel had begun to realize that no Protective Force personnel would be attempting to enter the reactor room. In fact, no one would. They had placed their charges on the three inlet pipes nearest the east wall where they could be seen from the window where they had spotted Otis earlier. That way Jorge could see them. He had one of the three remote detonators. Samuel and Ansel each had one as well. The charges were also wired to each other in such a way that any attempt to remove any one of them would immediately detonate all three. There was an eerie silence in the huge room. "How long are we supposed to stay in here", Ansel asked? "Until Jorge shows up in that window and waves us out, I guess", Samuel replied.

Both of them were getting hungry. They could swear there was a faint smell of spaghetti in the air. Luis was getting hungry too. It was dark up on the plus 55 roof and windy. Had Jorge forgotten about him? "Hey!" Luis thought he heard a voice from around the corner on the west side. "Hey, you still up here. Want some spaghetti", yelled Henry. "Yes please", Luis replied with a smile. "It's cold up here!"

Janine had come up to the plus 15 level to find a copy machine. She had to be sure no one saw her as she slipped quietly past the lunchroom and conference room. Luckily no one was in the lunchroom and the door to the conference room full of hostages was only slightly ajar. Janine had decided from the beginning she wasn't going to wait for Jorge to arrange safe transportation out of L Area. She had the security badge off one of the men now floating in the spent fuel storage pool below. It wasn't difficult to modify. There was a copy machine in the secretary's office next to the day supervisor's office. The photo on her Illinois driver's license was all she needed. It was even the correct size. Once she had a copy of her license, she carefully cut out the photo and glued it over the one on the badge. Changing the name was almost as easy. The name 'Jane Jones' appealed to her.

Henry went back to the control room. Luis stopped off in the lunchroom to eat, where he found Jane Jones all alone in her E&I Mechanic coveralls washing up her plate. "Yeah, I smelled the spaghetti downstairs. Besides, I seemed to have run out of 'customers' for the spent fuel storage pool. Have you seen the blue glow down there? Beautiful!" "Some other time", Luis replied. "By the way", she added. "The name is 'Jane Jones' and somebody had better escort me into the conference room with the other hostages or someone's going to get suspicious." Luis smiled. Any other time if he had grabbed her by the arm he would have ended up in the hospital. But this time she couldn't object.

"Look what I found", said Luis. "There was another one in the building. Keep an eye her, OK?" Silas looked startled, then gave Luis a thumbs up. "Take a seat over there", Silas barked, pointing to the back of the room. "And keep your mouth shut." Jane Jones was shaking with fear. Her head was down in a cowered posture. She wasn't planning to talk to anyone. She hated the phrase 'wolf in sheep's clothing'. But it aptly described what she enjoyed most. If there was some insidious plot being

Assault on L

hatched amongst the hostages, she would be there to insure it didn't succeed.

Luis was quickly back in the lunchroom having a second helping. Ansel and Samuel came in a few minutes later. Both went straight for the pot of spaghetti on the stove. "Your spaghetti is a hit", said Silas, as Crosby was brought back into the lunchroom to make another pot. Crosby shrugged his shoulders. He was tired of being held captive, as were all the others in the room. No one knew how long this would continue. It might be days. Their families would be worried about them of course. But they had no way to let them know they were alright, at least for now. Presumably personnel on C Shift had been turned away at the gate when they showed up just before midnight. It was now well after 1:00 am.

It took less than a minute for Samuel to notice Blythe sitting at the nuclear console, and Otis standing close behind her. It was already clear that Janine preferred the Dutchman over him. He hated losing, but maybe n that case it was just as well. But here was a new challenge, and his rival had gotten there first. It appeared Otis had already established a relationship with Blythe, although he noticed she never smiled at him. Should he push Otis off his perch or accept another loss. Russians weren't supposed to lose to the Dutch. It was supposed to be the other way around. But then Jorge wouldn't tolerate an open confrontation between team members. Reluctantly he decided to accept defeat again, at least for the moment.

It was well past the end of their shift. Leland had worked a double shift many times before, particularly at Christmas time when you got holiday pay plus time and a half for overtime. A few shifts at two and half times your normal salary meant you could afford some really nice gifts for the kids. But this was very different. No one knew when, or even if, they would be going home. His children were only three and five. They wouldn't miss him until about 7:00 am. Then they would be asking where's Daddy? Their mother wouldn't know what to tell them. If only he could get a message to her to let her know he was alright. Their house in Allendale was in a modest neighbourhood. He was sure the people next door would be able to help, at least for a day or two. He didn't want to think about it, but if something did happen to him his brother would be the first to look after her and the kids. He had a sizable life insurance policy, partly paid for by the company. That gave him some peace of mind as well.

Assault on L

Crosby never tired of cooking for the shift before. But cooking for these guys irritated the hell out of him. He even thought of putting something in the food. But there was nothing in the lunchroom cabinets like that, plus he didn't want his co-workers to get sick. Everyone was eating from the same pot. Actually, he fancied himself a pretty good cook. No one disagreed. Otherwise they would become the shift cook. Nobody else wanted the job, so he was assured of no complaints. For the first year after his divorce he lived off Kentucky Fried Chicken and Wendy burgers. Once a week he would order pizza just to have something different. Then he got an electric slow cooker. That let him do a pork loin or a roast without having to be there. He would put it on when he left for work and then return home at the end of his shift to a hot meal. Working shifts didn't matter. The slow cooker didn't care whether it was 5:00 pm or 1:00 am. He wished he could order a pizza right now and slip the delivery man a note. But there were no food deliveries to L Area in the best of times. And this certainly wasn't the best of times.

Jared and Ferbis were the two youngest Reactor Operators on B Shift. Both had young families. Jared's daughter was one. Ferbis' son was three. Their wives played bridge at the Ehrhardt Baptist Church on Wednesday evenings. They carpooled with one of the Maintenance Mechanics who lived in Lodge. Lodge was an even smaller community than Ehrhardt. Carpooling did save them quite a lot on gas. And they learned a lot about each other during the hour-long drive to and from work. Jared hated changing diapers. Ferbis claimed to be an expert at it and gave him lessons on way to L Area one Thursday. The Maintenance Mechanic in the back seat pretended to be asleep. Neither Ferbis nor Jared had a mortgage to worry about. Both rented but had plans to move to a place of their own. And it wouldn't be in Ehrhardt.

Martin was the quiet one on B Shift. He never said much, either about himself or anything else. Blythe and Leland had both learned he was an excellent chess player. They never played him anymore because he always won. Besides they weren't there to play games, as MacMahon would remind them. The best they could do was set up a board at the beginning of the shift, and then make a move or two during their break. Sometimes they never even saw each other all shift, with Leland in the control room most of the time and Martin in minus 40 level or in one of the 108 buildings. Everyone could see the board sitting there, but no one ever touched it. They only looked at the pieces, considered for a moment what they would do in that situation, and then went back to work. Maybe they would finish the game by the end of the shift. More often they wouldn't.

'Whoever these people are they've obviously had some experience at keeping hostages from planning an escape', thought Murphy. Initially Jorge kept watch over the two in the control room, plus Blythe at the nuclear console about half the time. Henry and Silas took turns watching the ones in the conference room, rotating them in and out of the lunchroom, and for toilet breaks. Jane Jones was treated like the others, or maybe a bit rougher at times. She had excellent hearing and if there was anything said between the hostages, she would hear it. She could pass along anything she heard the next time Henry escorted her to the toilet.

In the conference room Henry had a captive audience, quite literally. He regaled them with stories of his adventures in the jungles of Viet Nam when he was only 23, and how many Viet Cong he had killed. For the most part his audience found his descriptions disgusting rather than entertaining. In fact, Henry had never been closer to Viet Nam than Taiwan. He never mentioned those he had killed there. Neither did the Taiwanese government. Henry considered himself one of the best con artists who ever lived. In 1967 a high-ranking Taiwanese official had agreed to let Henry 'eliminate' a political rival 'free of charge' after Henry bragged about his prowess as an 'international assassin'. Henry considered it an 'audition' for a more permanent high paying position on this man's 'private security team'.

In fact, the only man Henry had ever killed up to then was his Commanding Officer, during a drunken brawl at a bar two miles from the Fort Irwin National Training Center in the Mohave Desert in California. Being absent without leave (AWOL) from the United States Army, he had to look for somewhere to hide for a few years. Henry's first assassination was a bit messy. He was asked to perform another as a further demonstration. In the end Henry had spent 18 years in Taiwan and had assassinated over thirty individuals at the behest of the Taiwanese government. During all that time he was given modest 'living arrangements' but was never paid a single Taiwan dollar. Then when his sponsor was assassinated and all his records destroyed, Henry had to leave quickly.

Communication between hostages was quite difficult for the first eight hours. No one was permitted to sit closer than six feet from another. There were usually three hostages in the conference room in chairs that were widely separated. Three or four hostages were in the lunchroom, in chairs at separate tables. Adding the two or three in the control room

Assault on L

made nine. They were moved every several hours, always one at a time, from conference room to lunchroom to control room and back to the conference room again. It was almost impossible for any of them to pass information or coordinate an attempt to overcome their armed captors.

"We have cots and blankets if you want to use them", Tyler offered, as everyone was showing signs of fatigue by 3:00 am. "They're just in case we get snowed in or there's some disaster outside and the next shift gets delayed. We've also got enough food and water for about a month." He was hoping Jorge or Otis would say something like 'Oh, we'll be gone after tomorrow'. No one said anything. "Anyway, some of us have to sleep OK?" Jorge motioned to Henry to make some accommodations. "I want you two right here in the control room though. He pointed at Tyler and Murphy. "You can sleep right where you're sitting. Same for her." He pointed at Blythe. "You can take over, right Otis?" Otis nodded. Actually, there wasn't much to do. Reactor power was being maintained by computer control. It could stay that way for a few days without him doing anything. By then they would be gone.

None of the other hostages recognized Jane Jones. She seemed so traumatized she could barely speak. By 4:00 am the rotation routine and rules about not talking had become a bit lax. "I just finished my E&I training last week", Jane whispered to Martin. "This is my first assignment." "Lucky you", he replied. "I didn't see you on the Shift Roster", Murphy commented. "Guess they forgot to put me on it", she replied, as she began sobbing again. "We aren't going to get out of here alive, are we?" "Yes, we are", Murphy replied. "We just have to wait for the right moment". Jane nodded. Then began to cry again. 'There won't be a right moment. No one's going off script while I'm here', she thought to herself.

Jorge was beginning to feel invincible. They had pulled it off without losing a single member of the team. He had expected to lose half of them. He had complete control of the building. No Protective Force personnel dared to show their faces. Once the package was picked up and safely delivered, everyone could just walk right out and fly away. All except him of course. He had a special surprise planned. Today he was invincible. Tomorrow he would achieve immortality!

Assault on L

Chapter 8

Captain Lowe was on the phone to his management in the Site Main Administration Area within minutes after the strike team entered the building. "Yes sir. It appears Brownlie and his team have gone rogue…… Yes sir, they were firing live rounds…… Yes sir, they must have known. One of our guys reported hearing gunfire in the woods just before they launched their attack. They must have been checking their weapons…… Yes sir, two dead and two wounded….. We do have men in the building. They are all in the below grade areas….. No sir, no one has reported seeing anyone down there yet. Yes sir, everyone is on live ammunition now. Whenever they show up down there we'll take them out….. Yes sir, I'm quite sure about that!" He hung up the phone and yelled to his second in command. "Chopper inbound!"

Lowe spotted it coming over the treetops. It landed on the west side in the open field about 40 meters from the main personnel entry building. The chopper had barely touched the ground when men in full SWAT gear began jumping out. They made a dead run to the entry building and shoved their way through the turnstiles that had been set to freewheel, setting off all four metal detectors simultaneously. They were out the other side of the building and into the courtyard within seconds. They had been trained to take up a defensive posture to prevent the adversaries from coming out of the large building in front them. Except in this case the adversaries had no intention of coming out, not for twenty-four hours at least.

Two ambulances arrived in another ten minutes. One man had a severe bullet wound to the thigh. The other had been hit in the forearm. Both were losing a lot of blood. The two men who'd been killed in the courtyard were loaded into the ambulances as well. Twenty minutes later they both sped away. Captain Lowe suddenly realized how quite it was. His reinforcements were in place. His casualties had been dispatched. The adversary team had disappeared into the main reactor building but hadn't shown up where his men were inside.

Lowe considered his Protective Force unit to be the best on site. Having drilled so many attack scenarios, they functioned like a well-oiled machine. Except tonight they were beaten, and badly. With two men dead and another two seriously wounded, Lowe's head was spinning. What had just happened was simply inconceivable. He had been trained not to react emotionally, but to keep a cool head and think clearly in a crisis. He found it very hard to do any of those things at the moment. He knew all the personnel in his unit like family. They were like his brothers and sisters. The two that had just been killed in the courtyard had young families. Their wives expected to see them walk through the door tonight alive and well. But that wasn't going to happen now.

Lowe felt an overwhelming sense of guilt, only he wasn't sure what he was guilty of. Certainly not negligence or dereliction of duty. Everything had been done by the book. He wasn't at fault. He couldn't see how anyone was. He stood outside the entry portal building, staring at the courtyard where it happened. It seemed impossible and yet he had to accept it and move on. His unit was waiting for instructions. They didn't need a commander with a brain freeze. They needed guidance.

"So what do I do next", he asked himself in an unsteady voice? Before he had time to consider his own question, gun fire erupted on the east side of L Area. Lowe ran around the building in time to see several of his men outside the PIDAS crouched over a man dressed in camouflage lying on the ground. "We got one of them", they yelled. Captain Lowe had to look through the two PIDAS fences to see what was happening about twenty meters away. "Damn", he heard one of them say. "He's firing blanks", the other man yelled. "What the hell is going on, Captain?"

Maybe this was a member of Brownlie's team that hadn't gotten the word to use live ammo. Or maybe he had been assigned to simply create a diversion on the east side. "He's still alive", one man yelled. "Name on the badge is Thompson, sir." Lowe was on the phone again. "We need another ambulance in L Area, stat!" It suddenly occurred to him to check the woods where Brownlie and his team, with the exception of Thompson apparently, had been located before the attack. Two men were dispatched to survey the area along the wood line. It took them about 20 minutes to find them. They radioed back. "All dead, sir. Brownlie, Jonesy, O'Hara, Sarco and Brennen. Repeat, all dead, sir." Lowe felt a sudden chill. The last time he felt fear like this was twenty years ago outside a village in Viet Nam. This wasn't a botched exercise and Brownlie hadn't gone rogue. The bad guys inside the building were the 'real McCoy'. But where the hell were they?

Protective Forces in reactor areas performed two vital functions. One was to intercept and eliminate any team of armed adversaries before they could reach critical areas within the reactor building. The other was to operate the personnel entry and control equipment in the main entry portal building. Although the former was most important, Lowe and his men spent 99.9% of their time on the latter. Anyone having clearance to work in L Area must enter through one of four parallel lanes located inside the entry portal building. Each lane included first a metal detector, second an explosives detector and third a floor-to-ceiling turnstile. The turnstile would only unlock after it received an acceptable response from the previous devices. All four lanes were performance tested frequently with small weapons and dummy explosives hidden in various places on the body. And of course, each employee had to present their badge to a security guard on duty. The guard was required to touch the badge to make sure it hadn't been tampered with.

Captain Lowe and his men were briefed frequently on methods and weapons an adversary might use to gain entry to the area and to the reactor building. At every such briefing the focus was on keeping the bad guys away from certain areas of the reactor building that were below grade. No one ever explained in detail why that was important, only that if the adversary was allowed to reach something called the 'crosstie header' they could cause the reactor to melt down with disastrous consequences. What he couldn't understand is why in this instance none of the adversaries had shown up at that location. He had martialled his forces to the minus 20 and minus 40 levels shortly after the strike team entered the building. Surely, they could overwhelm any adversary team in a matter of minutes. That would bring this whole ugly episode to an end.

Was it possible that other vulnerabilities existed elsewhere in the building that no one had mentioned? Is that where the adversaries had gone? Before he could instruct the SWAT team to retake the building Lowe had to know where the bad guys were. Phone calls with his management had not been much help. "Use your best judgement", was their answer.

Two of Captain Lowe's men reported hearing several explosions on the plus 55 roof where the filter compartments were located. "When", Lowe asked? "About twenty minutes after the strike team went inside the building, sir." 'So that's where they've gone', he thought. If that's where they were all of his men were exposed in the lit-up courtyard. Snipers on that roof could easily pick off anyone they wanted. He ordered everyone to take cover in the nearest building. He made a call to request a chopper to fly over and take a look.

Assault on L

It was a quarter of an hour before the chopper showed up. It came in from the north, banked around the building at a thousand feet, then moved in toward the building roof with spotlights on. "I don't see anyone on the roof, sir. But there's a lot of damage up here, mostly between the concrete building and the metal box cars. No snipers that we can see", radioed the chopper. "Roger that", Lowe replied. Maybe they had retreated back inside the building. None of this was making any sense at all.

Luis saw the chopper's lights coming in over the trees. He wasn't expecting it to be interested in his location. He hid between two of the huge filter compartments until it had left. He had already tried to get into the building but both the personnel access door and the large roll door on the opposite side were closed and locked. He was stuck on the roof in the dark until someone came to let him in. Had the rest of the team made it inside? Would any of them think to come let him in off the roof? If only he had a sniper rifle with him. It would be like shooting fish in a barrel.

The Emergency Operations Center (EOC) at the Savannah River Site is activated only in the event of a site emergency that could affect the offsite population or threaten the safety of a significant portion of the employees onsite. Normal staff consists of one or two personnel, but balloons to twenty or more as needed to coordinate site-wide emergency response activities when needed. Security emergencies require members of the site security contractor in the EOC as well as DOE and operations management. At 11:00 pm on a Friday night senior managers of the various site organisations expected to be at home asleep or at least getting ready for bed. It was nearly 11:30 before the last of them could be contacted. As they began to arrive, each took their place around the large oval table in the basement of the Main Administration Building. It was after midnight when the DOE Site Manager began to brief the assembled staff on the events of that evening in L Area. As part of that briefing, he played a recording of the demands made by the adversaries now in control of L Reactor.

Obviously, the Reactor Operations Manager and the Reactor Technical Manager were going to be key players in determining if the threat of causing a reactor meltdown was credible. The Site Security Manager would be responsible for retaking the building and rescuing the hostages, if possible. Site meteorological personnel would need to predict where any radioactive contamination might be deposited and the potential exposure to the public. The Separations Operations Manager would have to determine the feasibility of meeting the adversary's demand for plutonium if all else failed. All other site organisations would need to provide support, including Site Medical, Site Transportation, etc. And of course, there were the public relations staff, providing press releases and guidance on what could be said at the inevitable press conference. In this case a senior representative of the FBI had also been called in from the local office in Augusta. The one person that wasn't at the table was the hostage negotiator. He had a cubicle all to himself.

Either the DOE Site Manager or the Operations Site Manager directed the activities in the EOC. They were usually the first people to arrive and the last people to leave after the emergency was over. Some emergencies were over in hours, some took days. This one might set a record for its duration. As soon as the DOE Site Manager finished his initial briefing each person at the table immediately began figuring out who would relieve them at the end of the first 12 hours. Most of the managers in the room were already exhausted from nearly a year of constant inspections, interrogations, safety reviews, security reviews, and other activities bordering on outright harassment. The hoard of 'independent experts' hired by the DOE had added so much to their workload that most had lost their usual enthusiasm for their jobs. They and their staffs were already worn down. This had the potential to affect their judgement and decision making. For them this 'real' crisis in L Area couldn't have come at a worse moment.

The EOC was normally a 'limited access area'. With few exceptions you had to wait for someone to let you in. Tonight the door was propped open. "Ms. Johnson, can your people prepare a package as described and have it ready by 2:00 pm tomorrow", asked the DOE Site Manager? "You've got to be kidding", she replied with a smile. "Do I look like I'm kidding, Ms. Johnson?" His eyes were boring a hole in her 46-year-old forehead. Her smile quickly faded. "Yes sir, we can do that if we start right away. But surely..." He cut her off. "Then you better get started, just in case." He immediately turned to his right. "Mr. Suelle, can your men retake the building before these guys can detonate their explosives?" "No sir. We've just moved all Protective Force personnel out of the building. We suspect the adversary team is in the control room and maybe on the roof of the building as well. The area is surrounded. We'll take them out if they try to leave the building, sir", Suelle replied. "I don't think we can wait for that", said the DOE Site Manager.

"Mr. Metz, can these people really cause a reactor meltdown?" Metz didn't answer immediately. "Mr. Metz?" "It's possible. We need to know exactly where the explosives are", Metz responded. "Since no one reported seeing them in the below grade levels of the building, we have to assume they haven't placed any charges there, at least not yet. Your negotiator has talked with a member of the operations staff in the control room. From that vantage point the only portion of the reactor he can see is the inlet plenum and 'forest'. We believe they may have placed explosive devices on three of the six inlet nozzles. We are working as fast as we can to determine the potential consequences of detonating these charges", Metz added.

"I don't need the details", said the Site Manager. "I just need to know if they can make good on their threat. Even if there is some release of contamination our filter system will catch most of it, correct?" "No sir, the filter compartments have been disabled. I'm afraid the release would occur from the roof level." The Site Manager looked over at the meteorology team. "Does that make a difference?" "Yes sir, I'm afraid it makes a big difference to the local population within twenty miles of the site." There was a moment of silence in the room. "Alright ladies and gentlemen, we have less than five hours before the local press wakes up and our phones start ringing. The national media won't be far behind. We've got just that long to come up with some answers. Mr. Carlton, as the Operations Manager for the reactor areas you will be first to address the press. We won't be able to hold them off past 9:00 am. If I were you, I'd be prepared for 8:00."

Assault on L

Floor plan labels: 7 ft. Video Screens; Communications and Support Groups; Static Display Boards; Emergency Operations Center (EOC); Bunks

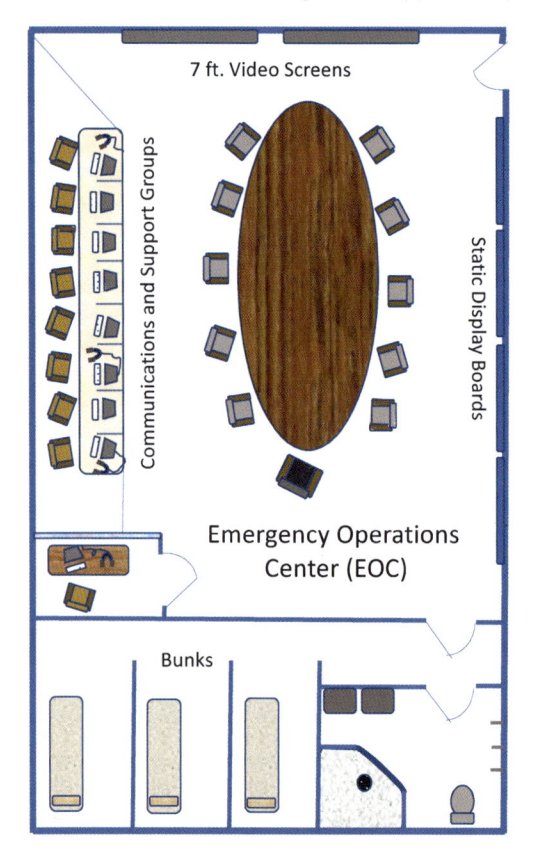

The Emergency Operations Center was designed during the 1960's to deal with site emergencies of every potential variety. As technology advanced the EOC was upgraded. A major upgrade was completed in the early 1980's. The two seven-foot-high video screens on the north wall of the main conference room displayed the status of activities by all organizations involved in the emergency, as well as the local and wider area weather conditions.

Part of one screen displayed a running timeline, with completed actions in blue and pending actions in red. There were several static boards for posting the latest information on conditions in the facility having the emergency. In addition to the large table in the center of the room for the principles, there were other workstations for support organizations, meteorologists, media consultants, and communications operators.

The operations contractor had its own security group, responsible for nuclear material control and accountability, classification of documents, repair of personnel intrusion detection equipment, maintenance of personnel entry control equipment, and studying the vulnerability of facilities to terrorist attack. Specialists from that organization were often called to the EOC during security exercises. Mr. Smith from the Vulnerability Assessment group was the lucky individual on this occasion. The EOC contained state of the art equipment for direct communications with state and federal law enforcement agencies, generating press releases, and producing high-quality presentation materials. Located in another part of the Main Administration Building, a large conference center was equipped with audio-visual systems and seating for one hundred members of the news media.

Minimal staff in the EOC, on duty 24-7, guaranteed immediate response to an emergency prior to the arrival of senior managers, media consultants, meteorologists, and other professionals able to sort, organize and display information in a timely manner. Periodic exercises were conducted in the EOC, including mock press conferences with surrogate press representatives. A number of senior managers had also survived one or more professional media training sessions, and therefore knew what to expect from the press. On this occasion, however, the emergency, the representatives of the press, and the questions were real. It was 8:35 am. Carlton was the first to face them, in spite of having not slept in nearly twenty-six hours. "Ladies and gentlemen, I have a prepared statement to read to you. Copies will be provided at the end of the briefing."

> *At approximately 9.00 pm last night a group of terrorists took control of L Reactor. They have provided a list of their demands and threatened to cause a reactor meltdown if these demands are not met. We are in the process of determining whether their demands can be met, while simultaneously evaluating whether their threat of a reactor meltdown is credible. Our Protective Force has the facility surrounded, so there is no possibility of their escape. It is our assessment at this time that these people may be prepared to commit suicide to accomplish their goals. However, negotiations with those inside the reactor building are continuing. We expect this to be a protracted event, possibly requiring days to resolve. Until it is resolved we will be providing press briefings every four hours so that you can keep the public appraised of the situation.*

"Now I'll take any questions you may have."

"Mr. Carlton, should we be evacuating Aiken, Augusta and other communities around the site?" The local reporter asking the question was well known for trying to 'get ahead of the narrative', as it was called. He liked to postulate the worst possible scenario and then goad the spokesperson into giving it credibility by their answers.

Assault on L

"Such action is not deemed necessary at this time. There has been no release of radioactive contamination and the public is currently in no danger. Should that situation change we will notify you immediately", replied Carlton.

"Has the L Reactor been shut down, and if not why not?" This was a 'gotcha question', implying that someone had failed to do the obvious. Therefore, they must be incompetent. "The reactor is still operating at full power. We have various means of shutting it down but have determined that doing so at this time might further aggravate the situation and our negotiations with persons occupying the building."

"What are the terrorist's demands?" "I'm sorry I'm not able to discuss that subject at this time." "But you do know what their demands are, right?" "Yes, but I can't discuss any of that for reasons of operational security." Actually, this was a national newspaper reporter. Carlton was surprised any of them had arrived on the scene so quickly. National media knew quite well that questions about the 'terrorist's demands' couldn't be answered. She was just testing him out. Maybe he would make a mistake and reveal information that he shouldn't.

"You have hundreds of security guards with guns running all over the place out there. How come they didn't stop these guys from taking over the L Reactor building?" More questions on competence. The reporter was hoping a spokesman from one contractor organization might throw the other contractor under the bus. "The Protective Force has done an admirable job of containing this emergency. They have lost seven men in the process. Two more of their men are in the hospital at this moment. Personally, I believe they did everything possible to prevent these people from gaining access to the L Reactor building. They will continue to take every action possible to resolve this situation. However, their efforts alone will not do so. We have martialled every resource this site has to determine the best ways to resolve this situation without impact to the citizens of the States of Georgia and South Carolina. I am confident we will do so. Thank you for your questions. There will be another briefing in three and a half hours." Carlton was certain he wasn't being paid enough.

The DOE Site Manager had been relieved at 7:00 am. One of the two Assistant Site Managers was now in charge of EOC operations. "Mr. Metz, do you have any new information for us?" Metz was suffering from lack of sleep, like most others in the room. He had phoned his brother in New Ellenton about taking care of the animals on his farm, since he wasn't sure how long it would be before he could leave the EOC. Some of the other managers could stay away from home for a week without any serious consequences. Farming wasn't like that. Livestock had to be fed and watered at a minimum. His brother was a 'city dweller' but he was sure he could manage the place for a few days. Of course, if Metz had a wife she could have helped out as well. But somehow he had never managed to find time for one.

"We have to get the reactor shut down, sir", Metz replied. Our analysis confirms that if cooling to the reactor is degraded or lost completely while it's at full power almost all the fuel assemblies will melt. If some water does manage to reach these fuel assemblies after melting begins the resulting steam explosion will likely lift the plenum off the top of the reactor, in spite of the weight of the safety rod and control mechanisms sitting on top."

"If we can get the reactor shut down, we may be able to limit the damage and possibly prevent any melting at all. It all depends upon which inlet nozzles are damaged. Emergency cooling water enters the reactor through only two of the six inlet nozzles. Depends upon whether they randomly picked one of both of those two. Can your hostage negotiator find out which inlet nozzles have explosive charges on them?" "No", replied the Assistant Site Manager. "We've been unable to re-establish contact with the control room."

"Can't we take control of the reactor remotely", asked Metz's boss, the Site Operations Manager. "We have a Remote Operations Center for the reactors, right?" "Yes, we already tried that. The Remote Ops Center is up here in the Main Administration Area. It's not in a protected area, though. It can request control. If the reactor control room has been abandoned and no one responds to the request, then the remote operations center becomes active within five minutes and we can shut down the reactor. We made the request and someone in the L Reactor control room denied it. We tried several times with the same result." "Isn't there some way to override the control room?" "No. Otherwise anyone could simply walk into the Remote Ops Center and take over a reactor without firing a shot."

"How about if we cut electrical power to the building. That will shut down the reactor and put them in the dark, won't it", asked the Assistant Site Manager? "Not quite", Metz replied. "Emergency lights in the control room run on long-life batteries. And I'm afraid such a blatant act on our part would be an obvious violation of the terrorist's instructions.

Assault on L

They would probably detonate their explosives immediately. The outcome would be slightly better than if the damage occurred with the reactor at full power, but I don't think we should risk it."

"Can we reach the explosive charges and disable them without them seeing us?" "No. They would see us very clearly through the reactor room observation window. And even if we did reach the explosives, they may have wired them such that any attempt to tamper with any one charge will result in detonation of the other two. It would be impossible to disable all three simultaneously." "Simultaneously", asked the Assistant Site Manager? "Within a millisecond of each other", Metz replied. "And there may be other explosives we don't know about."

"We need to shut down the reactor without it looking like we did it", Metz continued. "If it looks like the reactor just shut down on its own, we can deny that we did anything against their instructions, while buying some time for the reactor to cool down. And there's one more problem. We need to get inside the below grade areas of the building and determine if they have placed explosives anywhere else. Otherwise we might find a way to beat them at their game, only to fall into some other trap they've set for us." The Assistant Site Manager looked around the room. "Who's going to do that", he asked? "We'll do that", replied the Site Protective Force representative. "Three of our men are still missing. Some of the adversaries might venture out into the building. There could be trouble if we run into them." "That's very risky", replied the Assistant Site Manager. "They can't blame us for trying to find our missing men", he replied. "We do have to know if they've set other charges", Metz added.

Saturday was usually quiet in the Protective Force contractor's head offices. All the managers were usually enjoying their weekend, while only a few personnel manned the communications systems. This Saturday morning was quite different. "Good morning ladies and gentlemen. By now you've probably heard about the incident in L Area last evening. We got our butts kicked and lost seven good men. Three more are in University Hospital in Augusta, one in critical condition, and three others are unaccounted for. In all likelihood these three are dead as well. This certainly is not the exercise we planned. The situation in L Area has not been resolved. Our orders are to stand by and prevent the adversaries from leaving the building. Use of lethal force is authorized. Use your best judgement. Do what you have to do." There was complete silence in the room. The gravity of the situation was weighing on every man and woman present. "And now I think it would be appropriate if we have a minute of silence for our comrades who have sacrificed their lives in the performance of their duties...."

"I'm sure some of you have questions", said the Protective Force Assistant Manager. "Are we going to retake the building, sir?" "Not at this time. The adversaries have threatened to cause damage that could adversely affect the public in both Georgia and South Carolina. Experts are evaluating this threat to determine if it is credible. Until the threat is better defined, we have been instructed to maintain a perimeter around the reactor building but not attempt to enter.

"The three men who are missing. Do you think they are inside the building?" "That is most likely."

"Why can't we go in and get them, sir?" "When the time is right, we will do exactly that", replied the Protective Force Assistant Manager. "But right now, we have to wait for orders to do so."

"That's crap, sir!" "Yes, Captain, it is crap. But for now, we will have to sit in it."

Carlton returned from the press briefing just in time to hear the meteorological update. "Forecast winds are out of the south for next eight to ten hours. Neglecting the releases of Krypton 85 and Xenon 135, and using the source terms given to us by the Reactor Technical engineers for strontium 90, cesium 137 and iodine 131, we would need to evacuate Augusta, Aiken and all points northwest for approximately 150 miles. That means Newberry, Greenwood, Anderson, Spartanburg, possibly Ashville, North Carolina,..."

"Yes, that's enough. I get the picture", the Assistant Site Manager replied. His face was contorted as he stared silently at the top of the table. "What CAN we do Mr. Metz? Mr. Carlton? Anyone?" "I'm afraid the answer is 'nothing' at the moment", said Carlton. "Our best people are working on the problem", Metz replied. "And now some of us have to get some sleep. The Assistant Site Manager nodded his disappointment. He pointed to a soundproof area where there were bunks. Most of the other principals who had responded the previous night had already been replaced by other senior managers in their organizations. Another tray of coffee and Dunkin Doughnuts appeared on the table.

A sense of helplessness seemed to permeate the filtered air in the EOC. This area of the main administration building had the ability to isolate its air supply from the rest of the building. Filter systems were designed to remove contaminants from the ambient air, allowing people to remain in the EOC even if the environment outside contained significant radioactivity, hydrogen sulphide (used in heavy water production), or other toxic gases. In the worst case, the emergency management team could be moved to a facility about 20 miles away from the site, hopefully outside the public evacuation perimeter. This alternate EOC was considerably smaller than the primary, but it had all the necessary capabilities. No one was thinking they might have to evacuate the Main Administration Area, but the possibility had to be acknowledged.

Coincidently the Assistant Site Manager had been thinking about ventilation in the L Reactor control room. "That's it", he said. Everyone looked up with a start. "We'll inject sleeping gas into the air intake and knock them all out. Then we can just walk right in and retake the building." "Sorry, all reactor control rooms have filtration systems similar to the one for this room", Metz replied. "We installed them after a chlorine leak almost forced us to abandon a reactor control room several years ago. Your sleeping gas would never reach them." The Assistant Site Manager's face fell, as he took his seat again.

"Mr. Roland, have you and Ms. Johnson determined that your people in 200 F Area can prepare a package that meets the demands of the adversary team in L Area?" "Yes sir, we can probably have such a package ready by 2:00 pm. However, we would strongly recommend some alternative means of resolving this incident be developed. This quantity of Plutonium 239 in the hands of terrorists or a rogue nation could result in hundreds of thousands of American deaths in the event they were able to build a bomb and deploy it in a major city", replied Roland. "Yes, Mr. Roland. Thank you for stating your position so eloquently! They could kill a lot of people. And the guys sitting in the control room of the 105 L building right now might easily kill a great deal more than that number if we don't give them what they want! All they have to do is push a button. What would you like me to do, SIR!" It was clear that nerves were beginning to fray. And the clock was ticking. "Can you deliver the package of plutonium on time or not? YES or NO!" "YES SIR!" "And make sure everyone understands", said the Assistant Site Manager, looking slowly around the room, "that the mere existence of that package, and everything to do with it is classified 'Top Secret'!" The large clock on the wall said 11:00 am.

Members of the press were expecting another briefing at 12:30 pm. The press briefing room was already beginning to fill back up. Media representatives were jockeying for seats near the front. It was almost noon. Metz emerged from the bunk area of the EOC. It was his turn in the barrel. Someone handed him a statement to read. He finally found his glasses in his shirt pocket. 'It's a wonder I didn't crush them during my nap', he thought. It was almost 12:30 pm. 'Showtime', Metz said to himself, as he emerged from a side door onto the temporary stage that had been hastily erected. "I have the latest statement from the Department of Energy to read to you." He cleared his throat.

> *Efforts to resolve the situation in L Reactor are ongoing. Threats made by the adversaries in the L Area control room are being analysed. We have not been able to completely discredit these threats, but a number of means to mitigate the potential consequences are in place. There has been no release of radioactive contamination and there is currently no danger to the public. We remain confident we can negotiate a satisfactory resolution to this incident and will let you know as soon as that occurs.*

"Now I'll take any questions you may have."

"Mr. Metz, has the L Reactor been shut down or is it still operating?" "The reactor is still operating at full power." "Are you planning to shut it down and if so when?" "We continue to believe that shutting down the reactor at this time would simply aggravate the situation in L Area. The reactor can operate on computer control for long periods with little intervention by operators. There are experienced operators in the facility that can perform any actions that might become necessary", said Metz.

Suddenly there were fifty hands in the air. "You mean there are hostages in the building? How many hostages? Have any hostages been killed?" "Yes, there are hostages in the building." "How many?" "I am not able to give you a number at this time." "More than 10?" "Possibly." "Have any hostages been killed?" "We don't know if any have been killed." "Have the terrorists threatened to kill some of the hostages?" "Yes."

"And you still won't tell us what they are demanding." "Sorry, I cannot discuss that subject for operational security reasons." Metz could sense the press were become more and more hostile. As prearranged, a member of the DOE public relations group stepped forward and declared an end to the briefing. "I'm sorry that is all we have time for. There will be another briefing in four hours." He looked at his watch. That would be two hours after the package had been picked up in 200 F Area, or evacuation had begun for everyone in this building and in cities and communities within 150 miles north of the site.

Metz was shaking his head as he entered the EOC again. "It's getting rough out there", he muttered. What he really wanted was some more sleep, but if his people were going to deliver a breakthrough, he wanted to be awake for it. They still had an hour to come up with a way to eliminate the threat of a reactor meltdown. That would leave just thirty minutes to take whatever action they had developed. He was immediately on the phone with his engineers.

"What's the worst-case scenario, Bill?" "Worst case is the plenum shifts, the rods can't drop into the core, and we lose 60% of the heavy water flow in the first 20 seconds. That gives us 82% melting in five minutes. That's if the charges are on inlet nozzles 2 and 5. Best case is 21% melting if the charges are not on nozzles 2 and 5, assuming they haven't taken out our emergency cooling water piping in minus 20 level."

"What if we can get the reactor shut down before they blow the inlet nozzles", Metz asked? "You mean if we can ink the reactor and don't need the safety rods?" "Yes, suppose we could ink it somehow?" "Then if the emergency cooling water comes in both nozzles, we might prevent melting altogether. If only one nozzle, then maybe less than 8% to 10% melting." "OK, thanks very much Bill."

"We've got to get into minus 20 level and disable any explosives, if they placed any there", reported Metz. Everyone at the table was nodding agreement. "The Assistant Site Manager looked at the Protective Force representative. "Make it happen, Captain" "Yes sir", he replied, as he bolted from his chair toward the communications desk. 'Was an hour enough time to search all below grade areas of the building?' he wondered. Captain Lowe had gotten only a few hours' sleep himself. "Understood", he replied. He knew who he wanted.

"We've been instructed to re-enter the building and search below grade areas for explosive charges on pipes down there. DO NOT attempt to enter any area above ground level. If you find anything suspicious DO NOT TOUCH IT! The demolition team is standing by. They will take over while you get out of the building. We still have three men missing. If you find them, bring them out if you can. It's possible you may encounter some of the bad guys. Avoid them if possible but defend yourselves if necessary. Good luck, gentlemen!"

Assault on L

Two teams of four entered the building through the two 108 buildings on either side of the reactor building. Each team then split into pairs, with one pair going to minus 40 level and the other staying on minus 20 level. Although they had precious little time, they had to move cautiously in case any of the adversaries were in that part of the building. It was Ansel's turn to sweep the below grade areas. As he came around the corner in one of the hallways he spotted them. He got off several shots, before being hit in the shoulder and in the chest. One of the Protective Force was hit in the chest and fell onto his back, but his Kevlar vest saved him from serious injury.

"One bad guy taken out", they radioed back to Captain Lowe. "Roger that", he replied. "Any sign of our guys?" "Negative", they answered. There was a noise off to the far left. One went to investigate, while the other remained at the location where Ansel had fallen. "OK, stand up." There was man in grey coveralls crouched in the corner of a small electrical repair area in the southwest corner of that level. He put his hands on his head. It was plain to see he wasn't armed. "I'm an E&I Mechanic. I work here", he managed. Sweat covered his forehead.

The other man arrived to see who his partner was talking to. "What the hell are you doing here", he asked? "I know I was supposed to be in the lunchroom…, for the security exercise, I mean. Name's Grogan." He held out his badge for them to see. "But there was a faulty alarm from Disassembly, and it wouldn't stop. The Senior sent me down to disconnect it. It only took a few minutes. But when I was coming back out of Disassembly, I heard voices in the personnel entrance hallway. When I looked, I saw a lady in dirty grey coveralls, talking to one of your guys. I had never seen her in L Area before."

"Anyway, as soon as your guy turned his back, she kicked him from behind and then it looked like she broke his neck. I watched her drag the body past the doorway and under the stairs to plus 15. I could see she was coming into Disassembly, so I hid in one of the clothing cabinets. I could see her sometimes through the slats in the cabinet door. It wasn't long before I saw her and some other fellow dump two more of your guys into the storage pool. I thought she was never going to leave. Finally, she went up the stairs. That was my chance to get down here to my shop on minus 20 level and hide."

"Why didn't you just leave the building", asked one of the pair. "I figured I'd get shot by you guys. I could hear gunfire outside." "Yes, you probably would have", the other man admitted. "So, you've been hiding here for the past fourteen hours?" "Yeah man, what else could I do. I ate up all my snacks I had hidden here in my shop. I figured this would all be over by now and I could get out." They radioed Captain Lowe to let him know about Grogan. He in turn called the EOC to let them know as well. Metz sat up in his chair. "There's an E&I Mechanic in minus 20 level? Ask him if he knows where the gadolinium nitrate tanks are located", said Metz. The lady at the communications desk relayed the message to Lowe.

The room was absolutely quiet. Everyone was waiting for the answer. "Yes, he does", she finally replied. "Good", said Metz, acting like a five-year-old on Christmas morning! "Tell him…. His name is Grogan, right? Tell Grogan to go the gadolinium nitrate tanks and find one of the pneumatic lines going to the actuators on the valves. Doesn't matter which one. Either one will do." He gave the lady talking to Captain Lowe time to relay his words. Everyone waited. Then she gave a thumbs up. "OK, now tell Grogan to cut or drill a hole about a sixteen of an inch in diameter into one of those pneumatic lines. He will hear air escaping." She relayed the message. They waited again. Then another thumbs up.

Metz collapsed into his chair as if he had just finished running a marathon. "That should do it", he exclaimed! "Do what", asked the Assistant Site Manager? "Shut down the reactor", said Carlton. "The Supplementary Safety System injects gadolinium nitrate, or 'ink', into the heavy water circulating through the reactor. Gadolinium nitrate is a very strong neutron absorber. It suppresses the reactivity of the core and stops the nuclear chain reaction. The only way to restart the reactor is to remove the gadolinium nitrate using specially prepared deionizer columns. The fastest we've ever been able to that is 78 hours with a team of twenty people. It will be impossible for these guys."

"And", Metz added, "It will happen slowly this time, rather than all in ten seconds like it's designed to do. The guys in the control room won't be able to stop it. I'm guessing they won't be able to explain it either, or reasonably blame us for violating their instructions." "Let's hope you're right", said the Assistant Site Manager. The clock on the EOC wall read 1:40 pm. Protective Force personnel in the Main Administration Area reported sighting an unauthorized helicopter passing overhead and travelling towards 200 F Area. "Is the package ready for delivery, Mr. Roland", asked the Assistant Site Manager? "Yes sir, it is."

Assault on L

Chapter 9

All was quiet in the L Reactor control room. Jorge looked at his watch. Only another hour and a half. After the package was picked up and he received the confirmation code, whatever happened next would all be up to him. It almost seemed too easy, or was it? Every hour someone had to go into other areas of the building to check that his instructions were being followed. He sent Ansel down to minus 20 level around 13:00 hours. He should have returned by now. He kicked the side of one of the cots set up in the day supervisor's office. "Hey Luis. Go see what's keeping Ansel. He's late coming back." Luis didn't move. "HEY LUIS", yelled Jorge! Luis sat up slowly, shook the cobwebs out of his head, and turned to look at Jorge. "OK, Ok, I'm going", he replied with a raspy voice.

Jorge had a look in the conference room where Silas was watching over the hostages. Several were asleep on cots, while others had fallen asleep in their chairs. There were only nine cots and now there were fifteen people needing sleep. That meant they would have to 'hot bunk'. Jane Jones was on one of the cots. Jorge tried not to grin. 'She's earned it', he thought. He also glanced into the lunchroom to find Henry playing chess with one of the reactor operators. "You winning Henry", Jorge asked? "No", Henry replied with a frown.

Back in the control room, Jorge noticed Samuel had moved a chair around in front of the reactor room observation window. He was resting his head on the railing with eyes half shut. "Hey, wake up in there! Don't want them sneaking up on us and pulling our charges off", Jorge yelled. He was well aware that even if they did get into the reactor room, they'd never get past the first charge before they were blown up into the ceiling.

Blythe was still at the nuclear console, looking a bit tired. She had gotten a few hours' sleep while sitting there but was still a bit groggy. The oversized 'executive style' chair at the nuclear console had a high back and was well padded. It reclined slightly and swivelled, making the Senior Reactor Operator's job as comfortable as possible. Actually, there wasn't anything she needed to do. Otis was standing behind her as usual just in case she tried to reach the SCRAM button. Jorge took up his usual stance in front of the hole in the panel with a big metal ring inside. He wasn't sure what it did, although Murphy had tried to explain. Henry had tried to explain the chemistry involved, but Jorge wasn't interested. He only needed to know that no one was allowed anywhere near that ring.

Blythe was the first to notice a change in the High Level Flux Monitors. That is what she had been trained to do, after all. The recorder pens were dropping gradually. The control computer was withdrawing control rods to bring reactor power back up, but it wasn't able to stop the decline. The effects of xenon building in from fission product decay were accelerating the process. Reactor power was now down to 90%. Blythe pretended everything was normal, but it wasn't long before Otis noticed as well. "Hey what's happening. Get the power back up", he yelled.

Jorge came over for a look. "Those bastards! They're trying to shut it down. Tell me how they are doing that", he screamed, putting his Glock 19 to Blythe's head. She was shaking. "I don't know", she whispered. "Get away from there." He motioned her to get out of the chair so Otis could take over. Otis tried to withdraw the control rods but they were already 95% out. There was nothing he could do. About five minutes had passed and reactor power was now down to 80%. Jorge looked at Murphy. Murphy shrugged his shoulders. "Beats me!"

"Go get Henry", Jorge shouted, waving Otis toward the door. "I'm two moves away from checkmate", replied Henry. Otis brushed the chess pieces onto the floor. "NOW", he said! When Henry entered the control room he realized what was going on. "It has to be the gadolinium nitrate. That's the only explanation." "No it isn't", yelled Jorge. "You said they had to pull this ring in the hole in the wall. Nobody's gone near it. See." He pointed his pistol at the metal ring. "They must have done it from somewhere else in the building", Henry replied. "Damn", Jorge shouted. "Where's Ansel? Where's Luis?" Everyone suddenly realized neither of them had come back from minus 20 level.

"OK, I'll show those bastards." Jorge pulled the detonator out of this pocket. "The reactor's still at 50% power. That will do just fine." "Wait", said Henry. "The package won't be delivered if you blow it all now. Wait until after 14:00 hours and the package has been picked up. It's only a few more minutes. 50% power, 20% power, it won't make that much difference. At least let's accomplish our mission. If Ansel and Luis are lost and we don't accomplish the mission, then they will have died for nothing!" Jorge facial expression began to relax slightly. "Yeah, you're right. We're still holding four aces. They can't afford to call our hand. They won't dare!"

Assault on L

The clock in the EOC read 1:53 pm. "The reactor remote operations center can still monitor conditions in L Reactor even though it can't gain control", said Metz. "They've been watching the power drop in L Reactor. It's down to 20% and dropping fast. Can we stop them from delivering the package", he asked? "With the reactor shut down there may be no melting in the reactor core at all. And even if a small percentage of the fuel assemblies melt the release of contamination will be manageable. The effects on the public will be much less than if we let these guys get away with the plutonium. Can we stop the delivery?" The Assistant Site Manager looked at Roland. "Yes, we can", Roland replied with a smile. He picked up the phone and dialled the 200 F Area Manager. "Don't make the delivery", he shouted into the phone. "I repeat. Abort delivery of the plutonium!" He had to wait for confirmation. His face dropped. He put down the phone. "We're too late. The helicopter arrived ten minutes early and took off four minutes ago with the package."

The Assistant Site Manager slammed his fist down on the table. Roland continued, "They hovered at 500 feet and dropped a small box with a note in it. It reads, 'Receipt Code is BROMBURG459327'." "What the hell does that mean", asked Suelle? "It's what the adversaries in L Reactor are waiting for", said Carlton. It tells them the plutonium has been picked up. We have to find a way to contact them and give them the code! We may still be able to talk them down, especially now that they have what they want. We kept our end of the bargain. Now they need to keep theirs."

The Assistant Site Manager motioned for the negotiator to come out of his cubicle. "Abrams, did you talk to these guys in L Area last night?" "No sir, that was Stevens. He's home asleep", he replied. "OK, can you get through to the L Reactor control room now?" "I've been trying but no one answers. I've tried other phones in the building as well but they're just not picking up." "Keep trying. And if you get them tell them we have something they want", said the Assistant Site Manager. Abrams walked back to his cubicle. He was just about to pick up his head set and call the L Reactor control room for the thirtieth time when the phone rang. "Whatever you guys are trying it won't work", said Jorge. He had found the number for the EOC posted on the wall above the day supervisor's desk. "Has the package been picked up as we instructed?" "Yes, sir", Abrams replied. "It left ten minutes ago." "I don't believe you. You have ten seconds to convince me or I'll blow your reactor into little bits and pieces." Abrams ripped his headset off and ran out to the table. "I've got five seconds to give him the number", he panted. "Please read it correctly", said Metz! Abrams grabbed his headset again and struggled to get it on. "Here it is. It reads:

- Bravo
- Romeo
- Oscar
- Mike
- Bravo
- Uniform
- Romeo
- Golf
- 4
- 5
- 9
- 3
- 2
- 7

"Did you copy that, sir", asked Abrams? No one could hear him, but he could see everyone in the room was staring at him through the glass window. There was no response. "I'm sorry, sir. I said did you copy that", Abrams repeated. "Yes", came the reply. "I'll contact you when we are ready to talk", said Jorge. The line went dead. Abrams gave a thumbs up. Everyone in the room stood up and shook hands. "Ladies and gentlemen", said the Assistant Site Manager in a loud voice. "I suggest you all sit back down. We are not out of the woods yet. Not by any means. We have a press conference scheduled in an hour and a half. What are you going to tell them Mr. Carlton?"

Jorge replaced the receiver on the phone in the day supervisor's office. He had a blank look on his face. "Mission accomplished", he announced. Henry smiled. Jorge didn't. They had done what they were paid to do. Was that the end of it? No, not until the package was safely delivered to an Iranian oil tanker in international waters about 40 miles off the South Carolina coast. At least that's what he had been told. He could blow up the reactor now, while the helicopter was still over land. But they would definitely be tracking it and would blow it out of the sky the minute they were told he had detonated his charges in the reactor room. So now it was all about waiting again.

"It's Paris Island, sir. They have the chopper over Estill, South Carolina. The tracking device in the package is working perfectly. They will be able to track it even in international waters. If it's dropped at sea the Coast Guard will be able to recover it." The Assistant Site Manager looked relieved. "So, how do we get those guys out of our reactor building?" "Until we get the delivery code we'll just have to wait", said Carlton. "That chopper can't make it across the Atlantic. It must be planning to rendezvous with a ship out there", Suelle suggested. "The Coast Guard can tell us what ships are within the chopper's range. They have several Cutters in the area. It shouldn't take long for them to board and search the vessel."

The Assistant Site Manager looked at the weather map being displayed on one of the two large video screens. "Prevailing winds are shifting, sir", volunteered one of the meteorologists without being asked. Looks like we have a cold front from Canada moving down through Tennessee and north Georgia. Winds will be out of the northwest by later this evening." That was good news. If there was a release from L Reactor it would be carried southwest over Charleston, then out to sea. In the worst-case scenario, evacuation of less than a half million people to the southeast of the site would be easier than evacuating tens of millions to the northwest. It was time for another press conference. Carlton prepared himself for another pummelling.

"Ladies and gentlemen, I have another statement from the Department of Energy."

> Our negotiations with those in control of the L Reactor building are continuing. We believe we have reached agreement on several key points. However, several others remain unresolved. The reactor has been shut down. While this lessens the potential consequences of any accidental or deliberate actions by the adversaries in the building, a reduced level of threat remains. Multiple means to mitigate this threat are in place. No radioactive contamination has been released and there is currently no danger to the public. Negotiations toward a satisfactory resolution to this incident will continue until all remaining threats are eliminated.

"May I have your questions please?"

"Have you determined how many terrorists are in the L Reactor building?" "No, we have not. We have only been able to communicate with one of them. There are obviously others as well, but we still don't know how many", he replied.

Assault on L

"What do they want?" "They have made a number of demands. Some have been satisfied, others are as yet unresolved." "Why can't you tell us their demands?" "For operational security reasons I cannot discuss the specifics of what they have asked for. Once we have regained control of the facility and this incident has been fully resolved we may be able to release more information."

"Have these people said what organization they represent? Do you think they might be working for a foreign power?" "They have not indicated an allegiance to any organization in the United States or in a foreign country. We don't know what 'cause' they may be serving with this action."

"How many hostages are they holding at this time? Have they killed any hostages?" "The adversaries took control of the building on the evening shift approximately eighteen hours ago. The normal shift compliment is around ten individuals. We believe the number of hostages is around that number."

"So, you're saying none of the hostages have been killed?" "We cannot determine at this time if all the hostages are still alive."

"They may have killed some of them?" "It's possible, but we can't be sure of that." "And none of the hostages have escaped?" "None to my knowledge." Carlton suddenly remembered the E&I Mechanic Grogan. But then technically he was never a hostage.

"What happens if you don't give these people what they want? Can you be specific?" "Hypothetically speaking, there could be some release of radioactive contamination from the reactor building in the worst-case scenario. However, I must add that this is highly unlikely."

"So, we don't need to evacuate yet, but we might have to in a day or two?" "There is no danger to the public at this time. In the extremely unlikely event that some contamination is released a limited evacuation of the public in areas immediately down wind of the site might be necessary. Procedures for such an event are in place. It might be helpful to review those procedures, but it would be very premature to take any actions outlined in those procedures at this time."

"Someone saw a helicopter fly over this area a couple of hours ago. Was that one of yours?" "I'm sorry I can't comment on that." Carlton looked toward the DOE public relations team standing to one side. "I'm sorry that is all we have time for. We'll hold another press briefing in four hours. Thank you, ladies and gentlemen."

Jorge was able to contain his anger, but only just. "I think it's time we showed them who's in control here", he announced. "We'll give them a 'two for one special', just like at Walmart. Henry, you and Samuel take four of the hostages up to the roof and shoot them. Then toss the bodies off so the guys on the ground can see we mean business. For every one of our guys they kill, we'll give them two bodies in return."

"But we don't know that Ansel and Luis are dead", replied Henry. "Doesn't matter", Jorge replied. "Do what I said. Do it NOW!" Henry found Samuel in the lunchroom eating. "Come on, we've got a job to do." Samuel shoved one more piece of ham into his mouth and followed Henry into the conference room. "You and you …", said Henry. "And you", Samuel added. "No", Henry replied. "Not him. Then I won't have anyone to play chess with." Martin had never considered the ability to play chess a critically essential skill, until now.

They also decided against Crosby. He was the cook, although now that the reactor was shut down, maybe Otis could cook something other than spaghetti and beef stew. With Ferbis and Jared in tow, they entered the control room. "Henry motioned to Tyler and Blythe to join the group." Otis objected. "Not her!" "Why not" Jorge replied? "The reactor's shut down. We don't need her anymore." "We might", Otis pleaded. He had a chauvinistic objection to removing a woman this attractive from the world simply for revenge.

Jorge starred at Otis for a moment. He knew what Otis had in mind. Then Silas added his objection as well. Women were always the 'innocents' in Silas's mind. At least until he met Janine. She was a singular conundrum he really couldn't sort out. Jorge shrugged. "OK, take Leland then." He motioned for Leland to join the group. "We've got some cleaning up to do on the roof. You gentlemen are going to help", he announced. After they left the control room things got very quiet. "We're still one cot short though", Jorge shouted, just to break the silence.

Of course, Blythe realized she was being spared for a purpose; one she never would have agreed to under normal circumstances. As a female she was vulnerable in ways the others weren't. Her life had been threatened, but so far no one had made any sexual advances. Otis looked the type who might at some point, but the leader of the group seemed to be against such distractions. That was probably enough to keep everyone's private desires in check. Although he hadn't hesitated to kill MacMahon without provocation, Blythe considered Jorge to be her best chance to avoid getting raped by one of the others. Silas seemed strangely sympathetic towards her as well. Her emotions began to change from primal fear to apprehension as Blythe contemplated a more frightening prospect - that Jorge and Silas might both be killed, and what might happen to her then.

Protective Force personnel had completed their search of the below grade areas of the reactor building. They reported their findings to Captain Lowe. Metz was relieved to hear there were no other explosive charges. They had just finished removing the bodies of two adversaries killed in minus 20 out of building. Grogan had shown them four other bodies in the spent fuel basin in Disassembly. Unfortunately, all four had floated some distance away from where the floor grating had been removed. Captain Lowe was appraised of their location but made the decision to leave them there. He considered it too risky to try to retrieve the bodies, especially since the adversaries had demanded again that all personnel stay out of the reactor building. He had deduced by process of elimination who three of them were. The fourth could be one of the adversaries or a member of the operations staff. With all four floating face down it was impossible to see their badges.

In the EOC Metz was again concerned that the adversaries might plant additional explosives on the crosstie header to disable the emergency cooling water system. If that system failed, then the threat of melting the entire reactor core was back in play. "Whatever else we can do; we need to protect against loss of the emergency cooling water system. I think we should keep a small group of Protective Force personnel in minus 20 level to protect the crosstie header. We can't let them reach that location. Even if they don't have any explosives left, they could still disable the system if given enough time to work on it." The Assistant Site Manager looked at Suelle. "We can keep a team of four in minus 20 level. But I can't guarantee they won't be seen or that there won't be another skirmish", Suelle replied. "That will have to do", Metz nodded.

It took a while to get Tyler, Jared, Ferbis and Leland up to plus 55 level of the building. The roar of two giant ventilation exhaust fans echoed off the inside walls of the building. Thanks to Luis they were sucking outside air in through ruptured ductwork, pushing it through the filter compartments on the plus 55 roof and immediately back out again through the 200-foot stack. The reactor building supply fans located on the other end of the building were pushing a small air flow through the building and the reactor room, but it was negligible compared to the normal exhaust air flow. Most importantly, the air pressure in the reactor room was now higher than the ambient air pressure outside the building. Samuel kept watch while Henry opened the big roll door on the east side. There was less likelihood the two of them could be overpowered by the hostages if they went out this way.

"Alright gentlemen, if you will line up facing the side of this aluminum boxcar I'll explain what we have to do. Each of the men took their place about two feet apart. Tyler began reciting the Lord's Prayer. Leland joined in. When they finished, Henry shot three of them in the back of the head with his Glock 19. Samuel hesitated momentarily, then did the fourth. All four bodies were only about fifteen feet from the edge of the roof. One by one Samuel and Henry dragged them over to the edge and pushed them off. Although they couldn't see the ground immediately adjacent to the building, they could hear the sickening thud as each body hit the cement below. It wouldn't be long before they were found, along with a handwritten note from Jorge. It read, "For every one of ours, two of yours will die".

Immediately after coming back in from the roof, Henry motioned to Samuel to find a way to shut off the giant exhaust fans. "They're making too much noise", yelled Henry. Samuel shrugged his shoulders. Why did it matter? Henry motioned again by drawing his hand across his throat. Samuel found a long metal pole and wedged it between an electrical conduit and the pedestal supporting one of the fans. He twisted the pole around until it pulled the conduit out its panel. The fan began to spin down from loss of power. He did the same on the other fan that was running, and on the third fan that was idle. It took a few minutes for the fan impellers to stop rotating. Then all was quiet. "Good", said Henry.

"What did we do that for", asked Samuel? "Because I wanted to", Henry replied. In the control room all the lights on the exhaust ventilation graphic panel were now bright red. All the lights on the supply air system were still green. Jorge liked it when he could see a pattern to things. The graphic panel for building ventilation was now symmetrical. All the lights on the top half were green, all the lights on the bottom half were red. 'Top half live, bottom half dead', he mused. He liked having the air pressure inside the building higher than outside.

Suelle left the table in the EOC to take an urgent call from Captain Lowe. "Bad news", he announced upon his return. "We've recovered four bodies from the concrete apron on the east side of the building. All four were shot in the back of the head. It was clearly an execution. The note on one of them reads 'For every one of ours, two of yours will die'. Badges identified them as Jared, Tyler, Ferbis and Leland."

"BASTARDS", Carlton screamed, as he rose from his chair! Silence fell over the room. Carlton took the stairs two at a time. He was quickly out the door and onto the grassy area between A Wing and B Wing where it was raining. Bent over, he felt unable to catch his breath and thought he might throw up any second. Everyone in the EOC remained silent until Carlton returned about ten minutes later, his hair and shirt wet. "Sorry", he said. The Assistant Site Manager nodded. "Are your men in minus 20 level safe", he asked, turning to Suelle? "Yes sir. They can defend themselves. Those four souls couldn't." "Do we know where that chopper is", asked the Assistant Site Manager? There was no immediate answer. "For God's sakes, find out will you?"

Carlton was wondering how he was going to notify the next of kin for those operations personnel who had been killed. There was nothing in the EOC procedures about doing that. The death of an employee was something no manager ever expected to face. In this case the Operations Manager was expected to visit the next of kin personally and offer his condolences. Of course, this was clearly an extraordinary event. But then, come to think of it, anytime one of his employees died at work it would be considered an extraordinary event! He certainly couldn't leave the EOC at this moment. He asked the site operator for the home phone numbers for Leland, Tyler, Ferbis and Jared. He knew Tyler from L Reactor Restart Team. He must have been introduced to Leland, Febris and Jared at some time or other. At least he could call their wives and let them know what had happened. One of the EOC operators tried all four residences with no success. Their families must have already called the site to find out why their husbands hadn't come home yesterday morning after their regular shift. There was no way he could make this any less horrific.

Suelle had the same problem. Only he had ten families to notify. And like Carlton he took that responsibility personally. It would be easy to delegate to Captain Lowe, but his plate was full. Besides Brownlie and his crew didn't work for Lowe. It was all moving too fast. Someone should have thought about how to handle such notifications. But nobody had. "By the way, Mr. Suelle. How are your men in the hospital doing? Are their wounds serious? Are they out of danger?" It was a legitimate question and a courteous one. Suelle was embarrassed he didn't know the answer. "I'll call he hospital again and see how they are doing", he replied. In fact, he hadn't had time to call the hospital at all! It struck him how the entire process of managing a crisis had been carefully spelled out in the EOC's working procedures, but nobody had thought through the human aspects at all. It really was a disgrace.

The EOC communications operator suddenly turned to Carlton. "I have a Mrs. MacMahon on the phone for you. She can't reach her husband in L Area and doesn't know where he is. She needs to get an urgent message to him. One of his daughters has been taken to the hospital with a high fever." Carlton broke out in a cold sweat. What could he tell her?

Of course, Carlton couldn't know that MacMahon's body and the bodies of three Protective Force personnel were still floating face down under the metal grating that served as the floor over a vast spent fuel storage basin. The bodies had drifted about twenty feet and were now under a section of grating that was welded in place. Retrieving them would take hours that nobody had at the moment, especially with the building under terrorist control. Leaving them until later was the only option, in spite of what Captain Lowe had promised his men earlier. Lowe had determined by process of elimination who was missing from his roster. But no one outside the building had any way of knowing how many more hostages had been killed beyond the four that were thrown off the roof.

"The chopper's about fifteen miles out in the Atlantic", came the delayed reply. "Coast Guard has them on radar but not visual. The tracking device on the package is putting out a strong signal. There are several ships in the area. The only one of any size is an Iranian oil tanker about 18 miles out from Charleston." "Stay in contact with them", said the Assistant Site Manager. "We don't want to lose that package. As soon as they send us the 'delivery code' the Coast Guard can go in and get it." "What if they don't send the code", Metz asked? "I think they will", said Suelle. "They want their guys out of L Area. And they know that's the only way they're going to get them back." "You're assuming these people in the control room intend to calmly walk out of the reactor building and just fly away", said Carlton. "Yes", the Assistant Site Manager replied. "I'm assuming that at least some of them expect to do exactly that". "All we can do is wait", Roland added.

It came sooner than they expected. "I'm getting a message via short wave radio, sir. It reads, 'Delivery Code is Bromfield346229'. "Call the supervisor's office in L Reactor and give them the code," yelled Metz. The communications operator turned in his chair and made the call. He let it ring eight times but there was no answer. "Now what", said Metz. Three minutes later the operator's phone rang. "Did you get my message", asked Jorge? "Yes sir", replied the operator, pointing his finger at Abrams to pick up the call in his cubicle. "Yes sir", said Abrams. "And we have a message for you. It reads 'Delivery Code is

- Bravo
- Romeo
- Oscar
- Mike
- Foxtrot
- India
- Echo
- Lima
- Delta
- 3
- 4
- 6
- 2
- 2
- 9

"Did you copy that, sir", asked Abrams? Again, there was no reply. The line was silent. He was about to repeat the code when the line went dead. "Did they get the code", asked the Assistant Site Manager? "I don't know", Abrams replied. "I don't know!" "What's he playing at", said Suelle? The Assistant Site Manager shook his head. He didn't dare give a green light to recover the package until L Area acknowledged the delivery code. What was he supposed to do now? "Abrams", yelled Carlton. Abrams couldn't hear him inside the cubicle. Carlton went to the cubical door and tapped on it. "Try to get him back", he yelled. Abrams nodded. He was trying.

The Assistant Site Manager stood up from the table. "OK, we're out of options. I need a vote on whether we should tell the Coast Guard to recover the package. All in favor? Suelle raised his hand. Carlton raised his. Metz wasn't sure but decided to raise his hand anyway. Roland's hand was in the air. Abrams didn't get a vote. He was too busy to notice anyway. "Call the Coast Guard and ask them where the package is", said Suelle. They had to wait for an answer. "An object about five feet long has been dropped into the sea. It has been recovered by the Iranian tanker. The tanker is changing course toward the southeast."

Assault on L

"Tell the Coast Guard to board the Iranian tanker and recover the package. They'll have to find some excuse to search the ship if the Captain refuses to cooperate. They are authorized to use lethal force if necessary", said the Assistant Site Manager. "The Iranians will no doubt turn this into an international incident", said Carlton. "No doubt", the Assistant Site Manager replied. "But getting back 30 kg of plutonium will be worth it!"

"The Coast Guard wants a detailed description of the package they're looking for, sir". The communications operator was looking at the Assistant Site Manager again. He turned to Roland. "It's a long wooden box, about 65 inches long, containing 13 compartments each 2 inches wide", Roland replied. "There are 12 blocks of borated paraffin, each 3 inches thick, between the compartments. Thirteen metal 'buttons', each about the size and shape of an ice hockey puck, are in plastic bags, one in each compartment. That's the plutonium. Under no circumstances are they to remove anything from the box. If these items are placed too close together the consequences could be deadly. Make sure they understand that." The operator relayed the information to the Coast Guard. "Is there a radiation hazard they need to worry about?" "No", Roland replied. "Plutonium 239 is primarily an alpha emitter. A sheet of plastic or paper is enough to prevent significant radiation exposure."

Roland turned back around in his chair to find everyone staring at him to explain. "A spherical untamped critical mass of Plutonium 239 is about 11 kg. Obviously, each of the metallic buttons weighs much less than that, but if they remove several of them from the box and get them too close to each other they could create a 'criticality'. They'll see a blue flash of light and the buttons may fragment from the heat generated. Anyone close to the criticality will likely receive a massive beta-gamma radiation dose. They will probably be dead within a few days."

Jorge was sitting at the day supervisor's desk when Henry walked in. "The remaining hostages are starting to realize their comrades aren't' coming back from the roof. They might try to start something if they think they aren't going to get out of here alive." "Then shoot them", Jorge replied, without looking up. He seemed to be staring at a hole in the wall. After a few moments, he glanced up at Henry. "You still here", he asked? Henry turned to walk out. "We've received the delivery code", Jorge added in a subdued voice. "The Iranians have the package." "Iranians", said Henry? "Yeah, Iranians. Who the hell did you think was paying for all this anyway", Jorge replied with a smile? "So we can get out of here, then", said Henry? He was already starting to think about how far his $25 million could take him. Jorge didn't answer.

Assault on L

Jorge's father was Portuguese. His mother was Japanese. He was raised by his maternal grandmother from the age of 7 until he was nearly 16. He had heard all his grandmother's stories about how beautiful her country was before the war. There was so much culture. They would walk in the garden and talk about it for hours. Or just sit and watch the giant oriental carp twist their golden bodies between the lily pads in the pond. Eventually the events at Hiroshima and Nagasaki would creep into the narrative, although she spared him the gory details of badly burned children and the horrible way people died from radiation poisoning.

'These aren't the people who dropped the bombs. The nuclear material for those weapons wasn't made here.', he thought. Still, someone had to pay. Americans needed to understand what it's like to have your country contaminated with radioactivity; to worry about getting cancer because of radioisotopes in the air you breathe and the water you drink. Of course, there would be evacuations and mitigation measures. But people would still worry about how well those measures were working. And many would have to leave their homes and communities and not be allowed to come back for years. Or maybe never... Surely there was justice in what he was doing.

Jorge was reluctant now to send anyone else into the below grade areas of the building. In spite of his demand that no one enter the building, he expected there would be a Protective Force presence there. At the moment it seemed better to coexist, rather than have any more confrontations. He was safe in the control room. His explosives were safe in the reactor room. He had the detonator in his pocket. He could push the button before they could do anything. He wondered about the rest of the team though. They had done the impossible. Now they would be more interested in leaving with their winnings. Samuel and Otis had the other two detonators. He doubted either of them would push the button. It was up to him now. It was a personal thing. For him alone!

Assault on L

Chapter 10

Captains of U. S. Coast Guard Cutters rarely qualify for hazardous duty pay, but some days were certainly more interesting than others. Torrison wondered if this might be the one he would be telling his grandkids about. Except he didn't have any grandkids, or children, or even a wife for that matter. It reminded him that he needed to do something about that the next chance he got. The problem with Iranian tankers is you never knew how many men were on board or how well they were armed. The waterline on this one showed it was full. It was headed toward Charleston harbor, but had suddenly reversed course and was headed back out to sea. 'Why would they do that', Captain Torrison wondered?

The package on board was sending out a strong signal. But how much of a fight would they put up to keep it? He only had a crew of sixteen on the Cutter. Would that be enough? He could call for Naval Destroyer support but that would definitely create an international incident. And it would take too long. He couldn't afford to wait. The Iranian ship was nearly back to international waters. A peaceful boarding to conduct a maritime safety inspection would have to do. At least the weather was good. The sky was about as blue as he had ever seen it.

The Coast Guard Cutter easily caught up with the cumbersome tanker. Still 300 meters away it radioed the huge ship. "This is the U. S. Coast Guard requesting permission to conduct a safety inspection of your vessel per requirements of international maritime law. Do we have your consent to come along side and board your vessel?" There was no response. The ship was proceeding slowly toward the limit of U. S. territorial waters. Captain Torrison switched to broadcast the request over the loudspeaker. There was still no response.

He tried the radio again. "This is the U. S. Coast Guard requesting permission to conduct a safety inspection of your vessel per requirements of international maritime law. Do we have your consent to come along side and board your vessel?" The captain of the Iranian tanker knew if he refused, they would attempt to board anyway. That would only draw more unwanted attention. He decided to radio back to the Cutter. "U. S.

Assault on L

Coast Guard your request is acknowledged. You have permission to board this vessel."

Torrison was relieved. He had serious concerns about trying to board against a hostile reception. Pulling the Cutter alongside, he and twelve of his crew climbed the narrow steel ladder until all of them stood on the deck of the ship. It was like being on a floating island. The ship was so massive you barely realized you were in a rolling sea. The Iranian Captain offered a brisk salute. "Welcome aboard Captain." "Name's Torrison. Sorry for the inconvenience, sir." The captain of the tanker failed to state his name in return. He simply nodded. "Please conduct your inspection. I will be in my cabin if you need assistance." He turned crisply and walked away. He had no intention of helping these men find what they were after. If they found it, so be it!

Most of the crew on the tanker wore side arms, as was the custom in their country. The crew of the Coast Guard Cutter wore side arms as well. Neither party had any desire to use their weapons. Torrison considered them more for show anyway. They had much more serious weaponry on board the Cutter if needed. He deployed his men in various directions. It was a very big ship. There were so many places one could hide a wooden box five feet long and a little more than a foot square. The tracking device had confirmed the package was on board but could not pinpoint its location more accurately than plus or minus 30 meters. It did indicate that it was somewhere on the level of the crew's quarters.

None of the Iranian sailors were pleased about having their quarters searched so a cursory look in each cabin was judged sufficient. After an hour they had turned up nothing. Torrison decided he needed the Iranian Captain's help. Whether he would get it was anyone's guess. Torrison knocked, then opened the door to the Captain's Quarters to find the Iranian Captain sitting at his desk. On the floor was a long wooden box with its floatation device still attached, and still wet after being dragged from the sea. Torrison directed one of his men to open it carefully. The box contained a number of blocks of paraffin, but no plutonium.

"It appears we've both been searching for the same prize, Captain, but all we've found is the box it came in", said the Iranian Captain. Torrison was suspicious. "If you have removed the contents of the package, I'm afraid your men are in grave danger. If these items are placed too close to each other the consequences may be deadly." The Iranian Captain smiled. "The only danger either of us faces in this case is one of extreme embarrassment. It appears we have been outbid for the material. I suspect the punishment for you will be far less severe than what we will face when we return to our home port." The look of fear in the Iranian Captain's eyes seemed genuine. Torrison was further convinced when the Iranian Captain asked if asylum could be arranged for him and his crew in the United States of America. The tanker and the oil were the property of Iran and would have to be returned, of course.

It was close to 7:00 pm when they got a radio message from the Coast Guard some twenty miles south east of Charleston. "They've recovered the package", reported the communications operator in the EOC. "The Iranian Captain turned it over to them." Everyone applauded and began shaking each other's hands as though they had anything at all to do with the success. "Wait", added the operator, raising his hand in the air. "It's empty. The box is intact but there's no plutonium. The Iranian Captain claims they saw a helicopter drop something into the sea not far from their location. When they retrieved it, they found nothing inside except blocks of wax." "Ask them what happened to the helicopter", said Suelle. There was a few minutes delay before the EOC operator could raise the Coast Guard on the radio again. "They say the helicopter banked south before disappearing off their radar. It may have landed on another ship or simply gone out of range."

"So, we don't know where the plutonium is?" The Assistant Site Manager's mouth was ajar. "I'm afraid that's correct, sir", replied the operator. Everyone in the EOC fell back into their chairs again. After a few moments of silence, Roland felt the need to comment. "I wonder if they know how to handle those buttons." "I hope they don't" Carlton replied. "I hope they stacked them all on top of each other, created a criticality, and crashed their helicopter into the sea. We won't get our plutonium back, but we'll know it's somewhere at the bottom of the Atlantic where it can't be used to make a weapon!"

"Unlikely", said Metz. "My guess is they know exactly how to handle metallic plutonium. They probably know as much about it as we do. They wouldn't have gone to all this trouble without having procedures in place in case they succeeded." Heads began to nod around the table. "I suggest we turn our focus back to the people in L Reactor. We still have a problem there. We need to start dealing with it more aggressively. And we have another press briefing coming up in less than an hour. Whose turn is it in the barrel", he asked looking around the room.

About 170 miles due south of the Iranian tanker, a helicopter was nearing it true destination in the Atlantic off the Florida coast east of Orlando. It flew only 80 feet above a lightly rolling sea to avoid being on anyone's radar. Technicians on board had already begun their assay of the plutonium buttons before the chopper was even out of Savannah River Site's airspace. When they equipped the chopper, they had several choices. They could use either active or passive non-destructive analysis (NDA) to determine if the plutonium buttons were the real thing.

They could use active NDA to 'interrogate' each button using a neutron source, and then measure the button's response spectra. But that would mean having another source of neutrons on board in close proximity to so much fissile material. Somehow that didn't seem a good idea from a nuclear safety point of view. Or they could use passive NDA using either a Ge(Li) detector or a Na(I) detector. Although the Ge(Li) detector would give more accurate results, it would only operate at liquid nitrogen temperatures. Cryogenics on a helicopter was another bad idea. And they didn't need the exact amount of plutonium in each button. They only wanted to be sure it was actually plutonium and not an inert fake.

The Na(I) detector operated at room temperature and was faster than the other methods as well. It based its results on the Plutonium 239's 413.69 keV and 375.03 keV gamma rays and their weak neighbors. Only one problem remained. For Plutonium 239, 90% of the detectable gammas come from the outer 0.6 cm. If the plutonium button was a composite, with a plutonium 'skin' more than 0.6 cm thick over an inert substrate of relatively equivalent density, then the Na(I) NDA would not detect a forgery. Technicians considered that situation highly unlikely because 1) there would be no reason to ever create such an abomination at any of the facilities at the Savannah River Site, and 2) there wasn't time to fabricate something that exotic with less than twenty-four hours' notice.

Actually, the technicians and the pilot of the chopper were more worried about the transfer of the buttons. They only had a short time to move them before they reached the Iranian tanker and radioed the delivery code. One mistake and they would all die a horrible slow death from radiation poisoning. Each button had to be removed from the Savannah River Site package and placed carefully in their own specially designed container. The two were remarkably similar, each made out of wood with borated paraffin blocks to separate the plutonium buttons. The new container was made of highly polished walnut however, whereas the one made by the Savannah River personnel was only oak. Presentation was important. Their customer needed to feel he was getting his money's worth after all!

Only one button could be moved at a time, and always with caution to avoid moving it near another button. Without the paraffin blocks the minimum spacing between buttons had to be even greater. It was the third button that almost killed them all. One technician, wearing gloves as an extra precaution, dropped it when the chopper hit a pocket of turbulence. "Sorry", the pilot yelled back. But it was too late. The button was on the floor and sliding toward the others. It went under the seat and popped out the other side just as the second technician stuck his boot out to stop its progress. "Don't do that again", yelled the second technician over the roar of the engine. "I won't", replied the first technician with a relieved look. "No, I meant that for the pilot. He has to stop bouncing us around like that. I aim to collect my money!"

The press briefing room was packed. "Mr. Roland, are all of the hostages in L Reactor still alive? What are you doing to get them out?"

"Have you convinced the terrorists in the building to release some of the hostages? Have any of the terrorists been killed?"

Roland had been wondering why his boss hadn't shown up in the EOC to relieve him. She was probably at home having a quiet dinner. Rank has its privileges.

Assault on L

Chapter 11

Ten minutes after Henry let everyone know that the plutonium had been delivered 'Jane Jones' was down the stairs and into the spent fuel storage area. She quickly crossed nearly 80 meters of floor grating covering the water filled basin to the far door that led outside. She cracked the door open just far enough to see who was in the courtyard.

Two Protective Force personnel had taken up positions behind an earthen berm about 40 meters away. She closed the door, took several deep breaths, then threw the door open and began a slow and somewhat awkward run toward their position. Both men ducked behind the berm with weapons ready, then took a more casual stance as she reached them. "Please help me", she wheezed, pretending to be out of breath. "I hid in the bathroom, and then slipped out while they were distracted." "How many are there", asked one of the men, without bothering to examine her badge? "Only four of them and four operators", she replied. "They're all in the control room. Can you please get me out of here?"

One of them escorted her to the personnel entry building; the one she had climbed over less than 24 hours earlier. Obviously, they intended to question her about the terrorists in the control room. Once inside the entry building, she passed out, undoubtedly overwhelmed by her ordeal of being held as a hostage for so long. It was fifteen minutes before the ambulance arrived. She appeared semiconscious during that time, babbling about her childhood and her favorite toys when she was only three. Interrogation would have to wait, obviously!

Unable to walk, they placed her on a stretcher and bundled her into the ambulance for the trip up to the Site Medical Unit in the Main Administration Area. An EMT sat next to her in the back of the ambulance. They had been on the road for about 10 minutes when 'Jane Jones' reached out with her right hand and plunged a pair of seven-inch scissors into the EMT's chest. She leapt off the stretcher and placed her hand over the shocked look on his face so he couldn't scream. Her free hand hammered the scissors further into his chest. He struggled for almost a minute before collapsing onto the floor of the ambulance.

Assault on L

The driver heard the struggle in the back and pulled over to the shoulder of the road. When he opened the rear door, he felt a sharp kick to the throat that crushed his larynx. Jane Jones jumped down out of the ambulance, leaving the driver grabbing his throat and gasping for air. After dragging the EMT out onto the gravel beside the driver, she slammed the door shut. She had already removed the EMT's green uniform. It was a bit loose, but it would have to do. Once in the driver's seat she set out for the security barricade at the entrance to the Main Administration Area.

She found the switch for the siren and red warning lights as she approached the barricade, while maintaining her speed. Both security guards were quickly out of the guard house to raise the barricade for what was an obvious medical emergency. Jane Jones held her badge up to the windshield as her ambulance passed through the barricade at a little over 5 miles an hour. "I hope they get to the hospital in time", one of the security guards commented. Once past the barricade there was only a 90 degree turn to the right and a 105 degree turn to the left. Then directly across the highway and onto Green Pond Road. She began to relax as she passed Green Pond Baptist Church on the left. The ambulance didn't take kindly to the rut filled dirt road to the farm, but it covered the distance.

She left it in front of the barn while she grabbed all her stuff, put everything in a green duffle bag, made up her bed nice and neat, and looked around to be sure she had left nothing behind. The ambulance was back out onto the highway in only eighteen minutes. In another half hour she was through the center of Aiken and out to the Aiken Medical Center on the north side of town. Would anyone notice an extra ambulance parked to one side of the hospital emergency entrance? Probably not. There was a public toilet inside the main building not far from the ER entrance, where she discarded the EMT uniform. She removed a short black shirt and cream colored silk blouse with a loosely overlapping front from the small green duffel bag she had packed at the farm. She left the silk blouse a bit open just for good measure. A pair of black pumps with five inch heals completed the 'look' she wanted.

It didn't take long to catch a ride on the busy road that ran past the hospital and looped around the north side of the Aiken area. The driver was a nice-looking gentleman in his mid-fifties. He took a side road off the main highway, then pulled off into a secluded area at her suggestion. After she disposed of his body, she was quickly back on the highway, and then onto Interstate 20 headed toward Columbia. She parked the dark green Mercedes in the long-term lot, bought her ticket and boarded the flight. It took off within an hour and began climbing to 35,000 feet. She had quite literally vanished into thin air.

"Where's Jane Jones", Samuel asked? "Haven't seen her for over an hour", Henry replied. "Maybe she's in the toilet." Jorge couldn't help overhearing. "Maybe she's just vanished. I hear she does that from time to time. Some call her 'The Magician'." "She'll probably turn up in a little while", said Otis. "No, she won't", Jorge replied. He had a suspicion she had left the building. Jorge had always considered Janine an opportunist. Her skills of deception were superior even to her talent for the martial arts. He never underestimated her ability to think farther ahead than anyone else on the team, including himself. Yes, she was an opportunist, but he had to accept her at face value in order to guarantee the success of the mission. As to whatever else she was thinking about he couldn't even hazard a guess.

Jorge knew the time had come for negotiation. He had to get the rest of team onto a chopper and up to the Augusta Airport where a Gulfstream Jet was waiting. He couldn't push the button in his pocket until the Gulfstream was safely out of United States airspace. Well, he could actually. But he did give them his word they could leave when the mission was completed. And THEIR mission was completed. He picked up the phone in the day supervisor's office and dialled the EOC. The communications operator picked up the call, but immediately switched it to Abrams in the cubicle. Abrams raised his hand to let everyone know he was talking to the adversaries in L Reactor again.

Jorge spoke in an artificially calm voice. "This is the L Reactor control room. Thank you for complying with our demands earlier today. Now we just have one more request. Some of us need some transportation. One of your security team's helicopters will do. We'll expect them at exactly 22:00 hours on the front lawn of L Reactor area, on the west side, halfway between the double security fence and the wood line. Cut the lights at 100 feet before you land. We will execute one hostage for every minute you're late. And you know what will happen after we run out of hostages, don't you? I'm sure you are all ready to get this over with. I know I certainly am!" The line went dead. Abrams quickly relayed this information to the room. The DOE Site Manager had returned to the EOC about half an hour earlier, just as Roland was returning from the 8:00 pm press briefing. He gave Abrams a thumbs up, then looked at Suelle. "I'm on it", Suelle replied.

Assault on L

It was obvious to Murphy, Blythe, Crosby and Martin that something was up. Martin had beaten Henry at chess three times but lost to him just before Otis finished making beef lasagne for everyone. That was the last of the beef, however, so their situation definitely had to change. Crosby was happy that he didn't have to cook any more. He did learn a few things from watching Otis. Jorge seemed more restless than ever, while Henry, Silas and the others acted more like it was Christmas eve. Was it almost over? Jorge came into the lunchroom with an announcement. "You will all be leaving soon. The chopper will be here in twenty minutes to take some of us away from this god forsaken place. I will stay behind to make sure they don't try to stop you leaving. Everyone did what they were supposed to do. For that I am extremely grateful. Don't spend all your money in one place. Blythe, you'll be going on the chopper as well, just as an added bit of insurance. You other three will make the trip to the chopper. Once everyone else is on board you are free to go. Thanks to us you all have something interesting to talk about on the 6:00 am news!"

Otis had thought about taking Blythe with them when they left. He knew she wouldn't go willingly. She was nearly eight years younger. But in time maybe she would see him in a different light. It was selfish of him he knew. But maybe he could make her happy now that he was rich. At 21:50 hours they emerged from the main personnel entrance onto the concrete apron outside. There were Protective Force personnel everywhere, but only in a defensive posture. Captain Lowe held the door open at the personnel entry building. They made their way through the exit turnstile, then out the other door and into the darkness. They could hear the helicopter in the distance.

Blythe was pushed along in front of the group, while Murphy, Crosby and Martin were kept as shields in the line of fire from the Protective Force. Suddenly there it was, loud and blowing up dust all around them. It was difficult to see in the dark. The four of them appeared as ghostly figures moving aimlessly within a hazy cloud in the dappled light from the entry control building. Captain Lowe managed to get some photos using an infrared camera. Perhaps someone could identify one or two of them later.

The chopper hovered for a moment, then turned off its spotlights. The outline of the chopper against the black pine forest created a dreamlike image. As it touched the ground, they could barely make out the open doorway in the windblown darkness. Silas was the first to enter, then Henry, then Samuel. Otis had Blythe by the arm as she reluctantly climbed in. Otis was right behind her. Samuel was already thinking of ways to eliminate Otis. Surely Blythe would prefer him over the Dutchman. Why couldn't Jorge have sent Samuel out into the building to be killed instead of Ansel or Luis? Otis slammed the door shut. Murphy, Crosby and Martin ran toward the personnel entry building, shielding their eyes from the dirt and dust being thrown up by the chopper.

Henry had his Glock 19 pressed firmly to the pilot's neck. As the rotors began to rev up, Otis suddenly yelled out. "Wait!" He pulled Blythe from her seat, slid open the door and tossed her out onto the ground. "I'm sorry. It wouldn't have worked out." He slid the door shut again. "Go", he shouted. As the Protective Force helicopter lifted off Murphy, Crosby and Martin were already running back to see if Blythe was injured. They reached her as the helicopter cleared the trees heading north east. "I'm fine", she said as they helped her to her feet. She started to laugh. "I survived", she blurted out. "I made it!" Her knees suddenly went weak and she was on the ground again. "Get a stretcher", yelled Murphy.

All four of them were anxious to go home as soon as possible. Their families and Blythe's fiancé had all been notified they were safe and unharmed. But first Captain Lowe needed to know everything Murphy and the others could tell him about the one remaining terrorist in the control room and what else he might be planning. "First of all, we need to know where the explosives are", he asked? "We heard them say there were three charges on three adjacent inlet nozzles", Murphy replied. "Which ones?" "Don't know. Only Tyler ever got to see out the reactor room window. Then they took him up on the roof and we never saw him or Ferbis or Leland or Jared again." Captain Lowe explained how they found the four of them on the ground after they had been shot and pushed off the roof. Murphy shook his head. "We were afraid of that. Each us expected to be next." "So, we don't know which three nozzles they placed the charges on?"

Assault on L

"Well sort of", Murphy replied. "There are six inlet nozzles. The emergency cooling water comes in through two of them on opposite sides of the plenum. If the three charges are on 'adjacent' nozzles, then one of the emergency cooling nozzles will survive intact. He drew a simple diagram.

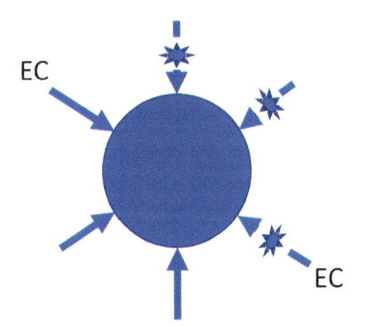

EC

EC

"No matter how they've arranged the charges we'll be able to get emergency cooling water into the reactor through one nozzle or the other, as long as the charges are on three adjacent nozzles." Captain Lowe realized he needed to get this information to the EOC immediately. When he returned he picked up where he left off. "They seemed to know the layout of the building, but not the equipment in it", Murphy added. "And obviously they didn't know much about heavy water reactors like ours."

"They seemed to think that by placing their explosives all on one side of the reactor they might shift the 'forest' of control and safety rods, so that the reactor couldn't be shut down. The Supplementary Safety System of gadolinium nitrate saved us. I don't know how you managed to activate it. We had no chance of doing it from the control room." "That idea came from the EOC actually, but an E&I Mechanic in the building figured out how to make it work", said Lowe. "You mean Grogan?" "Yes, that's him", Lowe replied. "Ahh! MacMahon forgot to put him on the shift roster." "Thank God he did", said Lowe!

Captain Lowe spent another half hour with Murphy, then it was Crosby's turn. "Can you describe these guys? Did any of them speak with an accent", asked Lowe? "Yeah, the one they called Luis. He had a strong Spanish accent." "You mean like Cuban or Mexican?" "No, like from Spain." "Any others?" "The man in charge. His name was Jorge, like George in Spanish. He was telling everyone what to do. Nobody had any interest in crossing him. He's still in there." "In the control room you mean?" "Yeah. That's where he was when we left." "Anything else?"

"Yeah, this one guy had the hots for Blythe. Kept standing behind her, real close. He seemed to know a lot about nuclear reactors, but not like ours. He was a really good cook too! I usually cook for B Shift. Nobody ever complained. But this guy was really good. Until we ran out of beef." "Anything else", Lowe asked? "Well, yes. There was an E&I Mechanic. A young lady. Jane Jones. She didn't come out with us. She must still be in the building." Murphy was concerned they might have killed her as well. "Relax", Lowe replied. "She's on her way to the hospital. She seemed completely overwhelmed by the whole experience. I'm sure she'll be fine." "OK, good", Murphy replied. The E&I Mechanic named Grogan had seen 'Jane Jones' in action in the spent fuel storage area. But he had already gone home.

Blythe was next. "One of their guys, middle aged I would say, seemed to understand how nuclear reactors work, but obviously had never seen one like this. He kept asking about the 'pressurizer' and 'high pressure injection pumps'. Stuff like that. He seemed to know a lot about nuclear power plants that run at hundreds of pounds of pressure and very high temperatures. He wouldn't believe that we operate with only 5 psi helium blanket gas. He just couldn't get his head around that somehow." "Did he take over the operation of the reactor", Lowe asked? "Not really. He seemed satisfied that it was on computer control. There were times when he let me sit at the nuclear console, either because he was tired or bored. When he went for a sleep sometimes there was no one in the chair. If there was a rod drive out incident the safety computers would have SCRAM'ed the reactor. We were all hoping for that, but it didn't happen."

"Did they ever say what they wanted? Why were they threatening to blow up the reactor?" "Not that I heard. We had no idea if this was going to go on for a few hours or a day, or maybe even a week. When Tyler and the others disappeared, we began to fear the worst. But then the one guy in charge left the control room and didn't come back for over an hour. After that all the others seemed more upbeat, like they were expecting to get out of there. Murphy and Crosby were cooking up a plan... Sorry, no pun intended. They were planning to rush one of the older guys in the lunchroom, with a pan of hot grease. But they decided against it when it started to look like it might be over soon."

Martin didn't have much to add, except that the one they called Henry was obsessed with beating him at chess. "I could see he was getting pissed about it, so I let him win one game. He seemed to calm down a bit after that. He kept his pistol on the table right next to him. Messed up my concentration, you know? I didn't want to die over a chess game!" According to statements by Murphy and the other hostages the one terrorist left in the building was unlikely to leave the control room. He had to keep an eye out the reactor room window to make sure no one attempted to remove the explosives.

"Just as a point of interest, Mr. Smith, did your vulnerability assessment team ever consider a scenario for L Reactor like the one we've been dealing with for the past twenty-four hours?" Smith never liked being in the EOC. Too many managers way above his pay grade, asking tough questions. "We've analysed hundreds of reactor sabotage scenarios, but I have to admit we've never done one quite like this", Smith replied with a painted smile. "Why the hell not, sir", asked the DOE Site Manager? Metz came to Smith's rescue. "We can still win this", he suggested. "Obviously, this man has a score to settle. He's not like the others. This is personal. He believes there's some sort of justice in blowing up our reactor. We need Abrams to convince him otherwise." Metz looked over to the negotiator's cubicle to discover Abrams had left, probably for home. Another man was sitting there with a questioning look on his face. "We've got to keep him talking. The longer he talks the more the decay heat drops in the reactor core, and the less melting we will have, especially now that we know one of emergency cooling lines will survive the explosives."

Metz had been on the phone getting a fresh set of estimates on how much melting they could expect. "Our best estimate is 10% to 14% melting if we lose three adjacent inlet nozzles and emergency cooling comes in through only one nozzle." "So your estimate has gone up from the numbers you gave us earlier", asked the DOE Site Manager? "Only slightly. There is some uncertainty about how the emergency cooling water will flow across the plenum and down the fuel assemblies." The DOE Site Manager looked confused.

Assault on L

Metz attempted an analogy. "The inlet plenum sitting on top of all the fuel assemblies in the reactor is a lot like the bottom of your grandmother's old metal colander. It's round and flat and full of holes. Imagine water coming in through the side of the colander in only one place. That water will flow across the flat bottom of the colander with some of it going down each of the holes that it comes across. If there is a lot of water, it will make it all the way across the colander to the opposite side. Even the holes on the opposite side will get some water, although not as much as the holes on the side nearest where the water came in. Are you with me so far?" Everyone in the room nodded their heads. Metz smiled. Having an audience in the palm of your hand was very satisfying.

Emergency Cooling Water

"OK, now assume that less water is coming in the side of the colander. This time the water goes down the nearest holes but doesn't make it all the way across to the opposite side. There are some holes on the far side that don't get any water at all. The water's all gone before it gets there. In the case of the emergency cooling water going into L Reactor only through one inlet nozzle, there isn't enough water to make it all the way across to the fuel assemblies on the opposite side of the reactor. Those fuel assemblies won't get any water at all and they will melt. We estimate up to 14% of the fuel assemblies won't get any cooling water and will melt."

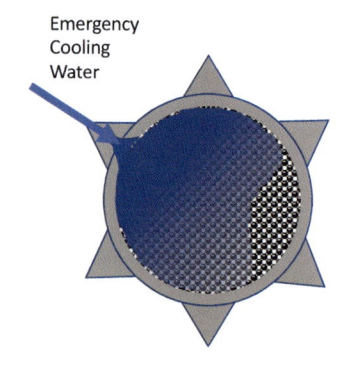

"Also, a lot depends on how hot the fuel gets before the emergency cooling water starts coming in. If the fuel gets too hot the water flowing down some of the fuel assemblies will flash to steam and steam pressure will blow it back out the top of those assemblies. That phenomenon is incredibly difficult to mathematically model." "What's your worst-case estimate, then", The Site Manager asked, with a slight frown. He was clearly struggling to understand the technical details that he had repeatedly asked Metz not to give him. "15%", Metz replied, with no further explanation.

Assault on L

A new group of meteorologists had arrived a few hours earlier. They took center stage now. By scaling the source terms to represent 15% fuel melting they were able to give a new estimate on the spread of radioactive contamination under current weather conditions. "Winds for the next few hours should remain out of the west northwest at 12 to 15 miles per hour. Using the new source terms we will need to evacuate everyone from here to Charleston along a cone that encompasses Barnwell, Fairfax, Ehrhardt, Branchville, St. George, Walterboro, Cottageville, Summerville, Goose Creek, North Charleston, Charleston, Isle of Palms, Johns Island, Folly Beach, Kiawah Island, Edisto Island and Edisto Beach." One of the support staff displayed a chart on one of the seven-foot video screens.

Communities in the Plume

City/Town	Population (1980)
Charleston	93,729
North Charleston	72,547
Mount Pleasant	45,307
Summerville	30,770
Goose Creek	26,621
Johns Island	14,660
Walterboro	6,503
Barnwell	5,940
Bamberg	4,604
Allendale	4,546
Isle of Palms	3,831
Williston	3,656
Edisto	3,046
Fairfax	2,578
Hampton	2,553
Estill	2,549
Folly Beach	2,376
St. George	2,130
Kiawah Island	1,428
Branchville	1,190
Yemassee	1,165
Meggett	1,071
Cottageville	797
Ehrhardt	680
Edisto Beach	422
Sycamore	222
Lodge	125
Ulmer	105
Rural Residents	11,321
Total	**346,473**

The DOE Site Manager's mouth was hanging open. "Jesus Christ", he exclaimed, as he pushed back from the table! His action was clearly a subconscious attempt to escape from the situation he found himself in. On the other hand, he had just realized that his budget problems would be solved if he no longer had to spend huge sums of money fixing all those deficiencies the 'independent experts' had identified in L Area. For a moment he was having mixed emotions. "We've got to talk this guy down", he finally announced. All heads nodded agreement with the obvious. 'It would be far worse if the wind had continued out of the south southeast', thought Metz.

"What about the people in L Area and other site facilities to the southeast", asked Suelle? He was concerned about his men in L Area should there be a release. And the hostages were still in L Area being questioned. Shouldn't they all be evacuated just in case this madman blew up the reactor? It might allow the last of the terrorists to escape but it seemed pretty clear that wasn't his intention. "Yes", get them all out now", replied the Site Manager, with a sudden worried look on his face! The press had already asked repeatedly about casualties. Ten Protective Force personnel had been lost and five more operations staff as well. Losing even more people trying to kill this guy, especially after he detonated his explosives, would look ridiculous. "We'll have to abandon the security barricade at the south end of Highway 125. That might allow unauthorized personnel enter the site", added Suelle. "I'd say you're a bit late in preventing that", Carlton replied, with one raised eyebrow!

Jorge figured it would take the helicopter about eighteen minutes to reach the Augusta Airport on the Georgia side of the river. Another ten minutes to get them off, across the tarmac and onto the Gulfstream. Fifteen minutes more to taxi and take off. That would put them in the air at about 22:50 hours. At the Gulfstream's cruising speed, they should be safely out of U. S. airspace by 23:50. He planned to detonate the explosives at midnight. In the EOC all ears were waiting for another code word that would let the one remaining terrorist in the L Reactor control room know that his comrades were safe. Some still expected him to surrender. Surely, he had achieved all he could hope for. It was time to put an end to this nightmare.

In fact, it only took the helicopter sixteen minutes to reach the Augusta airport. It was only 23 miles if you flew northwest straight across the river. It was a much longer trip by car, as all of the senior managers at the site knew quite well. Augusta airport officials had been warned that a large black helicopter would be landing there sometime before 10:30 pm. No one was to interfere. A freshly fuelled Gulf Steam jet was waiting for them. The helicopter landed on the tarmac at 22:17 hours. All those aboard jumped out of the sliding door and began to run across the tarmac toward the Gulf Stream about 30 meters away. The door on the Gulf Stream was open and the small staircase was down. No one bothered to greet the pilot or ask his nationality. By 22:30 they were all aboard and the stairs had been pulled up.

Their first glimpse of the pilot was when he popped open the rich wood grain door and stuck his head out to inform them of a delay. "The service truck was late. We are still being refuelled. It will be another fifteen minutes before we can take off. There is nothing we can do." He disappeared behind the door again. Anxiety began to build of course. They were supposed to be in the air before 22:40 hours. Everyone who had a watch kept looking at it. They were still safe but the anxiety was building.

"Do you think he'll really do it", asked Samuel? "Blow it up you mean", Henry answered? "Yeah, will he really go through with it?" "I think he will", Henry replied. "For him that's what this was all about. It's why he came to this party."

"I bet he won't", Silas added. "But I don't think they will take him alive." "If they do, he won't rat us out will he", Otis asked? "Never", Henry replied. "But they won't take him alive, so stop worrying!"

Otis sat back in the luxurious seat. "Neat ride though, huh?" Otis felt their accommodations worth a comment, as if no one else had noticed the plush interior of the aircraft. Just as Henry was about to ask, the pilot poked his head through the doorway again. "We are now ready to depart. Please make sure your seatbelts are securely fastened. There will be no food or refreshments served on this flight. We apologize for the inconvenience. We didn't have much time to prepare. He gave a mock salute and disappeared behind the door again. 'Middle eastern', Silas thought. 'Hope his Pilot Cert. is up to date.'

The twelve passenger Gulf Stream GIII began to taxy out to the runway. It took off into a north-westerly wind at 23:05 hours, then banked sharply to head in a south-easterly direction toward the Atlantic. At 23:10 hours an F-16 with the 9th Air Force took off from Shaw Air Force Base just northeast of Sumter, South Carolina. It would stay outside the Gulfstream's commercial radar range. The F-16's radar was much superior, however. The pilot of the F-16 could see them, but they couldn't see him.

Mr. Sangle in the EOC negotiator's cubicle was trying to reach the L Reactor control room every five minutes. The cords for the phone at the Senior Supervisor's desk and the ones in the day supervisor's office and the secretary's office had all been yanked out of the wall. Jorge didn't want to talk to anyone. And he didn't want to take his eyes off the explosives on top of the reactor. "Isn't there another phone in the Crane Control Room where they watch the refuelling operations through the reactor room window", asked Metz? "Yes, there is", Carlton replied. "Tell Sangle to try that number."

The sound of a phone ringing pierced the peaceful silence of the L Reactor control room. Jorge jumped. It was on a small shelf under the console about two feet from him. He could reach it without leaving the reactor room window. But he didn't want to. Sangle waited another five minutes then called again. Still Jorge didn't answer. Another five minutes went by and the phone rang again. Jorge grabbed the cord and was about to give it a hard yank when he suddenly stopped. "Maybe I should say a few parting words to them", he said out loud to no one. He thought it fitting that he answer as Murphy had done. "105 L control room", he said in a calm voice. Sangle suddenly stood up in his cubicle. Everyone knew what that meant.

Captain Lowe had his orders. "Lock it all up, ladies and gentlemen", he shouted as soon as he hung up the phone. "Lock all the turnstiles and lock up all weapons in the safes. We're all getting out of here." He found Murphy, Blythe, Crosby and Martin in one of the side rooms. "When can we go", Blythe asked? She had called her fiancé, but he was still worried. "We're all going, right now", said Lowe. "Everybody!" "Use your personal vehicles if you have one. Anybody that carpooled, find someone with a vehicle and get in it. Everyone drive north to the Main Administration Area. I repeat – no matter where you live or which direction you were planning to head, everyone must drive north." The word went out over every PA system and phone line on the site. All personnel south and southeast of L Area were to evacuate immediately.

Captain Lowe lived in one of the oldest and nicest homes in Barnwell. It belonged to his father, and his grandfather before him. His last act before leaving L Area was to call his wife. "Find the kids and get over to your sister's house in Orangeburg", he said. "In the middle of the night? They're all asleep at this hour", she replied. "Yes, tonight, right now. You have to go now!" "I don't know where they are. It's Saturday night. They don't usually come home 'til 12:30 or 1:00 am." "Do you know where they might be", he asked, sounding a bit out of breath? "What's wrong", she asked? "Can't say. Just find them, throw some stuff in a suitcase and get to Orangeburg as soon as possible. If nothing happens you can all come back home in the morning." "If what happens?" There was no answer. The line was dead. She could sense panic in his voice. He didn't panic easily. She had only seen it happen twice in the twenty-one years they had been married.

Her second phone call found them. "Dad says we have to go now", she insisted. "We'll be home in an hour", her daughter replied. "NO! NOW", she screamed. "OK, Ok." Seventeen is not the age you want your kids to be. When they are fourteen, they listen, most of the time. When they are twenty-two, they listen because their parents have become much smarter in the last few years. When they're seventeen their parents are idiots. She could tell something was terribly wrong. She decided to listen to her idiot mother just this once.

By the time she pulled onto the circular driveway her mother had packed the SUV and was waiting. Both she and her brother wanted to go back in the house to get a few things. "Get in right now", her mother insisted. She looked scared. Suddenly they were scared as well. "Will aunt Beth be up this late", she asked? "Yes, I just woke her up to tell her we were coming", her mother replied. "It's just for the night, Dad says." She looked at her hands on the steering wheel. She had left her diamond wedding ring on the dresser in the bedroom. Oh well, she could get it when they came back home next morning.

Blythe found her car in the parking lot. Crosby got in with her. Captain Lowe had instructed all four of them to report to the Main Administration Area for more interviews with the Federal Bureau of Investigation. Lowe spotted Murphy and Martin headed toward the twelve-passenger van that was assigned to L Area. Day supervision used it frequently to make trips up to their bosses' offices, Monday through Friday. "Hey you guys. You don't need that thing. You can ride with us", yelled Lowe. "No thanks", Murphy yelled back. "We'll be along in a few minutes." Martin was as quiet as usual until Murphy opened up the back of the van and started unlatching the fourth bench seat. "What the hell are we doing", Martin inquired? Murphy had been watching the direction of the wind ever since they had come out of the reactor building. It was steady toward the south east. "We're not sitting for a bunch more interviews with the FBI. We've got something much more important to do." Martin could see there was no point in arguing, especially since he was outranked.

Murphy had seen the look in Jorge's eyes more times than he cared to remember. He had seen it on the battlefield. It was the look of a soldier about to go into combat, when he didn't think he would be coming back. This man wasn't going to back down. He wasn't going to turn himself in.

Assault on L

And Murphy suspected no one had been able to notify the families of Jared or Ferbis that their husbands and fathers weren't coming home. It was a responsibility he felt very personally. And, as if that were not enough, he would need to convince them they had no time to grieve because they had to leave everything they owned behind and evacuate the area immediately. "We have to do something for Ferbis and Jared." Murphy looked at Martin. Martin looked puzzled, then smiled. "Yes", he said with fist pump. "But we have to hurry." They managed to get the fourth seat and the third seat out onto the pavement, where they left them. The two bench seats that remained would be adequate for the task.

Getting from L Area to Ehrhardt wasn't that easy. First you had to travel due east across the site to the Barnwell barricade, then through Snelling and Barnwell, and on about 30 miles down the low country highway. It took the government van about forty-five minutes to get there, breaking he speed limit all the way. Murphy knew where they lived even though he had never been to either address. He dropped Martin off near one address and proceeded to the other. They had rehearsed their lines on the way down. They knew they had to have their story straight. Murphy knocked on the door at the Jared house. The lights were still on. Jared's wife had become worried when her husband didn't come home from work the night before. Where could he have been for the past twenty-four hours? She had called their friends and several hospitals in the area, then the local police. But no one had seen him. Now there was a strange man at the door. What was he doing here at this late hour?

"Mrs. Jared, Hi. My name is Murphy." He showed her his security badge. "I work with your husband in L Area. He's been detained and asked me to let you know. Something's happening at the site and he wants you to go to a hotel in Columbia right away. He will meet you there as soon as he can. OK?" She looked confused. "Yes, Mr. Murphy. I've heard my husband talk about you often. Won't you come in. Where is my husband? Has he been hurt? What's this all about?" "I'm sorry there isn't more time to explain. Your husband asked that you gather as much of the baby's things, clothes and family items as you can. It may be some time before you'll be able to return home. We have a van with lots of room."

"That's most kind of you to offer but why can't he come home? Can't all this wait until he gets here?" "No mam, I'm afraid he won't be coming here. He will meet you in Columbia. It's imperative that we leave right away." She stared at him for a moment, then her expression became pained. There was a tear in her eye. "Yes sir, I'll be right with you. Just give me a few minutes."

Martin had essentially the same conversation at the Ferbis house, only Mrs. Ferbis wasn't convinced she and her three-year-old should get into a van with a stranger in the middle of the night. When Murphy arrived at the Ferbis house, Mrs. Jared immediately got out of the van and went inside. Fifteen minutes later the four of them came out with three suitcases. Martin got in the front seat with Murphy. The two women and their children took the second bench seat. It was fifteen minutes past midnight when they left Ehrhardt. Thanks to one man's twisted desire for revenge, both children would have to grow up without their fathers.

No one said anything for the next half hour. For another hour after that the two women talked softly. Neither Murphy nor Martin could tell what they were saying. The van was noisy and the ride a bit bumpy over the South Carolina back roads. Murphy kept the radio off, in case there was something on the news. They arrived at the Holiday Inn on the west side of Columbia along Interstate 20 around 2:00 am. Everyone had fallen asleep except for Murphy, who was driving. He and Martin helped both women with their luggage. It was obvious they had both been crying.

The hotel clerk was a bit startled to see someone arriving at that hour. It would be morning soon. Checkout time was 11:00 am. It was hardly worth paying for a room for only nine hours. Murphy had a quiet conversation with the clerk while everyone else had a seat in the lobby. When he returned, he knew the moment of truth had arrived. "OK, ladies I've arranged a room for each of you for two weeks." Both ladies just nodded. "And now I have to admit to being a liar. When I told you that your husbands would be joining you here, that was not the truth." He expected both women would react to that statement but neither of them did. Both remained calm and said nothing.

"The truth is", he continued, "both of your husbands were killed by a group of terrorists last evening in L Area. We have brought you here because it is very likely the terrorists will cause a release of radioactivity that will blow toward Ehrhardt. In fact, they may have already done so." Mrs. Ferbis was crying again. Mrs. Jared just looked at Murphy with kind eyes. "My husband used to say to me, 'If there ever comes a time when I cannot be there for you, a man named Murphy will be.'" She put her arms around him and gave him a big hug. It was the greatest compliment he could ever have imagined. "We knew what you were going to tell us the entire way here. And we knew how difficult it would be for you to say it.

We will be fine. I have some cash." Murphy couldn't hold back the tears either. "You won't need it", he said. "Both rooms are paid in full. The United States government owes you both a great deal more than that!"

Assault on L

Chapter 12

Sangle held the phone out in front of him for the DOE Site Manager to take it. He shook his head and pushed the phone back toward Sangle. "This is what I pay you for, OK!" His brow broke out in a sweat! "To whom am I speaking", said Sangle in an unsteady voice. "You know who the hell you're speaking to. Let's not waste each other's time. Am I on speaker?" "Yes, sir you are", Sangle replied, as he switched from his headphones to the PA system in the EOC. "Good", Jorge replied.

"You must have figured out by now there is nothing you can do to stop me from blowing up your nuclear reactor and contaminating at least a portion of your country. You are probably wondering why? It has nothing to do with ideology or politics or revenge by a foreign government. The action I'm taking is not a geopolitical statement. It's a personal one. Americans owe a debt that has not been paid. After tonight you will be able to finally mark that debt 'Paid in Full', even though the payment amounts to only a small fraction of what is owed."

"Americans have historically treated money and human suffering as commodities that can be exchanged, one for the other. The American government gave great sums of money to help rebuild Japan after the war; but, with exception of those who fought in the war, Americans never suffered in any real sense. Thousands of Americans were not treated for burns or radiation poisoning. In fact, the mainland of America has never even been bombed. The American approach to human suffering is to throw lots of money at the problem and then claim to be the moral leaders of the western world. The weapons used to destroy Hiroshima and Nagasaki in 1945 killed more human beings in a fraction of a second than had ever been possible before. That can hardly be considered moral leadership."

"My actions tonight will not directly kill more Americans, beyond those who died here in the last twenty-four hours. But it will inconvenience a lot of people in this country. Many will be worried and will have to make decisions more difficult than they ever imagined. I'm sure your government will be able to spend lots of money on mitigation, but people's lives will be disrupted. Thousands won't be killed in a fraction of a second, but millions will have their lives disrupted for years to come. That is my legacy and my price for marking your account 'Paid in Full'."

About half the people in the EOC felt a chill run up their spine, as they realized they had families or close friends living in an area about to become a disaster zone. Each began calling to warn as many as they could. Maybe this guy was bluffing. But most likely he wasn't. At least they could give people a head start. A communications specialist on duty and one of the meteorologists in the room realized they might not see their homes again for months, or maybe years. "All right people", announced the Assistant Site Manager. "Let your families know. Then it's back to work. There's nearly fifty communities plus over a dozen State officials we have to notify. Tell them a call for immediate evacuation of their populations is imminent, but not confirmed. We will notify them as soon as we know which way this thing is going to go. Now let's get with it, people!"

"Shaw, this is 'Flycatcher'. I have visual, turning southwest now toward Mexican air space. No surface vessels or other aircraft in the area."

"Roger, 'Flycatcher'." "Permission to arm the weapon?" "Permission granted." He estimated they were about 130 miles off the western coast of Florida, as he flipped the arming switch on one of his Sidewinder missiles.

The pilot of the Gulfstream noticed another aircraft had appeared on his radar, directly behind him. "Shaw, this is 'Flycatcher'. Request authorization to launch the weapon?" There was a slight pause.

"'Flycatcher', you are authorized to launch the weapon. Take the shot Colonel!"

The F-16 shuddered slightly as the Raytheon AIM-9 Sidewinder left its cradle under the left wing. All aboard the Gulfstream were asleep, except for the pilot. They died dreaming of how they were going to spend their twenty-five million.

Jorge hung up the phone, then ripped out the cord. His watch read 11:45 hours. The L Reactor control room was unbelievably quiet again. With

Assault on L

more than twenty feet of concrete between him and the outside world, no natural sounds or even man-made ones could leak in. One annunciator alarm broke the silence. Jorge walked across the control room and smashed the small square box on the annunciator panel with the butt of his M-16. All was quiet again. He quickly returned to the window looking out onto the top of the reactor.

This was the hardest time for him. He had spent days all alone before. He could deal with it, but he wouldn't say he enjoyed it. All around the world people were estimating their life expectancies in decades or years. If they were in the hospital, maybe it was days or hours. One way or the other his could be counted in minutes. He figured he had about fourteen of them left.

It never occurred to him before to burden other people with his personal opinions. One was that snipers were the unsung heroes of the battlefield. They always worked alone, sometimes waiting for hours or even days to get the right shot. And they often made the critical difference between success or failure of the mission. It's one thing to charge a fortified position firing your weapon indiscriminately just to keep the opposing forces from poking their heads up. It's quite another to see a man's, or woman's, head in the cross hairs of your scope. The combat experience was much more personal for a sniper. Rarely did they get to see the bullet hit its target. At a distance of 1000 meters the bullet takes almost a full second to arrive. During that time, you usually have to start moving towards your next position.

Not all of his hits had been headshots. And not all of his targets had been wearing uniforms. Some were considered 'diplomats', although they probably couldn't spell the word, much less define it. They were dressed in crisp white jackets adorned with ribbons and metals to advertise their achievements or their elevated positions in the government. Powerful people didn't carry sceptres anymore. They wore their symbols of authority on their breast pocket. It was risky to stay in place and watch the hit. But on those two occasions it was worth it. The scope on a sniper's rifle gave you a view that no one else could share. It was your reward for patience and perseverance. It was such a rush, like when a roller coaster tops out and begins to accelerate in a downward spiral. A small red spot that began to grow bigger and bigger on the chest of the white jacket. The startled look on the target's face the moment they realized what was happening. Acceptance of the fact that they would soon be dead. Now he knew how they felt.

Another thing that didn't make sense to Jorge was how in the middle ages kings would lead their armies as they charged an opposing force. Of course, it inspired their men to fight with great courage. But they were foolish to take such a tremendous personal risk. In 1485 Henry Tudor's victory at the Battle of Bosworth Field over Richard III changed England for the next 500 years. Had Richard behaved in a less cavalier manner, he might not have lost the battle or the throne. In 1743 George II became the last British King to lead his men into battle at Dettingen. It took 250 years for political leaders to realize putting yourself out in front is a reckless thing to do. After another 250 years it was obvious that lesson had been forgotten in the middle eastern countries of the world. A sniper could take full advantage of their stupidity at every opportunity. Jorge had personally taken out four platoon commanders that way.

Why weren't snipers respected for their skills? It took weeks and weeks of practice to be able to hit a silver dollar at a distance of 2000 meters. You had to compensate for the wind and the air temperature. And of course, the weapon had to be maintained like the surgical instrument that it was. There were so many factors to take into account. Soldiers returning from battle always got a warm reception from the public. They were a band of heroes. Somehow a sniper was something less. Something sinister. As if sniping was taking unfair advantage, or against the rules of combat. The truth was there were no rules of combat. It was survival and winning, by any means possible. Why did the public not see that?

During the American Revolution in 1775 British soldiers wore bright red uniforms and marched in straight lines. That was how it was done in Europe. The rebels fighting for the right to create a new country saw that as foolish. They wore green and brown clothing for camouflage and ambushed the British from behind trees and rocks. There were many reasons why the rebels won the War of Independence, but not playing by the rules was one of them. As far as Jorge was concerned there were no rules: not in combat, and not in L Reactor tonight. The result was all that mattered.

There had been other 'nuclear accidents' but none of them had released enough radioactive contamination to require a response anything like what happened in Hiroshima and Nagasaki. The experience of the Japanese people was unique in all the world. For Americans, only the 1979 loss of coolant and partial core meltdown of a reactor at Three Mile Island in Pennsylvania even came close. The amount of contamination released was very low. The average local radiation exposure was equivalent to a chest x-ray. The maximum local exposure was equivalent to a year's background radiation. The number of excess cancer deaths in the area was estimated to be negligible. Tonight would change all that. Tonight all the sanctimonious politicians and bureaucrats in the American government would discover that they weren't as clever as they thought. That they weren't as prepared as they thought. That they weren't as resourceful as the Japanese people had been in the face of a disaster they thought to be impossible.

Seconds after he pushed the little red button on the brown plastic box in his pocket, they would be coming through the door firing their M-16s in all directions. They were probably staged just down the hallway right now. At least his death would be quick, unless of course they were incredibly poor shots. Only a handful of people knew his name at this moment. In less than an hour the whole world would know his name. It was the only form of immortality he admired. People who had given their life for a reason. The Egyptian Pharaohs had their pyramids. His tomb would be an even larger structure, strangely similar to the pyramids in a way. The Egyptians didn't have concrete of course. If they had, maybe the tombs of the Pharaohs would have looked something like the building he was going to die in.

On the other hand, if they didn't come fairly soon, he would have to do it himself. He had contemplated eating his Glock 19 several times. This time he would actually have to do it! Jorge's grandmother had never shown him photographs of Nagasaki and Hiroshima and the people who lived there. She had them. He was sure of it. When he was in his teens, he had seen pictures on the news and in magazines on occasion. He couldn't imagine why they were published. They were too horrible to look at.

The only thing that gave him pause was the fact that these people in South Carolina and Georgia, and maybe further away than that, had done him no harm. They had done his grandmother no harm. They had done the Japanese people no harm that he was aware of. The people who operated this reactor and others at the Savannah River Site didn't make the material that was used in Fat Man and Little Boy. This entire complex wasn't built until a decade later.

But he wasn't killing tens of thousands of Americans in a mere fraction of a second. There would be some deaths from latent cancers and other indirect effects. But no one was going to be incinerated in blinding flash of light. What these people in South Carolina and Georgia, and perhaps beyond, would suffer is inconvenience. For some it would mean serious inconvenience, like losing their homes and possessions. Their families would have to move somewhere else and find new jobs and new friends. And there would be a cost. He hoped the cost to the State and Federal governments would be nearly as much as they had spent in reparations to the Japanese Islands after the war. These things seemed to him a fair compensation. And people would remember him for it. Kindly or unkindly, they would remember him.

Sometimes a bit of information can be priceless. Had he known the whole of L area had been abandoned, Jorge could have walked right out of the control room, down the stairs, and out the main personnel entrance of the building. He could have climbed over the double fence, walked back around L Lake and made it back to South Carolina Highway 125 in less than ninety minutes. It would have been easy to catch a ride to the southern security barricade where surprisingly there would be no security guards to ask any questions. Once off the site he could have gone anywhere in the world he wanted, at least until Interpol caught up with him. But then his grandmother, looking down from above, might never have forgiven him for not going through with it.

The midnight hour had arrived. Jorge had to assume the Gulf Stream was safely on its way and out of United States air space by now. He took the small brown plastic box out of his pocket and placed it on the table. He didn't expect to hear anything through the three feet of lead glass and oil. Would he get to watch for a minute or two before they came rushing in with weapons firing? Would they run out of the building instead hoping to escape from the spreading contamination? Which way was the wind blowing? He had no idea. He slammed his fist down onto the small red button, quickly before he changed his mind.

As he suspected there was no sound, only a slight shuddering through the thick concrete walls of the building. It was difficult to see. A piece of metal hit the window with a muted thud. It put a crack in the outside pane, but he could still see through it. Pillars of smoke from the explosions hung in the air like ghostly figures. Water was gushing out onto the floor. Then steam mixed with hot water began to spray out of the open fissures. Jorge realized no one was going to come and save him. He shoved the barrel of his Glock 19 past his tongue until he could feel the cold steel against the back of his throat. Then he pulled the trigger. Jorge must have realized at the last second that his body would be almost completely decomposed before anyone re-entered the L Reactor building to find it slumped over the railing in front of a completely opaque reactor room window. No pictures would ever be published.

"Mexico City International Airport reports a Gulf Steam GIII out of Augusta, Georgia is late arriving. According to their flight plan, it should have landed there two hours ago", a Federal Aviation Administration operator in Jacksonville, Florida announced.

His supervisor looked at his notes for the midnight to 8:00 am shift. Then he found it near the bottom. "Tell them we will begin a preliminary investigation. We'll handle it from here. They can strike that one off their list", replied his supervisor.

The FAA operator looked confused. His supervisor smiled. "After you've been in this job for a while, you'll learn that the 'Rich and Famous' don't always go where their flight plan says. It's the only way they can get away from the press and the paparazzi. That Gulf Stream may have gone anywhere within 3,500 miles. Don't give it another thought, OK?"

Assault on L

Chapter 13

The DOE Site Manager and all the others in the EOC had to wait as Sangle tried in vain to re-establish contact with the control room. Would there be no opportunity to reason with this man, no chance to talk him down? They had to assume the worst.

Someone was due to brief the press at midnight. No one volunteered. No one had even a clue what to tell them. "Go tell them we need a half hour delay", bellowed the DOE Site Manager. He was physically tired and mentally exhausted. He could no longer distinguish between the two. "That won't be long enough", said Metz, who was barely able to keep his eyes focused on the status boards. "It will have to be", the Site Manager replied. "Metz, you're up!"

He was just about to leave for the press briefing room when a call came in from the reactor remote operations center. "We're receiving multiple high radiation alarms from monitors all around the south east side of L Area. If the release is occurring at the plus 55 roof level, that means most of it is passing over the ground level monitors nearby. So actual releases are probably ten-fold what we are seeing."

Metz looked at his watch. It was 12:35 am. Fortunately, he didn't have a printed press release for them, because he couldn't have read it.

"Ladies and gentlemen, I have good news and bad news to report. The good news is that the hostage situation in L Reactor has been resolved with no further casualties. The bad news is that there has been some damage to the reactor. We are monitoring a small release of radioactive contamination from the reactor building at this time. There is no cause for alarm and the public is in no danger at the moment. We will keep you advised if there are any changes to this situation."

"Should some of the communities around the site be prepared to evacuate?" "It's too early to tell if there will be a need to evacuate areas outside the site boundary, but it is possible, yes."

Assault on L

Fifty hands shot into the air. Metz's knees folded under him. He grabbed one side of the podium to keep from falling. "I'm sorry ladies and gentlemen. We will have to continue this briefing in half an hour", said the DOE Public Relations specialist who had just arrived an hour earlier. It was nearly 1:00 am on a Sunday morning. All anybody wanted to do was go home and go to bed!

It was nearly 5:00 am before anyone could estimate the extent of the release. Representatives of the press had given up and gone home. The EOC was full of new faces. The other Assistant Site Manager was in charge. He was thinking he'd missed all the fun, but he soon discovered otherwise. Helicopter flyovers on the northwest (upwind) side of L Area estimated the radiation levels around the reactor building to be as high as 1000 rads/hr. Smoke could be seen coming out of the ruptured ducts between the filter compartments and the concrete building. The radiation level on the roof could only be guessed at, but some estimates put it as high as 4,000 rads/hr.

Someone suggested spraying or dumping some sort of sealant onto the ruptured ducts, but that would require getting much closer than anyone dared, even in a helicopter. Steam could be seen coming out as well. That meant the pressure inside the reactor room must be well above the outside atmosphere. That pressure would simply blow the sealant away as soon as it was applied.

Metz had gone home to bed. Sanders had taken his place in the EOC. "What's your best estimate of the core damage in the reactor", asked the Assistant Site Manager? "I just received latest numbers", Sanders replied. "They think about 20% of the core has melted, or has gotten hot enough that fission products are diffusing through the semi-molten aluminium cladding on the some of the fuel assemblies. Emergency cooling water continues to flow out into the half million-gallon containment basin. We have to assume that most of it is going through the reactor. Otherwise the entire core would be molten by now. All of that water has been filling up the 50,000-gallon tank we installed during the L Reactor restart upgrades, but it will overflow into the open basin in another 12 hours. At that point we will have to add tritium and radioiodine evaporation to the overall release term. Looks like that might be trivial compared to what is coming out of the roof."

Next it was the Emergency Operations Director's turn. "Communities to the southeast of the site began evacuation of all residents at 2:00 am this morning. That action is still in progress, especially in Allendale, Fairfax,

Hampton, and Ehrhardt. Winds are blowing the plume southeast at 6 to 8 miles per hour, but they will likely pick up again by early morning. Monitors in Ehrhardt were showing elevated radiation readings at approximately twenty-five times normal background at 4:30 am. As you can imagine the public was not happy about sirens going off at 2:00 am in the morning. They were told they had fifteen minutes to gather up what they could carry, throw it in the trunks of their cars or trucks and leave the area as fast as possible. Police are still active in getting people out in all areas except Martin. Even the police have abandoned that community."

"As you know we've done these drills before, but never had people actually on the roads. Most of the coastal roads are not major highways. It may take some time to get everyone out of the path of the plume." "It's a miracle the winds are not out of the southeast like early yesterday", said the Assistant Site Manager. "Yes sir. If the winds were out of the southeast, we wouldn't be sitting here!" "We'd be in Augusta", asked Suelle? The meteorologist shook his head. 'And I would be out $1000 for two tickets to the Masters on the 14th of next month', thought the Assistant Site Manager. This was the first year in the past ten he had been able to get Masters Golf Tournament tickets for Sunday.

Augusta, Georgia was, of course, well known as the home of the Masters Golf Tournament, held there each spring. A much larger city than Aiken, it still offered a number of scenic venues for those who wanted a 'peaceful life in the deep south'. The Savannah River formed the south-eastern boundary of the city, and of the State of Georgia. North Augusta was a small community on the South Carolina side of the river. It offered more affordable housing, and a two percent lower sales tax. "Masters Week, as the locals called it, was the busiest week of the year in Augusta. If you lived there, you left town that week if you could. Renting your house out to a famous golfer for the week could easily net you enough for a first-class holiday almost anywhere you wanted to go.

But there was another reason for leaving. Traffic! The population of Augusta roughly doubled for one week a year. All the hotels were packed full, having settled for about 30% occupancy the other 51 weeks of the year. Getting into a restaurant was nearly impossible that week as well. If you did stay in town it was worth taking the kids for a short drive out to the Augusta Airport sometime during the week. There they would see one of the largest collections of private planes, including Gulfstream Jets, Cessna single and twin engines, Beechcraft and many others. Augusta seemed to attract at least one or two private jets on any given week during the rest of the year as well.

Assault on I

Evacuation of large populations is difficult in the daytime. It was much worse in the darkness. There was no moon to give even the slightest illumination. Most people found they had enough gas in their cars or trucks to get them away from danger under normal circumstances. Although it wouldn't be hurricane season for another three months, most people made a habit of keeping their gas tank at least half full. Those who hadn't soon discovered all the gas stations were closed at 3:00 am, except maybe a few in Charleston. Local, State and Federal Emergency Management organizations were accustomed to having several days to prepare for an evacuation. This time they only had a few hours at best. It simply wasn't enough time.

In addition to the local population, others had to be warned to stay away from the affected area. The Federal Aviation Administration put out warnings to all airports and airlines to avoid the airspace above southern South Carolina. This impacted a large number of flights out of Hartsfield Jackson International Airport in Atlanta. Even though contamination was not detected above 20,000 feet, no one wanted the inconvenience and expense of having to decontaminate their planes. There were also ships off the South Carolina coast that had to be warned to leave the area, at least temporarily until comprehensive surveys had been completed to determine how far into the Atlantic the plume reached.

Local, State and Federal officials quickly found they were duplicating each other's efforts, even though they had supposedly practiced this sort of thing many times. Police realized they would have to go door to door in some communities. Those with impaired hearing took their hearing aids out at night when they were asleep, so they didn't hear the sirens. Some communities didn't have sirens, or the sirens didn't work due to lack of maintenance. More than a hour after evacuations began, local law enforcement was still finding groups of people in churches who had decided God would protect them from danger. And of course, there were those who insisted on 'riding this one out'. It was hard to convince them that 'riding this one out' wasn't possible. The danger wasn't going to pass over them in a day or two. It was going to stay, for weeks or months. Nobody knew how long it would be.

Dawn found huge traffic jams on US Highway 17 in both directions. A helicopter flyover of Sycamore at 5000 feet showed no activity in the streets or surrounding areas at 6:00 am. Evacuations were never expected to be 100% effective, but it did look like almost everyone had gotten out.

Assault on L

Contamination seemed to be confined below 3000 feet altitude, but this was only fifteen miles from L Area and on the edge of the plume. Further downwind the plume would likely reach much higher, requiring the use of specially equipped helicopters brought in by Federal Emergency Management.

Another press briefing had been scheduled for 6:00 am. Representatives from the national media were there as well as local press. The room held seats for one hundred. On this occasion many had to stand.

"Mr. Sanders, have all the terrorists been killed?" "Yes", he replied. "All of them?" "Yes, all of them." "How many were there?" "There were seven in the building." "Who were they?" "We don't have the names at this time. The FBI will be providing that information as soon as possible."

"What organization or 'cause' did they represent?" "We were not able to determine their affiliation or motives." "Why won't you tell us about their demands? What did they want?"

"I am still not able to discuss that topic with you. That information may become available at a later time."

"How many casualties did you suffer in taking them out?"

"Our Protective Force lost ten men. Five operations people lost their lives as well."

"Were they killed by the terrorists?"

"Yes."

"We've heard there is smoke coming out of the reactor building. Is the reactor on fire?

Is the building on fire?

What is it that's burning?"

"Nothing in the building is burning. Water and stainless steel don't burn. Some very fine particulates are being carried in the air leaving the building. They appear as smoke when viewed from a distance." That statement wasn't completely true. Uranium can burn in a technical sense if it gets hot enough. No one really knew how hot the reactor core might get in this situation.

"What damage did they do to the reactor?" "We cannot enter the building at this time to survey the damage. We believe they were able to rupture some of our cooling water piping. As a result, some of the reactor core has been damaged, releasing a small amount of radioactivity. That has resulted in the need to evacuate some communities to the southeast of the facility, at least temporarily."

"How many communities have been evacuated?" "We will have that list for you a bit later this morning."

"How many people have been affected by the evacuation order?" "Again, we will have that list for you shortly."

"Can you tell us the radiation levels in the communities that have been evacuated?" "We will be conducting aerial surveys throughout the day. That data will be reported to you as we have it. The levels are significantly above background levels. That is why we asked for the evacuations, as a precaution."

"Is there anyone in L Area now?"

"No, L Area has been evacuated."

"How long before you can go into the L Reactor building and look at the damage?"

"It may be months before that is possible." 'Or years', Sanders was thinking.

"Is there anything in L Area that needs attending to?"

"Yes, we will need to top up the water levels in the spent fuel storage basin periodically, but we have ways of doing that." 'We'll have to find a way', he worried.

"How can we get the names of the terrorists? What made them do this? Who were these people?"

"I'm sorry, you'll have to ask the FBI for that information."

Sanders looked at the DOE Public Relations representative. "I'm sorry ladies and gentlemen. That is all we have time for. There will be another briefing at 10:00 am this morning."

Sanders fell back into his chair in the EOC with newfound respect for his boss. Metz had warned him it would be tough. 'I think I don't want his job after all', Sanders mumbled to himself. The Assistant Site Manager had just called for a meteorological update. "No change in wind direction, but winds are up to 10 miles an hour." "Those people in Allendale better hurry up", said Sanders, suddenly realizing that he said that out loud. "Excuse me, Mr. Sanders?" "Sorry sir. I just meant that it's going to get worse. As the winds pick up they will aspirate more of the contaminated air out of the building. The release is going to get worse rather than better." Everyone looked at him, then rocked back in their chairs. This whole thing was far from over. Very far!

By 8:30 am the EOC had finally managed to establish communications link up with local law enforcement in Allendale, Fairfax, Brunson, Hampton, Varnville, Ulmer, Sycamore, Islandton, Ashton, Erhardt, and Lodge. The South Carolina State Police and Highway Patrol were tied in as well. Suddenly there was so much information it was impossible to follow who was doing what.

People in the EOC began to realize they were no longer in charge of anything. They had become observers at best, and irrelevant at worst. There were so many people on the roads that in most places no one was going anywhere fast. Adding to the confusion were the residents of North Charleston and Charleston, 104 miles southeast of L Area, who had seen the early news and had begun fleeing toward either Savannah or Myrtle Beach.

The Charleston metropolitan area was accustomed to evacuations caused by approaching hurricanes. There were defined evacuation routes that took people away from the coast, and even plans for switching major highways to 'both lanes going north' when necessary. In this case, however, those routes were useless. People needed to go east or west along the coast. Those roads were woefully inadequate for moving nearly 350,000 people out of harm's way in a matter of hours.

Local communities within 20 miles of the site maintained a supply of potassium iodide tablets as a precaution against an accidental release of the fission product Iodine 131. Most of these supplies were found to be considerably older than the recommended shelf life of six years.

Nevertheless, these were being distributed by local law enforcement where possible. Areas further south didn't have such supplies, and there were no pharmacies open at 3:00 am on a Sunday morning. Iodine 131 has a short half-life of only 8.5 days, but if inhaled it concentrates in the thyroid gland, resulting in prolonged radiation exposure. Potassium iodide saturates the thyroid reducing the amount of time radioiodine stays in the body. Radioiodine also deposits on grass in fields, where it is eaten by grazing cows. That meant that all milk produced in the area of the plume would be unfit for human consumption for several months and would have to be destroyed.

Carol and Pat were in their early sixties, but still managed to keep their small farm near Walterboro going. There were a dozen chickens and a large vegetable garden to tend. Each Wednesday they would take the eggs and surplus vegetables to the local market and sell them for enough cash to pay the electric bill and buy gas for their truck. They also had a blue 1981 Ford Escort which they only drove about once every two weeks. For reasons Pat could never quite explain to Carol's satisfaction, he kept the Escort gas tank full. Just in case.

It was a friend of Carol's who lived in Charleston that woke them at 3:10 am that Sunday morning. "I have insomnia, you know? So, I was watching CNN Headline News and they suddenly began announcing evacuations in South Carolina. Something's happened at the 'bomb plant' up there. They're telling everyone to go to Savannah or Myrtle Beach; like immediately. Just throw something in a suitcase and go. It'll probably only be for a couple days, but you gotta go NOW!"

Pat pulled on his coveralls and Carol threw on a dress. No time for makeup. She swiped all her cosmetics off the dresser and into an oversized handbag. She would put it on later. Pat went out to the hen house, unlocked the gate and left it open. He didn't know when he would be back so the chickens would have to fend for themselves in the field. Despite not having been driven for almost two weeks, the Ford Escort started on the first try. It was only half a mile down the gravel road to a paved road. They turned onto it and soon passed the Faith Baptist Church on their left. Another mile and a half and they were on the access ramp to Interstate 95 going south.

It seemed unusually busy for 4:00 am. But the traffic was moving at a normal 65 miles an hour. It normally took them about an hour to drive to Savannah, but it was nearly two hours this Sunday morning. Traffic started getting congested about ten miles out of the city. They were hoping to find a hotel room in Savannah for a few days until this whole thing blew over. After trying a number of places, it became obvious they had arrived too late. Every room in Savannah was already taken. "We'll have to go to Atlanta", Carol suggested. Pat nodded.

It was 148 miles on Interstate 16 to Macon, then another 72 miles on Interstate 75 to Atlanta. They reached the Atlanta Airport around noon. "What are you doing", asked Carol? "We're not flying anywhere, are we?" "No, no. I just want to use their phones. You know, the ones that let you talk to all the hotels with no charge." "We're paying $8 in the parking garage just so you can use the phones?" "Trust me, Carol. Atlanta is very big place. It will be worth it." The first eight hotels he called were already full for that night. Obviously, there had been a surge in bookings as soon as people saw the news on CNN that morning. On the ninth call he got lucky.

"Come on. We've got a room." "Where", said Carol, always the sceptic? "At the Airport Hilton", he replied. "It's only as short distance from here." "The Hilton! Your rich uncle Carl in Dallas is the only one that can afford to stay at the Hilton! It's cost us a fortune." "It's only for a couple of nights. So we'll run up a bill on our credit card. We hardly ever use the silly thing. Let's live a little for a change, OK?" She wasn't sure this was a good idea. There was still a frown on her face. "Come on, it'll be fun! We need to get the car washed on the way."

The 'Marketplace' right in the middle of downtown Charleston was always busy on a Sunday morning. Three full city blocks of tented stalls, with local people selling everything from baskets made from local palmetto palms, to T-shirts with any slogan one could image, to jewellery and trinkets of all descriptions. But this was no ordinary Sunday. Word had gone out and people were scared. By noon officials had already started to measure readings two- or three-times normal background levels. Many had left the city and were attempting to take US Highway 17 to get away from the plume, either south to Savannah or north to Myrtle Beach. It was gridlock in both directions.

Others had decided to close all their windows and doors and shelter in place. Law enforcement had warned these people they might have to abandon their homes later when radiation levels were higher. But just like during hurricanes there would always be some who were convinced they were better off staying put. They were sure they could put up with anything for a couple of days.

Assault on L

Survey teams had little problem getting into the Charleston area. All the traffic was going the other way. Once they were in the city, they found the streets empty. It was an eerie sight. Like something out of a disaster movie. Except this was no movie!

Most of the people in the EOC at the Savannah River Site and gone home to watch it on CNN. A few were still there. They were getting hourly reports from survey crews, state and local law enforcement about radiation levels and conditions on the ground in most of the communities south east of L Reactor.

The Federal Government was sending additional resources to help the State of South Carolina deal with the situation. It soon became clear that the States of Georgia, Florida, North Carolina and even Tennessee were being flooded with refugees, as more than 250,000 citizens spread out over the south-eastern United States looking for accommodations. All of them expected it would only be for a few days, like during a hurricane. None suspected how long it would be before they could return to their homes and communities.

Carol had to admit the room at the Airport Hilton in Atlanta was lovely. And expensive! But it was better than the alternative of sleeping in the car for the next several days. Their suite had the biggest bathtub she had ever seen. Pat called his uncle Carl in Dallas to let him know they had been evacuated. "Yeah", said Carl. "I saw it on the news. You can always come here for a while if it gets too bad." Pat couldn't imagine leaving the farm in Walterboro for very long. There was too much to do there. And he would never think of taking a handout from his uncle anyway. "It'll only be a few days", he replied. "Thanks for the offer."

"A section of the hallway on the fourth floor formed a mezzanine that looked out over the vast lobby and breakfast area of the hotel. By 8:00 am Monday morning they were starving. The breakfast buffet offered a variety of meats and egg dishes, as well as fresh fruit and hot or cold cereals of all descriptions. Both went back for seconds, then ventured down the stairs and out the revolving door in the rear to the lot where the blue Escort was parked. A leisurely walk around the local area and back to the front of the hotel almost made them forget why they were there. Walterboro seemed far far away.

Once back in their room Carol discovered CNN was reporting on the evacuation and the terrorists who made it necessary. The Federal Bureau of Investigation was speculating about who these people were and what they might have hoped to accomplish by taking over L Reactor. "While none of the individuals have been identified we suspect they were part of a geopolitical organization and wanted to make a statement of some sort. Unfortunately, they inadvertently caused damage to the reactor before making their demands known."

"If they were killed, then you have their bodies. Isn't that correct? You must have photographs that can be compared to those in your own database and others like Interpol." "Yes, and that information is obviously part of the investigation, which is being conducted as we speak. I'm sure the Bureau will release that information once the investigation is completed. As you know, the Bureau is not allowed to comment about ongoing investigations."

The CNN reporter quickly switched to a map showing the areas of South Carolina being affected by the plume of radioactivity. "My God", Carol gasped! The area being evacuated was much larger than either of them had realized. Next on the screen were still photographs and some video of the streets in Charleston. The 'Market' had been abandoned. Stalls were still full of merchandise. Tent flaps were moving back and forth in the light breeze. It looked as though all human life there had instantly vanished without a trace. Another video showed areas along the edge of the sea. The parks were there with their Civil War canons, huge oak trees and fresh green lawns.

All the old colonial style homes with rainbow pastel exteriors stood silently in a row along the street. There were no people. All the parking lots were empty as well. Another video of Fort Sumpter showed the island completely deserted, as though it was just a page in a history book. Charleston had been evacuated before, sort of. Every few years a hurricane would take aim at the city and most of the residents would leave as a precaution, but this looked different somehow. Carol began to cry. Pat tried to comfort her, but there was a tear in his eye as well. He began to wonder if they would be left with nothing more than memories of their favorite Great City of the South.

For the few souls still manning the EOC there was good news and bad news again. A helicopter survey of the 50-million-gallon earthen basin in L Area measured lower radiation levels than expected. Apparently, the half million-gallon tank had done a good job of containing the tritium and soluble fission products in the heavy water and initial emergency cooling water. As the tank overflowed and the earthen basin began to fill, the evaporation and diffusion of radioiodine and other radioisotopes from the water into the air above the basin was decreasing. Calculations indicated the releases from the basin would have been significant in isolation, but they added a negligible amount to the much larger release coming from the reactor building roof.

The bad news was that the smoke observed coming from the reactor building roof had increased roughly two-fold. The wind remained out of the north west but had increased to 10 to 12 miles per hour by noon on Sunday. This enhanced the aspiration from the building, which was already at slightly higher pressure than outside. Radiation levels around the reactor building had increased to 1,200 rads/hr.

State agencies began radiation surveys using specially equipped helicopters around 11:00 am on Sunday morning. The EOC could expect data on radiation levels in Barnwell, Ehrhardt and Charleston at 6:00 am, noon, and 6:00 pm each day. The survey at noon on Sunday showed radiation readings of 100 times normal background in Barnwell, 20 times normal background in Ehrhardt, and three times normal background in Charleston, where evacuation efforts were agonizing slow.

"Those will be going up", said the Assistant Emergency Management Director for the site. "Anyone around any hotspots in the Barnwell area may begin to experience some mild symptoms of radiation sickness in the next few weeks. Those in Ehrhardt have a few more hours at best. They need to all be out before dawn tomorrow." "We're going to have increased levels of cancer in these areas for decades to come", added the representative from the site's Medical Department. His comment won him the honor of holding the next press briefing at 2:00 pm.

Dr. Shielly entered the briefing room with some trepidation. He was pleasantly surprised to find only three reporters in attendance. It was almost laughable – this huge room with 100 chairs and only three people sitting there. Apparently, the news media had become much more interested in the evacuation of Charleston, relying on local reporters in the Charleston area and an occasional helicopter view of highways choked with cars and trucks going about five miles per hour at best. "Can you give us the latest radiation data from your aerial surveys please", one reporter asked? The doctor just happened to have those figures hot off one of the seven-foot-tall display screens.

The reporter took down the figures, but appeared puzzled about what they meant. Obviously, he had been instructed to ask that question without knowing what to do with the data once he had it. Dr. Shielly made the mistake of volunteering to help him understand the numbers. "Barnwell has been evacuated. However, if someone were there, over time they would receive a sufficient radiation dose that they would likely become ill. Their risk of having cancer in the next decade or two would go up significantly compared to the normal population. Their chance of dying from that radiation exposure would be about 3%." "You mean 3% of the population of Barnwell is going to die", asked the reporter? "No, no", replied the doctor. He suddenly remembered the old adage. 'When you're in a hole, stop digging!'

By 6:00 am on Monday the radiation levels had risen as predicted. Barnwell was up to 120 times normal background, Ehrhardt was at 30 times normal background, and Charleston was 10 times normal background. Everyone willing to leave the Ehrhardt area had left. Charleston was still struggling, however, and they were running out of time. No one expected Charleston would see radiation levels as high as Ehrhardt or Barnwell, but they might get high enough to substantially increase the risk of cancer for those who couldn't or wouldn't leave. Local law enforcement and State Police were doing everything they could to keep things moving. By early Monday morning they estimated 25% of the metropolitan population still had not been able to leave the area.

Carol and Pat began to realize things in Walterboro won't going to get back to normal anytime soon. CNN was reporting rising radiation levels at noon on Monday. Pat was worried about his vegetable garden. Everything would be contaminated and unsellable whenever he got back there. The chickens would survive, of course, but their eggs would be unsafe to eat, maybe for weeks. How would he know when they were safe? He didn't have a Geiger counter, or whatever they used these days to check for radioactive contamination. His world was suddenly upside down, and he had no idea how to right it. All he could do was not let Carol know he was worried, and that wouldn't be easy!

In the case of a hurricane very sturdy structures with floors well above ground level can be used as shelters for those who can't evacuate. Charleston was no stranger to large scale evacuations. A large number of buildings were designated as storm shelters. In this instance, there were no safe shelters. Everyone had to leave. For the nine hospitals in the Charleston area that was a problem. Roper, Bon Secours St. Francis, Pinehaven, Vibra, Apollo and several Veterans Administration hospitals had to get all their patients to safety in a very short period of time. There weren't nearly enough ambulances and the roads leading toward Savannah and Myrtle Beach were already choked with vehicles. Even with their sirens blaring there would be no way for them to get through. Some might be airlifted but only a very few.

The myriad of small islands in the Charleston area was another problem. There were few roads off the islands, in fact none at all in some cases. Those who could make it to land in boats had no vehicles once they were ashore. People with larger boats would have to head out to sea, then head either northeast or southwest at whatever speed they could manage. There would be little spare moorage in either Savannah or Myrtle Beach, so they would have to travel further along the coast to find refuge. At least they could escape the plume of radioactivity rather than being stuck on US Highway 17.

CNN reported on Monday afternoon that traffic was moving again toward Myrtle Beach, following an accident caused by someone trying to drive around the queue on the right shoulder. A bridge abutment suddenly blocked their progress. Their last second attempt to merge back in resulted in a seven-vehicle pileup. It took about 90 minutes for the ambulance to reach the victims. "This is ridiculous", Carol felt compelled to comment! Another news report quoted State officials who said radiation levels in all locations southwest of Barnwell were still rising steadily. The EOC had been following the evacuations and rising radiation levels.

Much to everyone's relief no more press briefings had been scheduled at the Savannah River Site. The press seemed satisfied to get their information from State and local government officials. A skeleton crew in the EOC was keeping a log of reported readings for official records. At 6:00 pm Monday the average level in Barnwell was 130 times normal background. Ehrhardt was at 50 times normal background. In North Charleston the average was 30 times normal background. Aerial surveys on site confirmed slightly higher than normal radiation readings at P Reactor. P Reactor happened be shut down for refuelling. That facility and others had been evacuated. The reactor remote operations center reported at 6:00 am Monday morning that radiation levels on the roof of the L Reactor building had reached 1,500 rads/hr.

The primary concern now was how to get the remaining 15% of the population of the Charleston metropolitan area to safety. The State Highway Patrol admitted late Monday evening there was simply nothing more they could do. They estimated about 1% of the population had refused to leave. Another 3% could not be moved. This included hospital patients in multiple locations. The only recourse for these people was to put the hospital ventilation systems on full recirculation mode. That would minimize leakage of outside air into the building, but of course the buildings weren't airtight. Experts estimated radiation exposures to these individuals and healthcare professionals could be reduced by 80% by such actions. Surface decontamination procedures would have to be carried out inside the hospital every few hours. That would have to do. Military installations in the area faced a similar problem. Sheltering in place and use of personal protective equipment were maximized. Some other locations, such as the Brookgreen Gardens in Charleston, simply could not be abandoned completely because of the animal population being kept there.

State politicians in Columbia, South Carolina had already begun to estimate the economic impacts of the accident at the Savannah River Site. Since this was the property of the Federal Government, state authorities assumed the folks in Washington, DC would foot the bill. Or more accurately, Federal tax dollars would cover most of the economic damage. Early indications were that Federal officials might not agree with that assessment. People would want to be compensated for loss of their farms, or businesses, or other livelihoods. Damage to property values would have to be assessed. Insurance companies would have to find loopholes allowing them to avoid payment of claims. Perhaps this was an act of God? Or perhaps an act of war? All the exclusion clauses were being carefully scrutinized by a host of lawyers in South Carolina, only two days after the incident began. Companies were quick to threaten lawsuits as well. Could they sue the Department of Energy for the damages and lost business, as well as the impact of all these refugees in their communities? Lawyers in seven states were working feverishly to find precedents.

Then there was the loss of State tax revenue from Charleston and other communities that had been evacuated. A significant portion of the State's operating funds came from taxes collected in this part of the State. Columbia could hardly expect Washington to compensate the State of South Carolina for all of that. Over 300,000 citizens had been displaced, unable to earn wages or conduct business. Most of these people had been living from paycheck to paycheck. What meagre savings they had would be depleted in a matter of days, or certainly weeks. They would be expecting either the State or Federal government to give them money to live on, at least until things returned to normal. Neither the federal nor state governments had any mechanism in place to distribute 'free money' to these people, even for those who received their annual tax refunds by direct deposit. The Governor of South Carolina and other politicians immediately realized their re-election hopes were nil if they failed to respond to this emergency generously and quickly.

By noon Tuesday it became obvious to everyone they were not going to be allowed back into their areas of residence for weeks or even months. Radiation levels were continuing to rise. Barnwell was at 155 times normal background. Ehrhardt was at 65 times background. North Charleston was at 45 times background. Wednesday evening's numbers were higher still, at 180 times background in Barnwell, 100 times background in Ehrhardt, and 55 times background in Charleston. Carol watched the CCN news at 7:10 pm. She pleaded with Pat to call his uncle in Dallas. "We may never see our farm again", she sobbed! "It's lovely here in Atlanta but we can't stay here." They had already run up a bill at the Airport Hilton that would take them a year to pay off. Carl had been watching CBS News in Dallas.

"Hi Pat, I was wondering how long you would wait to call. I knew you wouldn't accept if I offered. But now you have no choice. There will be two tickets on Delta Airlines for you at the Hilton in the morning. You can pick them up at the desk. Flight leaves at 1:20 pm. Don't worry about the hotel bill. I've already paid it. Just get on the plane. We'll sort everything out when you get here. I don't drive anymore, but I'll send someone to Love Field to pick you up around 2:30. Don't forget to change your watches. My love to Carol." Pat was overwhelmed. He started to cry and wasn't even able to manage a 'Thank You' as he hung up the phone.

Some were lucky like Pat and Carol. The had relatives or close friends that could take them in until they could find new jobs and places to live. Others weren't lucky and had to fall on the social safety net for unemployment payments and social housing, where such things existed. Parents knew it would be years before the youngest of their children would be able to understand why they had to climb out of bed in the middle of the night, leave their toys behind, climb into the backseat of the car, and possibly never see their childhood home again.

Angie's father was a patient in one of the largest hospitals in Charleston with a fractured hip. The hospital insisted he couldn't be moved. And besides they didn't have any ambulances left to transport him. They were doing their best to isolate the ventilation systems for the various wards, but they couldn't promise no contamination would get in. Everyone wondered if the Charleston municipal water supply might become contaminated as well. Nobody knew how long they would have to survive without being resupplied with food, bottled water, oxygen tanks, and other necessities. A dedicated staff of doctors and nurses had volunteered to stay and take care of the patients, but for how long? Angie's husband Robert had pleaded with the hospital authorities to let them put her father in their large van. They had quickly rigged it so it would hold a gurney for him to lie on while they drove to Myrtle Beach, and further if all the hospitals there were full. Angie was a retired nurse. She could administer morphine if the ride became too painful for him.

The hospital refused to release Angie's father into her care. They were afraid of being sued for malpractice. Of course, that was the last thing on Angie's mind. She would happily sign any waiver they put before her. All she wanted was to get Robert and her father to safety, but the hospital wouldn't budge. Eventually she found two orderlies who were packing up to leave Charleston. She persuaded them to delay just long enough to get her father out of the ward, into the parking lot, and into the van. Robert had to pay them $1000 each for twenty minutes work. But to her it was worth it. The hospital management didn't bother to interfere. They were sure their lawyers could argue successfully that this rogue act by a patient's family absolved them of any responsibility in the matter.

What Angie hadn't planned for was how long it would take them to get to Myrtle Beach. All the morphine was gone after five hours on the road. She did her best to comfort her father, but he was clearly in great pain. There was nothing more to do. Finally, a police car came up the shoulder. Angie stood in its path forcing him to stop. One of the policemen was about to arrest her when she managed to make him understand their plight. He radioed for a medical helicopter. It was another hour before it showed up, but it did take her father the last 12 miles to a hospital in Myrtle Beach. It was another three hours before Angie and Robert were able to see him again. He clasped her hand and smiled, then fell back asleep. The two of them had to leave him there while they looked for a place to stay. The nearest was in Wilmington, North Carolina. And it was $210 per night!

By Thursday there were over 250,000 'Pats and Carols' and 'Angies and Roberts', about half of them traveling north and northeast through South Carolina and into North Carolina. The other half were traveling west and northwest into Georgia. Some even made it into Alabama, Florida and Tennessee. A few hundred arrived in Mobile and New Orleans by boat. Six states were already asking Washington for money to support refugees fleeing Charleston and areas north of the city.

Assault on L

Jesse couldn't help but chuckle as he watched CNN's coverage of the evacuations. Several days earlier he and Maggie had threatened the local Sherriff with a 12-gauge shotgun when he showed up around dawn at their farm a few miles south of Barnwell. Jesse hadn't fired that shotgun in years, but it was loaded, and he was pretty sure he could take that Sherriff's head clean off with it if he got too pushy about them leaving. When the Sherriff explained that all of their neighbors were evacuating and the stores and gas stations and doctors would all be closed, Maggie gave him an earful. "Maybe all them people is nice folks. I don't really know, but we can do without 'em anyway. Things will be nice and quiet with all of 'em gone. That suits me and Jesse just fine. Now you get back in your little police car with the fancy lights on top and git off our land, ya hear!" Jesse half expected someone would come back in an hour and he might have to use that shotgun, but nobody did.

"Look at all these fools stuck on Highway 17 going nowhere, Maggie", he shouted toward the kitchen. Maggie emerged from the doorway, drying an oversized soup bowl with a dishtowel. She stood behind the couch where he was sitting and watched for a few moments. "Amazing how many people will believe anything the government tells 'em", she commented. "They sure as hell didn't run us off our land, did they", said Jesse? "Nope, not even if they bring the army out here. We ain't a budgin'", she replied, shaking her head. She had never been prouder of Jesse than that morning when he told the Sherriff it was all a hoax. The cool morning air smelled as fresh as ever and no government scientist was going to tell them otherwise.

On Thursday evening the EOC logged a reduction in radiation readings for Barnwell. It was down to 140 times background. Ehrhardt and Charleston were still seeing increases. Ehrhardt was up to 120 times background. Charleston was up to 65 times background. The 6:00 am Friday helicopter survey of the L Reactor building reported a significant reduction in the smoke coming from the building roof. Radiation level on the roof was about 2000 rads/hr. Data for Friday noon showed Barnwell at 90 times background, Ehrhardt at 100 times background, and Charleston at 75 times background. There was cause for optimism.

It was Saturday noon before things began to turn around, with Barnwell at 75, Ehrhardt at 80, and Charleston at 55 times normal background radiation levels. At 6:00 am on Saturday there was very little smoke coming from the L Reactor roof. Radiation level on the roof was 1,800 rads/hr. No one in the EOC ever expected to post a weekly chart like this one. One week after the assault on L Reactor and the U. S. Department of

Assault on L

Energy was already preparing for the 'mother of all critiques'! They had to find a scapegoat to offer up as a sacrifice during the inevitable Congressional Hearings.

Radiation Levels	Time	Reactor Bldg	Barnwell	Ehrhardt	Charleston
Sunday	4:30 am	1,000 rads/hr	25X	5X	–
Sunday	6:00 am		40X	7X	–
Sunday	Noon	1,200 rads/hr.	100X	20X	3X
Monday	6:00 am	1,500 rads/hr	120X	30X	10X
Monday	Noon		125X	45X	20X
Monday	6:00 pm		130X	50X	30X
Tuesday	6:00 am	2,000 rads/hr	140X	55X	40x
Tuesday	Noon		155X	65X	45X
Tuesday	6:00 pm		160X	70X	45X
Wednesday	6:00 am	2,200 rads/hr	165X	80X	50X
Wednesday	Noon		175X	90X	50X
Wednesday	6:00 pm		180X	100X	55X
Thursday	6:00 am	2,400 rads/hr	170X	100X	60X
Thursday	Noon		160X	110X	65X
Thursday	6:00 pm		140X	120X	65X
Friday	6:00 am	2,000 rads/hr	100X	110X	70X
Friday	Noon		90X	100X	75x
Friday	6:00 pm		85X	90X	70X
Saturday	6:00 am	1,800 rads/hr	75X	85X	65X
Saturday	Noon		75X	80X	55X
Saturday	6:00 pm		75X	75X	50X

Assault on

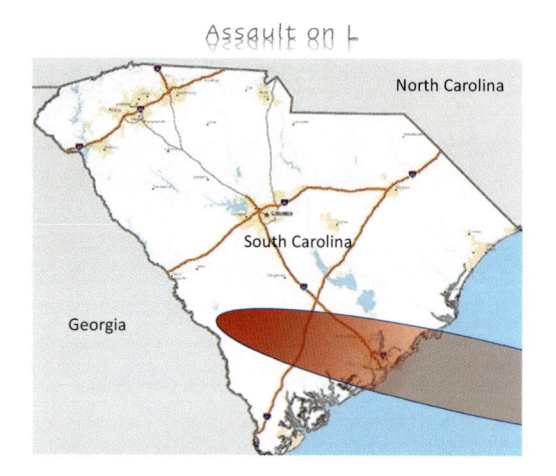

Assault on L

Chapter 14

It had been nearly two weeks since the incident in L Reactor. Radiation levels everywhere between Barnwell and Charleston remained stubbornly high. A parade of 'talking heads' on CNN confidently predicted Charleston would remain uninhabitable for at least eight months, possibly a year. However, one contemporary conspiracy theorist insisted there was no radiation release from L Reactor at all.

"The government wants to double the size of the Savannah River Site by grabbing all the land for 20 miles south east of the current Site", he claimed. "This is just a way to get everybody off that land in a hurry so they can start a lot of new construction there." "Construction of what", asked the CNN news anchor? "God only knows", he replied. "It's all secret of course." "OK, but where's your proof?" The news anchor pretended to be sceptical. "If you look at a map of South Carolina and then the outline of the current Savannah River Site, it's as plain as day! The government will insist a big chunk of land south of the Site is so contaminated that the public can never go back there. To control access to that land they'll just extend the boundary of the Site to include that additional 250 square miles. How convenient!"

"Obviously, they will need to transport a lot of new construction materials and equipment for the new facilities. All of that will come in through the Port of Charleston, with nobody there to see it. It'll probably take about six months to get everything through the port. Then they can let the public start coming back into the Charleston area. Once the highways are clear of everything being transported up to the new Site, they can allow the public back into the areas north of Charleston, maybe up to Ehrhardt and Allendale. And the tax money to pay for all these new secret facilities will be appropriated by Congress as 'funds needed for decontamination and clean-up as a result of the L Reactor release....', which never actually happened at all. You see how clever they are?"

Somehow CNN managed to get aerial photographs of a number of areas that had been evacuated. By comparing photos from different days, they found evidence that some people had not left as they were instructed. There were tractors in one field, and then in a different field a few days later. Cars were parked in different places. Fields that hadn't been ploughed were showing fresh planting a week later. "It's impossible to guarantee that everyone has left these areas", replied one of the emergency management spokespersons. She was embarrassed to admit that the government had no reliable way to determine that everyone had evacuated. "Local police suspected some citizens were hiding when they went door to door in the middle of the night. There are always people who believe that George Orwell got it right when he wrote his book '1984'. He was just off by two years! These people believe that this evacuation is a violation of their personal freedom and civil liberties." "Some people are still there then", asked the reporter? "Undoubtedly some of them have continued on like nothing has happened. Either they don't believe radioactive contamination is real because they can't see it, or they think they're immune."

"Their food and water will be contaminated, won't it", the reporter pressed? "Of course. And their internal and extremal exposure to radiation will make them sick in some cases. However, they will resist anything that smacks of the government controlling the population, like the census every ten years. They don't believe in that either. It's all about 'Big Brother' spying on them and controlling their freedom." "If they get radiation sickness, where will they get medical attention? Or even buy gasoline?" "There's no place to get either in the areas that have been evacuated! They're on their own." "How bad might it get for some of them?" "Depends on how much radiation exposure they get", she replied. "And without dosimetry no one will ever know until they develop symptoms."

"Although we have aerial radiation survey results for large areas, there may be local 'hot spots' where contamination levels are several times higher than the average for the area. For example, if the aerial survey for the Barnwell area is 100 times normal background, there may be some 'hot spots' where it's 200- or 300-times background at ground level. And that only accounts for the external dose. Any ingestion or inhalation of radioisotopes, like iodine, cesium or strontium, will add substantially to an individual's total exposure. The highest radiation rates the public might experience are in areas just outside the Site boundary about 9 miles from L Reactor. Based on the few surveys we've done to date, average levels there are almost 500 times normal background. I really hope no one decided to stay there." She had a chart that showed what might happen.

Exposure Times Normal Background	Consequences of 1 Year's Exposure	Symptoms within Hours	Symptoms within Days or Weeks
3	None - Like a Full Body CT Scan	None	None
30	Limit for Nuclear Worker	None	None
120	Increased Latent Cancer Risk	None	None
300	Latent Cancer Probable	Nausea within 6 Hours	Possible Hemorrhage
500	Multiple Cancers, Possible Organ Failure	Nausea within 2 Hours	Dizziness, Disorientation
1500	Fatal for 50% of population *	Nausea, Diarrhea, Headach, Fever	Weakness, Fatique, Hair Loss
2000	Fatal in One Month**	Nausea, Diarrhea, Headach, Fever	Weakness, Fatique, Hair Loss
3000	Fatal in One Week **	Nausea, Diarrhea, Headach, Fever	Weakness, Fatique, Hair Loss

* With Medical Care
** With or Without Medical Care

The DOE was already four days into its formal critique of the incident. Suelle, Metz, Carlton, Sanders, Smith and others found themselves before a government firing squad. Unlike the press briefings, this time there was no obfuscating who knew what and when. Of course, everything that was said in the EOC and during the press briefings had been recorded. Following almost a year of constant inspections and safety reviews, the DOE Critique following the L Reactor incident was seen by the management and staff in the reactor areas as a further insult. In spite of their best efforts they were being slowly beaten into the mould of the incompetent contractor.

Assault on L

The motive for the government's critique was as transparent as the windows in the Forrestal Building in Washington. In no way was the DOE at fault for what had happened at L Reactor. Obviously, these government contractors had failed to deal with the situation properly. Much better to admit they had hired incompetent contractors that to accept direct responsibility for the event itself. Failure to select the right contractors was an administrative error, committed by a nameless person somewhere in their organization. That hapless person would be found and summarily fired. So...., problem solved!

Most 'witnesses' feared their careers were finished. It was similar to the lions and the Christians in the Roman Colosseum. All the Christians were condemned to death from the start. It was only a matter of how long it took! To add insult to injury, several of the government's panel of 'experts' worked for a rival company that wanted to win the contract for operating the site the next time it came up for rebid. The whole thing was a blatant violation of the government's own code of ethics.

The panel of inquisitors typically numbered eight or more for each session. The room chosen for their performance was simultaneously too small on their end and too large on the end where the victim was told to sit. The wallpaper was a dingy brown. You knew just by being there you were in deep 'you know what'! The color of the wallpaper confirmed it. Each 'witness' was assured this was an impartial inquiry, not about finding fault or placing blame. Then each was asked to justify the decisions they made and the actions they took. It was all being recorded, of course, so that each of the government panel members could prove a) they were there and not off fishing in Alaska, and b) they were able to come up with such brilliant questions as to leave the witness speechless. And so it began!

"Mr. Suelle, can you explain for our panel how a group of terrorists managed to stage their assault on L Reactor to coincide with a secret security exercise in such a way that your forces were firing blanks against an adversary armed with live ammunition", asked the chief inquisitor? "No sir I cannot. Each of my men insists they told no one about the security exercise", Suelle replied. "Is it possible one of your men who was killed in the attack informed someone about the exercise?" "Excuse me, are you implying that one of my men might have tipped off the terrorists?" Suelle found the insinuation highly offensive. "I can assure you, sir. None of my men would do such a thing!" "By the way how are the three men in the hospital", asked another member of the panel? Suelle felt he was being patronized with false empathy. "All three will survive. Thank you", Suelle replied.

"OK, is it possible that one of the men who is now deceased might have inadvertently mentioned the date and time of the security exercise to a family member or friend, and that conversation was overheard?" "Sir, most of these men had families. I have not intruded while they are still grieving for their loss to ask them if they were told about some security exercise. It's extremely unlikely they would have the slightest clue what I was talking about." "The FBI will have to ask them at some point." "Yes sir. That is their job. My job is to protect the facilities in my charge from attack by an adversary, foreign or domestic", said Suelle. "Would you say you did that job well?" "Yes sir", Suelle replied. There were a few chuckles amongst the panel members. "I think some of us would disagree with you there!"

Suelle recognized three members of the critique panel as being DOE 'independent experts' who had been in L Area almost daily for the past ten months. He decided to launch his own counter offensive. "Mr. Chairman, I notice that three of your fellow panel members have been frequent visitors to L Area during the past few months. However, all three were conspicuously absent on the night of the security exercise and the incident we are discussing. Perhaps they had advance knowledge of the security exercise and knew to stay away that evening. Perhaps one of them leaked information about the exercise?" Suelle put on his most professional smile. The chief inquisitor looked a bit off balance but recovered quickly. "Your question is out of order, sir." He glanced over to one side at the clerk who was recording the proceedings. "You will delete Mr. Suelle's last remarks from the record", he ordered. She nodded.

Another panel member took over. "Your men at the barricade just off Highway 125 stopped the truck carrying the terrorists and searched it. Is that correct, Mr. Suelle?" "Yes sir. They examined the cargo the truck was carrying and passed it through." "Would you agree that if they had given the truck a proper search the terrorists would never have gotten on the Site property, never reached L Area, and never blown up the reactor?" "No sir, I cannot agree", Suelle replied. The inquisitor never heard Suelle's answer or chose to ignore it.

"Now we have a huge swath of South Carolina to clean up solely because two of your men didn't do their job!" "Not quite", Suelle promptly replied. "If those two men had thoroughly searched the truck and discovered the terrorists, they would have been killed at the security barricade. The terrorists would then have proceeded to their destination somewhere near L Area in less time than it would have taken for anyone to realize that something had happened at the barricade."

"But you still could have apprehended the terrorists in L Area long before the security exercise took place later that evening, right?" "Only if we had some idea of where they had gone", Suelle replied. "The Savannah River Site extends over 300 square miles. There are more than 200 miles of paved roadways on the Site property. There are a great many more unpaved roads as well. All anyone would have found at the barricade was two dead security guards. Who killed them? What sort of vehicle were they in? How many of them were there? What might they be planning to do? Where should we look first? Maybe they were hoping to steal nuclear material from the Separations Area. They could be hiding in the woods almost anywhere around any number of Site facilities. Or maybe they weren't on the Site at all. Maybe the two guards were killed by terrorists in a vehicle leaving the Site with stolen material, rather than entering the Site."

After four hours without a break the government's panel had managed to question Suelle's integrity and/or insult his intelligence on at least twelve occasions. He couldn't remember when he had been so thoroughly mugged in broad daylight. The members of this panel had managed to completely destroy whatever respect Suelle might have held for this supposed fact-finding process.

For all his faults, Suelle considered his integrity to be beyond question. His military record was spotless. He had also received more media training than anyone in the EOC. He had to wonder why the DOE had not asked him to conduct one of the press briefings. Perhaps his age had something to do with it. He was nearer retirement that the others. Maybe they thought he wasn't up to the task. Or maybe it was the fact that he had never married. It wasn't that he never found the right girl in all those years. He found her alright, when he was only 26. He asked her to wait a year until he came back from deployment in South Korea. They had planned the wedding and everything. The week before he returned to the States, she and her brother died in the crash of a Cessna 180 during a thunderstorm near Lafayette, Louisiana. Suelle never recovered from the loss. There would never be anyone like her again. He vowed he would never settle for second best. His house in the Westside area of Augusta was decorated with photos of the wife he couldn't have.

Assault on L

Metz was next. After five days of inquiry it appeared the government's panel was just getting started. Metz suspected they must be getting paid by the hour, or maybe by the question. "Mr. Metz, I believe your people were the ones that estimated the effectiveness of the emergency cooling water system to prevent melting in the L Reactor. Is that correct?" "That's correct", Metz replied. "Your original estimate was that there might not be any melting at all if at least one of the emergency cooling supplies remained intact and functioning?" "That is correct. Anywhere from no melting up to 10% melting was judged to be most likely." "So can you explain why your people got it so completely wrong, because an estimated 20% of the reactor core in fact has melted, as judged by the fission product releases and radiation levels that have been measured in the past twelve days?" He put a chart up on the overhead screen showing the calculated isotopic spectrum released from the L Reactor building to date.

Assault on L

Radionuclide	Est. % Core Released	Half Life	% After 1 Week	% After 1 Month	% After 3 Months	% After 6 Months	% After 1 Year
^{99}Mo	1.00%	66 hrs	17.129%	0.046%	0%	0%	0%
^{132}Te	7.00%	77 hrs	22.040%	0.137%	0%	0%	0%
^{133}Xe	20.00%	5.24 days	39.615%	1.769%	0.001%	0%	0%
^{131}I	11.00%	8.05 days	54.731%	7.235%	0.038%	0%	0%
^{140}Ba	1.00%	13.4 days	69.622%	20.645%	0.880%	0.008%	0%
^{141}Ce	0.70%	32.50 days	86.132%	52.179%	14.206%	2.018%	0.042%
^{103}Ru	1.00%	39.27 days	88.377%	58.371%	19.888%	3.955%	0.159%
^{89}Sr	0.80%	50.5 days	90.839%	65.795%	28.482%	8.112%	0.667%
^{95}Zr	0.70%	65 days	92.807%	72.235%	37.691%	14.206%	2.040%
^{242}Cm	0.70%	163 days	97.067%	87.836%	67.767%	45.923%	21.179%
^{144}Ce	0.70%	234 days	97.948%	91.361%	76.259%	58.154%	33.919%
^{106}Ru	0.70%	1.02 yrs	98.705%	94.480%	84.337%	71.127%	50.684%
^{134}Cs	7.00%	2.07 yrs	99.360%	97.241%	91.948%	84.545%	71.544%
^{239}Np	0.70%	2.36 yrs	99.438%	97.576%	92.902%	86.307%	74.550%
^{240}Pu	0.70%	6.56 yrs	99.798%	99.121%	97.386%	94.840%	89.973%
^{85}Kr	20.00%	10.76 yrs	99.877%	99.463%	98.398%	96.822%	93.761%
^{241}Pu	0.70%	14 yrs	99.905%	99.587%	98.767%	97.548%	95.170%
^{90}Sr	0.80%	28.79 yrs	99.954%	99.799%	99.398%	98.800%	97.621%
^{137}Cs	7.00%	30.17 yrs	99.956%	99.808%	99.426%	98.855%	97.729%
^{238}Pu	0.70%	87.7 yrs	99.985%	99.934%	99.802%	99.605%	99.213%

"Looking at the half-life of some of these radioisotopes it's obvious that many of them will persist in the environment for a very long time", one of the panel members continued. "Over 50% of the contamination will still remain after a full year. That is true for nearly half the isotopes listed – the ones that are shaded. We're going to be cleaning up cesium, plutonium, neptunium and strontium down there for years to come. It's hard to know where to start!"

"Our calculations were based on mathematical models of how the emergency cooling water enters the plenum at the top of the reactor and distributes to 600 individual fuel assemblies. Several of the fluid flow phenomena involved in these calculations involve rather large uncertainties. These phenomena have never been tested under controlled conditions", Metz replied. "You mean until now!" His tormentor was smiling. Metz frowned. "Sir, I wouldn't call what has happened in L Reactor a 'test conducted under controlled conditions'." "But you do admit you were wrong", he asked, again with a smile? "We were inaccurate", replied Metz. Then he thought to add, "Would it have made any difference if we had predicted 20% melting instead of 10%?" Many of the panel members looked taken aback. "We'll be asking the questions here, Mr. Metz. As for what difference it might have made if you had gotten it right, we'll be the ones to decide that too!"

At work Metz was the consummate professional engineer. At home on his farm somewhere between Aiken and New Ellenton he was quite different. The farm offered peace and quiet he could never find at work. All his chickens were anonymous, but the four pigs had names. The pigs all knew their names, even if no one else did. Metz's office at work was constantly busy. People seemed to drift in and out seeking his opinion about all sorts of reactor safety questions. That is what his organization did. People would postulate this or that scenario and his people would attempt to calculate the most likely consequences. Scenarios ranged from rupture of cooling water pipes that might flood the reactor building, to steam explosions in the reactor upon loss of cooling, to how much pressure it might take to rupture the casings on the giant exhaust fans that kept the reactor room at lower pressure than the ambient air pressure outside.

Metz was well known for his unique document filing system. More than any other organization, his people produced documents, hundreds and hundreds of documents. He used to tell young engineers conducting research, "If it isn't documented, then it never happened!" Metz had a unique filing system. He piled documents on his desk, on top of the bookcase, wherever he could put them. They were stacked in the order they came in, i.e., chronologically. When someone came looking for a document Metz would ask for the date it was issued. He would then go to one of the stacks, run his finger slowly down the stack, and then stop. Reaching into the stack at that point he would pull out the requested document. No one else could understand it, but it worked for him.

Metz passed Carlton in the hallway. "They've adjourned for the day. It is 3:00 pm after all", said Metz with a grin. "I think you're up at 9 in the morning."

Indeed, it was Carlton's turn the next morning. "I believe you had nine operations personnel in the L Reactor building when the terrorists took over. Is that correct, Mr. Carlton?" "That's correct", Carlton replied. He recognized several members of the panel as 'independent experts' who had been given carte blanche tours of his reactor buildings. "I'm sure you know as well as I do just how hard it is to keep a nuclear reactor running. There are so many ways to cause a reactor shut down. With nine people in the building why did it take tehm so long to shut it down?"

"I am unable to answer that question, sir, because I wasn't there. It's quite likely none of my people were allowed to stay in the control room. They may have been held somewhere else in the building where they had no access to the reactor instrumentation or control systems." "You can't say that for sure, because you weren't there, right?" "Right." "You don't think that any of your operations people might have helped the terrorists to keep the reactor running?" "No sir, I most certainly do not", Carlton replied. He highly resented the tone of the question. He gave serious thought to getting up and walking out of the room. But he had been instructed to cooperate with these baboons.

Carlton and his staff had been loyal to their customer, even when programs were underfunded, or demands were at times unreasonable. It was now clear that the DOE had no intention of reciprocating. They refused to defend their contractors' actions in front of their own hired 'independent experts' and had abandoned them completely during a real crisis in L Area. He knew he would find it difficult to continue to work for people who he could no longer respect.

Carlton never knew his real parents. He was given up for adoption at six months of age. At least that's what the official records said. He was raised by foster parents, changing households five times before he was 16. He was unusually bright, though, and when he was offered a scholarship to Georgia Tech, he took it, and graduated six months ahead of schedule with a bachelor's degree in Chemical Engineering. Atlanta being so near the Savannah River Site, it was natural to interview there. They gave him three job offers. He took the one he wanted most. It seemed he was destined to succeed, spending less than four years at each professional level, and less than three years in any management position. On his forty-third birthday he received a call from the man who originally hired him to ask if he would accept the position of Reactor Operations Manager. Carlton was a workaholic but tried to spend time with his only son whenever possible. At times that was difficult. Three years ago his wife left him.

Sanders wasn't quite as patient as Carlton. After being filleted by the press on two separate occasions, it no longer mattered to him whether he got that promotion or not. He didn't have as much to lose as the others. Why not speak his mind. "Mr. Sanders, you mentioned in a press briefing that there was nothing burning in the reactor building. Is that correct?" "To the best of my knowledge that is correct." "Do you mean you admit making that statement, or that the statement itself was accurate?" "Both, sir." There was a slight pause, as if Sanders response might have short circuited his inquisitor's prepared follow up.

"OK, so how did you know that nothing was burning since no one has been able to get inside the reactor building to actually see what is going on?" "My answer was based on my knowledge of the physical properties of uranium, aluminium, stainless steel and water. The reactor is primarily composed of these four things and none of them burn", he replied. "So, oxides of uranium and aluminium don't exist?" "I didn't say that. What I said was they don't burn. They don't produce smoke when they oxidize. That was the premise of the press reporter's question." His inquisitor paused again. Clearly this man was not going to let him get away with anything. He decided to change the subject.

Sanders had two engineering degrees, one in Chemical Engineering and another in Mechanical Engineering. The engineering job market was quite lean about the time he was due to graduate, so he decided to stay in school an extra year and get two degrees instead of one. It also kept him out of Viet Nam. Sanders was a family man with a moderate sized house in the Woodside subdivision in Aiken. He was very proud of his twin daughters, both blonde like his wife, and both destined to be engineers someday if he had any say in the matter. His wife wasn't sure about that but had wisely decided to postpone the debate until they were in their teens. Having presented papers at several international conferences, Sanders could go toe to toe with any 'expert' who might wander into his area of expertise. He enjoyed being Metz's 'second in command' most of the time. The last several weeks was definitely the exception.

Smith was quite certain his pay grade was not high enough that he should have to submit to questioning in this forum. Surely that was something unique in the job description for the more senior managers. "Mr. Smith, your organization looks at facilities like L Reactor and determines how they might be vulnerable to a terrorist attack. However, you have never warned anyone about the one we've just experienced. Why is that?" "Sorry, we have never postulated an attack where the Protective Force was essentially unarmed." "You don't have to apologize, Mr. Smith. Everyone makes mistakes sometimes." "No what I meant to say was that if the Protective Force had been in its normal posture their weapons and procedures would have been effective in taking out most of the terrorists before they reached the building. In addition, the doors to the building are normally locked. That would have delayed the terrorists long enough for a full Protective Force response to have completely eliminated them."

"That's all speculation on your part, isn't it?" "No sir. We have conducted many tabletop exercises where the adversaries were eliminated long before they could enter a facility." "Isn't it true that back in December there was an actual security exercise where the adversary team was able to enter the L Reactor building and reach their designated target in the minus 20 level?" "Yes, but we identified a number of security enhancements to prevent such a scenario from succeeding again." "So, you had a practice drill, the bad guys won, then you added some improvements, and the bad guys succeeded again. This time for real! That's two failures in a row, isn't it?" "This scenario was completely different from the one in December." Smith began to gather his notes in preparation for walking out of the room. "Unfortunately, in this case you won't get another opportunity to finally get it right!" Smith was nearly out the door and barely heard his inquisitor's parting remark.

Smith would be the first to agree that tabletop exercises were distinctively artificial and not the best way to determine each facility's vulnerabilities to a terrorist attack. However, there were only four members on his Vulnerability Analysis team and budgetary constraints on the number of scenarios that could be analysed. They had been promised advanced computer software used by the U. S. Military that would allow his team to conduct much more realistic simulations. All of that was nearly a year overdue.

Smith enjoyed playing military style board games with his two teenage sons at his home in North Augusta. They surprised him sometimes with their insights into how one might get around security systems. On alternate weekends when the boys were with his ex-wife, he could do some work at home. The problem was almost all his work involved documents that were classified Secret or at a minimum Unclassified

Controlled Nuclear Information, or UCNI. Bringing any of that information home was strictly forbidden.

Captain Lowe didn't like firing squads, especially when he was the one wearing the blindfold. "Captain Lowe, is it true you shot one of your own men? I believe his name was Thompson." "No sir, I didn't shoot him. He was dressed as an adversary for the security exercise that was supposed to take place that night. One of my men shot him thinking he was another of the real adversaries. He's recovering in the hospital", Lowe replied. "So, you admit your men aren't capable of distinguishing real adversaries from ones that are only pretending." "Not in this one unique instance." "Is it true that your men also rescued an E&I Mechanic by the name of Jane Jones? You even called an ambulance for her. Isn't that correct?" "Yes sir."

"Except there is no one by that name on the site's list of employees. And she never turned up at Site Medical or any of the hospitals in the area. Do you think she might have been a terrorist in disguise?" "It's possible", Lowe replied. "So that's twice in twenty-four hours when your men couldn't tell the good guys from the bad guys." "Yes sir." "Do you think your men might need some additional training, so they don't make the same mistakes if there's a real attack on another Reactor Area?" "I'm sure there will be some lessons learned from this incident", Lowe answered. "We all certainly hope so!" The entire panel had another chuckle, this time at Captain Lowe's expense.

Lowe, his wife and daughters were living at her sister's house in Orangeburg until they he could find a house to rent, at least temporarily. It was a bit crowded. They knew it might be some time before they could retrieve her wedding ring and other memorabilia from their house in Barnwell. All their clothes and household furnishings could be a total loss. The family might have to start over from scratch. At least they had some clothes and one of their cars.

In their effort to get paid for another week's work, the DOE panel of inquisitors decided to turn their attention to the reactor operations personnel who were held hostage in the L Reactor building for twenty-four hours. Murphy wasn't interested in being fodder for their smear campaign. Carlton had already given him a 'heads up' about what to expect. "Mr. Murphy, we're all familiar with the famous 'Stockholm Syndrome'. That's where people held captive become friendly with their captors and may even sympathize with their cause after a period of time. Do you think anything like that might have occurred during your time as a hostage in L Reactor?" Murphy had promised himself he would remain calm and answer the questions in a professional manner. He could feel his blood pressure rising on the very first question. "No sir, none of us ever experienced what you are describing at all. Our only interest was survival. We had no idea when we might be shot, like our Shift Senior Supervisor, without any provocation at all."

"What I'm asking is did you cooperate with the terrorists? When they told you to take some action in the control room, did you comply?" Murphy was sure his face must be getting even redder than it usually was. "They never asked any of us to take any action in the control room or anywhere else. Most of the time we were forced to sit in a conference room and do nothing, or the lunchroom where we could eat." "They never asked you to operate any of the equipment in the building, not even once?" "No sir, not once", Murphy replied. He could see the frustration in the face of his opponent in this little chess match. He was determined to weather the attack. "And there was nothing you could do to shut down the reactor during the entire twenty-four hours?"

"The reactor was eventually shut down." "Yes, but not through any action of yours. Isn't that correct?" "What would you have done with a gun pointed at your head? Would it have been worth one or several of us getting killed trying to reach the SCRAM button?" Murphy tried his best to remain civil. "In our collective opinion, at least you should have tried", said one of the other panel members. Murphy felt it coming. He couldn't stop it. "With all due respect, gentlemen, you can all take your collective opinion and shove it up your collective ass!" He stood up and walked, as professionally as possible, out of the room.

It was the end of the week and the DOE Site Manager had instructed the DOE panel to 'wrap it up'. There was only one more person to question. Blythe walked calmly to the solitary chair at one end of the room and sat down. "Can you explain to us what actions you took to maintain reactor power steady at the request of the terrorists in the control room of the L Reactor building. We're told you were at the nuclear console when the terrorists burst into the control room. Is that correct?" "I was sitting at the nuclear console when the terrorists entered", Blythe replied. "From my location I could not see what was happening. I heard the sound of a gunshot but could not see that MacMahon had been killed. One of the men pointed a weapon at me. He told me to stand up and move away from the nuclear console or I would be shot where I sat. I could not reach either the SCRAM button or the Supplementary Safety System switch.

Both were about four feet away. I was not interested in committing suicide, so I moved away as I was told."

"But there were times later on when you were allowed to sit at the nuclear console, correct?" "Correct." "So when you were sitting at the console, you were maintaining reactor power at a constant level?" "No sir. The computer was maintaining reactor power at a constant level." "You took no action yourself, then?" "None was required or requested."

"But you could have hit the SCRAM button while you were sitting there. You chose not to. Why was that?" "One of the men was always standing between me and the SCRAM button and SSS switch. I would have had to turn around and reach around his body to get to them." "We've been told this man appeared to find you very attractive. Was the feeling mutual? Did you find him attractive?" "I found him and all the rest of them disgusting", she replied! The look she gave them convinced them to abandon that line of questioning.

"There was another woman besides yourself being held as a hostage. Is that correct?" "Yes, I did see another woman wearing an E&I Mechanic's coveralls." "Were you able to speak with her at any time during your captivity?" "No, I only saw her briefly. They kept me in the control room most of the time. There were never more than three of us in the control room. I don't remember seeing her there at all." "So you don't know what happened to her?" "No. She may have managed to escape before we were brought out to the helicopter. She wasn't with us then." There was some muffled discussion among the panel members, while Blythe sat quietly. There appeared to be some disagreement about what to ask her next. After about five minutes, they dismissed her. Whatever someone had wanted to ask must have been deemed too vile even for their taste.

Assault on L

Chapter 15

Having survived numerous press briefings and the Department of Energy's inquisition, the managers who served in the EOC during the incident in L Reactor were just happy to get back to their regular jobs. Of course, their duties were far from regular at the moment. Most of their scheduled meetings were related to the releases that were still occurring from L Reactor, albeit at a reduced rate. Getting to sit in your own office for at least few hours a day was a welcome change. All that was left for the EOC was to keep staff at the Site informed.

All the actions were being directed by State and Federal Emergency Management officials. It rained several times during the first few weeks following the initial release. That meant that some of the contamination had been captured in the ground water. Every air, soil and water monitoring team in the United States was now fully engaged in the exclusion zone in South Carolina south east of the Savannah River Site.

No environmental monitoring and radioactive clean-up activities on this massive a scale had been attempted anywhere on earth since 1945. Many federal emergency management officials hadn't even been born yet in 1945. They had to review what was done forty years earlier and develop a comprehensive plan using modern methods and technology. At a minimum the plan had to prescribe resources and costs for:

1. Sealing off the L Reactor building at some future time when it was judged safe to do so. Radiation exposure to workers involved in that activity had to be managed and minimized. Some new robotics and other technologies would likely be needed for sealing off the building, as well as for cleaning up the area around it.
2. Creation of a temporary exclusion zone extending 50 miles southeast of the Site boundary, for a duration of 6 months. Access controls would have to be put in place at all roads and ingress points.
3. Creation of a long-term exclusion zone extending 20 miles southwest of the Site boundary, for a duration of 18 months. Access controls would have to be put in place at all roads and ingress points.
4. Resettlement of approximately 150,000 people who were displaced by the event. This had to include temporary housing and schooling for those who lived in the temporary exclusion zone, and permanent housing and schooling for those who lived in the long-term exclusion zone.

5. Frequent medical reviews and health care for 100,000 people exposed to radiation levels 5 times or more normal background radiation levels for more than 24 hours.
6. Future costing for 30,000 people who would be receiving benefits payments for 10 years.
7. Control of food, water, and agricultural products, such as hay and straw, in the exclusion zones to prevent the spread of contamination outside the zones.
8. Research to find possible ways to make contaminated food safe.
9. Long term monitoring of environmental radiation levels in both zones. This would include extensive sampling of natural flora and fauna, ground water, continuous air sampling, and sampling of domestic livestock.
10. Radioactive and toxic waste clean-up and disposal in the Savannah River Site's low-level waste burial ground. 100,000 tons of it would have to be buried right next to all that tomato farmer's dirt that had been excavated from an area near Palomares, Spain when two American hydrogen bombs accidently fell and disintegrated on land along the Spanish Andalusian coast in 1966.

At the summary level, the government's L Reactor Release Environmental Monitoring and Clean-up Plan estimated the total cost over the next ten years to be at least $500 billion, not adjusted for inflation. This was compared to the total cost to build the Savannah River Site in the early 1950's of just over $1.1 billion. Even adjusting that number for inflation, the total cost of the L Reactor incident would be many times the cost of the original construction. Captain Lowe was relieved to learn he could return to his family home in Barnwell in six months, but he and his family would face an enormous task of cleaning and decontaminating literally everything there. Mrs. Lowe had left the house with all the windows shut. That might mean most of the contents of the house was relatively clean.

As soon as he was released from the DOE inquisition, Suelle used the first opening on his calendar to visit University Hospital in Augusta. Thompson was doing well. He thought they might release him to go home in another three or four days. They had removed one bullet from his left thigh and another from his shoulder. The shoulder wasn't a problem but the wound in his thigh would likely prevent him from walking for several more weeks. Then there would be a month or two of physical therapy before he was back to normal. "Don't rush it", said Suelle. "Take as much time off as you need. I don't believe anyone will be trying to attack L Area again for quite some time." Both men shook their heads.

"Sir, can you explain what happened to the rest of my team? Captain Lowe said they were all found dead in the woods. What the hell happened to them?" Thompson was visibly upset. He needed answers for his own piece of mind. He felt like the lone survivor of a plane crash. Why was he in the hospital rather than with the rest of the team in the morgue? Suelle found Thompson's question more difficult to answer than any he had faced from the press. "Somehow a group of real terrorists found out exactly when and where we were going to conduct our next Force on Force exercise in L Area. They must have been in position before you and the rest of Brownlie's team arrived. From the positions of the bodies it looks like Brownlie, Jonesy, O'Hara, Sarco and Brennen were all ambushed from a short distance away. We found shell casings in an area about twenty meters from where they fell."

"They only reason you are here, Thompson, is because you deployed to the east side of the area to create a diversion for the exercise. It's likely the terrorists saw you moving away from the others before they could make their kills. Once you were apart from Brownlie and the team they didn't have the time or the need to take you out. You're a lucky man!" "I certainly don't feel lucky, sir", Thompson replied. "You will. Trust me. It'll just take a while", said Suelle. The two men shared a firm handshake. Thompson had to stop and think to use his good arm.

Suelle made similar visits to the other two men who were wounded in the L Area attack. Their wounds were worse due to the type of ammunition Jorge and his people were using. One of the men had to have a new hip made of titanium. The bullet that hit him tore away so much bone that simple repair was impossible. He would walk again but not without months of physical therapy. The other man had lost his right forearm. The bullet had completely severed the bones below the elbow. A prosthesis was being designed for him at government expense. All three men were in private rooms and receiving the best care the government could provide.

Carlton made a similar visit to pay his condolences to the MacMahon family. His wife and twin daughters were upset that their husband and father could not be given a proper funeral because the body could not be recovered. Murphy had described to Carlton how MacMahon died. Obviously, the body was still in the reactor building somewhere. Of course, Carlton could not give Mrs. MacMahon those details. All he could tell her was that her husband valiantly gave his life in an effort to prevent terrorists from causing the disaster that had been unfolding for the past several weeks. MacMahon's body would be provided with a proper burial as soon as practicable.

Assault on L

Murphy checked up on the families of Ferbis and Jared. Mrs. Ferbis' sister had come down from Charlotte, North Carolina to pick them up and take them back with her. Her sister had a large ranch style house with plenty of room until they could find a place of their own. The government provided more than enough money for them to live on, and even a down payment if they wanted to buy a place. Mrs. Jared had accepted the government's offer of a three-bedroom apartment in Columbia. She had given up her career as a legal clerk when she got married but found there were plenty of jobs available in the Columbia area. Tyler and Leland's next of kin had been evacuated and no one knew how to contact them. Leland's brother hadn't been able to find Leland's family since they left Allendale. Carlton had left word that if they contacted the Site, he needed information about how he could reach them.

Suelle made every effort to personally contact the next of kin for Brownlie, Jonesy, and Brennen. Brownlie's brother lived in New Jersey and Jonesy's parents still lived in Carbondale, Illinois. Brennen had left the line on his Employment Application blank where it asked for the name and address of the person to contact in an emergency. No next of kin could be identified. O'Hara's relatives all lived across the Atlantic in Ireland. They were grateful for Suelle's call but didn't seem all that upset. Perhaps if they had seen anything of him over the past decade, they would have been more concerned. That left Sarco. His wife and three children lived in Martinez, a popular area on the north side of Augusta. Suelle arrived at their door about 2:00 pm on a Saturday after calling ahead to make sure they were home.

"Come in Mr. Suelle", his wife replied politely. She ushered him into the den and shut the door where the three boys couldn't hear. Then she began. Suelle was familiar with the phrase 'stand and take', but he had never experienced anything like this. Over the next twenty minutes he was forced to endure the most incandescent torrent of profanity he had ever heard. Mrs. Sarco blamed him personally, and that 'damn bomb plant' in general, for her husband's death. It was clearly his fault her three children were now fatherless. No amount of the government's money could ever take his place. In fact, she considered the compensation she had been offered an insult of the highest order! She planned to make her views known to every member of the news media she could contact. Since she never offered him a seat, all he could do was apologize, turn around and walk back out the door. As he sat in his car, he had to admit that for him that was the worst moment of the entire incident. It only reinforced his growing feelings of guilt.

Assault on L

Both Carlton and Suelle attended the funerals of all those who died during the incident in L Area. Suelle was finding it more and more difficult to sleep the last few weeks, making him wonder if he might need counselling to help him cope with it all. Murphy identified Otis and Ansel. They were buried at South Carolina taxpayer's expense.

By the third week Sanders and his team calculated all melting in the reactor had ceased. There was no longer enough heat generated by fission product decay for fuel assemblies to release further contamination. They estimated the reactor room was still filled with a spectrum of fission product isotopes, however. Wind would continue to aspirate both gases and particulate matter from the building for several more weeks, or maybe even months. And each time it rained contamination was leaching into the ground around the reactor building as well. Radioactive decay of the various isotopes and local weather conditions would determine the rate at which radiation levels in the countryside would diminish over time. Rain would reduce the airborne material but increase the groundwater contamination levels. Some radioisotopes had relatively long half-lives. It was impossible to predict just how long it might be before people could return to some areas. The only way to know when it was safe was to sample the air, ground water, soil and natural vegetation as extensively as humanly possible.

All the resources of the State and Federal governments were being thrown into the effort. There were even programs to harvest deer and other animals periodically. Deer and other grazing animals are nature's collectors of vegetation samples. Over time they concentrate the radioisotopes found on the leaves and grasses they eat. By harvesting some of the deer and other animals, technicians would be able to tell how the radioactivity was migrating through the local environment. A number of students working at the Georgia Ecology Laboratory at the Site might well be able to base their doctorate thesis on such research. If one could ignore the horrific cost to local populations and to society in general, this event offered an unparalleled opportunity to the scientifically minded.

All those who evacuated in the middle of the night and into the morning naturally wanted to return to their homes, even if it was only to retrieve precious family memorabilia or other items of great value. Mrs. Lowe, for one, wanted her diamond wedding ring. It was sitting on her dresser in the bedroom. At least she hoped it was still there. The State of South Carolina had commandeered nearly 500 school buses from across the state and was organizing daily trips for people to go back home and get what they could collect in thirty minutes. Some would have to wait just over a month to make the trip, but it was better than nothing. Per the same advice initially given to all refuges, everything had to be washed, including the clothes you were wearing when you returned. Everyone was asked to shower, whether they thought they needed it or not. All luggage had to be wiped down. Every school bus had to be washed after every trip into the exclusion zone.

A different plan had to be devised for hospital workers and others who could not evacuate. All those who were required to stay in the exclusion zone rotated out after three days. Buses were used again to bring people back and forth from hospitals, nursing homes, and other vital facilities. The federal government created a list of 'essential workers' who maintained electric utilities, telephone systems and other indispensable services. Those who volunteered were rotated every three days. Everyone working in the exclusion zone wore a pocket dosimeter. These were exchanged weekly and read by technicians so that a log of everyone's exposure could be maintained. Individual radiation exposures were limited according to the same federally mandated standards applied to workers at the Savannah River Site and other DOE nuclear facilities.

And as if State and Federal governments didn't have enough on their plate, every one of the hundreds of people in the United States who may have protested against building the Savannah River Site, or any similar facilities, over the past thirty years suddenly decided this was the perfect time to renew their objections! There were marches in Washington, DC, Atlanta and Columbia, and even a small demonstration in Augusta. Banners were everywhere bearing 'I told you so!' messages in various phrases. Some demonstrators even appeared along Highway 17 attempting to prevent essential workers and refugees from returning to the exclusion zone. The nuclear disarmament people joyfully chimed in. There was clearly something to celebrate. Over 300,000 people were now homeless. What could be more glorious?

Protestors attempted to block Highway 17 in one location by using one of their signature methods. They sat down in the road, handcuffed themselves together in groups of twenty and refused to be moved by the police. One of the local sheriffs had seen this before. He and two of his deputies found a nice big South Carolina red ant bed not far away. They dug up three washtubs full of red ants and pored them over the protestors. It didn't take long before the protestors decided to vacate the roadway and let the busses pass. Law enforcement in Atlanta had a harder time with demonstrations there. It seems they couldn't find any red ant beds in the city.

Assault on L

CNN was there to cover all the demonstrations and protests of course. They even pulled reporters out of retirement to cover all the venues. "You say they shouldn't have ever built the reactors at Savannah River Site in the first place", asked one Washington reporter, standing in the middle of the National Mall in front of the Museum of Natural History. "That's right. Biggest waste of money in the history of this country. Now look at what they've done. It's going to cost even more to clean up the mess they've made in Charleston. That place will never be the same", he replied, waving an American flag. "Wouldn't you agree that nuclear weapons were necessary during the cold war to prevent the Russians from launching their missiles at us?" "No, no. You don't get it, do you! The only reason the Russians have nuclear weapons is because the United States has them. We started the whole thing in Japan. Then we decided those bombs weren't big enough. Wiping out an entire city wasn't enough. We had to have the 'H bomb' so we can wipe out several cities with one strike. Russians got scared so they had to develop the same thing. Now nobody can back down."

Another protest group in Atlanta was calling for the Department of Energy to be abolished. They felt the Department of Defence should have been in charge of operating the Savannah River Site from the beginning. "The stuff they've been making down there is for weapons used by the military. If the military had been in charge, they would have built an army base all around those reactors. Those terrorists would have been dead before they got within a mile of those reactors." "You think the Department of Energy didn't do enough to protect against a terrorist attack", asked the reporter? "Obviously not. The facts speak for themselves. Look at Fort Knox in Kentucky. It's called a 'fort' for a reason. There are hundreds of troops there to prevent anyone getting near our gold reserves. It's going to take more than a few gold bars to pay for cleaning up Charleston, right?"

The demonstration in Columbia, South Carolina had a different message. The people there were scared of another release like the one from L Reactor, but with the wind blowing north east along Interstate 20. "Are you afraid this sort of thing could happen again", asked the reporter? "You bet I am! I've lived here in Lexington for the past 40 years and watched them build that 'bomb plant'. Everybody knew it was going to go wrong someday. I'm just surprised it didn't happen a lot sooner. Of course, they keep everything secret down there. Nobody knows what they're really doing. They say that if you fly a plane over the Site the radiation beams coming up from those buildings will knock the plane out of the sky. That's why they won't let anyone fly over the place. I think it's just 'cause they don't want any of us to see what they're really doing." "What do you think they're doing then", she asked? "I heard they're experimenting on aliens. You know, like they're doing at that Area 51 in Nevada. It's right next to another DOE site where they used to test the 'A-bombs'. That's another place they won't let anyone fly over."

The national tabloids saw an opportunity to boost their sales as well. Several of them offered considerable sums to the four hostages who had escaped the ordeal in L Reactor with their lives. All four refused the offers. Then things got nasty. One of the tabloids pushed a story that Blythe had been raped by one or several of her captors. She was forced to publicly deny it. Then another story came out that she had fallen in love with one of the terrorists. Maybe she was even pregnant with his child. Again, she denied it all, but they refused to stop. Eventually she had to hire several lawyers who threatened to sue the tabloids for deformation of character and anything else they could think of. The American Civil Liberties Union volunteered to pay her legal expenses. There were comments made about Murphy and Crosby and Martin as well, but they didn't seem to have the same 'news value' as the stories about Blythe, and quickly faded away.

There was suddenly a lot of public unrest about the Department of Energy. The protests hadn't escaped the notice of top officials in the Forrestal Building in Washington, DC. As if the emergency management problems in South Carolina weren't enough, now they had a revitalized public campaign for nuclear disarmament to deal with as well. For several days now every time the Secretary of Energy looked out her fourth-floor window all she could see was people picketing the Forrestal Building carrying signs that reminded her of the war in Viet Nam. One sign read, "Make Babies, Not Bombs!". Another read, "Remember Charleston!" A third said, "No More Nukes!" Her political position was rather tenuous at the moment, not because of the happenings in South Carolina, but because of the lack of progress on receiving spent nuclear fuel back from foreign countries. The United States, under a number of previous Secretaries of Energy, had loaned fissile material to other countries who wanted it for research in building reactors to generate electricity. These efforts had now concluded. The spent nuclear fuel was still the property of the United States. But now the U. S. didn't want to take it back.

The inconvenient answer, of course, was that the Unites States didn't have anywhere to put it. All their storage facilities were already full of their own spent fuel. Like so many government initiatives over the years there was enough money to begin the project but no money to finish it. Building new storage facilities would cost money the DOE didn't have. And an environmental impact study would have to be done. The outcome of that study would depend on where the new spent nuclear fuel storage facilities

Assault on L

would be located. The DOE's Environmental Impact Statement would have to spell out which of the fifty States would be home to the new project. Unsurprisingly not one of the States had volunteered. In fact, all fifty were adamantly opposed to 'putting this mess in their backyard'.

"Isn't there a facility somewhere in our vast empire that has unused spent fuel storage capacity", asked the Secretary of Energy at her weekly staff meeting? Everyone around the table simply shook their heads. "I'm told the Receiving Basin for Offsite Fuels at Savannah River Site is not completely full at the moment. However, people there say any available space is already allocated", replied one of her underlings. "Allocated for what", she asked? "RBOF at Savannah River is sometimes used to temporarily store their own spent fuel from the reactors on site. It only stays there until it can be sent to the Separations Facilities where they dissolve it and separate out the plutonium", he replied. "And what if the reactors weren't making spent fuel anymore", she asked with a wry smile? "Then there would be lots of space in the spent fuel storage basins in each of the reactor areas." "Including L Area?" "Maybe, after about five years and a lot of decontamination." Her demeanour instantly changed. Suddenly all was right with the world!

Assault on L

Chapter 16

The Federal Bureau of Investigation in Washington had begun its investigation using the infrared photos Captain Lowe had been able to take as the terrorists were boarding the helicopter in L Area. The images were admittedly rough, but the Bureau had some ways to enhance them. One of the images failed to match anything in the state or national databases. Another wasn't clear enough to be of any use. They were able to find matches for the remaining two photos. One was of a 29-year-old man named Samuel who held a security clearance for work with a government contractor in Arlington, Virginia.

In fact, he had been helping to develop technology for new security systems design. That had to be more than a coincidence! The other photo turned up nothing in the national database but there was a match with someone named Silas in the South Carolina driver's licence records. Digging deeper, investigators discovered this man Silas had been living in the Aiken area for several years and purchased a farm at auction over a year ago. The next step was to visit the farm.

For the local FBI team, the visit to the farm answered many questions. Seven individuals had left amble evidence behind. Used airline boarding passes indicated two of the them had travelled from Germany and another from Spain. The boarding passes could be used by agents in Washington to query the airlines and identify the passenger's names and other information. Another left a one-way ticket stub from San Francisco. Samuel had probably come directly from Arlington, Virginia. Silas had probably been living there since he bought the place.

One of the two bodies removed by the Protective Force before L Area was evacuated appeared to be of Spanish heritage. The other was Austrian. It was like a mix and match puzzle. Who was connected to which set of articles found in the farmhouse? One collection of items was different from the others. The owner was obviously experienced at remaining anonymous and wasn't planning to return. The first unanswered question was why there were eight beds.

"Can anyone tell me which of these guys stayed behind and blew up L Reactor after the others left?" The other three agents all pointed to the collection of items that were anonymous. "Had to be this one", she replied. "And why is that", the lead agent asked? "Because the others all seemed to be enjoying life. You can tell by their clothes and other items. Life wasn't going to end here for them", another agent added. "This one had given up on life", said the third agent. "He's left nothing for us because he had nothing left to leave." The lead agent paused to look back over the entire scene. "I believe you're right!"

There were three sets of tire tracks in the dirt leading to the barn. One was much wider than the other two. "One set of tracks is from the old pickup truck we found in the barn.", she commented. "The second is from a van of some sort. Its tracks are on top of all the others, so it was the last one here. And the other vehicle is much larger and heavier." "You mean like a delivery truck of some sort." "Yes. And the security people at SRS have gone back through their records and discovered a Walmart truck entered the site on the morning of the attack on L Area, but there's no record of it leaving."

"OK, we need to check all the Walmart stores and warehouses in the area for a missing delivery truck. What's next?" "These vertical marks on the wall of the barn. They must have been practicing something." "And we've detected residue from explosives on some of the straw in the barn." "This is the place alright!" The lead investigator was nodding his head. There were plenty of fingerprints to be taken, as well as other bits and pieces that might identify who these people were.

Except for Samuel, none of the prints matched anything in the database at the J. Edgar Hoover Building in Washington. Interpol did turn up something, however. One set of prints found all over the farm matched someone on their 'most wanted' list. They only knew him as 'Jorge'.

During the early years of the Iran-Iraq war, both sides employed a number of mercenaries, particularly for clandestine operations against individual military leaders. The Interpol dossier on 'Jorge' listed him as primarily a hired assassin, charged with killing almost a dozen 'important individuals' both in Iran and in Iraq over a three-year period. His loyalty was more to Iran, according to people who knew him. Iraqi police arrested him on one occasion about a year ago, but he managed to escape by bribing several of the guards at a local jail. Iraq issued a standing warrant for his arrest and extradition. Iraq officials promised 'Jorge' would be afforded a fair trial before they hung him, seven times.

Assault on L

Follow up with the airlines identified the two German passengers from Frankfurt and the Spanish passenger from Barcelona. The passenger from San Francisco had a criminal record in Taiwan, but law enforcement officials there refused to provide further information. From interviews with Murphy and the others, the FBI knew the names the terrorists called themselves. They never showed any concern for hiding their identities in front of Murphy or any of the other hostages. It was no surprise that the names on the boarding passes were different from what they called themselves. Blythe believed the one called Henry was from San Francisco, because he kept referring to 'fisherman's wharf'. He fancied himself a seafood aficionado, although some of his 'fishing tales' were hard to believe. The one they called Silas had several other names as well. All of them had to be researched.

Henry was suspected of killing nearly a dozen individuals in Taiwan and Hong Kong, but his records were sealed. Someone had paid a lot of money to make sure his fingerprints and other information were kept hidden. The FBI judged his profile to be one of a political assassin, with strong ties to someone in a powerful position who might want to use his services again in the future. The one called Silas was a complete enigma. He had a South Carolina driver's license for the past three years. Prior to that he didn't seem to exist. The FBI referred to such people as sleepers. They move to a country and establish a fictitious history based on forged documents, such as a birth certificate or Social Security number. Usually 'sleepers' are sponsored by a foreign government that provides them with the financial means to live quietly in an area until they are needed.

What they could learn about Samuel suggested he was a 'sleeper' as well, and a very successful one. His fake documentation must have been good enough to convince the United States government to grant him a security clearance for work in Arlington. Samuel's knowledge of security systems design and operation must have been invaluable to the rest of the group. Otis had been hiding as an assistant chef in Frankfurt. The Belgian Authorities had nearly caught up with him when he left Germany for South Carolina. There was a $100,000 price on his head according to some sources in Brussels. Fortunately for him his father owned a restaurant in Noordwijk and let him 'play' in the kitchen when he was growing up. Ansel was suspected of blowing up several government office buildings in Austria, but he was never charged. No one had ever been able to find any evidence of explosives that would link him to these incidents, even though he had detailed knowledge of them.

The FBI had sufficient evidence that Jorge was now deceased to convince Interpol to close the file on him. Even though all the individuals who had stayed at the farm were now dead, evidence of their connections with other terrorist groups or previous criminal activities was valuable to the Bureau. Much of it was deemed classified, however, and not included in their final report on the events in L Area.

The Department of Energy had a problem, not only in South Carolina but in Washington. It had to consider how it would present this whole 'Savannah River Site' matter during Congressional Hearings scheduled to begin within days. Another embarrassing truth was that the Department of Defence currently had more plutonium than it knew what to do with. And with a half-life of 21,400 years, none of it was going away anytime soon. Tritium in weapons would have be replaced more often, but there were other ways to produce tritium. The billion-dollar question was 'Did the DOE need to operate the reactors at the Savannah River Site any longer?'

The easiest way out for the DOE was to say NO. That was the ultimate answer to all the Congressional questions about how they were going to prevent a recurrence of what happened in L Area. "We're shutting them all down", said the Secretary of Energy. "You're shutting them down", the Congressman asked? "Did I hear you correctly? You're shutting them all down?" "Yes, Congressmen. They are no longer needed. The world is awash with plutonium. DOD says they have enough. Time to declare the mission of the reactors at Savannah River Site completed."

The entire Congressional panel was slightly stunned. No one had given them a 'heads up' this was coming. No one from the Department of Defence had briefed them about being 'awash in plutonium'. This announcement looked opportunistic at best, and downright foolish at worst. However, she had made up her mind and no one was going to change it. The operations contractor for the site was notified only minutes before the announcement appeared on the CNN news at 6:00 pm. Everyone who worked at the site, and everyone who didn't, learned of the decision at the same time. That made the job easier for operations management at the site, but only for the first twenty-four hours.

The Governor of South Carolina was immediately on the phone to Washington demanding to know what was going on. With an economic and public disaster involving nearly 11% of his state, how was he supposed to deal with a major layoff of personnel by the state's largest employer? Many people who were to be laid off had just lost their homes.

Assault on L

Now someone had to tell them their jobs were gone as well? The Secretary of Energy listed patiently, then explained that it wasn't her problem. She told the Governor to have a nice day.

DOE's critique of events in L Reactor finally ended after three long weeks. By then most operations on the site were back to normal. P Area had mostly escaped the radiation plume, but not the government's decision to leave the reactor shut down permanently. The south security barricade on South Carolina Highway 125 had been spared as well. Of course, it really didn't matter. No one would be driving in that direction for a very long time. The government's panel of inquisitors ran out of 'witnesses' after questioning every person remotely involved in the incident. Their report provided no new information and few insights into how things might be improved. One recommendation stood out, however. The current site operations contractor was definitely incompetent and needed to go. And they knew who was best suited to take their place, at slightly higher cost to the government, of course.

By contrast with the Department of Energy, it took the local FBI team only one week to finish collecting evidence at the farm. It was all just for the record of course. There was no one left alive to prosecute. But they did have to file a field report that would be included in the full report being compiled in Washington. A survey of local Walmart stores revealed the delivery van was stolen from the Aiken Walmart. The driver had disappeared. His body was never found. All that merchandise that had been dumped from the delivery van was found, but not by the FBI. Some scavengers discovered it and had removed the entire lot.

Agents interviewed security guards at the entry barricade off Highway 125 and were able to piece together how the delivery van got onsite. The ravine where it had been dumped was never searched. Radiation levels were too high that close to L Area. All agreed they had enough to file their field report by the end of the week. What wasn't in their report was the practice area Janine had created in the woods some distance from the farmhouse. It wasn't in their report because they never found it!

Assault on L

Chapter 17

She sits quietly in a yellow chase lounge on her terracotta patio wearing nothing at all. The loosely woven silk and bamboo canopy overhead flaps gently in the fresh sea breeze, causing the sunlight to play patterns on the tiles. Crystal blue-green waters of the Mediterranean match the color of her eyes. She owns the beach for 300 meters in both directions. Private security makes sure no one is on it.

She enjoys the company of a White Russian - the drink, not the man. Her broker calls to ask if she wants to buy shares of Apple stock at a bargain price. "They only have a tiny bit of the market share compared to Microsoft", he says. "This guy Steve Jobs has some really great ideas though." She agrees. "Buy ten million shares at $4 per share."

Who could blame her for taking the Saudi's offer? The Iranians shouldn't have assumed they were the only player.

She has the New York Times delivered to the door of her six-bedroom 17th Century luxury villa each morning. The April 29th edition reports the possibility of a nuclear accident in a place called 'Chernobyl' somewhere in the Ukraine. Could this be a coincidence? Another nuclear accident only a month after the one in South Carolina? Some conspiracy theorists think there has to be a connection.

It's only four days until her 28th birthday. Maybe she'll throw a party for some of her new French friends.

She slips on a black Karategi, just as her instructor arrives for her daily martial arts workout. As always it begins with a ceremonial bow. From Okinawa, he now lives in Marseille at her convenience. They converse in Japanese. Of all the martial arts, Tae Kwon Do is her favorite. She has learned several things from him in the past three weeks, but he would readily admit being no match for her in a real fight. She almost killed him one afternoon when he accepted a ride back to Marseille in her metallic blue Lamborghini Countach.

Assault on L

Page five of yesterday's New York Times reported the results of the latest radiological survey of the area around Charleston, South Carolina. About one-third of the metropolitan population has been taken into the city on buses and given thirty minutes to collect clothes and personal items that could easily be decontaminated. No one from the Charleston area would be moving back into their homes for another five or six months.

Two men having a pint in a pub in Geneva think they know where she is. They would readily admit, however, such information is perishable. "They don't call her 'The Magician' for nothing", said one. "Yah, she could vanish into thin air at any moment", replied the other. They both laugh as they clink their glasses together.

The weather was turning cloudy in southern France. It might rain.

You Only Die Once

DeathLore

Someone once said the only good thing about dying is you only have to do it once! I remember people telling me drowning is a horrible way to die. How would they know, I wondered? Now one last burst of adrenaline spiked the length of my body like a massive electric shock. My worst fears confirmed - oblivion was certain to arrive before I reached the surface. I had gone too deep and couldn't get back. How could I have made such a stupid mistake! My lungs were on fire, like inhaling pepper spray in pure form. My mind raced through all the scenarios. Someone will pull me from the water at the last moment. No, another mistake – I was diving alone. Rescue was impossible! This was my final moment!! The overwhelming urge to inhale would not be denied. As my lungs filled with liquid, blackness began closing about me. Gradually, paralyzing terror transmuted into a peacefulness I hadn't expected. A voice spoke softly. 'It must be someone who had passed on before me, mom or dad, perhaps...' The voice grew louder... "Session End", it said. It repeated.

Points of light began replacing the darkness, a few at first, then more and more until images began to materialize. I became aware of a couch beneath me, supporting my weight. A touch on my hand and I realized someone in a bright orange uniform was standing next to me. "You'll probably need an hour or so to recover from your session. We're here to make sure you suffer no ill effects as stipulated in your contract with us. EsCyberScope is very proud of its 99.9% recovery record. Would you like a drink of water?" I managed to shake my head, wondering if I would ever want to drink anything again. 'What happened to the other 0.1%', I suddenly wondered?

In fact, it took the full hour before I felt well enough to leave the EsCyberScope laboratory. Technicians there pride themselves on being accurate. While waiting for the world to reconstitute itself I began to wonder if the architect for this place ever considered that some people are afraid of heights. All the walls were tinted glass. I lay inches away from one of those glass walls, looking down at the ants scurrying back and forth on the streets many floors below. Perhaps we were all just ants in a giant colony, going through our daily motions, foraging for food and shelter, trying to survive one day at a time.

The elevator ride down to ground level left my legs a bit rubbery, but the feeling of real people bumping into you on the street can be quite refreshing, even when it's 112 degrees. If I managed it properly the credit EsCyberScope had just made to my account would be enough to get me through another six months. Four hours work for 180 days of minimalist living! OK, so it might be the worst four hours imaginable, and those occasional five-second flashbacks were unsettling, but there certainly are more interesting ways to die than being penny-less and freezing to death under a bridge somewhere. I should know because they say I've experienced two of them. Or maybe three or four. I'm not sure.

Efforts to map the human brain began in earnest in the third decade of the 21st Century. By 2055 such studies had found the brain to be an extremely dynamic organ, capable of instantly remapping itself to cope with an almost infinite variety of external and internal stimuli and stressors. Mapping of the brain was found to depend heavily upon its stress environment, with hundreds of unique stressors being investigated over three decades. Considered the ultimate external stressor, the death experience proved to be problematic however since the law prohibited actually killing people to map their brain's reaction to end of life. Use of chemically enhanced virtual reality to convince subjects they were dying without actually killing them proved to be lawful solution, even as the ethics were still being debated.

The long-term effect of chemically leveraged enhanced virtual reality (CLEVR) on 'research volunteers' was declared, without evidence, to be minimal. Most of those who agreed to 'experience death in the laboratory' were homeless people who would be well compensated for accepting the risk of future problems, mental or physical. If anyone did suffer long-term effects, the state would provide medical care. On rare occasions 'mishaps' at EsCyberScope were revealed to the public, but state-run news media quickly moved on. 'Nothing to see here', they insisted.

My name is George, and although I can't afford a permanent place of residence, I am not lazy or ignorant and have an engineering degree to prove it. I make an effort to know as much about what's going on in the world as most people. One spring day five years ago I decided to 'go walk about' as the Australians like to call it. South Texas looks a lot like Australia, judging by the pictures I've seen - I've never actually been outside the continental U.S. After cancer took my wife of 30 years what did I need with a four-bedroom house in the Woodlands? There were too many memories, many of them quite painful. I no longer wanted that house or any house for that matter.

You might think $350,000 would allow me to live well in the Houston area for quite some time. 'Quite some time' turned out to be less than three years. Then it was life on the streets or get a job. 'Been there, done that', I thought. A job meant rules to follow, people telling me what to do and when to do it. No thanks! 'Like the birds in the sky I'll take my chances with whatever the Lord provides, simple and uncomplicated.' Food wasn't a problem. There are plenty of city-funded soup kitchens in north Houston. Keeping clean was more difficult. Funny how, in the middle of the 21st Century, you could eat for free, but soap and a hot shower costs $20.00. $1.00 more to use the public toilet. At least I didn't have to clean it. Apparently nobody did.

I think it was Sam who put me onto the thing at EsCyberScope. He claimed he was younger than me, but he didn't look it. He died sixteen months later but I never made the connection. "What they put you through is absolutely horrible, but the pay is fantastic", Sam insisted. One thing about life on the streets. There are no surnames. That way when the authorities come asking questions you can truthfully answer, "I don't know anybody by that name". Sam showed me the building but wouldn't go inside. It's one of the tallest buildings in Houston, with huge glass panels that act like mirrors, lighting up everything across the street late in the day. I looked up and tried to count the floors, but my neck started hurting before I could finish. It was more than thirty! Sam was missing three fingers on his right hand. He pointed skyward with the one finger he had left. "They're on the 27th floor, I think. Not sure, but there's a directory on the wall on the ground level." Sam's hearing was almost gone. I nodded that I understood. Homeless people can't afford hearing aids.

"I won't need to go there for two more months", Sam declared, now staring at his worn-out shoes. It was as if a doctor had just told him he had two more months to live. After recovering from my first session at EsCyberScope I understood what he meant. It was an indescribable feeling, for no particular reason, that life was both artificial and temporary. There must have been others like Sam who went there from time to time, but only Sam would admit it. He claimed the drugs they used were 98% effective at blocking out your memory of everything that happened there, including signing your name on the waiver form in the front office. That's what he said, anyway.

People living on the streets age more quickly. At least it seems that way judging by what I see in the mirror at the public showers. Three years ago a dirty shade of grey began a full out invasion on both sides of my head. The auburn hair that no longer grows on top has relocated to my nose and ears. Wrinkles are breeding at an alarming rate on my forehead while my chin is rapidly disappearing. Not that my appearance matters much anymore. I certainly couldn't afford to buy dinner for an attractive woman if I should happen across one. Beards were considered sexy back in the 2020's, but having one nowadays is the unmistakable mark of poverty. Clothing from charity shops and the Salvation Army isn't as stylish as it used to be either. Most of the time I find the freedoms of living without restrictions exhilarating but trusting in the Lord to provide often falls short of expectations.

Walking away from your job, your house, your friends, all forms of social media, and society in general isn't difficult. Staying off all the societal networks is hard work, however. Fortunately, I've never been arrested, needed a passport, or held a government job that required me to be fingerprinted. To remain homeless, you must remain 'anonymous', and society doesn't like 'anonymous'. Nearly all of society's institutions insist on identifying you. Governments, banks, hospitals, etc. all want to identify you. "We'll be happy to help you", they say. "But first you have to tell us everything there is to know about you so we can cross-categorize you down to your toenails". You have to be tough and clever to remain anonymous.

No one carrying cash survives on the streets for more than a week. That means finding an institution that will keep safe what little money you have on a 'no questions asked' basis. When homeless communities began to exceed 10% of the population local governments in most major cities were forced to create such institutions to regain some measure of control over urban violence. But these places aren't advertised so you have to look for them. Mine only knows me as 'George236596714'. I can only access my funds in exchange for goods or services at public points of sale (PPOS). Homeless people have fully realized the dream of cashless living! Everyone is safer that way.

Homeless people have to shelter somewhere when they're not panhandling in the downtown part of the city. Winters are the worst, of course, even though it rarely freezes anymore this far south. The simultaneous rise in home mortgage rates and unemployment in the Houston area over the last four years caused many suburban homeowners to abandon their houses, as they found themselves owing substantially more than even the most optimistic selling price. Most of these homes are new enough to need little in the way of maintenance and now provide suitable shelter for the homeless, as long as we disturb the neighborhood as little as possible. There are no utilities, of course. Battery operated lights are also prohibited, and we can't open any windows. We don't need someone calling the cops to investigate whether a neighbor is being burgled. There are eight of us in 'our house' not far from where the Northline Shopping Center used to be. It's almost too far to walk to downtown - sometimes you can hitch a ride that will take you most of the way.

Doctors say walking is good exercise. I suppose it is if you do it only when you want to. If you're homeless and have no other way to get where you need to be, it's not regarded as 'exercise'. Cities are designed for cars and buses, not people on foot. It's amazing how much you take for granted when you own a car. When you're on foot it can be quite a challenge figuring out how to get from one side of a six-lane highway, like the Beltway 8 or the 610 Loop, to the other. I often feel like the pioneers in their covered wagons who had to figure out how to cross the Mississippi River. A five-minute drive in the car can be an hour long walk if there's a major highway between you and Walmart. I particularly try to avoid the areas west of downtown Houston where Interstate 10, the 610 Loop, and Highway 290 all come together. This impressive display of concrete spaghetti is five levels high and provides a more formidable barrier than the Great Wall of China. For the homeless it might as well be the Atlantic Ocean! The only way across is to hitch multiple rides, at least three or four. It can take most of the day.

People who travel a lot say they see the world - they don't really. You only really see the world up close and personal when you're on foot. Then you see the details, the cracks in the pavement and the litter everywhere. People in cars don't notice the large fissures in the walls between some of the shops. They don't see the thousands of dark alleys that lead to rows of dumpsters overflowing with glass and plastic waste that will never decompose. Tens of thousands of rusting storm sewer grates are invisible until you step on them. God knows what lives down there! Cities are beautiful from a distance, or even from a car window. They are actually quite ugly when you have to walk the streets.

The human nose is acutely sensitive to the smell of smoke, especially at night in total darkness. I was instantly awake and heard others scrambling about. "Get out", someone yelled. My sleeping bag was old, but I still wanted to save it. I grabbed up what I could and felt my way to the door. The smell of smoke was much stronger there. I felt the door itself and it was very hot. I didn't dare open it. A single window was the other option. As a crawled across the floor trying to stay below the smoke, I could feel vibrations emanating from above. The attic must be on fire and collapsing. I had little time left. Even less than I realized. The ceiling disintegrated before I could reach the window. Burning timbers and debris cascaded into the room like a fiery waterfall. It just kept coming.

I struggled to free myself only to be buried by the next wave of flaming plasterboard and insulation. After managing a few more feet I began to realize I wasn't going to make it. My sleeping bag had caught fire and I had to let go of it. Acrid smoke had reached the floor and I began to choke uncontrollably. They say most people caught in a house fire die of smoke inhalation rather than burning. Please, I prayed. Let it be true. But as I managed another foot of progress my skin began to blister. The pain along my arms and legs became unbearable. My clothes were on fire. Shock set in as blessed darkness began to carry me away from the agony. I looked back at my body burning now, engulfed in the flames. I felt nothing at all ……

A soft voice, unfamiliar yet comforting. "Session End". It repeated. Light crept in from somewhere and nowhere. Then faint images. The color orange. Words of encouragement. "……. an hour or so to recover from your session. We're here to make sure you suffer no ill effects as stipulated in your contract with us. EsCyberScope is very proud of its 99.9% recovery record. Would you like a drink of water?" I nodded. "Yes, please", I managed, feeling a bit hoarse for some reason. Had I heard those words before? No. Probably not. Then I threw up, choking myself in the process.

The hardest thing to maintain on the streets is your self-esteem. No one ever compliments you because you're invisible. Nobody sees you. That's a good thing. Most of the time you don't want to be remembered. You just want to be left alone. However, sometimes late at night, when you take stock of things, it hurts that no one cares about you. Others like you might say they care, but they don't really. It's not as though you'll be missed if you disappeared tomorrow. That's just the way it is. Nobody cares if your teeth rot. Dental care is way outside the budget for homeless people. So is medical care, other than an occasional visit to the Emergency Room when absolutely necessary. A homeless person feels completely alone and isolated while standing in a crowd of thousands. Depression is your fiercest adversary. It's hard work fighting it off every day. Psychiatric help is out of the question. An hour with one of those guys would consume your entire food budget for a month!

Not knowing (or caring) what day it is – that's another freedom homeless people enjoy. Most days are pretty much the same, so whether it's

DeathLore

Wednesday or Saturday doesn't really matter. There are exceptions, of course. This day was definitely one of them. Word spread quickly that the authorities were looking for someone. Six-foot-tall, olive complexion, auburn hair thinning dramatically on top with grey strands creeping in at the temples, and scruffy beard. If I had a twin that's what he would look like. Of course, nobody could remember seeing anyone like that in our area. I had to 'disappear' for a few days until things cooled off. There are places to hide - I won't say where, of course. The disadvantage is that news can't find you either. A week passed before I learned my twin was wanted for first-degree murder.

Actually, there was one other fellow in our group who once admitted going to EsCyberScope. Billy let it slip one night around 2 am, when it was just him and me and Sam huddled in the entrance alcove of a department store during a thunderstorm. He said he got the 'shakes' about 48 hours before he had to go there, but he didn't know why. Sam claimed that after ten sessions they wouldn't let you do it anymore, but he wasn't sure if he had had his ten. Billy was the only one who cried when we put Sam in the ground two months later. Sam had no family that anybody knew of. I suppose we were his family, just me and Billy. The state paid to bury Sam with just a small marble plaque over his head. He was a true minimalist so that would have been more than enough for him. We all suspected Sam's heart just gave out. Nobody said for sure.

He did look a lot older than the rest of us. His hair was white, not grey, and he walked with a bit of a limp, like his right leg didn't always get the message from his brain. He always had a smile for whomever he met. My mom would have liked Sam. "No harm in him", she would have said. No higher compliment could be paid. It was hard to believe we wouldn't be seeing Sam ever again.

Another thing you learn on the streets: Don't get too close to anybody. Just because you see them today doesn't mean they'll be there tomorrow. In fact, there's a better than even chance you'll never see them again. And the less you know about someone the less you can tell the authorities if they come looking. I was about 90% sure I hadn't murdered anyone. That left a 10% chance that I had but just didn't remember it. That wouldn't be the sort of thing most people would forget. Perhaps I should blame EsCyberScope for my not being like most people. Maybe other memories were blocked besides the ones from my sessions in their laboratory.

DeathLore

After a week hiding out, I decided to turn myself in to the authorities. That was the only way I could find out what evidence they had against me. Having generally avoided the police since becoming homeless, I wasn't sure what to expect. Common courtesy was a surprise, given that I represented the lowest level of society and had been accused of a most heinous crime. Even the coffee was considerably better than what I was used to. I was fingerprinted of course – so much for anonymity! The state provided me with Counsel, a young-looking, but bright, female attorney who cautioned me to keep my answers brief as well as truthful. She was quite attractive to a man of 58 years. But when she looked at me it was clear she had no interest whatsoever, other than seeing to it that I got a fair hearing.

The police interview room was pale green – walls, floor, ceiling, table, everything. The Houston Police Department must have gotten a special deal on that color paint. "Please tell me where you were on the night of the 23rd of July of this year", asked the rather thin looking Houston Metropolitan Police Detective. His uniform was freshly pressed, and shoes polished like a mirror. He was a most 'antiseptic' looking fellow – probably a compliment in his reality. It must have taken him a full hour to get dressed for work that morning. His stony facial expression left no doubt he would be challenging my answer to his question, even as I noticed his moustache was trimmed a bit shorter on one side than the other. I get distracted by things like that for some reason. It made me smile just a bit when I didn't mean to. Wonder what he thought of that?

I asked what day of the week that was, just to buy some time to think. "Thursday" replied my Counsel, rather too quickly. That information was no help. Then I remembered buying a donut at the Krispy Kreme shop less than a block away after leaving the EsCyberScope building. The date was in big red letters on the wall behind the counter in a banner announcing 'Dollar-Donut Day'. "I spent most of the night walking from north of the city to the downtown area", I replied. "Nobody would give me a ride that night." Then I thought to add, "You can ask the people at EsCyberScope. They will confirm I was at their place on the morning of July 24th." My Counsel returned a cautioning frown.

"It is your statement that you were on foot north of the city the night of the 23rd, and not in the Pasadena area around midnight. Is that correct?", asked the detective? His firm demeanor never changed. Neither did his moustache.

DeathLore

"Yes", I replied with a polite smile, having gained a piece of information.

"Suppose I told you there are witnesses who saw you commit murder in Pasadena around midnight on July 23rd", said the Detective?

"Do you have witnesses or not", interrupted Counsel? "Yes", replied the Detective, turning his gaze slowly toward her. "How many", she asked? "Five", he answered. She frowned, again.

I had never been in a police lineup before. It was quite a tedious and time-consuming process actually. "Turn to the left". "Now turn to the right". "Now look straight ahead". I didn't think the other guys looked much like me, but then no one asked my opinion. After nearly half an hour, three out of the five witnesses claimed I was definitely the man they saw in Pasadena that night. The other two were 'pretty sure'. Trial date was set for late February. It was two days before Counsel came to my cell to explain the case against me. She brought a law student with her – he was even younger.

"How are you George", she asked? It was rhetorical question – neither of them really wanted to know how I was. I could have admitted I slept better the past two nights than I had in the last two years. I chose not to. "OK, George, you stand accused of committing the crime of first-degree murder on the night of July 23, 2055. If convicted, you could be executed by electric shock, depending on how the jury finds. Texas is one of only three States than still has the death penalty for first-degree murder."

'Lucky me, that I live in Texas', I thought.

"The victim was a Pasadena resident, who happened to be out walking her dog just before midnight on July 23rd. You were seen approaching the victim from behind and striking her on the head with a length of steel pipe. It was single blow, but it crushed part of her skull and caused a massive cerebral hemorrhage, resulting in her immediate death. Several witnesses heard you say, "That will teach the bitch" as you ran away from the scene. That statement was judged sufficient to bring a charge of first-degree murder instead of second-degree murder. It appeared that you knew the victim and the assault was premeditated. What have you to say?"

"Who goes out to walk their dog at midnight?", was all I could think of. I raised my hand immediately by way of apology. I needed time to process what I had just been told. "First of all, I wasn't in Pasadena that night, or any other night. As far as I know I've never been in Pasadena."

"As far as you know", replied Counsel? I had to confess that I experience occasional memory loses, but I was 99% certain I had never been to Pasadena. "I don't know anyone in Pasadena, so I couldn't have known the victim. What motive would I have to kill this woman? What else can you tell me about her?"

Counsel gave me a condescending look. "She was 31 years old, single, wearing a dark grey track suit and had red hair. But you said you didn't know her."

"I'm trying to solve a puzzle, Counselor. I don't even know where to start, but I need all the information I can get. Can you help me?"

"I just told you all that was in the police report", she replied with a plastic smile.

"What about the witnesses? How could there have been five witnesses at that hour?"

"There were five witnesses because you attacked this woman within 20 feet of a popular bar, directly under a streetlight, just as the witnesses were coming out the entrance foyer. They may have had a few drinks, but they claim to have seen you clear as day."

"Red hair, you said?" "Yes", she replied. Why was that significant? I had no idea….

"Is there anyone who can testify that you were in north Houston on the night of July 23rd", asked Counsel?

"I doubt it." Even if they saw me that night they would be reluctant to testify. Homeless people don't get involved in such things, especially something like this. "But EsCyberScope can verify I was at their place between 10 am and 2 pm on the 24th. And there's the lady at the donut shop after that."

Counsel looked at the floor for a moment. "George, these people might be able to account for you that morning, but you need an alibi for the night before. That's when the murder occurred. And the witnesses are very confident they saw you commit the crime."

"Doesn't look good, does it?" "No", she replied.

Daily life in jail awaiting trial isn't necessarily better or worse than being on the streets. It's just different, and warmer. Neither the weather nor the calendar is of any concern. Nor is eating. The only real problem is you can't leave. On the streets if you get fed up with an area or group of people you just go somewhere else. Diplomacy was never a prominent part of my skill set. In jail diplomacy is paramount to survival. Get a group of ten people together and a hierarchy quickly forms. Someone takes the lead. With hundreds of people who can't leave, hierarchy dictates most everything. You can challenge the leader and spend lots of time in the infirmary, or you can just learn your place and stay in it. My Counsel seemed to show up about once a month. Apparently it was something she was required to do, only this time she had a request. "How would you like to go outside for a day?" "Sure", I replied, pretending I had a choice.

The Houston Chronicle was doing a 'human interest story' on first-degree murder cases awaiting trial. Bringing their audio/video studio to the jail was out of the question. They wanted me to come to them, shackled of course and with 'escorts'. It was nice to see sunshine and something other than the color grey. The video studio is on the 10th floor of the Chronicle Building, another modern mostly glass building in the center of downtown Houston. I've never been comfortable with heights. Why are buildings mostly glass these days? This one had an atrium right up the center, with a mezzanine leading to the offices on each floor. As soon as we exited the elevator on Floor 10 my heart started to race. With my wrists shackled to my waist and a policeman on each elbow, I had to go wherever they took me. Keeping my eyes fixed on the decorative wall opposite the railings, I could only hope the journey was a short one. I don't recall ever being so desperate for four solid walls around me.

Suddenly I was pushed backwards against the railing by someone exiting one of the offices. My restraints prevented me from grabbing or pushing off the railing to regain my balance. I felt myself going over backwards, while the guards made what seemed a half-hearted attempt to retrieve me. I was now facing upwards, watching the four mezzanines above me begin a surreal retreat. I felt the backs of my legs bounce off the railing, spinning me in mid-air so I now faced the marble floor on ground level. The human brain can process information at incredible speed, especially when stressed. Researchers claim that the mind can recall and even re-experience the significant memories of an entire lifetime in the time it takes to fall to one's death. When death is certain memories are enhanced, displacing reality in the precious moments of life that remain.

It was unquestionably my father's voice. There was a 'B' on my report card. I wasn't supposed to make 'B's', only 'A's'. "Why didn't you make an 'A'", he asked in a threatening voice? "I don't know", I said. "I tried; I really did." "Trying isn't good enough", he insisted. Go to your room and stay there until I tell you to come out." I spent a lifetime in my room that evening. It was one of many lifetimes I spent there in solitary confinement. It seems I was always being punished for not measuring up to Dad's ever escalating standards. I simply wasn't good enough to please him. He made that perfectly clear. Even my Chemical Engineering Degree from the University of Texas didn't satisfy him, because I didn't graduate top of my class. I suppose I could have. There were 52 Chemical Engineers in my graduating class. I came 6th from the top.

I always wondered what it would be like to have a brother or sister. Not that I really wanted one. But it would have given Dad someone else to criticize, taking some of the heat off me. The nice thing about being an only child is your things are always where you left them, well almost. The downside is there's no one to blame if something gets broken or you can't find something. And there's no one to solve your problems for you. It's all up to you. Succeed or fail, you have to do everything yourself. Asking for help is a sure sign of weakness. That's what Dad always said. As a teenager I found solace walking in the woods behind our house. A small creek about three feet wide ran through a ravine in those woods. I always took my single shot 22 calibre rifle with me. If I saw a squirrel, I would shoot at it. One day I hit one and killed it. It hit me like a thunderbolt. I had killed that squirrel for no reason at all. I had taken a life. Why? I didn't know. When I arrived back at the house Mom asked why I was crying. I said I didn't know. The death of that squirrel has haunted me ever since.

The year after graduation I met Samantha at a bar in downtown Austin. I was still looking for a job and thinking I needed to relocate closer to the gulf coast, maybe Baytown or League City. There were plenty of girls at University, but all were rather shallow and some downright dishonest. Samantha was a blue-eyed blonde, a few inches shorter than me, who had a math degree. She could add up the grocery list in her head before we got to the checkout. That had to be worth something! She also had a job.

Samantha and I were married three months later, before she had time to find somebody better. It was a year after that when the doctors told us Samantha couldn't have children. We had been trying, thinking I was the one with the problem. I was simultaneously relieved and disappointed. I really wanted a son. Moving to League City wasn't difficult. Neither of us had very much worth moving. My job offer from Exxon changed everything of course. In two years we were able to buy a house in the Woodlands just north of Houston.

Funny how you can take 'the good life' for granted for decades, and then suddenly with no warning your world crumbles around you. Cutbacks in the petrochemical industry due to reduced demand for petroleum-based products was inevitable I suppose. It had been forecast for over twenty years, so often no one took it seriously anymore. One Friday morning I was told my job had been made redundant. The following Thursday Samantha was diagnosed with stage four pancreatic cancer. Six months of chemotherapy and related treatments wiped out what savings we had. The government and health insurance companies talked a good story but seemed to vanish when she finally lost the fight. I started stacking the medical bills on the dining room table. It wasn't long before I could no longer see the top of the stack.

It was true what they say about the slowing of time when death is certain. The marble floor was rising to meet me at an accelerating pace. I must have screamed. Everyone screams they say. There was searing pain upon impact. A few incoherent images, then black emptiness.

Alcohol and disinfectant. I could smell it. No light, just the smell. I couldn't open my eyes, but I could hear distant sounds. Then closer ones. "He's awake", someone whispered. I tried to lift one arm, but it was restrained. Then the other arm. It was the same. Was I still in police shackles? No, my arms were at my sides, not in front of me. "Don't try to move", I heard. "Your restraints are to keep you from pulling off your monitors." I could hear the steady beat of a heart monitor – beep, beep, beep... "You've had a seizure. Please do not try to move." Suddenly there was bright light. Something had been removed from over my eyes. I opened them slowly.

The world had turned silver and white. Why can't hospitals ever have things that are red or blue or purple, not just silver and white? OK, the face standing over me was black, but her uniform was blindingly white. "What happened?", I managed. "How did I survive the fall?" "What fall", the face replied? "From the 10th floor. I was with my Counsel." The black face was replaced with a blank white ceiling. After a few moments the black face reappeared. "I'm told no one is scheduled to visit you until next week. You were found collapsed on the floor of your cell at the Harris County Jail. Can you remember what you were doing before you blacked out?"

I told her where I was and what I was doing, in as much detail as I could remember. Suddenly her face was replaced by a man with jet black hair, probably dyed, and moustache, trimmed evenly on both sides. At least he wasn't wearing white. "I'm Sergeant Clyve. Can you hear me?" "Yes", I replied. "You haven't been anywhere outside the Harris County Jail for nearly three months now. Your next visit with Counsel is scheduled for next Thursday. She will be notified that you have had an 'episode'. You will be returned to your cell at the Harris County Jail as soon as the hospital releases you and placed under 24-hour surveillance. Do you understand what I have just told you?" I nodded. It didn't mean I believed him. It just meant I didn't feel like arguing at the moment. Twenty-four-hour surveillance… 'I won't be able to take a crap without somebody watching me. How wonderful!' It turned out to be a video camera. I pretended it was one of hundreds, making it unlikely anyone was actually watching me after all.

Counsel did show up on Thursday just as I was told. She claims she hasn't visited me in the past month and knows nothing about an interview with the Houston Chronicle. I'm struggling to believe her, but then what choice do I have. "Trial begins in three weeks", she says. "I will be here every Thursday afternoon until then, so we can go over your testimony should I decide to put you on the stand. You are not required to testify in your own behalf but given the circumstances of the crime and the fact that there are a number of reputable witnesses it may be almost impossible to avoid." I nodded in agreement. "Are you certain there is no one who can give you an alibi?" I nodded again. She starred at me for a moment, then moved on.

"We have to place you somewhere other than Pasadena around midnight on July 23rd." Again, I mentioned the donut shop and my appointment with EsCyberScope the morning of the 24th. She isn't interested, preferring to study her papers for a few moments. "Alright we'll call them both. It's all we've got. What size suit do you wear?" "I think a 44 long", I guessed. "And lose the beard before you go to court, OK?" With that Counsel folded her notebook and called for the guard to let her out.

Another lifetime passed while I waited those last three weeks. Finally, the moment arrived. I thought I looked quite smart, clean shaven and wearing the navy-blue suit and yellow tie provided by Counsel's law firm. The shoes didn't match, but the jury probably wouldn't notice. Counsel was already at the defendant's table when I was brought in. She didn't look up as I was seated. The draperies framing the portico were pale blue silk tapestry. The carpet was burgundy. Our table was oak, while the Prosecutor had a darker and slightly larger one of mahogany. I could already see where this was going. In fact, everything in the courtroom was mahogany except for the defendant's table. It seemed as out of place as I did. Why was I cursed with noticing such things? All rose as the Judge entered the court room and took his place behind the ornately carved bench.

"Your client pleads 'not guilty'? Is that correct, Ms. Roberts?" "Yes, your Honor", Counsel replied. The Prosecutor for the State cracked a wry smile. It was obvious he considered this case a 'slam dunk'. The judge's expression left no doubt he agreed. "You may begin your opening statement, Mr. Owens". The Judge gestured toward the jury.

The State's opening statement was brief. Five witnesses saw me murder a woman in cold blood. It was obvious I knew the woman and had been planning to kill her for some time. I obviously didn't care who saw me commit this heinous act. Therefore, I didn't deserve leniency. I should get the death penalty, plain and simple. The Prosecutor spoke for a sum total of four minutes; whereupon my Counsel waived her right to an opening statement. The next two hours brought forth five witnesses of diverse backgrounds and impressive credibility. All were upstanding citizens in the community and had no reason to lie. At the end of their testimony even I could no longer be sure I didn't do it.

Finally, it was our turn. Counsel called as her first witness an employee from the donut shop, who confirmed that July 24th was indeed one of their 'Dollar-Donut Days'. However, she didn't remember seeing me there that afternoon, or any afternoon for that matter. One time in five years when you want someone to remember you and they can't do it! Anonymity isn't always a good thing. This lady couldn't confirm that I 'didn't look nervous', like I had just murdered someone the night before. She couldn't say that I 'didn't have blood on my clothes'. Surely there would be blood on my clothes if I just fractured a woman's skull less than 24 hours earlier. She didn't remember me at all. The Prosecutor was looking at his watch. He could probably make tee-time at the golf course that afternoon if he and the Judge could wrap this up in another couple of hours.

There was only one other witness. Counsel called a tall blonde headed gentleman to the stand. He looked to be in his early forties, well groomed, obviously well paid. "Can you tell the jury your name and occupation please", asked Counsel? "My name is Jason Osterhausenshire. I am the facilities manager at EsCyberScope, Houston office", he replied with a slight eastern European accent. Counsel looked down at her notebook. "Mr. Osterhausenshire, can you tell the jury whether the defendant in this case has ever visited your EsCyberScope facilities here in Houston?" She waited while the witness consulted his registration book. "Yes, this individual has volunteered to be a subject for research at our laboratory on six occasions." "Mr. Osterhausenshire, did the defendant volunteer for such research at any time in the month of July of last year?" "Yes, he signed into our facilities at 10 am on July 23rd for a confirmation of previous results recorded six months earlier." "Excuse me, Mr. Osterhausenshire, are you sure he signed in on the 23rd and not the 24th?" Counsel looked at me for confirmation. I couldn't give her any. Possibly they made a mistake about the date when I signed in that day. The witness consulted his records again. "Yes, it's quite clear on our documents. The defendant signed into our Houston laboratory at 10 am on the morning of July 23rd and didn't sign out until 2 pm on July 24th." He raised his eyes toward Counsel, then suddenly looked a bit puzzled....

"Is something wrong, Mr. Osterhausenshire", asked Counsel? The Prosecutor suddenly bolted upright from his chair. "Your honor I object." "On what grounds", asked the Judge? "Those records must be in error", replied the Prosecutor. "This man was in Pasadena committing murder that night. He couldn't have been at some laboratory downtown. It's not possible!", he screamed, waiving his hands in the air. Counsel asked the witness to check once more. "This man couldn't possibly have been in Pasadena on the night of July 23rd", replied Mr. Osterhausenshire. "No one enters or leaves our laboratory without signing our register. Rigorous access control is required by law and enforced electronically."

"Your Honor, may I have a moment to consult with my client", asked Counsel? The Judge nodded. She moved the chair closer to me as she took her seat and leaned in. "Do you understand this ", she whispered? "I must have gone there on the wrong day", I responded. "My appointments are only for four hours. That's all they pay me for. Four hours!" "Could you have been there for 28 hours, instead of 4, and not realized it?" "I'm not sure", I replied. Counsel sat back in her chair with a startled look. "What in hell do they do to you at that place?" "Never mind", I said. Counsel looked at the Judge for a moment, then back at me. "This witness just gave you an iron clad alibi for murder. Do you want me to challenge his testimony?" "Absolutely not", I replied!

Counsel stood in front of the table to address the court. "Your Honor the Defence asks that the charge of first-degree murder against this defendant be dismissed." The Prosecutor, still unconvinced of my innocence, objected and petitioned the court to subpoena EsCyberScope's records for the period in question in order to confirm their validity. The Judge nodded. "So ordered." My Counsel seemed only mildly annoyed. "No problem", she said. It was the first and only time she ever smiled at me. "You are the luckiest man I've ever met!" A brisk handshake and she was off to her next case. I never saw her again.

Another month passed while I waited for the court to rule on Counsel's motion that I be acquitted. During that time, I was allowed to sit in, without legal representation, on the Prosecutor's investigation of EsCyberScope's subpoenaed records, as long as I kept my mouth shut. The company provided a variety of witnesses, each testifying to the uncompromising rigor applied in the conduct of each of their activities. This culminated in an appearance by the Senior Vice President for EsCyberScope's operations worldwide.

The Prosecutor rose from his chair. "Mr. Hamphersaven, you are responsible for research activities at seven EsCyberScope laboratories in four countries. Is that correct?" "That is correct", he replied. "And you have conducted your own investigation into the discrepancies in admission records for your Houston facility for the month of July of last year. Is that correct?" "Yes, I have." "Can you give the court an explanation for these discrepancies?"

"Yes, I will attempt to explain what happened. A thorough review of our records for the period of July 23rd through July 24th of last year at our Houston laboratory has confirmed beyond any doubt that the subject in question spent 28 hours under the supervision of two of our researchers, although he was lead to believe that the time he spent there was only four hours. The subject mistakenly reported one day early for his appointment scheduled for July 24th. Realizing this, the two researchers on duty took advantage of subject's error and proceeded to conduct research protocols that were completely unethical and definitely not authorized by management at EsCyberScope. This involved a number of prohibited activities, including editing portions of the subject's brain map so that he would feel extreme hostility towards females with red hair, enhancing these edits with chemicals so they would persist after the subject was disconnected from our virtual reality equipment, transporting the subject to a location outside the laboratory where he was observed to attack and kill a female victim with red hair, transporting the subject back to the laboratory, and finally re-editing the subject's brain map to remove all memory of these actions."

I could barely believe what I was hearing. That was me this man was talking about. Feelings of rage, confusion and guilt raced through my mind. I had to clamp my hand over my mouth to keep from screaming in anger. A brief wave of nausea passed over me. How in God's name could they have done this to someone. The Judge looked dazed. The Prosecutor stood expressionless for a full minute, like a statue, frozen in disbelief. "Is it really possible to do as you have just described? Can you actually do that to a human being", he asked? "Yes sir, it is possible", Mr. Hamphersaven replied. His expression was extremely sincere and apologetic.

The Prosecutor struggled to compose himself. He looked down, shuffling his papers, trying to formulate his next question. "What could possibly cause these two researchers do such a thing", he asked. Mr. Hamphersaven looked uncomfortable as he cleared his throat. "Apparently they had a theory, untested of course, that our chemically enhanced virtual reality techniques had their limits – that those techniques couldn't cause a person to perform an act that violated his own moral code of conduct. It's been proven that a person under hypnosis can't be made to perform an act they believe is criminal or immoral. These researchers didn't believe the subject would commit a violent act. However, their efforts to test their theory by simulation in the laboratory had been inconclusive. The defendant's arrival for his appointment 24 hours early gave them the opportunity to test their theory in reality without anyone finding out. Or so they thought."

The Prosecutor suddenly remembered I was in the courtroom. He turned to look at me with newfound sympathy and perhaps even a glimmer of understanding. Then he turned back to face the Judge. "Your Honor I wish to call these two researchers as witnesses, and then charge them as accomplices to the crime of first-degree murder on July 23rd of last year." "You can't call them, your Honor", Mr. Hamphersaven interrupted. "We suspect they have fled the country some time ago. We have no idea where they are." "When did you learn of this", asked the Judge? "They failed to show up for work the first week in August of last year. After 30 days their employment at EsCyberScope was terminated. I only learned of this two weeks ago, when we discovered electronic records indicating the events I have just described for the court."

In the end it was the court's decision that, although I had committed the act, I could not legally be held responsible for murdering the woman in Pasadena on July 23rd. Before I was released on a balmy sunny afternoon in late March, the court ordered that I be provided 'psychological counselling' to help me deal with 'the guilt I must be experiencing' after learning that I killed someone. I decided to decline – more counselling was definitely not what I needed. It was anger I was feeling, not guilt. An anger management course might have helped, but it wasn't offered. It took me a few days to calm down. Life wasn't that bad actually. I had spent the entire winter where it was warm and dry. News reports mentioned a company called EsCyberScope had been fined $1.5 billion for illegal activities, including unauthorized research protocols indirectly responsible for the death of a woman in Pasadena. 'Indirectly?' Corporate spin was alive and well!

I did accept the new clothes the city provided upon my release from the Harris County Jail. That and being clean shaven must have made a difference. It was no problem hitching a ride out of the downtown area. They let me out less than a mile from the old neighborhood near where Northline Mall used to be. Nothing much had changed. Some faces were familiar, others weren't. Billy was the only one who realized I had been gone the past eight months. He didn't seem any worse for wear. Same old blue jean jacket, with a few holes for ventilation. Same worn out tennis shoes. He preferred the old Converse ones, like we wore to school when we were kids. Not sure where he got them, actually.

Billy had deep-set eyes, long white hair that would blow in the wind, and a low baritone voice. Any church choir would have been thrilled to have him, but he didn't like churches. Sometimes he would start to talk about what he did for a living before he became homeless. Then he would catch himself and go quiet. It had something to do with nuclear materials. That's all we could ever get out of him. Unlike many of us, Billy hadn't chosen to live on the streets. He made it clear he had no choice, but never said why. Even though he was only 5 foot 6 inches, just about everyone in our group looked up to him, morally or emotionally if not physically.

The old gang had moved houses. The homeowners next-door to the old house had too many noisy late-night parties. Our new house was much quieter. The average homeless person doesn't live past the age of 44. Those of us who are older have to band together, for protection from the younger ones. All we want is to live out our remaining days in peace and quiet. Nobody mentioned EsCyberScope. I began to wonder if my visits there, and even the trial, were just part of a bad dream. It was getting hard to tell what was real and what wasn't. Maybe reality was in fact just what you remembered. In that case if I didn't remember it then it didn't happen. Except I did remember Mr. Hamphersaven's testimony. That must have actually happened, or I wouldn't have been arrested and tried for murder. Or was I?

The days got longer then shorter again as the first autumn chill arrived. It wasn't cold yet, but that feeling of urgency had returned for all of us. It's what makes animals start storing up food, knowing that resources will be getting scarce and life will be getting more difficult very soon. When we were children we called it 'that going back to school' feeling. Everything seemed to be changing and not for the better. There would be no warm jail cell this winter. I needed to find a new sleeping bag, waterproof if possible, and without holes in it. Arms and legs seem to find the holes when you are trying to sleep. I didn't mind being cold occasionally when I was younger. Sometimes it was refreshing. But being cold and knowing that you will stay that way all night long tends to wear on you. Time moves ever so slowly between 1 am and 4 am. Being cold during those hours sucks the life out of you. It takes away hope and leaves you barren and empty. It's so easy to convince yourself that the darkness is permanent. That dawn will never come.

And then there's the fear of not waking up. Or not wanting to wake up. Is there anything worth waking up for? Why bother? Because you need the toilet and you don't want to soil what few things you have in this world. Can't let your sleeping bag get wet. And there's hunger of course. It grinds on you until to do something about it. Someone was shaking me. I was ignoring them. 'OK', I thought. 'I'll wake up.' Except this time it wouldn't happen. I could hear voices but couldn't open my eyes. I couldn't raise my right arm, or my left. I couldn't feel my legs either. What was wrong with me! Panic began to build but there was no release from it. "I think maybe he's passed", I heard them say. "I can't get a pulse." 'No, no, I'm alive I screamed', but there was no sound. I must be breathing. Surely they can see that I'm breathing! "Nope, no pulse and no respiration", she said. "We'll take this one directly to the morgue. No rush, no sirens, OK?" My brain was clearly working but nothing else was. That was impossible. Was I going to be buried alive? Please God no! No, they couldn't do that. The embalming process would surely kill me. 'There must be some way to let them know I'm alive.'

I could sense motion but nothing else. I was being moved, but where to? "Is Number 47 empty" I hear him ask? "No, I'm not finished with the autopsy on that one. Put him in Number 51." More motion. I could hear the door latch. Then deafening silence, perhaps for eternity. 'No one will hear me now', I thought. I had never been so totally alone. Death would be slow and agonizing. Hours seemed to pass. Then something touched my finger. Or did it? Was I imagining it? Was I hallucinating? There it was again. I could move my finger if I tried very hard. Then two fingers. Somebody please open up so I can signal that I'm alive. Gradually other body parts began to respond. I was coming out of it, whatever it was. I could feel the cold steel only inches above me. On both sides now, the same. I wasn't buried alive, but I might as well be. Then I heard the latch open. There was light and motion.

"Wakey, wakey!" The voice was familiar. "Billy?", I gasped! "Yeah man. You coming with us to the soup kitchen or are you just going to lie there all day?" "What", I finally managed? "Are you coming", he repeated. "We'll give you five minutes to get your crap together. Then we're leaving you. OK?" The world was slowly forming around me, but I remained very disoriented. True to their word they did leave without me. It was almost noon by the time things seemed back to normal, whatever normal was supposed to be.

A week later I decided to visit several of the nearest mortuaries and tell them about my dream, if that's what it was. One of the morticians listened with interest. "That sounds similar to what happened at our morgue. Paramedics brought in a homeless gentleman who they believed was deceased after suffering a heart attack. In fact, the man was in a catatonic state and recovered while in one of our storage lockers." "Which one" I asked? "Number 51, I think. Scared the hell out me when I opened it up and found this guy alive." I broke out in a cold sweat. "Who called the ambulance to pick up this fellow?" "Some place I never heard of, EsCyberScope or something like that." The next question was obvious. "About a week ago, right?" "Oh no", he replied. "That was two and a half years ago!"

What I find particularly annoying are these little flashbacks that happen without warning, usually at the most inopportune times. One morning the lady at the soup kitchen was trying to explain that their hours of operation, and some other policies, were going to change. She had just started speaking when suddenly I could hear two technicians at EsCyberScope going over their research results. "Yes, effects of these sessions on the conscious mind are blocked quite effectively, but we still don't fully understand what's happening to the subconscious", said one technician. "Do you think that could lead to subjects having a recurrence of a VR experience hours, days or weeks after they are no longer connected to the equipment in the lab", asked the other? "Yes, some subjects have reported just such episodes. Some became so disoriented they thought they were dying again." "Shouldn't we report this to the Laboratory Manager's level?" "No, no. The last guy that did something like that was fired the next day. Just keep your mouth shut, OK!" "So, George, do you understand these changes as I have explained them to you", she asked me? "What changes", I replied?

Actually, I didn't really care what 'changes' the soup kitchen was making. If they were open when I got there, I would eat some of whatever they had that day. You never really knew because the menu listed on the wall was almost never accurate. Meat loaf might be spelled 'fish', and apple pie might turn out to be chocolate cake. Not that I'm complaining, mind you. I like surprises as much as any man. And the food was quite tasty most of the time. There were exceptions. At least none of us ever got sick from eating there. All those stainless-steel countertops and cabinets had to be kept sanitary because the city inspectors would shut them down if they weren't. That's really the only thing I was happy to let the government do for me. The people that worked there were all volunteers, which means they were there because they wanted to be. And they treated homeless people as equals, not as the lowest possible level of humanity. That was a bonus.

Most people take their vacations in summer, when the kids are out of school. It should be obvious that I'm not most people. Besides, homeless people usually try to do the opposite of what 'most people' do. It's a matter of principle! What does a homeless person need a vacation from, you might ask? Boredom is the answer. Beaches on the Gulf Coast are much too crowded in the summer, but a delightful escape from the city in winter. If you don't mind the chill, Gulf Coast swimming in winter can be very invigorating. The beaches in Florida are mostly white sand and the waters are crystal clear, if you can get to them. What I can get to is Galveston Island. Hitching a ride to Galveston, day or night, is pretty easy. One fellow driving an antique Tesla Model 3 told me what his grandfather used to say. 'About a hundred years ago the highway between Houston and Galveston was empty marshland. There was nothing to see except grass and a fence here and there, until you were almost to the causeway over Galveston Bay.' Now, of course, it's nonstop housing developments and shopping centers as far as the eye can see. Unlike Florida, Galveston beaches are brown and smelly, and the water is completely opaque. You get used to it.

Galveston has survived any number of hurricanes and related bad weather, meaning it has lots of public places to shelter. As you might expect there are lots of homeless people there, even more in the winter. It's a place you can still experience on foot. Many of the buildings are more than 200 years old and well worth visiting just for historical purposes. The permanent residents in Galveston don't seem to mind homeless people quite as much as some places I've been. Sometimes they even let you hang around the docks when the shrimp boats come in around 5 am. The shrimp are lifted out of the holds and unceremoniously dumped onto conveyor belts that take them to the packing houses about 20 yards on shore. Only about 99.9% of the shrimp complete the trip. The other 0.1% fall off the belt in transit. If you're quick enough you can 'catch' enough jumbo shrimp in a quarter of an hour to boil up a gourmet meal.

There is one problem with swimming off Galveston Island. When the water is opaque you can't see what's in it, near you I mean. It could be the stinging tentacles of a Portuguese Man o' War, that trail out from its pinkish purple float sail for ten yards or more. Or it might be a sting ray lying just under the sand, until you step on it and feel the bony spine in its tail stab into your calf. I'm told the pain is absolutely paralyzing. Today there were no pinkish purple float sails in sight. And I had it on good authority from the hot-dog vendor up on the sea wall that it was the wrong time of year for stingrays as well. Wearing a bright green and black swimsuit from a newfound Salvation Army shop, I decided to take the plunge.

You have to go out quite a long way on Galveston beach before the water is up to your chest. It's difficult to swim in water much shallower than that, and I was determined to practice my breaststroke, if I could remember how. I hadn't gone more than a few yards when something caught my eye, then disappeared. A few moments later I saw it again. It was a dorsal fin. Perhaps a porpoise. There are lots of them in these waters. They chase the ferries that come over from Port Bolivar on the northeast mainland. I was some distance away in any case. I resumed my swim in a direction that would take me away from it, whatever it was. A few minutes later it was closer than before. Was it following me? Perhaps it was curious. I've never been in the water with a porpoise before. I hear they can be quite friendly. I decided to stand on the bottom and let it catch up to me. As I turned to face the shoreline someone was waving at me. What was that all about? 'I'm sure I don't have any friends here.' Now two people were waving and pointing. I turned to see a large dorsal fin no more than ten yards behind me. I realized this was no porpoise. He was hunting and I was his prey.

The shoreline was more than 100 yards away. The water would eventually get too shallow for my opponent as I moved toward it, but he was less than twenty feet from me now. There was no way I could cover even half the distance required to force him to break off his pursuit. I was his for the taking. My arms and legs were beginning to go numb, not just from the chill of the water. Shock was setting in. Perhaps he would drag me under, and I would drown before he began to dismember me. Suddenly a blast of air came from above. I could hear a loud roar of rotors overhead. It was an orange rescue chopper. They were lowering a cable and harness. My eyes focused on the approaching harness, then the dorsal fin, then back to the harness. Would it reach me in time? Faster please God, faster! Both the fin and the harness were getting closer. Which one would win? I pushed off from the sandy bottom and reached for the harness. Got it! I threw my arm over it and locked my wrist under my other armpit. No time to place the harness around me in the proper manner. It began to lift me slowly, as I felt sandpaper rub across my leg.

The murky brown water began to turn pink around me. He just had a taste. He would surely turn for a full bite. Instinctively I drew my legs up under me as far as they would go. They just cleared the surface as the large dorsal fin passed beneath them. Now I was a yard above the water, now two yards. They were winching me up as the chopper tilted its rotor forward and we began to move toward the beach. I could see an ambulance waiting and a paramedic standing by. "You were lucky today, my friend", he shouted, as my feet touched the ground and I let go of the harness. "I've been told that before", I replied. The wound on my lower thigh was bleeding badly, but the femoral artery had not been severed. It took sixteen stitches to close. "You'll have a 'battle scar, I'm afraid", declared the doctor. "Thanks Doc. I'll have to wear shorts next summer to show it off!" And I did just that. It wasn't a dream or a simulation. This time I had a four-inch scar to prove it.

DeathLore

Of course I wasn't the only one wearing shorts. Any of us lucky enough to have a pair of shorts wore them, and as little else as the law allowed, all summer long. For the homeless in Houston there wasn't much relief from the scorching summer temperatures and humidity. The best thing to do between 10 am and 4 pm was sleep, in a shady spot if you could find one. July and August temperatures reached 120 Fahrenheit two days out of five. Public fountains offered a way to get everything you were wearing as wet as possible. The high humidity ensured that you would stay that way for two or three hours, long enough to catch a midday nap. Salt tablets were free and publicly available almost everywhere. The downtown area was pretty much off-limits during summer months. Glass skyscrapers and asphalt streets absorbed and re-radiated the sunlight, adding another 5 degrees. No problem for all those people in airconditioned offices and shops, were we weren't allowed, of course.

October brought relief from the summer heat, but with it came fresh anxiety of facing another winter in a vacant house somewhere. We had to abandon our 'vacant house' each summer, as they turned into ovens from mid-April through late September. When unairconditioned houses became habitable again in October the search for winter shelter began, always in a new area where we weren't 'known'. If you want to remain anonymous you have to keep moving. Otherwise homeowners start to recognize you and call the cops. This October brought another unwelcome surprise. The news media reported a body being found in one of the backwaters of the Houston Ship channel. It had been in the water for quite some time. The victim was female and still had a few strands of red hair that hadn't rotted away. Death was caused by a blow to the head. Of course, it only took police computers about two milliseconds to find a similar case, dated July 23 two years earlier. That's also how long it took me to realize I needed to go into hiding again, as far away from Houston as I could possibly manage. I made it as far as La Grange before they caught up with me. It must have been that scruffy looking guy and his granddaughter in the old brown pickup truck who have me a ride after I got off I-10 just past Columbus. The dog and I got along just fine in the back. You just never know who's going to rat on you, or why!

There were no witnesses this time, except for one. The victim didn't die right away and had time to scribble a note describing her assailant. The body had decomposed quite substantially as had her clothes. The note had survived, of course, and was neatly folded in her jeans pocket in pristine condition. Apparently Bic ballpoint pen ink is quite insoluble. The police considered the note a 'dying declaration' and therefore unimpeachable, especially since her description matched the suspect they had in custody. The time, and even the date, of death couldn't be determined with accuracy, but it didn't matter since no one remembered seeing me for more than a week either before or after the period in question. Luck wasn't going to save me again.

I won't bore you with the details of the trial. It was brief and persuasive - the jury needed only an hour to convict. Even I was convinced I killed her, although I remembered none of it. EsCyberScope was subpoenaed as a witness on my behalf, but a junior member of their management team explained that all their records of my appointments with the company had been lost somehow during one of their 'housekeeping campaigns'. They weren't even given a fine for corporate negligence. Worst of all, the court elected to reconsider my acquittal of the murder on July 23 two years earlier. Double jeopardy prevented me being retried, but they could do the next best thing by giving me the death penalty in this case.

There certainly are many interesting ways to die. Most all of them are unpleasant, so it's good that I don't remember them. The electric chair has been used in Texas for well more than a century. Forty people were executed in Huntsville in the year 2000. In the first half of the 21st Century about half of the legal executions in the United States have taken place in Texas by electrocution, averaging about fifteen per year. I've been told it's relatively painless, because you become unconscious after only a few seconds. But no one has been able to confirm whether that is true, until now. Don't misunderstand. I am quite certain this is not a simulation at EsCyberScope or any other laboratory. It's not a research project run by semi-ethical management, desperately searching for a breakthrough that will guarantee them a large government grant for life. No, this the real thing - state sponsored and eminently legal. I am going to actually die in about 11 minutes. That's how long it takes them to strap you into the chair, so your muscle reflexes don't toss you out on to the floor before you are really and truly dead. And the steel helmet. That makes sure the electrical current passes through your brain, rather than just leaving you paralyzed. It's all tried and tested, and quite foolproof. But just in case the brain does survive for a few seconds or even minutes after death, I may be able to tell you what it's like.

I'm watching the large clock on the wall, as the minute hand ticks down the last few seconds of my life. It reminds me of the rocket launches back in the 1960's. We've all seen the old videos. 10 – 9 – 8 - 7 – 6 – 5 - - 4 ---- 3 ----- 2 -------1------. "We have lift off..." Fire shoots through my body. I am being 'microwaved', cooked from the inside out! First the large bones heat up, then the smaller ones, then the flesh around them. The smell of raw meat being seared in a frying pan fills my nostrils. My eyes see only red flashes, then nothing. I am totally blind. I hear nothing, perhaps there is nothing to hear. The unbearable pain ceases, but I am still conscious, just barely. When will it all go black? When will oblivion come? How long must I endure? There is a bright light in the distance. It is very far away but moving toward me. It's getting brighter. But now it stops. Why is it getting fainter? "I am here", I try to scream! But I have no voice. In fact, I have no body. No physical form. Now the light comes again, but then retreats as before.

Billy is waiting just outside the recovery room. "Doctor, have you ever known anyone to survive the Huntsville electric chair?" "No", the doctor replies, shaking his head slowly. "I would have said it's impossible. By some miracle your friend George is still alive, but only just. His heartbeat was very weak and erratic, but he refused to stop breathing after his execution. At that moment he became a problem for the medical profession rather than law enforcement. The Hippocratic oath requires that we keep him alive if possible. One of these machines keeps his heart beating and the other monitors his brainwave patterns, which remain remarkably strong. He might actually recover if he comes out of the coma."

"So, what happens then, Doc", Billy frowned? "If he recovers the courts will undoubtedly order another execution, presumably by electrocution here in Huntsville. Legally the State of Texas has no other means of carrying out his sentence." A tear forms in Billy's eye as he looks at George, and then the array of wires and machines keeping him alive. Slowly he bends down, putting his mouth close to George's left ear. "To hell with the courts", he whispers, as he pulls the electric plugs from their wall sockets. He then turns slowly to face the doctor. "I don't think George is going to make it this time", says Billy. The doctor's expression slowly changes from alarm to empathy. "I believe you're right."

Printed in Great Britain
by Amazon